By the same author

The Flea Palace

The Saint of Incipient Insanities

The Gaze

The Bastard of Istanbul

The Forty Rules of Love

The Happiness of Blond People

Honour

Black Milk

The Architect's Apprentice

Three Daughters of Eve

10 Minutes 38 Seconds in This Strange World

How to Stay Sane in an Age of Division

The Island of Missing Trees

There Are Rivers in the Sky

ABOUT THE AUTHOR

Elif Shafak is an award-winning British Turkish novelist, whose work has been translated into fifty-eight languages. The author of twenty books, thirteen of which are novels, she is a bestselling author in many countries around the world. Shafak's novel *10 Minutes 38 Seconds in This Strange World* was shortlisted for the Booker Prize and the RSL Ondaatje Prize. *The Island of Missing Trees* was a *Sunday Times* bestseller, and was shortlisted for the Costa Novel Award and the Women's Prize for Fiction. *There are Rivers in the Sky*, which won an Edward Stanford Award for Fiction, is her latest novel.

Shafak holds a PhD in political science, and is a Fellow and a Vice President of the Royal Society of Literature. She has been awarded the medal of Chevalier de l'Ordre des Arts et des Lettres and, in 2024, was awarded the British Academy President's Medal for 'her excellent body of work which demonstrates an incredible intercultural range'.

The Forty Rules of Love

ELIF SHAFAK

PENGUIN BOOKS

PENGUIN BOOKS

UK | USA | Canada | Ireland | Australia
India | New Zealand | South Africa

Penguin Books is part of the Penguin Random House group of companies
whose addresses can be found at global.penguinrandomhouse.com.

Penguin Random House UK,
One Embassy Gardens, 8 Viaduct Gardens, London SW11 7BW

penguin.co.uk

First published in the United States of America by Viking Penguin,
a member of Penguin Group USA Inc. 2010
First published in Great Britain by Viking 2010
Published in Penguin Books 2011
Reissued in this edition 2025
049

Grateful acknowledgement is made for permission to reprint
excerpts from the following copyrighted works:
'Only Breath' and 'Why Wine is Forbidden' from *The Essential Rumi*,
translations by Coleman Barks (HarperCollins).
Used by permission of Coleman Barks.
'Tattooing in Qazwin' from *A Year with Rumi: Daily Readings* by Coleman Barks.
Copyright © 2006 by Coleman Barks.
Reprinted by permission of HarperCollins Publishers.

Typeset by Jouve (UK), Milton Keynes
Printed and bound in India by Replika Press Pvt. Ltd.

The authorized representative in the EEA is Penguin Random House Ireland,
Morrison Chambers, 32 Nassau Street, Dublin D02 YH68

A CIP catalogue record for this book is available from the British Library

ISBN: 978-0-241-97293-9

Penguin Random House is committed to a sustainable future
for our business, our readers and our planet. This book is made from
Forest Stewardship Council® certified paper.

MIX
Paper | Supporting
responsible forestry
FSC® C018179

To Zahir & Zelda

When I was a child, I saw God,
I saw angels;
I watched the mysteries of the higher and lower worlds. I thought all men saw the same. At last I realized that they did not see. . . .

—SHAMS OF TABRIZ

The Forty Rules of Love

Prologue

Between your fingers you hold a stone and throw it into flowing water. The effect might not be easy to see. There will be a small ripple where the stone breaks the surface and then a splash, muffled by the rush of the surrounding river. That's all.

Throw a stone into a lake. The effect will be not only visible but also far more lasting. The stone will disrupt the still waters. A circle will form where the stone hit the water, and in a flash that circle will multiply into another, then another. Before long the ripples caused by one plop will expand until they can be felt everywhere along the mirrored surface of the water. Only when the circles reach the shore will they stop and die out.

If a stone hits a river, the river will treat it as yet another commotion in its already tumultuous course. Nothing unusual. Nothing unmanageable.

If a stone hits a lake, however, the lake will never be the same again.

For forty years Ella Rubinstein's life had consisted of still waters—a predictable sequence of habits, needs, and preferences. Though it was monotonous and ordinary in many ways, she had not found it tiresome. During the last twenty years, every wish she had, every person she befriended, and every decision she made was filtered through her marriage. Her husband, David, was a successful dentist who worked hard and made a lot of money. She had always known that they did not connect on any deep level, but connecting emotionally need not be a priority on a married couple's list, she thought, especially for a man and a woman who had been married for so long. There were more important things than passion and love in a marriage, such as understanding, affection, compassion, and that most godlike act a person could perform, forgiveness. Love was secondary to any of these. Unless, that is, one lived in novels or romantic movies, where the protagonists were always larger than life and their love nothing short of legend.

Ella's children topped her list of priorities. They had a beautiful daughter in college, Jeannette, and teenage twins, Orly and Avi. Also, they had a twelve-year-old golden retriever, Spirit, who had been Ella's walking buddy in the mornings and her cheeriest companion ever since he'd been a puppy. Now he was old, overweight, completely deaf, and almost blind; Spirit's time was coming, but Ella preferred to think he would go on forever. Then again, that was how she was. She never confronted the death of anything, be it a habit, a phase, or a marriage, even when the end stood right in front of her, plain and inevitable.

The Rubinsteins lived in Northampton, Massachusetts, in a large Victorian house that needed some renovation but still was splendid, with five bedrooms, three baths, shiny hardwood floors, a three-car garage, French doors, and, best of all, an outdoor Jacuzzi. They had life insurance, car insurance, retirement plans, college savings plans, joint bank accounts, and, in addition to the house they lived in, two enviable apartments: one in Boston, the other in Rhode Island. She and David had worked hard for all this. A big, busy house with children, elegant furniture, and the wafting scent of homemade pies might seem a cliché to some people, but to them it was the picture of an ideal life. They had built their marriage around this shared vision and had attained most, if not all, of their dreams.

On their last Valentine's Day, her husband had given her a heart-shaped diamond pendant and a card that read,

To my dear Ella,

A woman with a quiet manner, a generous heart, and the patience of a saint. Thank you for accepting me as I am. Thank you for being my wife.

Yours,
David

Ella had never confessed this to David, but reading his card had felt like reading an obituary. *This is what they will write about me when I die,* she had thought. And if they were sincere, they might also add this:

Building her whole life around her husband and children, Ella lacked any survival techniques to help her cope with life's hardships on her own. She was not the type to throw caution to the wind. Even changing her daily coffee brand was a major effort.

All of which is why no one, including Ella, could explain what was going on when she filed for divorce in the fall of 2008 after twenty years of marriage.

But there was a reason: love.

They did not live in the same city. Not even on the same continent. The two of them were not only miles apart but also as different as day and night. Their lifestyles were so dissimilar that it seemed impossible for them to bear each other's presence, never mind fall in love. But it happened. And it happened fast, so fast in fact that Ella had no time to realize what was happening and to be on guard, if one could ever be on guard against love.

Love came to Ella as suddenly and brusquely as if a stone had been hurled from out of nowhere into the tranquil pond of her life.

Ella

NORTHAMPTON, MAY 17, 2008

Birds were singing outside her kitchen window on that balmy day in spring. Afterward Ella replayed the scene in her mind so many times that, rather than a fragment from the past, it felt like an ongoing moment still happening somewhere out there in the universe.

There they were, sitting around the table, having a late family lunch on a Saturday afternoon. Her husband was filling his plate with fried chicken legs, his favorite food. Avi was playing his knife and fork like drumsticks while his twin, Orly, was trying to calculate how many bites of which food she could eat so as not to ruin her diet of 650 calories a day. Jeannette, who was a freshman at Mount Holyoke College nearby, seemed lost in her thoughts as she spread cream cheese on another slice of bread. Also at the table sat Aunt Esther, who had stopped by to drop off one of her famous marble cakes and then stayed on for lunch. Ella had a lot of work to do afterward, but she was not ready to leave the table just yet. Lately they didn't have too many shared family meals, and she saw this as a golden chance for everyone to reconnect.

"Esther, did Ella give you the good news?" David asked suddenly. "She found a great job."

Though Ella had graduated with a degree in English literature and loved fiction, she hadn't done much in the field after college, other than editing small pieces for women's magazines, attending a few book clubs, and occasionally writing book reviews for some local papers. That was all. There was a time when she'd aspired to become a prominent book critic, but then she simply accepted the fact that life had carried her elsewhere, turning her into an industrious housewife with three kids and endless domestic responsibilities.

Not that she complained. Being the mother, the wife, the dog walker, and the housekeeper kept her busy enough. She didn't have to be a breadwinner on top of all these. Though none of her feminist friends from Smith College approved of her choice, she was satisfied to be a stay-at-home mom and grateful that she and her husband could afford it. Besides, she had never abandoned her passion for books and still considered herself a voracious reader.

A few years ago, things had begun to change. The children were growing up, and they made it clear that they didn't need her as much as they once had. Realizing that she had too much time to spare and no one to spend it with, Ella had considered how it might be to find a job. David had encouraged her, but though they kept talking and talking about it, she rarely pursued the opportunities that came her way, and when she did, potential employers were always looking for someone younger or more experienced. Afraid of being rejected over and over, she had simply let the subject drop.

Nevertheless, in May 2008 whatever obstacle had impeded her from finding a job all these years unexpectedly vanished. Two weeks shy of her fortieth birthday, she found herself working for a literary agency based in Boston. It was her husband who found her the job through one of his clients—or perhaps through one of his mistresses.

"Oh, it's no big deal," Ella rushed to explain now. "I'm only a part-time reader for a literary agent."

But David seemed determined not to let her think too little of her new job. "Come on, tell them it's a well-known agency," he urged, nudging her, and when she refused to comply, he heartily agreed with himself. "It's a prestigious place, Esther. You should see the other assistants! Girls and boys fresh out of the best colleges. Ella is the only one going back to work after being a housewife for years. Now, don't be modest."

Ella wondered if, deep inside, her husband felt guilty about keeping her away from a career, or else about cheating on her—these being the only two explanations she could think of as to why he was now going overboard in his enthusiasm.

Still smiling, David concluded, "This is what I call chutzpah. We're all proud of her."

"She is a prize. Always was," said Aunt Esther in a voice so sentimental that it sounded as if Ella had left the table and was gone for good.

They all gazed at her lovingly. Even Avi didn't make a cynical remark, and Orly for once seemed to care about something other than her looks. Ella forced herself to appreciate this moment of kindness, but she felt an overwhelming exhaustion that she had never experienced before. She secretly prayed for someone to change the subject.

Jeannette, her older daughter, must have heard the prayer, for she suddenly chimed in, "I have some good news, too."

All heads turned toward her, faces beaming with expectation.

"Scott and I have decided to get married," Jeannette announced. "Oh, I know what you guys are going to say! That we haven't finished college yet and all that, but you've got to understand, we both feel ready for the next big move."

An awkward silence descended upon the kitchen table as the warmth that had canopied them just a moment ago evaporated. Orly and Avi exchanged blank looks, and Aunt Esther froze with her hand tightened around a glass of apple juice. David put his fork aside as if he had no appetite left and squinted at Jeannette with his light brown eyes that were deeply creased with smile lines at the corners. However, right now he was anything but smiling. His mouth had drawn into a pout, as though he had just downed a swig of vinegar.

"Great! I expected you to share my happiness, but I get this cold treatment instead," Jeannette whined.

"You just said you were getting married," remarked David as if Jeannette didn't know what she'd said and needed to be informed.

"Dad, I know it seems a bit too soon, but Scott proposed to me the other day and I've already said yes."

"But why?" asked Ella.

From the way Jeannette looked at her, Ella reckoned, that was not the kind of question her daughter had expected. She would rather have been asked "When?" or "How?" In either case it meant that she could start shopping for her wedding dress. The question "Why?" was another matter altogether and had completely caught her off guard.

"Because I love him, I guess." Jeannette's tone was slightly condescending.

"Honey, what I meant was, why the rush?" insisted Ella. "Are you pregnant or something?"

Aunt Esther twitched in her chair, her face stern, her anguish visible. She took an antacid tablet from her pocket and started chewing on it.

"I'm going to be an uncle," Avi said, giggling.

Ella held Jeannette's hand and gave it a gentle squeeze. "You can always tell us the truth. You know that, right? We'll stand by you no matter what."

"Mom, will you please stop that?" Jeannette snapped as she pulled her hand away. "This has nothing to do with pregnancy. You're embarrassing me."

"I was just trying to help," Ella responded calmly, calmness being a state she had been lately finding harder and harder to achieve.

"By insulting me, you mean. Apparently the only way you can see Scott and me getting married is me being knocked up! Does it ever occur to you that I might, just might, want to marry this guy because I *love* him? We *have* been dating for eight months now."

This elicited a scoff from Ella. "Oh, yeah, as if you could tell a man's character in eight months! Your father and I have been married for almost twenty years, and even *we* can't claim to know everything about each other. Eight months is nothing in a relationship!"

"It took God only six days to create the entire universe," said Avi, beaming, but cold stares from everyone at the table forced him back into silence.

Sensing the escalating tension, David, his eyes fixed on his elder daughter, his brow furrowed in thought, interjected, "Honey, what your mom is trying to say is that dating is one thing, marrying is quite another."

"But, Dad, did you think we would date forever?" Jeannette asked.

Drawing in a deep breath, Ella said, "To be perfectly blunt, we were expecting you to grow out of it. You're too young to get involved in any serious relationship."

"You know what I'm thinking, Mom?" Jeannette said in a voice so flat as to be unrecognizable. "I'm thinking you're projecting your own fears onto me. But just because you married so young and had a baby when you were my age, that doesn't mean I'm going to make the same mistake."

Ella blushed crimson as if slapped in the face. From deep within she remembered the difficult pregnancy that had resulted in Jeannette's premature birth. As a baby and then as a toddler, her daughter had drained all of her energy, which was why she had waited six years before getting pregnant again.

"Sweetheart, we were happy for you when you started dating Scott," David said cautiously, trying a different strategy. "He's a nice guy. But who knows what you'll be thinking after graduation? Things might be very different then."

Jeannette gave a small nod that conveyed little more than feigned acquiescence. Then she said, "Is this because Scott isn't Jewish?"

David rolled his eyes in disbelief. He had always taken pride in being an open-minded and cultured father, avoiding negative remarks about race, religion, or gender in the house.

Jeannette, however, seemed relentless. Turning to her mother, she asked, "Can you look me in the eye and tell me you'd still be making the same objections if Scott were a young Jewish man named Aaron?"

Jeannette's voice needled with bitterness and sarcasm, and Ella feared there was more of that welling up inside her daughter.

"Sweetheart, I'll be completely honest with you, even if you might not like it. I know how wonderful it is to be young and in love. Believe me, I do. But to get married to someone from a different background is a big gamble. And as your parents we want to make sure you're doing the right thing."

"And how do you know your right thing is the right thing for me?"

The question threw Ella off a little. She sighed and massaged her forehead, as if on the verge of a migraine.

"I love him, Mom. Does that mean anything to you? Do you remember that word from somewhere? He makes my heart beat faster. I can't live without him."

Ella heard herself chuckle. It was not her intention to make fun of her daughter's feelings, not at all, but that was probably what her laughing to herself sounded like. For reasons unknown to her, she felt extremely nervous. She'd had fights with Jeannette before, hundreds of them, but today it felt as though she were quarreling with something else, something bigger.

"Mom, haven't you ever been in love?" Jeannette retorted, a hint of contempt creeping into her tone.

"Oh, give me a break! Stop daydreaming and get real, will you? You're being so . . . " Ella's eyes darted toward the window, hunting for a dramatic word, until finally she came up with " . . . romantic!"

"What's wrong with being romantic?" Jeannette asked, sounding offended.

Really, what was wrong with being romantic? Ella wondered. Since when was she so annoyed by romanticism? Unable to answer the questions tugging at the edges of her mind, she continued all the same. "Come on, honey. Which century are you living in? Just get it in your head, women don't marry the men they fall in love with. When push comes to shove, they choose the guy who'll be a good father and a reliable husband. Love is only a sweet feeling bound to come and quickly go away."

When she finished talking, Ella turned to her husband. David had clasped his hands in front of him, slowly as if through water, and was looking at her like he'd never seen her before.

"I know why you're doing this," Jeannette said. "You're jealous of my happiness and my youth. You want to make an unhappy housewife out of me. You want me to be you, Mom."

Ella felt a strange, sinking feeling in the pit of her stomach, as if she had a giant rock sitting there. Was she an unhappy housewife? A washed-up mom trapped in a failing marriage? Was this how her children saw her? And her husband, too? What about friends and neighbors? Suddenly she had the feeling that everyone around her secretly pitied her, and the suspicion was so painful that she gasped.

"You should apologize to your mom," David said, turning to Jeannette with a frown on his face.

"It's all right. I don't expect an apology," Ella said dejectedly.

Jeannette gave her mother a mock leer. And just like that, she pushed back her chair, threw her napkin aside, and walked out of the kitchen. After a minute Orly and Avi silently followed suit, either in an unusual act of solidarity with their elder sister or because they'd gotten bored of all this adult talk. Aunt Esther left next, mumbling some poor excuse while chewing fiercely on her last antacid tablet.

David and Ella remained at the table, an intense awkwardness hanging in the air between them. It pained Ella to have to face this void, which, as they both knew, had nothing to do with Jeannette or any of their children.

David grabbed the fork he had put aside and inspected it for a while. "So should I conclude that you didn't marry the man you loved?"

"Oh, please, that's not what I meant."

"What is it you meant, then?" David said, still talking to the fork. "I thought you were in love with me when we got married."

"I was in love with you," Ella said, but couldn't help adding, "back then."

"So when did you stop loving me?" David asked, deadpan.

Ella looked at her husband in astonishment, like someone who had never seen her reflection before and who now held a mirror to her face. Had she stopped loving him? It was a question she had never asked herself before. She wanted to respond but lacked not so much the will as the words. Deep inside she knew it was the two of them they should be concerned about, not their children. But instead they were doing what they both were best at: letting the days go by, the routine take over, and time run its course of inevitable torpor.

She started to cry, unable to hold back this continuing sadness that had, without her knowledge, become a part of who she was. David turned his anguished face away. They both knew he hated to see her cry just as much as she hated to cry in front of him. Fortunately, the phone rang just then, saving them.

David picked it up. "Hello . . . yes, she's here. Hold on, please."

Ella pulled herself together and spoke up, doing her best to sound in good spirits. "Yes, this is Ella."

"Hi, this is Michelle. Sorry to bother you over the weekend," chirped a young woman's voice. "It's just that yesterday Steve wanted me to check in with you, and I simply forgot. Did you have a chance to start working on the manuscript?"

"Oh." Ella sighed, only now remembering the task awaiting her.

Her first assignment at the literary agency was to read a novel by an unknown European author. She was then expected to write an extensive report on it.

"Tell him not to worry. I've already started reading," Ella lied. Ambitious and headstrong, Michelle was the kind of person she didn't want to upset on her first assignment.

"Oh, good! How is it?"

Ella paused, puzzled as to what to say. She didn't know anything about the manuscript, except that it was a historical novel centered on the life of the famous mystic poet Rumi, who she learned was called "the Shakespeare of the Islamic world."

"Oh, it's very . . . *mystical.*" Ella chuckled, hoping to cover with a joke.

But Michelle was all business. "Right," she said flatly. "Listen, I think you need to get on this. It might take longer than you expect to write a report on a novel like that. . . ."

There was a distant muttering on the phone as Michelle's voice trailed off. Ella imagined her juggling several tasks simultaneously—checking e-mails, reading a review on one of her authors, taking a bite from her tuna-salad sandwich, and polishing her fingernails—all while talking on the phone.

"Are you still there?" Michelle asked a minute later.

"Yes, I am."

"Good. Listen, it's crazy in here. I need to go. Just keep in mind the deadline is in three weeks."

"I know," Ella said abruptly, trying to sound more determined. "I'll make the deadline."

The truth was, Ella wasn't sure she wanted to evaluate this manuscript at all. In the beginning she'd been so eager and confident. It had felt thrilling to be the first one to read an unpublished novel by an unknown author and to play however small a role in his fate. But now she wasn't sure if she could concentrate on a subject as irrelevant to her life as Sufism and a time as distant as the thirteenth century.

Michelle must have detected her hesitation. "Is there a problem?" she asked. When no answer came, she grew insistent. "Listen, you can confide in me."

After a bit of silence, Ella decided to tell her the truth.

"It's just that I'm not sure I'm in the right state of mind these days to concentrate on a historical novel. I mean, I'm interested in Rumi and all that, but still, the subject is alien to me. Perhaps you could give me another novel—you know, something I could more easily relate to."

"That's such a skewed approach," said Michelle. "You think you can work better with books you know something about? Not at all! Just because you live in this state, you can't expect to edit only novels that take place in Massachusetts, right?"

"That's not what I meant . . ." Ella said, and immediately realized she had uttered the same sentence too many times this afternoon. She glanced at her husband to see if he, too, had noticed this, but David's expression was hard to decipher.

"Most of the time, we have to read books that have nothing to do with our lives. That's part of our job. Just this week I finished working on a book by an Iranian woman who used to operate a brothel in Tehran and had to flee the country. Should I have told her to send the manuscript to an Iranian agency instead?"

"No, of course not," Ella mumbled, feeling silly and small.

"Isn't connecting people to distant lands and cultures one of the strengths of good literature?"

"Sure it is. Listen, forget what I said. You'll have a report on your desk before the deadline," Ella conceded, hating Michelle for treating her as if she were the dullest person alive and hating herself for allowing this to happen.

"Wonderful, that's the spirit," Michelle concluded in her singsong voice. "Don't get me wrong, but I think you should bear in mind that there are dozens of people out there who would love to have your job. And most of them are almost half your age. That'll keep you motivated."

When Ella hung up the phone, she found David watching her, his face solemn and reserved. He seemed to be waiting for them to pick up where they'd left off. But she didn't feel like mulling over their daughter's future anymore, if that was what they'd been worrying about in the first place.

Later in the day, she was alone on the porch sitting in her favorite rocking chair, looking at the orangey-red Northampton sunset. The sky felt so close and open that you could almost touch it. Her brain had gone quiet, as if tired of all the noise swirling inside. This month's credit-card payments, Orly's bad eating habits, Avi's poor grades, Aunt Esther and her sad cakes, her dog Spirit's decaying health, Jeannette's marriage plans, her husband's secret flings, the absence of love in her life . . . One by one, she locked them all in small mental boxes.

In that frame of mind, Ella took the manuscript out of its package and bounced it in her hand, as if weighing it. The title of the novel was written on the cover in indigo ink: *Sweet Blasphemy.*

Ella had been told that nobody knew much about the author—a certain A. Z. Zahara, who lived in Holland. His manuscript had been shipped to the literary agency from Amsterdam with a postcard inside the envelope. On the front of the postcard was a picture of tulip fields in dazzling pinks, yellows, and purples, and on the back a note written in delicate handwriting:

Dear Sir/Madam,

Greetings from Amsterdam. The story I herewith send you takes place in thirteenth-century Konya in Asia Minor. But I sincerely believe that it cuts across countries, cultures, and centuries.

I hope you will have the time to read SWEET BLASPHEMY, a historical, mystical novel on the remarkable bond between Rumi, the best poet and most revered spiritual leader in the history of Islam, and Shams of Tabriz, an unknown, unconventional dervish full of scandals and surprises.

May love be always with you and you always surrounded with love.

A. Z. Zahara

Ella sensed that the postcard had piqued the literary agent's curiosity. But Steve was not a man who had time to read the work of an amateur writer. So he'd handed the package to his assistant, Michelle, who had passed it on to *her* new assistant. This is how *Sweet Blasphemy* ended up in Ella's hands.

Little did she know that this was going to be not just any book, but *the* book that changed her life. In the time she was reading it, her life would be rewritten.

Ella turned the first page. There was a note about the writer.

A. Z. Zahara lives in Amsterdam with his books, cats, and turtles when he is not traveling around the world. Sweet Blasphemy *is his first novel and most probably his last. He has no intention of becoming a novelist and has written this book purely out of admiration and love for the great philosopher, mystic, and poet Rumi and his beloved sun, Shams of Tabriz.*

Her eyes moved down the page to the next line. And there Ella read something that rang strangely familiar:

For despite what some people say, love is not only a sweet feeling bound to come and quickly go away.

Her jaw dropped as she realized this was the contradiction of the exact sentence she had spoken to her daughter in the kitchen earlier in the day. She stood still for a moment, shivering with the thought that some mysterious force in the universe, or else this writer, whoever he might be, was spying on her. Perhaps he had written this book knowing beforehand what kind of person was going to read it first. This writer had her in mind as his reader. For some reason unbeknownst to her, Ella found the idea both disturbing and exciting.

In many ways the twenty-first century is not that different from the thirteenth century. Both will be recorded in history as times of unprecedented religious clashes, cultural misunderstandings, and a general sense of insecurity and fear of the Other. At times like these, the need for love is greater than ever.

A sudden wind blew in her direction, cool and strong, scattering the leaves on the porch. The beauty of the sunset drifted toward the western horizon, and the air felt dull, joyless.

Because love is the very essence and purpose of life. As Rumi reminds us, it hits everybody, including those who shun love—even those who use the word "romantic" as a sign of disapproval.

Ella was as bowled over as if she had read there, "*Love hits everybody, even a middle-aged housewife in Northampton named Ella Rubinstein.*"

Her gut instinct told her to put the manuscript aside, go into the house, give Michelle a call, and tell her there was no way she could write a report on this novel. Instead she took a deep breath, turned the page, and started to read.

Sweet Blasphemy

A Novel

A. Z. ZAHARA

Sufi mystics say the secret of the Qur'an lies
in the verse Al-Fatiha,
And the secret of Al-Fatiha lies in
Bismillahirrahmanirrahim
And the quintessence of Bismillah is the letter *ba*,
And there is a dot below that letter. . . .
The dot underneath the *B* embodies the entire
universe. . . .

ب

The Mathnawi starts with *B*,
Just like all the chapters in this novel. . . .

Foreword

Beset with religious clashes, political disputes, and endless power struggles, the thirteenth century was a turbulent period in Anatolia. In the West, the Crusaders, on their way to Jerusalem, occupied and sacked Constantinople, leading to the partition of the Byzantine Empire. In the East, highly disciplined Mongol armies swiftly expanded under the military genius of Genghis Khan. In between, different Turkish tribes fought among themselves while the Byzantines tried to recover their lost land, wealth, and power. It was a time of unprecedented chaos when Christians fought Christians, Christians fought Muslims, and Muslims fought Muslims. Everywhere one turned, there was hostility and anguish and an intense fear of what might happen next.

In the midst of this chaos lived a distinguished Islamic scholar, known as Jalal ad-Din Rumi. Nicknamed Mawlana—"Our Master"—by many, he had thousands of disciples and admirers from all over the region and beyond, and was regarded as a beacon to all Muslims.

In 1244, Rumi met Shams—a wandering dervish with unconventional ways and heretical proclamations. Their encounter altered both their lives. At the same time, it marked the beginning of a solid, unique friendship that Sufis in the centuries to follow likened to the union of two oceans. By meeting this exceptional companion, Rumi was transformed from a mainstream cleric to a committed mystic, passionate poet, advocate of love, and originator of the ecstatic dance of the whirling dervishes, daring to break free of all conventional rules. In an age of deeply embedded bigotries and clashes, he stood for a universal spirituality, opening his doors to people of all backgrounds. Instead of an outer-oriented jihad—defined as "the war against infidels" and carried out by many in those days just as in the present—Rumi stood up for an inner-oriented jihad where the aim was to struggle against and ultimately prevail over one's ego, *nafs*.

Not all people welcomed these ideas, however, just as not all people open their hearts to love. The powerful spiritual bond between Shams and Rumi became the target of rumor, slander, and attack. They were misunderstood, envied, vilified, and ultimately betrayed by those closest to them. Three years after they met, they were tragically separated.

But the story didn't end there.

In truth, there never was an end. Almost eight hundred years later, the spirits of Shams and Rumi are still alive today, whirling amid us somewhere. . . .

The Killer

ALEXANDRIA, NOVEMBER 1252

Beneath dark waters in a well, he is dead now. Yet his eyes follow me wherever I go, bright and imposing, like two dark stars ominously hanging in the sky above. I came to Alexandria hoping that if I traveled far enough, I could escape this piercing memory and stop the wail echoing inside my mind, that very last cry he gave out before his face drained of blood, his eyes bulged out, and his throat closed in an unfinished gasp, the farewell of a stabbed man. The howl of a trapped wolf.

When you kill someone, something from that person passes to you—a sigh, a smell or a gesture. I call it "the curse of the victim." It clings to your body and seeps into your skin, going all the way into your heart, and thus continues to live within you. People who see me on the street have no way of knowing this, but I carry with me the traces of all the men I have killed. I wear them around my neck like invisible necklaces, feeling their presence against my flesh, tight and heavy. Uncomfortable though it feels, I have gotten used to living with this burden and have accepted it as part of my job. Ever since Cain slew Abel, in every murderer breathes the man he murdered, that much I know. It doesn't disturb me. Not anymore. But then why was I shaken so badly after that last incident?

Everything was different this time, right from the start. Take the way I found the job, for instance. Or should I say instead the way the job found me? Early in the spring of 1248, I was working for a brothel patron in Konya, a hermaphrodite famous for her anger and wrath. My task was to help her to keep the harlots under control and intimidate the customers who didn't behave.

I remember the day vividly. I was hunting a harlot who had escaped the brothel to find God. She was a beautiful young woman, which sort of broke my heart, because when I caught up with her, I was going to ruin her face so bad that no man would ever want to look at her again. I was this close to catching the stupid woman when I found a mysterious letter on my doorsill. I had never learned how to read, so I took it to the madrassa, where I paid a student to read it for me.

It turned out to be an anonymous letter signed by "a few true believers."

"We have heard from a reliable source where you came from and who you really were," the letter said. "A former member of the Assassins! We also know that after the death of Hassan Sabbah and the incarceration of your leaders, the order is not what it used to be. You came to Konya to escape persecution, and you have been under disguise ever since."

The letter said that my services were urgently needed on a matter of great importance. It assured me that payment would be satisfactory. If interested, I was to appear in a well-known tavern that evening after dark. Once there, I had to sit at the table closest to the window, my back to the door, my head bowed down, and my eyes fixed on the floor. I would soon be joined by the person or persons who would hire me. They were going to give me all the information I needed to know. Neither when they arrived nor as they left, and at no point during our conversation, could I raise my head and look at their faces.

It was a strange letter. But then again, I was used to dealing with the whims of clients. Over the years I had been hired by all sorts of people, and most of them wished to keep their names secret. Experience had taught me that, more often than not, the more strongly a client strived to hide his identity, the closer he happened to be to his victim, but that was none of my business. My task was to kill. Not to inquire into the reasons behind my assignment. Ever since I left Alamut years ago, this had been the life I chose for myself.

I seldom ask questions anyway. Why would I? Most folks I know have at least one person they want to get rid of. The fact that they don't do anything about it doesn't necessarily mean they are immune to the desire to kill. In fact, everyone has it in him to kill someday. People don't get that until it happens to them. They think of themselves as incapable of murder. But it is just a matter of coincidence. Sometimes even a gesture is enough to inflame their tempers. A deliberate misunderstanding, a squabble over nothing, or simply being at the wrong place at the wrong time can bring out a destructive streak in people who are otherwise good and decent fellows. Anyone can kill. But not everyone can kill a stranger in cold blood. That is where I enter the picture.

I did the dirty work of others. Even God recognized the need for someone like me in His holy scheme when He appointed Azrael the Archangel of Death to terminate lives. In this way human beings feared, cursed, and hated the angel while His hands remained clean and His name unblemished. It wasn't fair to the angel. But then again, this world was not known for its justice, was it?

When darkness settled, I went to the tavern. The table by the window happened to be occupied by a scar-faced man who seemed to be in deep sleep. It occurred to me to wake him up and tell him to go somewhere else, but with drunks you never knew how they would react, and I had to be careful not to draw too much attention to myself. So I sat at the next available table, facing the window.

Before long, two men arrived. They sat on either side of me so as not to show their faces. I didn't need to look at them, though, to realize how young they were and how unprepared for the step they were about to take.

"You came highly recommended," said one of them, his tone not so much cautious as apprehensive. "We were told you were the best."

It felt funny, the way he said it, but I suppressed my smile. I noticed they were scared of me, which was a good thing. If they were scared sufficiently, they could not dare to do me wrong.

So I said, "Yes, I am the best. That is why they call me Jackal Head. I have never let my clients down, no matter how hard the task."

"Good." He sighed. "Because this might not be an easy task."

Now the other spoke. "See, there is this man who has made himself too many enemies. Ever since he came to this town, he has brought nothing but trouble. We have warned him several times, but he pays us no attention. If anything, he has become all the more contentious. He leaves us no other option."

It was always the same. Each time the clients tried to explain themselves before we cut a deal, as if my approval could in any way lessen the gravity of what they were about to do.

"I know what you mean. Tell me, who is this person?" I asked.

They seemed reluctant to give me a name, offering vague descriptions instead.

"He is a heretic who has nothing to do with Islam. An unruly man full of sacrilege and blasphemy. A maverick of a dervish."

As soon as I heard this last word, a creepy feeling spread over my arms. My mind raced. I had killed all sorts of people, young and old, men and women, but a dervish, a man of faith, was not among them. I had my superstitions and didn't want to draw God's wrath upon me, for despite everything I still believed in Him.

"I'm afraid I'm going to have to turn it down. I don't think I want to kill a holy man. Find someone else."

With that, I stood up to leave. But one of the men grabbed my hand and beseeched, "Wait, please. Your payment will be commensurate with your effort. Whatever your fee is, we are ready to double the price."

"How about triple?" I asked, convinced that they wouldn't be able to raise the amount that high.

But to my surprise, after a brief hesitation, they both agreed. I sat back in my seat, feeling jittery. With this money I could finally afford the price of a bride and get married and stop fretting over how to make ends meet. Dervish or not, anyone was worth killing for this amount.

How could I know in that moment that I was making the biggest mistake of my life and would spend the rest of my days regretting it? How could I know it would be so hard to kill the dervish and that even long after he was dead, his knifelike gaze would follow me everywhere?

Four years have passed since I stabbed him in that courtyard and dumped his body in a well, waiting to hear the splash that never came. Not a sound. It was as if rather than falling down into the water he fell up toward the sky. I still cannot sleep without having nightmares, and if I look at water, any source of water, for more than a few seconds, a cold horror grips my whole body and I throw up.

PART ONE

Earth

THE THINGS THAT ARE SOLID, ABSORBED, AND STILL

Shams

AN INN OUTSIDE SAMARKAND, MARCH 1242

Beeswax candles flickered in front of my eyes above the cracked wooden table. The vision that took hold of me this evening was a most lucid one.

There was a big house with a courtyard full of yellow roses in bloom and in the middle of the courtyard a well with the coolest water in the world. It was a serene, late-autumn night with a full moon in the sky. A few nocturnal animals hooted and howled in the background. In a little while, a middle-aged man with a kind face, broad shoulders, and deep-set hazel eyes walked out of the house, looking for me. His expression was vexed, and his eyes were immensely sad.

"Shams, Shams, where are you?" he shouted left and right.

The wind blew hard, and the moon hid behind a cloud, as if it didn't want to witness what was about to happen. The owls stopped hooting, the bats stopped flapping their wings, and even the fire in the hearth inside the house did not crackle. An absolute stillness descended upon the world.

The man slowly approached the well, bent over, and looked down below. "Shams, dearest," he whispered. "Are you there?"

I opened my mouth to answer, but no sound came out of my lips.

The man leaned closer and looked down into the well again. At first he couldn't see anything other than the darkness of the water. But then, deep down at the bottom of the well, he caught sight of my hand floating aimlessly on the rippling water like a rickety raft after a heavy storm. Next he recognized a pair of eyes—two shiny black stones, staring up at the full moon now coming out from behind thick, dark clouds. My eyes were fixed on the moon as if waiting for an explanation from the skies for my murder.

The man fell on his knees, crying and pounding his chest. "They killed him! They killed my Shams!" he yelled.

Just then a shadow scurried out from behind a bush, and with fast, furtive moves it hopped over the garden wall, like a wildcat. But the man didn't notice the killer. Seized by a crushing pain, he screamed and screamed until his voice shattered like glass and flew all over into the night in tiny, prickly shards.

"Whoa you! Stop screaming like a maniac."

"..."

"Stop that awful noise or I am going to kick you out!"

"..."

"I said shut up! Do you hear me? Shut up!"

It was a male voice that shouted these words, booming menacingly close. I pretended not to hear him, preferring to stay inside my vision for at least a bit longer. I wanted to learn more about my death. I also wanted to see the man with the saddest eyes. Who was he? How was he related to me, and why was he so desperately looking for me on an autumn night?

But before I could sneak another look at my vision, someone grabbed me by the arm and shook me so hard I felt my teeth rattle in my mouth. It yanked me back into this world.

Slowly, reluctantly, I opened my eyes and saw the person standing beside me. He was a tall, corpulent man with a hoary beard and thick mustache, curved and pointy at the tips. I recognized him as the innkeeper. Almost instantly I noticed two things about him: That he was a man used to intimidating people with tough talk and sheer violence. And that right now he was furious.

"What do you want?" I asked. "Why are you pulling my arm?"

"What do I want?" the innkeeper roared with a scowl. "I want you to stop screaming, for starters, that's what I want. You are scaring away my customers."

"Really? Have I been screaming?" I muttered as I managed to pull myself free from his grip.

"You bet you were! You were screaming like a bear with a thorn stuck in its paw. What happened to you? Did you doze off during dinner? You must have had a nightmare or something."

I knew that this was the only plausible explanation, and if I went along with it, the innkeeper would be satisfied and leave me in peace. Still, I did not want to lie.

"No, brother, I have neither fallen asleep nor had a bad dream," I said. "Actually, I never have dreams."

"How do you explain all that screaming, then?" the innkeeper wanted to know.

"I had a vision. That's different."

He gave me a bewildered look and sucked on the ends of his mustache for a while. Finally he said, "You dervishes are as crazy as rats in a pantry. Especially you wandering types. All day long you fast and pray and walk under the scorching sun. No wonder you start hallucinating—your brain is fried!"

I smiled. He could be right. They say there is a thin line between losing yourself in God and losing your mind.

Two serving boys appeared just then, carrying between them a huge tray stacked with plates: freshly grilled goat, dried salted fish, spiced mutton, wheat cakes, chickpeas with meatballs, and lentil soup with sheep's-tail fat. They went around the hall distributing them, filling the air with the scents of onion, garlic, and spices. When they stopped by my end of the table, I got myself a bowl of steaming soup and some dark bread.

"Do you have money to pay for those?" the innkeeper asked, with a flicker of condescension.

"No, I don't," I said. "But allow me to offer an exchange. In return for the food and the room, I could interpret your dreams."

To this he responded with a sneer, his arms akimbo, "You just told me you never had dreams."

"That's right. I am a dream interpreter who doesn't have dreams of his own."

"I should toss you out of here. Like I said, you dervishes are nuts," the innkeeper said, spitting out the words. "Here is some advice for you: I don't know how old you are, but I'm sure you have prayed enough for both worlds. Find a nice woman and settle down. Have children. That will help to keep your feet on the ground. What is the point of roaming the world when it's the same misery everywhere? Trust me. There is nothing new out there. I have customers from the farthest corners of the world. After a few drinks, I hear the same stories from them all. Men are the same everywhere. Same food, same water, same old crap."

"I'm not looking for something different. I'm looking for God," I said. "My quest is a quest for God."

"Then you are looking for Him in the wrong place," he retorted, his voice suddenly thickened. "God has left this place! We don't know when He will be back."

My heart flailed away at my chest wall upon hearing this. "When one speaks ill of God, he speaks ill of himself," I said.

An odd, slanted smile etched along the innkeeper's mouth. In his face I saw bitterness and indignation, and something else that resembled childish hurt.

"Doesn't God say, *I am closer to you than your jugular vein*?" I asked. "God is not someplace far up in the sky. He is inside each and every one of us. That is why He never abandons us. How can He abandon Himself?"

"But He *does* abandon," the innkeeper remarked, his eyes cold and defiant. "If God is here but does not move a finger when we suffer the worst ends, what does that tell us about Him?"

"It is the first rule, brother," I said. *"How we see God is a direct reflection of how we see ourselves. If God brings to mind mostly fear and blame, it means there is too much fear and blame welled inside us. If we see God as full of love and compassion, so are we."*

The innkeeper immediately objected, but I could see that my words had surprised him. "How is that any different than saying God is a product of our imagination? I don't get it."

But my answer was interrupted by a ruckus that broke out at the back of the dining hall. When we turned in that direction, we saw two rough-looking men yelling drunken gibberish. With unbridled insolence they were bullying the other customers, snatching food off their bowls, drinking from their cups, and, should anyone protest, mocking them like two naughty *maktab* boys.

"Somebody should take care of these troublemakers, don't you think?" hissed the innkeeper between clenched teeth. "Now, watch me!"

In a flash he reached the end of the hall, yanked one of the drunken customers from his seat, and punched him in the face. The man must not have been expecting this at all, for he collapsed on the floor like an empty sack. A barely audible sigh came out of his lips, but other than that he made no noise.

The other man proved stronger, and he fiercely fought back, but it didn't take the innkeeper long to knock him down, too. He kicked his unruly customer in the ribs and then stomped on his hand, grinding it under his heavy boots. We heard the crack of a finger breaking, or maybe more.

"Stop it!" I exclaimed. "You are going to kill him. Is that what you want?"

As a Sufi I had sworn to protect life and do no harm. In this world of illusions, so many people were ready to fight without any reason, and so many others fought for a reason. But the Sufi was the one who wouldn't fight even if he had a reason. There was no way I could resort to violence. But I could thrust myself like a soft blanket between the innkeeper and the customers to keep them apart.

"You stay out of this, dervish, or I'll beat the hell out of you, too!" the innkeeper shouted, but we both knew he wasn't going to do that.

A minute later, when the serving boys lifted up the two customers, one of them had a broken finger and the other a broken nose, and there was blood all over. A fearful silence descended on the dining hall. Proud with the awe he'd inspired, the innkeeper gave me a sidelong look. When he spoke again, it sounded as if he were addressing everyone around, his voice soaring high and wild, like a marauder bird boasting in the open sky.

"You see, dervish, it wasn't always like this. Violence wasn't my element, but it is now. When God forgets about us down here, it falls upon us common people to toughen up and restore justice. So next time you talk to Him, you tell Him that. Let Him know that when He abandons his lambs, they won't meekly wait to be slaughtered. They will turn into wolves."

I shrugged as I motioned toward the door. "You are mistaken."

"Am I wrong in saying I was a lamb once and have turned into a wolf?"

"No, you got that right. I can see that you have become a wolf indeed. But you are wrong in calling what you are doing 'justice.'"

"Wait, I haven't finished with you!" the innkeeper shouted behind my back. "You owe me. In return for food and bed, you were going to interpret my dreams."

"I'll do something better," I suggested. "I'll read your palm."

I turned back and walked toward him, looking hard into his burning eyes. Instinctively, distrustfully, he flinched. Still, when I grabbed his right hand and turned his palm up, he didn't push me away. I inspected the lines and found them deep, cracked, marking uneven paths. Bit by bit, the colors in his aura appeared to me: a rusty brown and a blue so pale as to be almost gray. His spiritual energy was hollowed out and thinned around the edges, as if it had no more strength to defend itself against the outside world. Deep inside, the man was no more alive than a wilting plant. To make up for the loss of his spiritual energy, he had doubled up his physical energy, which he used in excess.

My heart beat faster, for I had started seeing something. At first dimly, as if behind a veil, then with increasing clarity, a scene appeared in front of my eyes.

A young woman with chestnut hair, bare feet with black tattoos, and an embroidered red shawl draped over her shoulders.

"You have lost a loved one," I said, and took his left palm in my hand.

Her breasts swollen with milk and her belly so huge it looks as if it could rip apart. She is stuck in a hut on fire. There are warriors around the house, riding horses with silver-gilded saddles. The thick smell of burning hay and human flesh. Mongol riders, their noses flat and wide, necks thick and short, and hearts as hard as rocks. The mighty army of Genghis Khan.

"You have lost two loved ones," I corrected myself. "Your wife was pregnant with your first child."

His eyebrows clamped down, his eyes fixed on his leather boots, and his lips tightly pursed, the innkeeper's face creased into an unreadable map. Suddenly he looked old beyond his years.

"I realize that it's no consolation to you, but I think there is something you should know," I said. "It wasn't the fire or the smoke that killed her. It was a wooden plank in the ceiling that collapsed on her head. She died instantly, without any pain. You always assumed she had suffered terribly, but in reality she did not suffer at all."

The innkeeper furrowed his brow, bowed under a pressure only he could understand. His voice turned raspy as he asked, "How do you know all that?"

I ignored the question. "You have been blaming yourself for not giving her a proper funeral. You still see her in your dreams, crawling out of the pit she was buried in. But your mind is playing games with you. In truth, your wife and son are both fine, traveling in infinity, as free as a speck of light."

I then added, measuring each word, "You can become a lamb again, because you still have it in you."

Upon hearing this the innkeeper pulled his hand away, as if he had just touched a sizzling pan. "I don't like you, dervish," he said. "I'll let you stay here tonight. But make sure you are gone early in the morning. I don't want to see your face around here again."

It was always like this. When you spoke the truth, they hated you. The more you talked about love, the more they hated you.

Ella

NORTHAMPTON, MAY 18, 2008

Brimming over with the tension that followed the argument with David and Jeannette, Ella was so drained she had to stop reading *Sweet Blasphemy* for a while. She felt as though the lid of a boiling cauldron had suddenly been lifted, emitting old conflicts and new resentments in the rising steam. Unfortunately, it was no one other than she who had lifted that lid. And she had done it by dialing Scott's number and asking him not to marry her daughter.

Later in her life, she would deeply regret everything she'd uttered during this phone conversation. But on this day in May, she was so sure of herself and the ground beneath her feet that she could not for the life of her fathom any dire consequences from her intrusion.

"Hi, Scott. This is Jeannette's mom, Ella," she said, trying to sound jovial, as if calling her daughter's boyfriend were something she did all the time. "Do you have a minute to talk?"

"Mrs. Rubinstein, how may I help you?" Scott stammered, surprised but ever so civilized.

And in a no-less-civilized tone, Ella told him that although she had nothing against him personally, he was too young and inexperienced to marry her daughter. Upset as he might be to receive this call now, she added, someday in the not-so-distant future he would understand and even thank her for warning him in time. Until then she asked him to kindly drop the subject of marriage and to keep this phone conversation between the two of them.

There was a thick, dense silence.

"Mrs. Rubinstein, I don't think you understand," Scott said when he finally found his voice. "Jeannette and I love each other."

There it was again! How could people be naïve enough to expect love to open every door for them? They looked at love as if it were a magic wand that could fix everything with one miraculous touch.

But Ella didn't say any of this. Instead she said, "I understand how you feel, believe me, I do. But you are too young and life is long. Who knows? Tomorrow you might fall in love with someone else."

"Mrs. Rubinstein, I don't want to be rude, but don't you think the same rule applies to everyone, including yourself? Who knows? Tomorrow you, too, might fall in love with someone else."

Ella chuckled, louder and longer than she intended.

"I'm a married woman. I've made a choice for a lifetime. So did my husband. And that's exactly my point. Marriage is a serious decision, which needs to be considered very carefully."

"Are you telling me not to marry your daughter, who I love, because I might love an unidentified other in an indefinite future?" Scott demanded.

The conversation went downhill from there, filled with distress and disappointment. When they finally hung up, Ella headed to the kitchen and did what she always did at times of emotional unrest: She cooked.

Half an hour later, she received a call from her husband.

"I can't believe you called Scott to ask him not to marry our daughter. Tell me you didn't do this."

Ella gasped. "Wow, word gets out fast. Honey, let me explain."

But David interjected tensely, "There is nothing to explain. What you did was wrong. Scott told Jeannette, and now she's extremely upset. She'll be staying with her friends for a few days. She doesn't want to see you right now." He paused briefly. "And I don't blame her."

That evening Jeannette wasn't the only one who didn't come home. David sent Ella a text message informing her of a sudden emergency that had arisen. There was no explanation as to the nature of the emergency.

It was so unlike him and against the spirit of their marriage. He might flirt with woman after woman, could even sleep with them and spend his money on them for all she knew, but he had always come home and taken his place at the table in the evenings. No matter how deep the rift between them, she always cooked and he always ate, gladly and gratefully, whatever she put on his plate. At the end of each dinner, David never failed to thank her—a heartfelt thank-you that she always took to be a coded apology for his infidelities. She forgave him. She always did.

This was the first time her husband had acted this brazen, and Ella blamed herself for the change. But then again, "guilt" was Ella Rubinstein's middle name.

When she sat at the table with her twins, Ella's guilt gave way to melancholy. She resisted Avi's pleas to order pizza and Orly's attempts not to eat anything, forcing them to munch on wild rice with green peas and roast beef with mustard glaze. And although on the surface she was the same hands-on, concerned mother, she felt a surge of despair rise in her, a sharp taste in her mouth, sour like bile.

When dinner was over, Ella sat at the kitchen table on her own, finding the stillness around her heavy and unsettling. Suddenly the food she had cooked, the outcome of hours of hard work, seemed not only dull and boring but easily replaceable. She felt sorry for herself. It was a pity that, at almost forty, she hadn't been able to make more of her life. She had so much love to give and yet no one demanding it.

Her thoughts turned to *Sweet Blasphemy.* She was intrigued by the character of Shams of Tabriz.

"It could be nice to have someone like him around," she joked to herself. "Never a dull day with a guy like him!"

And somehow the image that popped up in her mind was of a tall, dark-looking, mysterious man with leather pants, a motorcycle jacket, and black hair that fell to his shoulders, riding a shiny red Harley-Davidson with multicolored tassels hanging from the handlebars. She smiled at the image. A handsome, sexy, Sufi motorcyclist riding fast on an empty highway! Wouldn't it be nice to get picked up while hitchhiking by a guy like that?

Ella then wondered what Shams would see if he read her palm. Would he explain to her why her mind turned from time to time into a coven of dark thoughts? Or how come she felt so lonely even though she had a large, loving family? What about the colors in her aura? Were they bright and bold? Had anything in her life been bright and bold lately? Or ever?

It was then and there, while sitting alone at the kitchen table with only a faint glimmer of light from the oven, that Ella realized that despite her high-flying words denying it, and despite her ability to keep a stiff upper lip, deep inside she longed for love.

Shams

AN INN OUTSIDE SAMARKAND, MARCH 1242

Burdened with loneliness, all fast asleep in separate dreams, were more than a dozen weary travelers upstairs at the inn. I stepped over bare feet and hands to reach my empty bedroll that reeked of sweat and mold. I lay there in the dark, mulling over the day's events and reflecting on any divine signs I might have witnessed but, in my haste or ignorance, failed to appreciate.

Since I was a boy, I had received visions and heard voices. I always talked to God, and He always responded. Some days I ascended all the way up to the seventh sky as light as a whisper. Then I descended into the deepest pits of the earth, suffused with the smells of soil, hidden away like a rock buried under mighty oaks and sweet chestnuts. Every so often I lost my appetite for food and went without eating for days on end. None of these things scared me, though in time I had learned not to mention them to others. Human beings tended to disparage what they couldn't comprehend. I had learned that firsthand.

The first person to misjudge my visions was my father. I must have been ten years old when I started seeing my guardian angel on a daily basis and was naïve enough to think that everyone else did as well. One day, while my father was teaching me how to build a cedar chest so that I could become a carpenter like him, I told him about my guardian angel.

"You have a wild imagination, son," my father said dryly. "And you better keep it to yourself. We don't want to upset the villagers again."

A few days before, the neighbors had complained about me to my parents, accusing me of acting strange and scaring their kids.

"I don't understand your ways, my son. Why can't you accept that you are no more remarkable than your parents?" my father asked. "Every child takes after his father and mother. So have you."

That was when I realized that although I loved my parents and craved their love, they were strangers to me.

"Father, I am from a different egg than your other children. Think of me as a duckling raised by hens. I am not a domestic bird destined to spend his life in a chicken coop. The water that scares you rejuvenates me. For unlike you I can swim, and swim I shall. The ocean is my homeland. If you are with me, come to the ocean. If not, stop interfering with me and go back to the chicken coop."

My father's eyes grew large, then small and distant. "If this is the way you talk to your father now," he said gravely, "I wonder how you will address your enemies when you grow up."

Much to the mortification of my parents, the visions did not disappear as I got older. If anything, they became more intense and gripping. I knew I made my parents nervous, and I felt guilty for upsetting them so, but the truth is, I didn't know how to end the visions, and even if I had, I don't think I would have. Before long I left my house for good. Since then Tabriz has become a smooth, sweet word, so fine and delicate that it melts on my tongue. Three scents accompany my memories of this place: cut wood, poppy-seed bread, and the soft, crisp smell of snow.

I have been a wandering dervish ever since, not sleeping in the same place more than once, not eating out of the same bowl twice in a row, every day seeing different faces around me. When hungry, I earn a few coins by interpreting dreams. In this state I roam east and west, searching for God high and low. I hunt everywhere for a life worth living and a knowledge worth knowing. Having roots nowhere, I have everywhere to go.

During my travels I have taken all sorts of roads, from popular trade routes to forgotten tracks where you wouldn't run into a soul for days on end. From the coasts of the Black Sea to the cities of Persia, from the vast steppes of Central Asia to the sand dunes of Arabia, I have passed through thick forests, flat grasslands, and deserts; sojourned at caravansaries and hostels; consulted with the learned men in age-old libraries; listened to tutors teaching little children in *maktabs*; discussed *tafsir* and logic with students in madrassas; visited temples, monasteries, and shrines;

meditated with hermits in their caves; performed *zikr* with dervishes; fasted with sages and dined with heretics; danced with shamans under the full moon; come to know people of all faiths, ages, and professions; and witnessed misfortunes and miracles alike.

I have seen poverty-stricken villages, fields blackened by fire, and plundered towns where the rivers ran red and there were no men left alive above the age of ten. I have seen the worst and the best in humanity. Nothing surprises me anymore.

As I went through all these experiences, I began to compile a list that wasn't written down in any book, only inscribed in my soul. This personal list I called The Basic Principles of the Itinerant Mystics of Islam. To me these were as universal, dependable, and invariable as the laws of nature. Together they constituted The Forty Rules of the Religion of Love, which could be attained through love and love only. And one of those rules said, *The Path to the Truth is a labor of the heart, not of the head. Make your heart your primary guide! Not your mind. Meet, challenge, and ultimately prevail over your* nafs *with your heart. Knowing your self will lead you to the knowledge of God.*

It had taken me years to finish working on these rules. All forty of them. And now that I was done, I knew I was nearing the final stage of my time in this world. Lately I had been having many visions in this direction. It wasn't death that worried me, for I didn't see it as an end, but dying without leaving a legacy behind. There were many words piled up inside my chest, stories waiting to be told. I wanted to hand all this knowledge to one other person, neither a master nor a disciple. I sought an equal—a companion.

"God," I whispered into the dark, damp room, "all my life I traveled the world and followed Thy path. I saw every person as an open book, a walking Qur'an. I stayed away from the ivory towers of scholars, preferring to spend time with outcasts, expatriates, and exiles. Now I am bursting. Help me to hand Thy wisdom to the right person. Then Thou can do with me as Thou wish."

Before my eyes the room was showered with a light so bright that the faces of the travelers in their beds turned lurid blue. The air inside smelled fresh and alive, as if all the windows had been pushed open and a gusty wind brought in the scent of lilies and jasmine from faraway gardens.

"Go to Baghdad," fluted my guardian angel in a singsong voice.

"What is awaiting me in Baghdad?" I asked.

"You prayed for a companion, and a companion you will be given. In Baghdad you will find the master who will point you in the right direction."

Tears of gratitude welled up in my eyes. Now I knew that the man in my vision was no other than my spiritual companion. Sooner or later we were destined to meet. And when we did, I would learn why his kind hazel eyes were eternally sad and how I came to be murdered on an early-spring night.

Ella

NORTHAMPTON, MAY 19, 2008

Before the sun had set and the children had come back home, Ella placed a bookmark in the manuscript and put *Sweet Blasphemy* aside. Curious about the man who had written the novel, she went online and Googled "A. Z. Zahara," wondering what would pop up but not expecting much.

To her surprise, a personal blog appeared. The colors on the page were predominantly amethyst and turquoise, and on top of the page a male figure with a long white skirt whirled slowly. Having never seen a whirling dervish before, Ella took a careful look at the picture. The blog was titled An Eggshell Named Life, and beneath it there was a poem with the same title:

Let us choose one another as companions!
Let us sit at each other's feet!
Inwardly we have many harmonies—think not
That we are only what we see.

The page was full of postcards from cities and sites all around the world. Underneath each postcard there were comments about that particular place. It was while reading these that Ella came across three pieces of information that immediately drew her attention: First, that the *A* in A. Z. Zahara stood for Aziz. Second, that Aziz regarded himself as a Sufi. Third, that at the moment he was traveling somewhere in Guatemala.

In another section there were samples of the photos he had taken. Most were portraits of people of all colors and stripes. Despite their stark differences, they resembled one another in one curious respect: All the people in all the portraits had something visibly missing. For some the missing element was a simple thing, like an earring, a shoe, or a button, while for others it was much more substantial, like a tooth, a finger, or sometimes a leg. Underneath the photos it read:

> *No matter who we are or where we live, deep inside we all feel incomplete. It's like we have lost something and need to get it back. Just what that something is, most of us never find out. And of those who do, even fewer manage to go out and look for it.*

Ella scrolled up and down the Web page, clicked on every postcard to enlarge it, and read every comment Aziz had made. At the bottom of the page, there was an e-mail address, azizZzahara@gmail.com, which she wrote down on a piece of paper. Next to that she found a poem by Rumi:

> *Choose Love, Love! Without the sweet life of*
> *Love, living is a burden—as you have seen.*

It was while reading this poem that a most peculiar thought flashed across her mind. For a fleeting moment, it felt as if everything Aziz Z. Zahara included in his personal blog—the pictures, the comments, the quotations, and the poems—were written for her eyes only. It was a strange and slightly supercilious thought, but one that made perfect sense to her.

Later in the afternoon, Ella sat by the window, feeling tired and slightly down, the sun heavy on her back and the air in the kitchen filled with the smells of the brownies she was baking. She had *Sweet Blasphemy* open in front of her, but her mind was so preoccupied she couldn't concentrate on the manuscript. It occurred to her that perhaps she, too, should write her own set of ground rules. She could name it The Forty Rules of the Sedentary, Suburban, Earthy Housewife.

"Rule Number One," she murmured. "Stop looking for love! Stop running after impossible dreams! There are surely more important things in life for a married woman about to be forty."

But her own joke produced an obscure discomfort in Ella, reminding her of bigger worries. Unable to hold herself back anymore, she gave her elder daughter a call. She got her answering machine.

"Jeannette, dear, I know it was wrong of me to call Scott. But my intentions weren't bad. I just wanted to make sure . . ."

She paused, deeply regretting not planning this message in advance. She could hear the soft rustle of the answering machine recording in the background. It made her nervous to think that the tape was rolling and time was running short.

"Jeannette, I'm sorry for the things I do. I know I shouldn't complain when I'm so blessed. But it's just that I'm so . . . unhappy—"

Click. The answering machine came to a stop. Ella's heart constricted with the shock of what she'd just said. What had come over her? She hadn't known she was unhappy. Was it possible to be depressed and not know it? Oddly enough, she didn't feel unhappy about confessing her unhappiness. She hadn't been feeling much of anything lately.

Her gaze slid to the piece of paper on which she'd written Aziz Z. Zahara's e-mail address. The address looked simple, unpretentious, and somehow inviting. Without giving it much thought, she went to her computer and started composing an e-mail:

Dear Aziz Z. Zahara,

My name is Ella. I am reading your novel *Sweet Blasphemy* in my capacity as a reader for the literary agency. I have only just begun, and I am enjoying it immensely. This, however, is my personal opinion and is not reflective of the views of my boss. Whether I like your novel or not, I have barely any influence on the final decision as to whether we will take you on as a client.

It seems like you believe that love is the essence of life and that nothing else matters. It's not my intention to get into a fruitless debate with you on this matter. Suffice it to say that I do not completely agree. But this is not why I am writing to you.

I am writing because the "timing" of my reading *Sweet Blasphemy* couldn't have been more bizarre. Currently I am trying to persuade my elder daughter not to marry so young. The day before, I asked her boyfriend to call off their marriage plans. Now my daughter hates me and refuses to talk to me. I have a feeling you two would get along well, as you seem to have very similar views on love.

I am sorry to pour my personal problems out to you. That wasn't my intention. Your personal blog (that is where I found your e-mail address) says you are in Guatemala. Traveling around the world must be quite a thrill. If you happen to come to Boston, perhaps we could meet in person and talk over a cup of coffee.

Best wishes,
Ella

Her first e-mail to Aziz was not a letter so much as an invitation, a cry for help. But Ella had no way of knowing this as she sat in the silence of her kitchen and composed a note to an unknown writer she didn't expect to meet now or at any time in the future.

The Master

BAGHDAD, APRIL 1242

Baghdad took no note of the arrival of Shams of Tabriz, but I will never forget the day he came to our modest dervish lodge. We had important guests that afternoon. The high judge had dropped by with a group of his men, and I suspected there was more than cordiality behind his visit. Renowned for his dislike of Sufism, the judge wanted to remind me that he kept an eye on us, just as he kept an eye on all the Sufis in the area.

The judge was an ambitious man. He had a broad face, a sagging belly, and short, stubby fingers, each with a precious ring. He had to stop eating so much, but I suspected that nobody had the courage to tell him, not even his doctor. Coming from a long line of religious scholars, he was one of the most influential men in the area. With one ruling he could send a man to the gallows, or he could just as easily pardon a convict's crimes, lifting him up from the darkest dungeons. Always dressed in fur coats and expensive garments, he carried himself with the grandeur of someone who was sure of his authority. I did not approve of his showy ways, but for the well-being of our lodge I did my best to remain on good terms with this man of influence.

"We live in the most magnificent city in the world," the judge pronounced as he popped a fig into his mouth. "Today Baghdad overflows with refugees running away from the Mongol army. We provide them safe haven. This is the center of the world, don't you think, Baba Zaman?"

"This city is a gem, no doubt," I said carefully. "But let us not forget that cities are like human beings. They are born, they go through childhood and adolescence, they grow old, and eventually they die. At this moment in time,

Baghdad is in its late youth. We are not as wealthy as we used to be at the time of Caliph Harun ar-Rashid, though we can still take a measure of pride in being a center of trade, crafts, and poetry. But who knows what the city will look like a thousand years from now? Everything might be different."

"Such pessimism!" The judge shook his head as he reached out to another bowl and picked a date. "The Abbasid rule will prevail, and we will prosper. That is, of course, if the status quo is not disrupted by the traitors among us. There are those who call themselves Muslim, but their interpretation of Islam is far more dangerous than threats from infidels."

I chose to remain silent. It was no secret that the judge thought the mystics, with their individualistic and esoteric interpretations of Islam, were troublemakers. He accused us of paying no heed to the sharia and thus disrespecting the men of authority—men like him. Sometimes I had the feeling he would rather have all Sufis kicked out of Baghdad.

"Your brotherhood is harmless, but don't you think some Sufis are beyond the pale?" the judge asked, stroking his beard.

I didn't know how to respond to that. Thank God just then we heard a knock on the door. It was the ginger-haired novice. He made a beeline toward me and whispered in my ear that we had a visitor, a wandering dervish who insisted upon seeing me and refused to talk to anyone else.

Normally I would have asked the novice to take the newcomer to a quiet, welcoming room, give him warm food, and make him wait until the guests had left. But as the judge was giving me a hard time, it occurred to me that a wandering dervish could dispel the tension in the room by telling us colorful stories from faraway lands. So I asked the novice to bring the man in.

A few minutes later, the door opened and in walked a man dressed head to toe in black. Lank, gaunt, and of indeterminable age, he had a sharp nose, deeply set pitch-black eyes, and dark hair that fell over his eyes in thick curls. He wore a long, hooded cloak, a wool garment, and sheepskin boots. There were a number of charms around his neck. He held a wooden bowl in his hand of the sort that mendicant dervishes carry to overcome their personal vanity and hubris by accepting the charity of others. I realized that here was a man who did not pay much attention to the judgments of society. That people could confuse him with some vagrant, or even a beggar, didn't seem to bother him in the least.

As soon as I saw him standing there, awaiting permission to introduce himself, I sensed he was different. It was in his eyes, in his elaborate gestures, written all over him. Like an acorn that might seem modest and vulnerable to ignorant eyes but already heralds the proud oak tree that it will turn out to be, he looked at me with those piercing black eyes and nodded silently.

"Welcome to our lodge, dervish," I said as I motioned for him to take a seat on the cushions across from me.

After greeting everyone, the dervish sat down, inspecting the people in the room, taking in every detail. Finally his gaze stopped at the judge. The two men looked at each other for a full minute, without so much as a word, and I couldn't help wondering what each thought of the other, as they seemed so very opposite.

I offered the dervish warm goat milk, sweetened figs, and filled dates, all of which he politely refused. When asked his name, he introduced himself as Shams of Tabriz and said he was a wandering dervish searching for God high and low.

"And were you able to find Him?" I inquired.

A shadow crossed his face as the dervish nodded and said, "Indeed, He was with me all along."

The judge interjected with a smirk he didn't bother to hide, "I never understand why you dervishes make life so complicated. If God was with you all along, why did you rummage around this whole time in search of Him?"

Shams of Tabriz bowed his head pensively and remained silent for a moment. When he looked up again, his face was calm, his voice measured. "Because although it is a fact that He cannot be found by seeking, only those who seek can find Him."

"Such wordplay," the judge scoffed. "Are you trying to tell us that we cannot find God if we stay in the same place all our lives? That's nonsense. Not everyone needs to dress in tatters and hit the road like you!"

There followed a ripple of laughter as the men in the room were eager to show their agreement with the judge—high-pitched, unconfident, and unhappy laughs from people used to toadying to superiors. I felt uneasy. Obviously it hadn't been a good idea to bring the judge and the dervish together.

"Perhaps I was misunderstood. I didn't mean to say one could not find God if he stayed in his hometown. That is certainly possible," conceded the dervish. "There are people who have never traveled anywhere and yet have seen the world."

"Exactly!" The judge grinned triumphantly—a grin that vanished upon hearing what the dervish uttered next.

"What I meant to say, Judge, was that one could not find God if he stayed in the fur coat, silk garment, and pricey jewelry that you are wearing today."

A stunned silence descended upon the room, the sounds and sighs around us dissolving down to dust. We all held our breath, as if expecting something bigger to happen, though what could have been more shocking, I didn't know.

"Your tongue is too sharp for a dervish," the judge said.

"When something needs to be said, I'll say it even if the whole world grabs me by the neck and tells me to keep quiet."

This was met with a frown from the judge, but then he shrugged dismissively. "As you will," he said. "In any case, you are the man we need. We were just talking about the splendor of our city. You must have seen many places. Is there a place more charming than Baghdad?"

Softly, his gaze moving from one man to another, Shams explained, "There is no question Baghdad is a remarkable city, but no beauty on earth lasts forever. Cities are erected on spiritual columns. Like giant mirrors, they reflect the hearts of their residents. If those hearts darken and lose faith, cities will lose their glamour. It happens, and it happens all the time."

I couldn't help but nod. Shams of Tabriz turned to me, momentarily distracted from his thoughts, with a friendly flicker in his eyes. I felt them on me like the heat of a sweltering sun. That was when I clearly saw how he merited his name. This man was radiating vigor and vitality and burning within, like a ball of fire. He was indeed Shams, "the sun."

But the judge was of a different mind. "You Sufis make everything too complicated. The same with philosophers and poets! Why the need for so many words? Human beings are simple creatures with simple needs. It falls upon the leaders to see to their needs and make sure they do not go astray. That requires applying the sharia to perfection."

"The sharia is like a candle," said Shams of Tabriz. "It provides us with much valuable light. But let us not forget that a candle helps us to go from one place to another in the dark. If we forget where we are headed and instead concentrate on the candle, what good is it?"

The judge grimaced, his face closing up. I felt a wave of anxiety wash over me. Entering into a discussion about the significance of the sharia with a man whose job was to judge, and often punish, people according to the sharia was swimming in dangerous waters. Didn't Shams know that?

Just as I was looking for an appropriate excuse to take the dervish out of the room, I heard him say, "There is a rule that applies to this situation."

"What rule?" asked the judge suspiciously.

Shams of Tabriz straightened up, his gaze fixed as if reading from an invisible book, and he pronounced:

"Each and every reader comprehends the Holy Qur'an on a different level in tandem with the depth of his understanding. There are four levels of insight. The first level is the outer meaning and it is the one that the majority of the people are content with. Next is the Batını—the inner level. Third, there is the inner of the inner. And the fourth level is so deep it cannot be put into words and is therefore bound to remain indescribable."

With glinting eyes Shams continued. "Scholars who focus on the sharia know the outer meaning. Sufis know the inner meaning. Saints know the inner of the inner. And as for the fourth level, that is known only by prophets and those closest to God."

"Are you telling me that an ordinary Sufi has a deeper grasp of the Qur'an than a sharia scholar?" the judge asked as he tapped his fingers on the bowl.

A subtle, sardonic smile curved the dervish's mouth, but he didn't answer.

"Be careful, my friend," the judge said. "There is a thin line between where you stand and sheer blasphemy."

If there was a threat in these words, the dervish seemed not to have noticed it. "What exactly is 'sheer blasphemy'?" he asked, and then with a sharp intake of breath he added, "Allow me to tell you a story."

And here is what he told us:

One day Moses was walking in the mountains on his own when he saw a shepherd in the distance. The man was on his knees with his hands spread out to the sky, praying. Moses was delighted. But when he got closer, he was equally stunned to hear the shepherd's prayer.

"Oh, my beloved God, I love Thee more than Thou can know. I will do anything for Thee, just say the word. Even if Thou asked me to slaughter the fattest sheep in my flock in Thy name, I would do so without hesitation. Thou would roast it and put its tail fat in Thy rice to make it more tasty."

Moses inched toward the shepherd, listening attentively.

"Afterward I would wash Thy feet and clean Thine ears and pick Thy lice for Thee. That is how much I love Thee."

Having heard enough, Moses interrupted the shepherd, yelling, "Stop, you ignorant man! What do you think you are doing? Do you think God eats rice? Do you think God has feet for you to wash? This is not prayer. It is sheer blasphemy."

Dazed and ashamed, the shepherd apologized repeatedly and promised to pray as decent people did. Moses taught him several prayers that afternoon. Then he went on his way, utterly pleased with himself.

But that night Moses heard a voice. It was God's.

"Oh, Moses, what have you done? You scolded that poor shepherd and failed to realize how dear he was to Me. He might not be saying the right things in the right way, but he was sincere. His heart was pure and his intentions good. I was pleased with him. His words might have been blasphemy to your ears, but to Me they were sweet blasphemy."

Moses immediately understood his mistake. The next day, early in the morning, he went back to the mountains to see the shepherd. He found him praying again, except this time he was praying in the way he had been instructed. In his determination to get the prayer right, he was stammering, bereft of the excitement and passion of his earlier prayer. Regretting what he had done to him, Moses patted the shepherd's back and said: "My friend, I was wrong. Please forgive me. Keep praying in your own way. That is more precious in God's eyes."

The shepherd was astonished to hear this, but even deeper was his relief. Nevertheless, he did not want to go back to his old prayers. Neither did he abide by the formal prayers that Moses had taught him. He had now found a new way of communicating with God. Though satisfied and blessed in his naïve devotion, he was now past that stage—beyond his sweet blasphemy.

"So you see, don't judge the way other people connect to God," concluded Shams. "To each his own way and his own prayer. God does not take us at our word. He looks deep into our hearts. It is not the ceremonies or rituals that make a difference, but whether our hearts are sufficiently pure or not."

I checked the judge's face. I could see beneath his mask of absolute confidence and composure that he was clearly annoyed. Yet at the same time, being the astute man that he was, he had detected a tricky situation. If he reacted to Shams's story, he would have to take the next step and punish him for his insolence, in which case things would get serious and everybody would hear that a simple dervish had dared to confront the high judge. It was therefore better for him to pretend there was nothing to be upset about and leave it there.

Outside, the sun was setting, painting the sky a dozen shades of crimson, punctuated now and again by dark gray clouds. In a little while, the judge rose to his feet, saying he had some important business to attend to. After giving me a slight nod and Shams of Tabriz a cold stare, he strode off. His men followed wordlessly.

"I am afraid the judge didn't like you much," I said when everyone had left.

Shams of Tabriz brushed his hair from his face, smiling. "Oh, that is quite all right. I am used to people not liking me much."

I couldn't help feeling excited. I had been the master of this lodge long enough to know that it was not often such a visitor came.

"Tell me, dervish," I said, "what brings someone like you to Baghdad?"

I was eager to hear his answer but also strangely fearful of it.

Ella

NORTHAMPTON, MAY 20, 2008

Belly dancers and dervishes spun in Ella's dream on the night her husband didn't come home. Her head resting on the manuscript, she watched as rough-looking warriors dined at a roadside inn, their plates piled high with delicious pies and desserts.

Then she saw herself. She was searching for someone in a bustling bazaar in a citadel in a foreign country. All around her, people moved slowly, as if dancing to a tune she couldn't hear. She stopped a fat man with a drooping mustache to ask something, only she couldn't remember the question. The man looked at her blankly and hobbled away. She tried to talk to several vendors and then shoppers, but no one responded to her. At first she thought it was because she couldn't speak their language. Then she put her hand to her mouth and realized with horror that her tongue had been cut off. With increasing panic she looked around for a mirror to see her reflection and figure out if she was still the same person, but there was none in the bazaar. She started to cry and woke up to a disturbing sound, not knowing whether she still had a tongue.

When Ella opened her eyes, she found Spirit frantically scratching at the back door. An animal had probably gotten onto the porch, driving the dog crazy. Skunks made him particularly nervous. The memory of his inopportune encounter with one last winter was still fresh. It had taken Ella weeks to remove that nasty odor from the dog, and even after she'd washed him in tubs of tomato juice, the smell lingered, reminiscent of burning rubber.

Ella glanced at the clock on the wall. It was a quarter to three in the morning. David was still not back, and perhaps he never would be. Jeannette had not returned her call, and in her pessimistic state Ella doubted she ever would. Seized by the terror of being abandoned by her husband and daughter, she opened the fridge and looked through it for a few minutes. The desire to scoop out some cherry vanilla ice cream warred with the fear of gaining weight. With no small effort, she took a step away from the fridge and slammed the door, a bit more harshly than necessary.

Then Ella opened a bottle of red wine and poured herself a glass. It was good wine, light and lively, with an underlying hint of bittersweetness that she liked. Only when she was filling the second glass did it occur to her she might have opened one of David's expensive Bordeaux. She checked the label—Château Margaux 1996. Not knowing what to make of that, she frowned at the bottle.

She was too tired and too sleepy to read anymore. So she decided to check her e-mail. There, among half a dozen junk e-mails and a message from Michelle inquiring about how the manuscript was going, she found an e-mail from Aziz Z. Zahara.

Dear Ella (if I may),

Your e-mail found me in a village in Guatemala called Momostenango. It's one of the few places left where they still use a Mayan calendar. Right across from my hostel, there is a wish tree bedecked with hundreds of pieces of fabric of every color and pattern you can imagine. They call it The Tree of the Brokenhearted. Those with broken hearts write down their names on pieces of paper and tie these to the branches, praying for their hearts to be healed.

I hope you won't find this too presumptuous, but after reading your e-mail I went to the wish tree and prayed that you and your daughter solve this misunderstanding. Even a speck of love should not go unappreciated, because, as Rumi said, love is the water of life.

One thing that has helped me personally in the past was to stop interfering with the people around me and getting frustrated when I couldn't change them. Instead of intrusion or passivity, may I suggest submission?

Some people make the mistake of confusing "submission" with

"weakness," whereas it is anything but. Submission is a form of peaceful acceptance of the terms of the universe, including the things we are currently unable to change or comprehend.

According to the Mayan calendar, today is an auspicious day. A major astrological shift is on its way, ushering in a new human consciousness. I need to hurry to send you this e-mail before the sun sets and the day is over.

May love find you when you least expect, where you least expect.

Yours sincerely,
Aziz

Ella shut off the laptop, moved to learn that a complete stranger in a remote corner of the world had prayed for her well-being. She closed her eyes and imagined her name written on a piece of paper tied to a wish tree, dangling like a kite in the air, free and happy.

A few minutes later, she opened the kitchen door and stepped out into the backyard, enjoying the unsettling coolness of the breeze. Spirit stood beside her, uneasy and growling, constantly sniffing the air. The dog's eyes grew small, then big and anxious, and his ears kept perking up, as if he had recognized in the distance something scary. Ella and her dog stood side by side under the late-spring moon, staring into the thick, vast darkness, similarly frightened of the things moving in the dark, frightened of the unknown.

The Novice

BAGHDAD, APRIL 1242

Bowing and scraping, I showed the judge to the door and quickly returned to the main room to collect the dirty bowls. I was surprised to find Baba Zaman and the wandering dervish in the same position as when I left them, neither one saying a word. Out of the corner of my eye, I checked them, wondering if it could be possible to carry on a conversation without talking. I lingered there as long as I could, arranging the cushions, tidying up the room, picking up the crumbs on the carpet, but after a while I ran out of reasons to stay.

Halfheartedly, I dragged my feet back to the kitchen. As soon as he saw me, the cook started to rain orders. "Wipe the counter, mop the floor! Wash the dishes! Scrub the stove and the walls around the grill! And when you are done, don't forget to check the mousetraps!" Ever since I'd come to this lodge some six months ago, the cook had been riding roughshod over me. Every day he made me work like a dog and called this torture part of my spiritual training, as if washing greasy dishes could be spiritual in any way.

A man of few words, the cook had one favorite mantra: "Cleaning is praying, praying is cleaning!"

"If that were true, all the housewives in Baghdad would have become spiritual masters," I once dared to say.

He threw a wooden spoon at my head and yelled at the top of his lungs, "Such back talk will get you nowhere, son. If you want to become a dervish, be as mute as that wooden spoon. Rebelliousness is not a good quality in a novice. Speak less, mature quicker!"

I hated the cook, but, more than that, I feared him. I had never disobeyed his orders. That is, until this evening.

As soon as the cook turned his back, I sneaked out of the kitchen and tiptoed to the main room again, dying to learn more about the wandering dervish. Who was he? What was he doing here? He wasn't like the dervishes in the lodge. His eyes looked fierce and unruly, even when he bowed his head in modesty. There was something so unusual and unpredictable about him that it was almost frightening.

I peeped through a crack in the door. At first I couldn't see anything. But soon my eyes adjusted to the semidarkness inside the room and I could make out their faces.

I heard the master ask, "Tell me, Shams of Tabriz, what brings someone like you to Baghdad? Have you seen this place in a dream?"

The dervish shook his head. "No, it wasn't a dream that brought me here. It was a vision. I never have dreams."

"Everybody has dreams," Baba Zaman said tenderly. "It's just that you might not remember them all the time. But that doesn't mean you don't dream."

"But I do not," the dervish insisted. "It is part of a deal I made with God. You see, when I was a boy, I saw angels and watched the mysteries of the universe unfold before my eyes. When I told this to my parents, they weren't pleased and told me to stop dreaming. When I confided in my friends, they, too, said I was a hopeless dreamer. I tried talking to my teachers, but their response was no different. Finally I understood that whenever people heard something unusual, they called it a dream. I began to dislike the word and all that it represented."

Upon saying this, the dervish paused as if he had heard a sudden sound. Then the strangest thing happened. He stood up, straightened his spine, and slowly, deliberately began to walk toward the door, all the while looking in my direction. It was as if he somehow knew I was spying on them.

It was as if he could see through the wooden door.

My heart pounded like mad. I wanted to run back to the kitchen but couldn't see how. My arms, my legs, my whole body froze. Through and beyond the door, the dark eyes of Shams of Tabriz were fixed upon me. As terrified as I was, I also felt a tremendous amount of energy rushing through my body. He approached, put his hand on the door handle, but just when I thought he was about to open the door and catch me, he stopped. I couldn't see his face from this close and had no idea what had changed his mind. We waited like that for an unbearably long minute. Then he turned his back, and as he paced away from the door, he continued with his story.

"When I got a little older, I asked God to take away my ability to dream, so that every time I encountered Him, I would know I wasn't dreaming. He agreed. He took them all away. That's why I never dream."

Shams of Tabriz now stood by the open windows across the room. Outside, there was a light drizzle, and he watched it pensively before he said, "God took away my ability to dream. But to compensate for that loss, He allowed me to interpret the dreams of others. I am a dream interpreter."

I expected Baba Zaman not to believe this nonsense and to scold him, as he scolds me all the time.

But instead the master nodded respectfully and said, "You seem to be an unusual person. Tell me, what can I do for you?"

"I don't know. Actually, I was hoping you could tell me that."

"What do you mean?" asked the master, sounding puzzled.

"For almost forty years, I have been a wandering dervish. I am skilled in the ways of nature, although the ways of society are still alien to me. If necessary, I can fight like a wild animal, but I myself cannot hurt anyone. I can name the constellations in the sky, identify the trees in the forests, and read like an open book the types of people the Almighty has created in His image."

Shams paused briefly and waited as the master lit an oil lamp. Then he continued. "One of the rules says, *You can study God through everything and everyone in the universe, because God is not confined in a mosque, synagogue, or church. But if you are still in need of knowing where exactly His abode is, there is only one place to look for Him: in the heart of a true lover.* There is no one who has lived after seeing Him, just like there is no one who has died after seeing Him. Whoever finds Him will remain with Him forever."

In that dim, flickering light, Shams of Tabriz seemed even taller, his hair falling to his shoulders in disorderly waves.

"But knowledge is like brackish water at the bottom of an old vase unless it flows somewhere. For years I prayed to God for a companion to share the knowledge accumulated inside me. Finally, in a vision in Samarkand, I've been told I should come to Baghdad to fulfill my destiny. I understand that you know the name of my companion and his whereabouts and will tell me, if not now, then later."

Outside, the night had settled, and a wedge of moonlight streamed in through the open windows. I realized how late it was. The cook must have been looking for me. But I didn't care. For once it felt good to break the rules.

"I don't know what kind of answer you are asking of me," murmured the master. "But if there is a piece of information I am destined to reveal, I know it will happen in due time. Until then you can stay here with us. Be our guest."

Upon hearing this, the wandering dervish bowed humbly and gratefully to kiss Baba Zaman's hand. That is when the master asked that bizarre question: "You say you are ready to deliver all your knowledge to another person. You want to hold the Truth in your palm as if it were a precious pearl and offer it to someone special. But opening up someone's heart to spiritual light is no small task for a human being. You're stealing God's thunder. What are you willing to pay in return?"

For as long as I live, I will never forget the answer the dervish gave then. Raising an eyebrow, he said firmly, "I am willing to give my head."

I flinched, feeling a cold shiver travel down my spine. When I put my eye to the crack again, I noticed that the master looked shaken by the answer as well.

"Perhaps we have done enough talking for today." Baba Zaman exhaled a sigh. "You must be tired. Let me call the young novice. He will show you to your bed and provide clean sheets and a glass of milk."

Now Shams of Tabriz turned toward the door, and I felt down to my bones that he was gazing at me again. More than that. It was as if he were looking through and into me, studying the pits and peaks of my soul, inspecting secrets that were hidden even from me. Perhaps he was involved with black magic or had been trained by Harut and Marut, the two angels of Babylon that the Qur'an warned us against. Or else he possessed supernatural talents that helped him to see through doors and walls. Either way he scared me.

"No need to call the novice," he said, his voice attaining a higher pitch. "I've a feeling he is nearby and has already heard us."

I let out a gasp so loud it might have woken the dead in their graves. In utter panic I jumped to my feet and scurried into the garden, seeking refuge in the dark. But an unpleasant surprise was awaiting me there.

"So there you are, you little rascal!" yelled the cook as he ran toward me with a broom in his hand. "You are in big trouble, son, big trouble!"

I jumped aside and managed to duck the broom at the last minute.

"Come here or I'll break your legs!" the cook shouted behind me, puffing.

But I didn't. Instead I dashed out of the garden as fast as an arrow. While the face of Shams of Tabriz shimmered before my eyes, I ran and ran along the winding trail that connected the lodge to the main road, and even after I had gotten far away, I couldn't stop running. My heart pounding, my throat dried up, I ran until my knees gave out and I could run no more.

Ella

NORTHAMPTON, MAY 21, 2008

Braced for a quarrel, David came home early the next morning, only to find Ella asleep in bed with *Sweet Blasphemy* open on her lap and an empty glass of wine by her side. He took a step toward her to pull her blanket up a little and make sure she was snugly covered, but then he changed his mind.

Ten minutes later, Ella woke up. She wasn't surprised to hear him in the bathroom taking a shower. Her husband could flirt with other women, and apparently even spend the night with them, but he would rather not take his morning shower anywhere other than his own bathroom. When David finished and walked back through the room, Ella pretended to be asleep, thus saving him from having to explain his absence.

Less than an hour later, both her husband and the kids had left, and Ella was in the kitchen alone. Life seemed to have resumed its regular course. She opened her favorite cookbook, *Culinary Artistry Made Plain and Easy,* and after considering several options chose a fairly demanding menu that would keep her busy all afternoon:

Clam Chowder with Saffron, Coconut, and Oranges
Pasta Baked with Mushrooms, Fresh Herbs, and Five Cheeses
Rosemary-Infused Veal Spareribs with Vinegar and Roasted Garlic
Lime-Bathed Green Bean and Cauliflower Salad

Then she decided on a dessert: Warm Chocolate Soufflé.

There were many reasons that Ella liked cooking. Creating a delicious meal out of ordinary ingredients was not only gratifying and fulfilling but also strangely sensual. But more than that, she enjoyed cooking because it was something she was really good at. Besides, it quieted her mind. The kitchen was the one place in her life where she could avoid the outside world altogether and stop the flow of time within herself. For some people sex might have the same effect, she imagined, but that always required two, whereas to cook all one needed was time, care, and a bag of groceries.

People who cooked on TV programs made it sound as if cooking was about inspiration, originality, and creativity. Their favorite word was "experimenting." Ella disagreed. Why not leave experimenting to scientists and quirkiness to artists! Cooking was about learning the basics, following the instructions, and being respectful of the wisdom of ages. All you had to do was use time-honored traditions, not *experiment* with them. Cooking skills came from customs and conventions, and although it was clear that the modern age belittled such things, there was nothing wrong with being traditional in the kitchen.

Ella also cherished her daily routines. Every morning, at roughly the same time, the family had breakfast; every weekend they went to the same mall; and on the first Sunday of every month they had a dinner party with their neighbors. Because David was a workaholic with little time on his hands, Ella was in charge of everything at home: managing the finances, caring for the house, reupholstering the furniture, running errands, arranging the kids' schedules and helping them with their homework, and so on. On Thursdays she went to the Fusion Cooking Club, where the members merged the cuisines of different countries and freshened up age-old recipes with new spices and ingredients. Every Friday she spent hours at the farmers' market, chatting with the farmers about their products, inspecting a jar of low-sugar organic peach jam, or explaining to another shopper how best to cook baby portabella mushrooms. Whatever she hadn't been able to find, she picked up from the Whole Foods Market on the way home.

Then, on Saturday evenings, David took Ella out to a restaurant (usually Thai or Japanese), and if they weren't too tired or drunk or simply not in the mood when they came home, they would have sex. Brief kisses and tender moves that exuded less passion than compassion. Once their most reliable connection, sex had lost its allure quite a while ago. Sometimes they went for weeks without making love. Ella found it odd that sex had once been so important in her life, and now when it was gone, she felt relieved, almost liberated. By and large she was fine with the idea of a long-married couple gradually abandoning the plane of physical attraction for a more reliable and stable way of relating.

The only problem was that David hadn't abandoned sex as much as he had abandoned sex with his wife. She had never confronted him openly about his affairs, not even hinting of her suspicions. The fact that none of their close friends knew anything made it easier for her to feign ignorance. There were no scandals, no embarrassing coincidences, nothing to set tongues wagging. She didn't know how he managed it, given the frequency of his couplings with other women, particularly with his young assistants, but her husband handled things deftly and quietly. However, infidelity had a smell. That much Ella knew.

If there was a chain of events, Ella couldn't tell which came first and which followed later. Had her loss of interest in sex been the cause of her husband's cheating? Or was it the other way round? Had David cheated on her first, and then she'd neglected her body and lost her sexual desire?

Either way the outcome remained the same: The glow between them, the light that had helped them to navigate the uncharted waters of marriage, keeping their desire afloat, even after three kids and twenty years, was simply not there anymore.

For the next three hours, her mind was filled with thoughts while her hands were restless. She chopped tomatoes, minced garlic, sautéed onions, simmered sauce, grated orange peels, and kneaded dough for a loaf of whole-wheat bread. That last was based on the golden advice David's mother had given her when they got engaged.

"Nothing reminds a man of home like the smell of freshly baked bread," she had said. "Never buy your bread. Bake it yourself, honey. It will work wonders."

Working the entire afternoon, Ella set an exquisite table with matching napkins, scented candles, and a bouquet of yellow and orange flowers so bright and striking they looked almost artificial. For the final touch, she added sparkly napkin rings. When she was done, the dining table resembled those found in stylish home magazines.

Tired but satisfied, she turned on the kitchen TV to the local news. A young therapist had been stabbed in her apartment, an electrical short had caused a fire in a hospital, and four high-school students had been arrested for vandalism. She watched the news, shaking her head at the endless dangers looming in the world. How could people like Aziz Z. Zahara find the desire and courage to travel the less-developed parts of the globe when even the suburbs in America weren't safe anymore?

Ella found it puzzling that an unpredictable and impenetrable world could drive people like her back into their houses but had almost the opposite effect on someone like Aziz, inspiring him to embark on adventures far off the beaten track.

The Rubinsteins sat at a picture-perfect table at 7:30 P.M., the burning candles giving the dining room a sacred air. An outsider watching them might assume they were a perfect family, as graceful as the wisps of smoke slowly dissolving in the air. Even Jeannette's absence didn't tarnish the picture. They ate while Orly and Avi prattled on about the day's events at school. For once Ella felt grateful to them for being so chatty and noisy and covering up the silence that would otherwise have rested heavily between her and her husband.

Out of the corner of her eye, Ella watched David jab his fork into a cauliflower and chew slowly. Her gaze dropped to his thin, pale lips and pearl-white teeth—the mouth she knew so well and had kissed so many times. She visualized him kissing another woman. For some reason the rival who appeared in her mind's eye was not David's young secretary but a big-bosomed version of Susan Sarandon. Athletic and confident, she showed off her breasts in a tight dress and wore high-heeled, knee-high red leather boots, her face shiny, almost iridescent with too much makeup. Ella imagined David kissing this woman with haste and hunger, not at all the way he chewed his cauliflower at the family table.

It was then and there, while having her *Culinary Artistry Made Plain and Easy* dinner and imagining the woman her husband was having an affair with, that something inside Ella snapped. She understood with chilling clarity and calm that despite her inexperience and timidity, one day she would abandon it all: her kitchen, her dog, her children, her neighbors, her husband, her cookbooks and homemade-bread recipes. . . . She would simply walk out into the world where dangerous things happened all the time.

The Master

BAGHDAD, JANUARY 26, 1243

Being part of a dervish lodge requires far more patience than Shams of Tabriz possesses. Yet nine months have passed, and he is still with us.

In the beginning I expected him to pack up and leave at any moment, so visible was his aversion to a strictly ordered life. I could see that it bored him stiff to have to sleep and wake up at the same hours, eat regular meals, and conform to the same routine as everyone else. He was used to flying as a lonely bird, wild and free. I suspect several times he came close to running away. Nevertheless, great as his need for solitude, even greater was his commitment to finding his companion. Shams firmly believed that one of these days I would come up with the information he needed and tell him where to go, whom to find. With this faith he stayed.

During these nine months, I watched him closely, wondering if time flowed differently for him, more rapidly and intensely. What took other dervishes months, sometimes years, to learn took him only weeks, if not days. He had a remarkable curiosity about everything new and unusual and was a great observer of nature. So many days I found him in the garden admiring the symmetry of a spiderweb or the dewdrops glistening on a night-blooming flower. Insects, plants, and animals seemed more interesting and inspiring to him than books and manuscripts. But just when I would start thinking he had no interest in reading, I would find him immersed in an age-old book. Then, once again, he could go for weeks on end without reading and studying anything.

When I asked him about this, he said one should keep the intellect satisfied and yet be careful not to spoil it. It was one of his rules. *"Intellect and love are made of different materials,"* he said. *"Intellect ties people in knots and risks nothing, but love dissolves all tangles and risks everything. Intellect is always cautious and advises, 'Beware too much ecstasy,' whereas love says, 'Oh, never mind! Take the plunge!' Intellect does not easily break down, whereas love can effortlessly reduce itself to rubble. But treasures are hidden among ruins. A broken heart hides treasures."*

As I got to know him better, I admired his audacity and acumen. But I also suspected there was a downside to Shams's unrivaled ingenuity and originality. For one thing, he was straightforward to the point of brusqueness. I taught my dervishes never to see the faults of other people and, if they did, to be forgiving and quiet. Shams, however, let no mistake go unnoticed. Whenever he saw anything wrong, he spoke out about it right away, never beating around the bush. His honesty offended others, but he liked to provoke people to see what came out of them in moments of anger.

Forcing him to do ordinary tasks was difficult. He had little patience for such jobs and lost interest in something as soon as he got the hang of it. When it came to a routine, he got desperate, like a tiger trapped in a cage. If a conversation bored him or somebody made a foolish remark, he got up and left, never losing time with pleasantries. Values cherished by most human beings, such as security, comfort, and happiness, had hardly any meaning in his eyes. And his distrust of words was so intense that often he went without speaking for days. That, too, was one of his rules: *Most of the problems of the world stem from linguistic mistakes and simple misunderstandings. Don't ever take words at face value. When you step into the zone of love, language as we know it becomes obsolete. That which cannot be put into words can only be grasped through silence.*

In time I became concerned about his well-being. For deep inside I sensed that one who could burn so fervently might have a tendency to put himself into dangerous situations.

At the end of the day, our fates are in the hands of God, and only He can tell when or how we each will depart the world. For my part I decided to do my best to slow Shams down and accustom him, as much as I could, to a more tranquil way of life. And for a while I thought I might succeed. But then came winter, and with the winter came the messenger carrying a letter from afar.

That letter changed everything.

The Letter

FROM KAYSERI TO BAGHDAD, FEBRUARY 1243

Bismillahirrahmanirrahim,

My dear brother Baba Zaman,

May the peace and blessings of God be upon you.

It has been a long time since we have last seen one another, and I hope my letter finds you in good spirits. I have heard so many wonderful things about the lodge you built on the outskirts of Baghdad, teaching dervishes the wisdom and love of God. I am writing this letter in confidentiality to share with you something that has been preoccupying my mind. Allow me to start from the beginning.

As you know, the late Sultan Aladdin Keykubad was a remarkable man who excelled in leadership in difficult times. It had been his dream to build a city where poets, artisans, and philosophers could live and work in peace. A dream many called impossible given the chaos and hostility in the world, especially with the Crusaders and Mongols attacking from both sides. We have seen it all. Christians killing Muslims, Christians killing Christians, Muslims killing Christians, Muslims killing Muslims. Warring religions, sects, tribes, even brothers. But Keykubad was a determined leader. He chose the city of Konya—the first place to emerge after the great flood—to realize his big dream.

Now, in Konya there lives a scholar you may or may not have heard of. His name is Mawlana Jalal ad-Din but he often goes by the name Rumi. I have had the pleasure of meeting him, and not only that, of studying with him, first as his teacher, then, upon his father's death, as his mentor, and, after years, as his student. Yes, my friend, I became a student of my student. So talented and judicious was he, after a point I had nothing else to teach him and started to learn from him instead. His father was a brilliant scholar, too. But Rumi has a quality that very few scholars ever have: the ability to dig deep below the husk of religion and pull out from its core the gem that is universal and eternal.

I want you to know that these are not solely my personal thoughts. When Rumi met the great mystic, druggist, and perfumist Fariduddin Attar as a young man, Attar said of him, "This boy will open a gate in the heart of love and throw a flame into the hearts of all mystic lovers." Likewise when Ibn Arabi, the distinguished philosopher, writer, and mystic, saw the young Rumi walking behind his father one day, he exclaimed, "Glory be to God, an ocean is walking behind a lake!"

As young as the age of twenty-four, Rumi became a spiritual leader. Today, thirteen years later, the residents of Konya look up to him as a role model, and every Friday people from all over the region flock to the city to listen to his sermons. He has excelled at law, philosophy, theology, astronomy, history, chemistry, and algebra. Already he is said to have ten thousand disciples. His followers hang upon his every word and see him as a great enlightener who will generate a significant positive change in the history of Islam, if not in the history of the world.

But to me Rumi has always been like a son. I promised his late father that I would always keep an eye on him. And now that I am an old man who is nearing his final days, I want to make sure he is in the right company.

You see, as remarkable and successful as he no doubt is, Rumi himself has several times confided in me that he feels inwardly dissatisfied. There is something missing in his life—an emptiness that neither his family nor his disciples can fill. Once I told him, though he was anything but raw, he wasn't burned either. His cup was full to the brim, and yet he needed to have the door to his soul opened so that the waters of love could flow in and out. When he asked me how this could be done, I told him he needed a companion, a friend of the path, and reminded him that the Qur'an says, "Believers are each other's mirrors."

Had the subject not come up again, I might have forgotten about it completely, but on the day I left Konya, Rumi came to me to ask my opinion on a recurrent dream that had been bothering him. He told me that in his dream he was searching for someone in a big, bustling city in a land far away. Words in Arabic. Delightful sunsets. Mulberry trees and silkworms waiting patiently in secretive cocoons for their moment to arrive. Then he saw himself in the courtyard of his house, sitting by the well with a lantern in his hand, weeping.

At the outset I had no idea what the fragments in his dreams indicated. Nothing seemed familiar. But then one day, after I had received a silk scarf as a gift, the answer came to me and the riddle was solved. I remembered how you were fond of silk and silkworms. I recalled the wonderful things I had heard about your *tariqa*. And it dawned upon me that the place Rumi saw in his dreams was none other than your dervish lodge. In short, my brother, I can't help wondering whether Rumi's companion lives under your roof. Hence the reason I write this letter.

I don't know if there is such a person in your lodge. But if there is, I leave it in your hands to inform him about the destiny that awaits him. If you and I can play even a minute role in helping two rivers meet and flow into the ocean of Divine Love as one single watercourse, if we can help two good friends of God to meet, I will count myself blessed.

There is, however, one thing you need to take into consideration. Rumi might be an influential man adored and respected by many, but that doesn't mean he does not have critics. He does. Furthermore, such a flowing-together might generate discontent and opposition and cause rivalries beyond our comprehension. His fondness of his companion might also cause problems in his family and inner circle. The person who is openly loved by someone who is admired by so many people is bound to draw the envy, if not the hatred, of others.

All of this might put the companion of Rumi in unpredictable danger. In other words, my brother, the person you send to Konya might never make it back. Therefore, before reaching a decision as to how to reveal this letter to Rumi's companion, I ask you to give the matter considerable thought.

I am sorry to put you in a difficult position, but as we both know, God never burdens us with more than we can bear. I look forward to your answer and trust that whatever the outcome, you will take the right steps in the right direction.

May the light of faith never cease to shine upon you and your dervishes,
Master Seyyid Burhaneddin

Shams

BAGHDAD, DECEMBER 18, 1243

Beyond dangling icicles and snow-covered roads, a messenger appeared in the distance. He said he came from Kayseri, and caused a stir among the dervishes, who knew visitors to be scarcer than sweet summer grapes at this time of the year. A messenger with a message urgent enough to be carried through snowstorms could only mean one of two things: Either something terrible had happened or something important was about to happen.

The arrival of the messenger set tongues wagging in the dervish lodge, as everyone was curious about the content of the letter handed to the master. But, shrouded in a cloak of mystery, he gave no hints whatsoever. Stolid and ruminant, and zealously guarded, for days he bore the expression of a man struggling with his conscience, finding it hard to reach the right decision.

During that time it wasn't sheer curiosity that prompted me to closely observe Baba Zaman. Deep inside, I sensed that the letter concerned me personally, although in what way I could not tell. I spent many evenings in the praying room reciting the ninety-nine names of God for guidance. Each time one name stood out: al-Jabbar—the One in whose dominion nothing happens except that which He has willed.

In the following days, while everyone in the lodge was making wild speculations, I spent my time alone in the garden, observing Mother Nature now cuddled under a heavy blanket of snow. Finally one day we heard the copper bell in the kitchen ring repeatedly, calling us all for an urgent meeting. Upon entering the main room in the *khaneqah,* I found everyone present there, novices and senior dervishes alike, sitting in a wide circle. And in the middle of the circle was the master, his lips neatly pursed, his eyes hazy.

After clearing his throat, he said, "*Bismillah,* you must be wondering why I summoned you here today. It is about this letter I received. It doesn't matter where it came from. Suffice it to say that it drew my attention to a subject of great consequence."

Baba Zaman paused briefly and stared out the window. He looked fatigued, thin, and pale, as if he had aged considerably during these past days. But when he continued to speak, an unexpected determination filled his voice.

"There lives an erudite scholar in a city not far away. He is good with words, but not so with metaphors, for he is no poet. He is loved, respected, and admired by thousands, but he himself is not a lover. Because of reasons far beyond me and you, someone from our lodge might have to go to meet him and be his comrade."

My heart tightened in my chest. I exhaled slowly, very slowly. I couldn't help remembering one of the rules. *Loneliness and solitude are two different things. When you are lonely, it is easy to delude yourself into believing that you are on the right path. Solitude is better for us, as it means being alone without feeling lonely. But eventually it is best to find a person, the person who will be your mirror. Remember, only in another person's heart can you truly see yourself and the presence of God within you.*

The master continued. "I am here to ask if any one of you would like to volunteer for this spiritual journey. I could just as well have appointed someone, but this is not a task that could be performed out of duty. For it can be done only out of love and in the name of love."

A young dervish asked permission to speak. "Who is this scholar, Master?"

"I can reveal his name only to the one who is willing to go."

Upon hearing this, several dervishes raised their hands, excited and impatient. There were nine candidates. I joined them, becoming the tenth. Baba Zaman waved his hand, gesturing at us to wait for him to finish. "There is something else you should know before you make up your mind."

With that, the master told us the journey was beset with great danger and unprecedented hardships, and there was no guarantee of coming back. Instantly all the hands went down. Except mine.

Baba Zaman looked me straight in the eye for the first time in a long while, and as soon as his gaze met mine, I understood he knew right from the start that I would be the only one to volunteer.

"Shams of Tabriz," the master said slowly and dourly, as if my name left a heavy taste in his mouth. "I respect your determination, but you are not fully a member of this order. You are our guest."

"I don't see how that could be a problem," I said.

The master was silent for a long, reflective moment. Then, unexpectedly, he came to his feet and concluded, "Let's drop this subject for the time being. When spring comes, we will talk again."

My heart rebelled. Though he knew that this mission was the sole reason I had come to Baghdad in the first place, Baba Zaman was robbing me of the chance to fulfill my destiny.

"Why, Master? Why wait when I am ready to go this very moment? Just tell me the name of the city and the scholar and I will be on my way!" I exclaimed.

But the master retorted in a cold, stern voice I wasn't used to hearing from him, "There is nothing to discuss. The meeting is over."

It was a long, harsh winter. The garden was frozen stiff, and so were my lips. For the next three months, I didn't speak a word to anyone. Every day I took long walks in the countryside, hoping to see a tree in blossom. But after snow came more snow. Spring wasn't anywhere on the horizon. Still, as low-spirited as I was outside, I remained grateful and hopeful inside, keeping in mind yet another rule. There was a rule that suited my mood: *Whatever happens in your life, no matter how troubling things might seem, do not enter the neighborhood of despair. Even when all doors remain closed, God will open up a new path only for you. Be thankful! It is easy to be thankful when all is well. A Sufi is thankful not only for what he has been given but also for all that he has been denied.*

Then finally one morning, I caught sight of a dazzling color, as delightful as a sweet song, sticking out from under the piles of snow. It was a bush clover covered with tiny lavender flowers. My heart filled with joy. As I walked back to the lodge, I ran into the ginger-haired novice and saluted him merrily. He was so used to seeing me fixed in a grumpy silence that his jaw dropped.

"Smile, boy!" I yelled. "Don't you see spring is in the air?"

From that day on, the landscape changed with remarkable speed. The last snow melted, the trees budded, sparrows and wrens returned, and before long a faint spicy smell filled the air.

One morning we heard the copper bell ring again. I was the first to reach the main room this time. Once again we sat in a wide circle around the master and listened to him talk about this prominent scholar of Islam who knew everything, except the pits of love. Again no one else volunteered.

"I see that Shams is the only one to volunteer," Baba Zaman announced, his voice rising in pitch and thinning out like the howl of the wind. "But I'll wait for autumn before reaching a decision."

I was stunned. I could not believe that this was happening. Here I was, ready to leave after three long months of postponement, and the master was telling me to put my journey off for another six months. With a plunging heart, I protested and complained and begged the master to tell me the name of the city and the scholar, but once again he refused.

This time, however, I knew it was going to be easier to wait, for there could be no further delays. Having endured from winter to spring, I could hold my fire from spring to autumn. Baba Zaman's rejection had not disheartened me. If anything, it had raised my spirits, deepening my determination. Another rule said, *Patience does not mean to passively endure. It means to be farsighted enough to trust the end result of a process. What does patience mean? It means to look at the thorn and see the rose, to look at the night and see the dawn. Impatience means to be so shortsighted as to not be able to see the outcome. The lovers of God never run out of patience, for they know that time is needed for the crescent moon to become full.*

When in autumn the copper bell rang for the third time, I walked in unhurriedly and confidently, trusting that now things would finally be settled. The master looked paler and weaker than ever, as if he had no more energy left in him. Nevertheless, when he saw me raise my hand again, he neither looked away nor dropped the subject. Instead he gave me a determined nod.

"All right, Shams, there is no question you are the one who should embark on this journey. Tomorrow morning you'll be on your way, *inshallah*."

I kissed the master's hand. At long last I was going to meet my companion.

Baba Zaman smiled at me warmly and thoughtfully, the way a father smiles at his only son before sending him to the battlefield. He then took out a sealed letter from inside his long khaki robe and, after handing it to me, silently left the room. Everyone else followed suit. Alone in the room, I broke the wax seal. Inside, there were two pieces of information written in graceful handwriting. The name of the city and the scholar. Apparently I was going to Konya to meet a certain Rumi.

My heart skipped a beat. I had never heard his name before. He could be a famous scholar for all I knew, but to me he was a complete mystery. One by one, I said the letters of his name: the powerful, lucid *R;* the velvety *U;* the intrepid and self-confident *M;* and the mysterious *I,* yet to be solved.

Bringing the letters together, I repeated his name over and over again until the word melted on my tongue with the sweetness of candy and became as familiar as "water," "bread," or "milk."

Ella

NORTHAMPTON, MAY 22, 2008

Beneath her white duvet, Ella swallowed past a sore throat, feeling worn out. Staying up late and drinking more than her usual limit several nights in a row had taken their toll. Still, she went downstairs to prepare breakfast and sat at the table with her twins and her husband, doing her best to look interested in their ongoing chatter about the coolest cars at school when all she wanted was to go back to bed and sleep.

All of a sudden, Orly turned to her mother and inquired, "Avi says our sister isn't going to come home again. Is that true, Mom?" Her voice reeked of suspicion and accusation.

"Of course that's not true. Your sister and I had a quarrel, as you know, but we love each other," Ella said.

"Is it true that you gave Scott a call and asked him to dump Jeannette?" Avi asked with a grin, apparently enjoying the subject immensely.

Ella glanced at her husband with widened eyes, but David raised his eyebrows and flipped his hands open to indicate it wasn't he who'd told them such a thing.

With practiced ease, Ella gave her voice the authoritarian tone she used when giving instructions to her children. "That's not quite right. I *did* speak with Scott, but I did not tell him to dump your sister. All I said was not to rush into marriage."

"I'm never going to get married," Orly announced with certitude.

"Yeah, as if any guy would want to have you as his wife!" Avi snapped.

While she listened to her twins tease each other, for reasons she couldn't understand Ella felt a nervous smile settle on her mouth. She suppressed it. But the smile was there, carved under her skin, as she walked them to the door and wished them all a nice day.

Only when she returned to her seat at the table could she get rid of the smile, and she did that simply by allowing herself to sulk. The kitchen looked as if it had been attacked by an army of rats. Half-eaten scrambled eggs, unfinished bowls of cereal, and dirty mugs cluttered the counter. Spirit was pacing the floor, eager to go out for a walk, but even after two cups of coffee and a multivitamin drink all Ella could manage was to take him out into the garden for a few minutes.

Back from the garden, Ella found the red light flashing on the answering machine. She pressed the button, and to her great delight Jeannette's melodious voice filled the room.

"Mom, are you there . . . ? Well, I guess not, or you would have picked up the phone." She chuckled. "Okay, I was so angry at you I didn't want to see your face again. But now I'm cool about it. I mean, what you did was wrong, that's for sure. You should never have called Scott. But I can understand why you did it. Listen, you don't need to protect me all the time. I'm not that premature baby who needed to be kept in an incubator anymore. Stop being overprotective! Just let me be, okay?"

Ella's eyes filled with tears. The sight of Jeannette as a newborn baby flashed across her mind. Her skin utterly red and sad, her little fingers wrinkled and almost transparent, her lungs attached to a breathing tube—she was so unprepared for this world. Ella had spent many a sleepless night listening to her breathing just to make sure she was alive and would survive.

"Mom, one more thing," added Jeannette, like an afterthought. "I love you."

On that cue Ella let out a deep breath. Her mind shifted to Aziz's e-mail. The wish tree had granted his wish. At least the first part of it. By giving her a call, Jeannette had done her part. Now it fell upon Ella to fulfill the rest. She called her daughter's cell phone and found her on her way to the campus library.

"I got your message, honey. Listen, I'm so sorry. I want to apologize to you."

There was a pause, brief but charged. "That's all right, Mom."

"No, it's not. I should have shown more respect for your feelings."

"Let's leave it all behind, shall we?" said Jeannette, as though she were the mother and Ella her rebellious daughter.

"Yes, dear."

Now Jeannette dropped her voice to a confidential mumble, as if afraid of what she was going to ask next. "What you said the other day kind of worried me. I mean, is that true? Are you really *unhappy*?"

"Of course not," Ella answered, a bit too quickly. "I raised three beautiful children—how can I be unhappy?"

But Jeannette didn't sound convinced. "I meant with Daddy."

Ella didn't know what to say, except the truth. "Your father and I have been married a long time. It's difficult to remain in love after so many years."

"I understand," said Jeannette, and, oddly, Ella had the feeling she did.

After she hung up, Ella allowed herself to muse over love. She sat curled up in her rocking chair and wondered how she, hurt and cynical as she was, could ever experience love again. Love was for those looking for some rhyme or reason in this wildly spinning world. But what about those who had long given up the quest?

Before the day ended, she wrote back to Aziz.

Dear Aziz (if I may),

Thanks for your kind and heartwarming reply, which helped me through a family crisis. My daughter and I managed to leave behind that awful misunderstanding, as you politely called it.

You were right about one thing. I constantly vacillate between two opposites: aggressive and passive. Either I meddle too much in the lives of loved ones or I feel helpless in the face of their actions.

As for submission, I've never experienced the kind of peaceful surrender you wrote to me about. Honestly, I don't think I have what it takes to be a Sufi. But I have to give you this: Amazingly, things between

Jeannette and me turned out the way I wanted only after I stopped wanting and interfering. I owe you a big thank-you. I, too, would have prayed for you, but it has been such a long time since I last knocked on God's door that I'm not sure if He still lives in the same place. Oops, did I speak like the innkeeper in your story? Don't worry, I'm not that bitter. Not yet. Not yet.

Your friend in Northampton,
Ella

The Letter

FROM BAGHDAD TO KAYSERI, SEPTEMBER 29, 1243

Bismillahirrahmanirrahim,

Brother Seyyid Burhaneddin,

Peace be on you, and the mercy of God, and His blessings.

I was very pleased to receive your letter and learn that you were as devoted to the path of love as ever. And yet your letter also put me in a quandary. For as soon as I learned you were looking for the companion of Rumi, I knew who you were talking about. What I did not know was what to do next.

You see, there was under my roof a wandering dervish, Shams of Tabriz, who fit your description to the letter. Shams believed he had a special mission in this world, and to this end he wished to enlighten an enlightened person. Looking for neither disciples nor students, he asked God for a companion. Once he said to me that he hadn't come for the common people. He had come to put his finger on the pulse of those who guided the world to the Truth.

When I received your letter, I knew that Shams was destined to meet Rumi. Still, to make sure every one of my dervishes got an equal chance, I gathered them and without going into any details told them about a scholar whose heart had to be opened. Though there were a few candidates, Shams was the only one who persevered even after hearing about the dangers of the task. That was back in winter. The same scene was repeated in spring and then in autumn.

You might be wondering why I waited this long. I have thought hard about this and frankly can offer only one reason: I have grown fond of Shams. It pained me to know that I was sending him on a dangerous journey.

You see, Shams is not an easy person. As long as he lived a nomadic life, he could manage it pretty well, but if he stays in a town and mingles with the townspeople, I am afraid he will ruffle some feathers. This is why I tried to postpone his journey as long as I could.

The evening before Shams left, we took a long walk around the mulberry trees where I grow silkworms. Old habits rarely die. Painfully delicate and surprisingly strong, silk resembles love. I told Shams how the silkworms destroy the silk they produce as they emerge from their cocoons. This is why the farmers have to make a choice between the silk and the silkworm. More often than not, they kill the silkworm while it is inside the cocoon in order to pull the silk out intact. It takes the lives of hundreds of silkworms to produce one silk scarf.

The evening was now coming to an end. A chilly wind blew in our direction, and I shivered. In my old age, I get cold easily, but I knew it wasn't my age that caused this shiver. It was because I realized this was the last time Shams would stand in my garden. We will not see each other again. Not in this world. He, too, must have sensed it, for there was now sorrow in his eyes.

This morning at the crack of dawn, he came to kiss my hand and ask for my blessings. I was surprised to see he had cut his long dark hair and shaved his beard, but he didn't offer an explanation and I didn't ask. Before he left, he said his part in this story resembled the silkworm. He and Rumi would retreat into a cocoon of Divine Love, only to come out when the time was ripe and the precious silk woven. But eventually, for the silk to survive, the silkworm had to die.

Thus he left for Konya. May God protect him. I know I have done the right thing, and so have you, but my heart is heavy with sadness, and I already miss the most unusual and unruly dervish my lodge has ever welcomed.

In the end we all belong to God, and to Him we shall return.

May God suffice you,
Baba Zaman

The Novice

BAGHDAD, SEPTEMBER 29, 1243

Being a dervish is not easy. Everybody warned me so. What they forgot to mention was that I had to go through hell in order to become one. Ever since I came here, I have been working like a dog. Most days I work so hard that when I finally lie on my sleeping mat, I can't sleep because of the pain in my muscles and the throbbing in my feet. I wonder if anybody notices how awfully I am being treated. Even if they do, they surely show no signs of caring. And the harder I strive, the worse it seems to get. They don't even know my name. "The new novice," they call me, and behind my back they whisper, "that ginger-haired ignoramus."

The worst by far is to work in the kitchen under the supervision of the cook. The man has a stone instead of a heart. He could have been a bloodthirsty commander in the Mongol army rather than a cook in a dervish lodge. I can't recall ever hearing him say anything nice to anyone. I don't think he even knows how to smile.

Once I asked a senior dervish if all the novices had to go through the trial of working with the cook in the kitchen. He smiled mysteriously and replied, "Not all novices, only some."

Then why me? Why does the master want me to suffer more than the other novices? Is it because my *nafs* is bigger than theirs and needs harsher treatment to be disciplined?

Every day I am the first to wake up, to get water from the nearby creek. I then heat up the stove and bake the flat sesame bread. Preparing the soup to be served at breakfast is also my responsibility. It is not easy to feed fifty people. Everything needs to be cooked in cauldrons that are no smaller than bathtubs. And guess who scrubs and washes them afterward? From dawn to dusk, I mop the floors, clean the surfaces, wipe the stairs, sweep the courtyard, chop wood, and spend hours on my hands and knees to scrub the creaky old floorboards. I prepare marmalades and spicy relishes. I pickle carrots and squash, making sure there is just the right amount of salt, enough to float an egg. If I add too much or too little salt, the cook throws a fit and breaks all the jars, and I have to make everything anew.

To top it all off, I am expected to recite prayers in Arabic as I perform each and every task. The cook wants me to pray aloud so that he can check whether I skip or mispronounce a word. So I pray and work, work and pray. "The better you bear the hardships in the kitchen, the faster you will mature, son," my tormentor claims. "While you learn to cook, your soul will simmer."

"But how long is this trial going to last?" I asked him once.

"A thousand and one days" was his answer. "If Scheherazade the storyteller managed to come up with a new tale every night for that long, you, too, can endure."

This is madness! Do I resemble in the least bit that loudmouthed Scheherazade? Besides, all she did was lie on velvet cushions twiddling her toes and make up fancy stories while she fed the cruel prince sweet grapes and figments of her imagination. I don't see any hard work there. She wouldn't have survived a week if she were asked to accomplish half of my work. I don't know if anyone is counting. But I surely am. And I have 624 more days to go.

The first forty days of my trial I spent in a cell so small and low that I could neither lie down nor stand up and had to sit on my knees all the time. If I longed for proper food or some comfort, was scared of the dark or the loneliness, or God forbid had wet dreams about a woman's body, I was ordered to ring the silver bells dangling from the ceiling for spiritual help. I never did. This is not to say I never had any distracting thoughts. But what's wrong with having a few distractions when you can't even move?

When the seclusion period was over, I was sent back to the kitchen to suffer at the hands of the cook. And suffer I did. But the truth is, as bitter as I might be toward him, I never broke the cook's rules—that is, until the evening Shams of Tabriz arrived. That night, when the cook finally caught up with me, he gave me the worst beating of my life, breaking willow stick after willow stick on my back. Then he put my shoes in front of the door, with their fronts pointing out, to make it clear it was time for me to leave. In a dervish lodge, they never kick you out or tell you openly that you have failed; instead they make *you* silently leave.

"We cannot make you a dervish against your will," the cook announced. "A man can bring a donkey to the water but cannot make him drink. The donkey should have it in him. There's no other way."

That makes me the donkey, of course. Frankly, I would have left this place a long time ago had it not been for Shams of Tabriz. My curiosity about him kept me anchored here. I had never met anyone like him before. He feared no one and obeyed no one. Even the cook respected him. If there ever were a role model for me in this lodge, it was Shams with his charm, dignity, and unruliness. Not the humble old master.

Yes, Shams of Tabriz was my hero. After seeing him, I decided I didn't need to turn myself into a meek dervish. If I spent enough time next to him, I could become just as brash, steadfast, and rebellious. So when autumn came and I realized that Shams was leaving for good, I decided to leave with him.

Having made up my mind, I went to see Baba Zaman and found him sitting, reading an old book by the light of an oil lamp.

"What do you want, novice?" he asked wearily, as if seeing me tired him.

As forthright as I could be, I said, "I understand that Shams of Tabriz is leaving soon, Master. I want to go with him. He might need company on the way."

"I didn't know you cared for him so much," the master said suspiciously. "Or is it because you are looking for ways to avoid your tasks in the kitchen? Your trial is not over yet. You can hardly be called a dervish."

"Perhaps going on a journey with someone like Shams is my trial," I suggested, knowing that it was a bold thing to say but saying it anyhow.

The master lowered his gaze, lapsing into contemplation. The longer his silence, the more I was convinced he would scold me for my insolence and call the cook to keep a better eye on me. But he did no such thing. Instead he looked at me forlornly and shook his head.

"Perhaps you were not created for life in a lodge, my son. After all, out of every seven novices that set out on this path, only one remains. My feeling is you are not fit to be a dervish and need to look for your kismet elsewhere. As for accompanying Shams on his journey, you will have to ask him about that."

Thus ending our conversation, Baba Zaman closed the subject with a polite but dogged gesture of his head and went back to his book.

I felt sad and small, but strangely liberated.

Shams

BAGHDAD, SEPTEMBER 30, 1243

Battling the winds, my horse and I sped away at the crack of dawn. Only once did I stop to look back. The dervish lodge resembled a bird's nest hidden among mulberry trees and shrubs. For a while Baba Zaman's weary face kept flickering across my mind. I knew he was concerned about me. But I saw no real reason for that. I had embarked on an inner journey of Love. How could any harm come out of that? It was my tenth rule: *East, west, south, or north makes little difference. No matter what your destination, just be sure to make every journey a journey within. If you travel within, you'll travel the whole wide world and beyond.*

Though I anticipated hardships ahead, that didn't worry me much. Whatever fate awaited me in Konya, I welcomed it. As a Sufi, I had been trained to accept the thorn with the rose, the difficulties with the beauties of life. Hence followed another rule: *The midwife knows that when there is no pain, the way for the baby cannot be opened and the mother cannot give birth. Likewise, for a new Self to be born, hardship is necessary.*

Just as clay needs to go through intense heat to become strong, Love can only be perfected in pain.

The night before I left the dervish lodge, I opened all the windows in my room to let the sounds and the smells of the darkness waft in. By the flickering light of a candle, I cut my long hair. Thick clusters of it fell to the floor. I then shaved my beard and mustache and got rid of my eyebrows. When done, I inspected the face in the mirror, now brighter and younger. Without any hair my face was cleared of a name, age, or gender. It had no past or future, sealed forever in this moment.

"Your journey is already changing you," said the master when I went to his room to say good-bye. "And it hasn't even started yet."

"Yes, I realized," I said softly. "It is another one of the forty rules: *The quest for Love changes us. There is no seeker among those who search for Love who has not matured on the way. The moment you start looking for Love, you start to change within and without.*"

With a slight smile, Baba Zaman took out a velvet box and handed it to me. Inside, I found three things: a silver mirror, a silk handkerchief, and a glass flask of ointment.

"These items will help you on your journey. Use them when need be. If you ever lose faith in yourself, the mirror will show your inner beauty. In case your reputation is stained, the handkerchief will remind you of how pure your heart is. As for the balm, it will heal your wounds, both inside and outside."

I caressed each object, closed the box, and thanked Baba Zaman. Then there was nothing else to say.

As the birds chirped and tiny dewdrops hung from the branches with the first light of the morning, I mounted my horse. I set off toward Konya, not knowing what to expect but trusting the destiny that the Almighty had prepared for me.

The Novice

BAGHDAD, SEPTEMBER 30, 1243

Behind Shams of Tabriz, I rode my stolen horse. Hard as I tried to keep a safe distance between us, it soon proved impossible to trail him without making myself apparent. When Shams stopped at a bazaar in Baghdad to refresh himself and buy a few things for the road, I decided to make myself known and threw myself in front of his horse.

"Ginger-haired ignoramus, what are you doing there lying on the ground?" Shams exclaimed from his horse, looking half amused, half surprised.

I knelt, clasped my hands, and craned my neck, as I had seen beggars do, and implored, "I want to come with you. Please let me join you."

"Do you have any idea where I am going?"

I paused. That question had never occurred to me. "No, but it makes no difference. I want to become your disciple. You are my role model."

"I always travel alone and want no disciples or students, thank you! And I am certainly no role model for anyone, much less for you," Shams said. "So just go on your way. But if you are still going to look for a master in the future, please keep in mind a golden rule: *There are more fake gurus and false teachers in this world than the number of stars in the visible universe. Don't confuse power-driven, self-centered people with true mentors. A genuine spiritual master will not direct your attention to himself or herself and will not expect absolute obedience or utter admiration from you, but instead will help you to appreciate and admire your inner self. True mentors are as transparent as glass. They let the Light of God pass through them.*"

"Please give me a chance," I implored. "All the famous travelers had someone to assist them on the road, like an apprentice or something."

Shams scratched his chin pensively, as if acknowledging the truth in my words. "Do you have the strength to bear my company?" he inquired.

I jumped to my feet, nodding with all my heart: "I certainly do. And my strength comes from within."

"Very well, then. Here is your first task: I want you to go to the nearest tavern and get yourself a pitcher of wine. You will drink it here in the bazaar."

Now, I was used to scrubbing the floors with my robes, polishing pots and pans till they sparkled like the fine Venetian glass I had seen in the hands of an artisan who had escaped from Constantinople long ago when the Crusaders had sacked the city. I could chop a hundred onions in one sitting or peel and mince cloves of garlic, all in the name of spiritual development. But drinking wine in the midst of a crowded bazaar to that end was beyond my ken. I looked at him in horror.

"I cannot do that. If my father learns, he'll break my legs. He sent me to the dervish lodge so that I could become a better Muslim, not a heathen. What will my family and friends think of me?"

I felt the burning glare of Shams on me and shivered under the pressure, just like the day I had spied on him behind closed doors.

"You see, you cannot be my disciple," he pronounced with conviction. "You are too timid for me. You care too much about what other people think. But you know what? Because you are so desperate to win the approval of others, you'll never get rid of their criticisms, no matter how hard you try."

I realized that my chance to accompany him was slipping away and rushed in to defend myself. "How was I to know you were not asking that question on purpose? Wine is strictly forbidden by Islam. I thought you were testing me."

"But that would be playing God. It is not up to us to judge and measure each other's devoutness," Shams answered.

I looked around in despair, not knowing what to make of his words, my mind pounded like dumpling dough.

Shams went on: "You say you want to travel the path, but you don't want to sacrifice anything to that end. Money, fame, power, lavishness, or carnal pleasure—whatever it is that one holds most dear in life, one should dispose of that first."

Patting his horse, Shams concluded with an air of finality, "I think you ought to stay in Baghdad with your family. Find an honest tradesman and become his apprentice. I have a feeling you might make a good merchant someday. But don't be a greedy one! Now, with your permission, I need to get going."

With that, he saluted me one last time, kicked his horse, and galloped away, the world sliding under its thundering hoofs. I hopped onto my horse and chased him toward the outskirts of Baghdad, but the distance between us got greater and greater until he was no more than a dark spot in the distance. Even long after that spot had disappeared on the horizon, I could feel the weight of Shams's stare on me.

Ella

NORTHAMPTON, MAY 24, 2008

Breakfast is the most important meal of the day. Being a big believer of this saying, every morning, weekdays and weekends alike, Ella made her way to the kitchen. A good breakfast, she thought, set the tone for the rest of the day. She had read in women's magazines that families who regularly had a proper breakfast together were more cohesive and harmonious than those in which each member rushed out the door half hungry. And though she firmly believed in this research, she had yet to experience the joyful breakfast the magazines wrote about. Her breakfast experience was a collision of galaxies where every member of her family marched to a different drummer. Everyone wanted to eat a different thing at breakfast, which was entirely against Ella's notion of eating together. How could there be unity at a table when one nibbled toasted bread and jam (Jeannette) while another chomped honey-puffed cereal (Avi) and a third waited patiently to be served scrambled eggs (David) and a fourth refused to eat anything at all (Orly)? All the same, breakfast was important. Every morning she prepared it, determined that no child of hers would begin the day munching on biscuits or some other junk food.

But this morning when she entered the kitchen, instead of brewing coffee, squeezing oranges, or toasting bread, the first thing Ella did was to sit at the kitchen table and turn on her laptop. She logged on to the Internet to see whether there was an e-mail from Aziz. To her delight, there was.

Dear Ella,

I was so happy to learn that things have improved between you and your daughter. As for me, I left the village of Momostenango yesterday at the crack of dawn. Strange, I stayed here only a few days, and yet when the time came to bid farewell, I felt sad, almost grieved. Would I ever see this tiny village in Guatemala again? I didn't think so.

Each time I say good-bye to a place I like, I feel like I am leaving a part of me behind. I guess whether we choose to travel as much as Marco Polo did or stay in the same spot from cradle to grave, life is a sequence of births and deaths. Moments are born and moments die. For new experiences to come to light, old ones need to wither away. Don't you think?

While in Momostenango, I meditated and tried to visualize your aura. Before long, three colors came to me: warm yellow, timid orange, and reserved metallic purple. I had a feeling these were your colors. I thought they were beautiful both separately and together.

My final stop in Guatemala is Chajul—a small town with adobe houses and children with eyes wise beyond their years. In each house, women of all ages weave magnificent tapestries. I asked a granny to choose a tapestry and said it was for a lady living in Northampton. After giving it some thought, she pulled a tapestry from a huge pile behind her. I swear to God, there were more than fifty tapestries of every possible color in that pile. Yet the one she chose for you was composed of only three tones: yellow, orange, and purple. I thought you might like to know about this coincidence, if there is such a thing in God's universe.

Does it ever occur to you that our exchange might not be a result of coincidence?

Warm regards,

Aziz

P.S. If you want, I can send you your tapestry via mail, or I can wait till the day we meet for coffee and bring it myself.

Ella closed her eyes and tried to imagine how the colors of her aura surrounded her face. Interestingly, the image of herself that popped up in her mind was not her grown-up self but her as a child, around seven years of age.

Many things came flooding back to her, memories that she thought she had long left behind. The sight of her mother standing still with a pistachio green apron around her waist and a measuring cup in her hand, her face an ashen mask of pain; dangling paper hearts on the walls, bright and sparkly; and the body of her father hanging from the ceiling as if he wanted to blend with the Christmas decorations and give the house a festive look. She remembered how she had spent her teenage years holding her mother responsible for the suicide of her father. As a young girl, Ella had promised herself that when she got married, she would always make her husband happy and not fail in her marriage, like her mother. In her endeavor to make her marriage as different from her mother's as possible, she had not married a Christian man, preferring to marry inside her faith.

It was only a few years earlier that Ella had stopped hating her aging mother, and though the two of them had been on good terms lately, the truth was, deep inside she still felt ill at ease when she remembered the past.

"Mom! . . . Earth to Mom! Earth to Mom!"

Ella heard a ripple of giggles and whispers behind her shoulder. When she turned around, she saw four pairs of eyes watching her with amusement. Orly, Avi, Jeannette, and David had for once all come to breakfast at the same time and were now standing side by side inspecting her as if she were an exotic creature. From the way they looked, it seemed they had been standing there for a while, trying to get her attention.

"Good morning, you all." Ella smiled.

"How come you didn't hear us?" Orly asked, sounding genuinely surprised.

"You seemed so absorbed in that screen," David said without looking at her.

Ella's gaze followed her husband's, and there on the open screen in front of her, she saw Aziz Z. Zahara's e-mail shining dimly. In a flash she closed her laptop, without waiting for it to shut down.

"I've got a lot of reading to do for the literary agency," Ella said, rolling her eyes. "I was working on my report."

"No you were not! You were reading your e-mails," Avi said, his face serious, matter-of-fact.

What was it in teenage boys that made them so eager to detect everyone's flaws and lies? Ella wondered. But, to her relief, the others didn't seem interested in the subject. In fact, they were all looking somewhere else now, focused on the kitchen counter.

It was Orly who turned to Ella, voicing the question for them all. "Mom, how come you haven't made us any breakfast this morning?"

Now Ella turned to the counter and saw what they had seen. There was no coffee brewing, no scrambled eggs on the stove, no toast with blueberry sauce. She nodded repeatedly as if agreeing with an inner voice that spoke an undeniable truth.

Right, she thought, how come she had forgotten the breakfast?

PART TWO

Water

THE THINGS THAT ARE FLUID,
CHANGING, AND UNPREDICTABLE

Rumi

KONYA, OCTOBER 15, 1244

Bright and plump, the gorgeous full moon resembled a massive pearl hanging in the sky. I got up from the bed and looked out the window into the courtyard, awash in moonlight. Even seeing such beauty, however, did not soothe the pounding of my heart or the trembling of my hands.

"Effendi, you look pale. Did you have the same dream again?" whispered my wife. "Shall I bring you a glass of water?"

I told her not to worry and to go back to sleep. There was nothing she could do. Our dreams were part of our destiny, and they would run their course as God willed it. Besides, there must be a reason, I thought, that every night for the last forty days I had been having the same dream.

The beginning of the dream differed slightly each time. Or perhaps it was always the same but I entered it from a different gate each evening. On this occasion I saw myself reading the Qur'an in a carpeted room that felt familiar but was like no place I had been before. Right across from me sat a dervish, tall, thin, and erect, with a veil on his face. He was holding a candelabrum with five glowing candles providing me with light so that I could read.

After a while I lifted my head to show the dervish the verse I was reading, and only then did I realize, to my awe, that what I thought was a candelabrum was in fact the man's right hand. He had been holding out his hand to me, with each one of his fingers aflame.

In panic I looked around for water, but there was none in sight. I took off my cloak and threw it on the dervish to extinguish the flames.

But when I lifted the cloak, he had vanished, leaving only a burning candle behind.

From this point onward, it was always the same dream. I started to look for him in the house, searching every nook and cranny. Next I ran into the courtyard, where the roses had blossomed in a sea of bright yellow. I called out left and right, but the man was nowhere to be seen.

"Come back, beloved. Where are you?"

Finally, as if led by an ominous intuition, I approached the well and peered down at the dark waters churning below. At first I couldn't see anything, but in a little while the moon showered me in its glittering light and the courtyard acquired a rare luminosity. Only then did I notice a pair of black eyes staring up at me with unprecedented sorrow from the bottom of the well.

"They killed him!" somebody shouted. Perhaps it was me. Perhaps this was what my own voice would sound like in a state of infinite agony.

And I screamed and screamed until my wife held me tight, drew me to her bosom, and asked softly, "Effendi, did you have the same dream again?"

After Kerra went back to sleep, I slipped into the courtyard. In that moment I had the impression that the dream was still with me, vivid and frightening. In the stillness of the night, the sight of the well sent a shiver down my spine, but I couldn't help sitting next to it, listening to the night breeze rustle gently through the trees.

At times like these, I feel a sudden wave of sadness take hold of me, though I can never tell why. My life is complete and fulfilled, in that I have been blessed with the three things I hold most dear: knowledge, virtue, and the capability to help others find God.

At age thirty-eight, I have been given by God more than I could ever have asked for. I have been trained as a preacher and a jurist and initiated into The Science of Divine Intuition—the knowledge given to prophets, saints, and scholars in varying degrees. Guided by my late father, educated by the best teachers of our time, I have worked hard to deepen my awareness with the belief that this was the duty God had assigned me.

My old master Seyyid Burhaneddin used to say I was one of God's beloved, since I was given the honorable task of delivering His message to His people and helping them differentiate right from wrong.

For many years I have been teaching at the madrassa, discussing theology with other sharia scholars, instructing my disciples, studying law and *hadiths,* giving sermons every Friday at the biggest mosque in town. I have long lost track of the number of students I have tutored. It is flattering to hear people praise my preaching skills and tell me how my words changed their lives at a time when they most needed guidance.

I am blessed with a loving family, good friends, and loyal disciples. Never in my life have I suffered destitution or scarcity, although the loss of my first wife was devastating. I thought I would never get married again, but I did, and thanks to Kerra I have experienced love and joy. Both of my sons are grown, although it never ceases to amaze me to see how different from each other they turned out to be. They are like two seeds that, though planted side by side in the same soil and nourished with the same sun and water, have blossomed into completely different plants. I am proud of them, just as I am proud of our adopted daughter, who has unique talents. I am a happy, satisfied man both in my private life and in the community.

Why, then, do I feel this void inside me, growing deeper and wider with each passing day? It gnaws at my soul like a disease and accompanies me wherever I go, as quiet as a mouse and just as ravenous.

Shams

KONYA, OCTOBER 17, 1244

Before passing through the gates of a town I've never visited, I take a minute to salute its saints—the dead and the living, the known and the hidden. Never in my life have I arrived at a new place without getting the blessing of its saints first. It makes no difference to me whether that place belongs to Muslims, Christians, or Jews. I believe that the saints are beyond such trivial nominal distinctions. A saint belongs to all humanity.

So when I saw Konya for the first time from a distance, I did what I always did. But something unusual happened next. Instead of greeting me back and offering their blessings, as *they* always did, the saints remained as silent as broken tombstones. I saluted them again, more loudly and assertively this time, in case they had not heard me. But once again there followed silence. I realized that the saints had heard me, all right. They just weren't giving me their blessing.

"Tell me what's wrong?" I asked the wind so that it would carry my words to the saints far and wide.

In a little while, the wind returned with an answer. "O dervish, in this city you'll find only two extremes, and nothing in between. Either pure love or pure hatred. We are warning you. Enter at your own risk."

"In that case there is no need to worry," I said. "As long as I can encounter pure love, that'll be enough for me."

Upon hearing that, the saints of Konya gave me their blessing. But I didn't want to enter the city just yet. I sat down under an oak tree, and as my horse munched on the sparse grass around, I looked at the city looming in the distance. The minarets of Konya glistened in the sun like shards of glass. Every now and then, I heard dogs barking, donkeys braying, children laughing, and vendors yelling at the top of their lungs—ordinary sounds of a city throbbing with life. What kinds of joys and sorrows, I wondered, were being lived at this moment behind closed doors and latticed windows? Being used to an itinerant life, I found it slightly unnerving to have to settle in a city, but I recalled another fundamental rule: *Try not to resist the changes that come your way. Instead let life live through you. And do not worry that your life is turning upside down. How do you know that the side you are used to is better than the one to come?*

A friendly voice yanked me out of my reverie. "*Selamun aleykum,* dervish!"

When I turned around, I saw an olive-skinned, brawny peasant with a drooping mustache. He was riding a cart pulled by an ox so skinny that the poor thing looked as if it could at any moment breathe its last.

"*Aleykum selam,* may God bless you!" I called out.

"Why are you sitting here on your own? If you are tired of riding that horse of yours, I could give you a lift."

I smiled. "Thanks, but I think I could go faster on foot than with your ox."

"Don't sell my ox short," the peasant said, sounding offended. "He might be old and frail, but he's still my best friend."

Put in my place by these words, I jumped to my feet and bowed before the peasant. How could I, a minor element in God's vast circle of creation, belittle another element in the circle, be it an animal or a human being?

"I apologize to you and your ox," I said. "Please forgive me."

A shadow of disbelief crossed the peasant's face. He stood deadpan for a moment, weighing whether I was mocking him or not. "Nobody ever does that," he said when he spoke again, flashing me a warm smile.

"You mean apologize to your ox?"

"Well, that, too. But I was thinking nobody ever apologizes to *me.* It's usually the other way round. I am the one who says sorry all the time. Even when people do me wrong, I apologize to them."

I was touched to hear that. "The Qur'an tells us each and every one of us was made in the best of molds. It's one of the rules," I said softly.

"What rule?" he asked.

"God is busy with the completion of your work, both outwardly and inwardly. He is fully occupied with you. Every human being is a work in progress that is slowly but inexorably moving toward perfection. We are each an unfinished work of art both waiting and striving to be completed. God deals with each of us separately because humanity is a fine art of skilled penmanship where every single dot is equally important for the entire picture."

"Are you here for the sermon, too?" the peasant asked with a renewed interest. "It looks like it's going to be very crowded. He is a remarkable man."

My heart skipped a beat as I realized whom he was talking about. "Tell me, what is so special about Rumi's sermons?"

The peasant fell quiet and squinted into the vast horizon for a while. His mind seemed to be everywhere and nowhere.

Then he said, "I come from a village that has had its share of hardships. First the famine, then the Mongols. They burned and plundered every village in their way. But what they did in the big cities was even worse. They captured Erzurum, Sivas, and Kayseri and massacred the entire male population, taking the women with them. I myself have not lost a loved one or my house. But I *did* lose something. I lost my joy."

"What's that got to do with Rumi?" I asked.

Dropping his gaze back to his ox, the peasant murmured tonelessly, "Everyone says if you listen to Rumi preach, your sadness will be cured."

Personally, I didn't think there was anything wrong with sadness. Just the opposite—hypocrisy made people happy, and truth made them sad. But I didn't tell this to the peasant. Instead I said, "Why don't I join you until Konya, and you'll tell me more about Rumi?"

I tied my horse's reins to the cart and climbed in to sit beside the peasant, glad to see that the ox didn't mind the additional load. One way or the other, it walked the same excruciatingly slow walk. The peasant offered me bread and goat cheese. We ate as we talked. In this state, while the sun blazed in an indigo sky, and under the watchful eyes of the town's saints, I entered Konya.

"Take good care, my friend," I said as I jumped off the cart and loosened the reins of my horse.

"Make sure you come to the sermon!" the peasant yelled expectantly.

I nodded as I waved good-bye. *"Inshallah."*

Although I was eager to listen to the sermon and dying to meet Rumi, I wanted to spend some time in the city first and learn what the townspeople thought about the great preacher. I wanted to see him through foreign eyes, kind and unkind, loving and unloving, before I looked on him with my own.

Hasan the Beggar

KONYA, OCTOBER 17, 1244

Believe it or not, they call this purgatory on earth "holy suffering." I am a leper stuck in limbo. Neither the dead nor the living want me among them. Mothers point me out on the streets to scare their misbehaving little ones, and children throw stones at me. Artisans chase me from their storefronts to ward off the bad luck that follows me everywhere, and pregnant women turn their faces away whenever they set eyes on me, fearing that their babies will be born defective. None of these people seem to realize that as keen as they are to avoid me, I am far keener to avoid them and their pitiful stares.

It is the skin that changes first, becoming thicker and darker. Patches of varying sizes, the color of rotten eggs, appear on the shoulders, knees, arms, and face. There is a lot of stinging and burning in this phase, but then somehow the pain withers away, or else one becomes numb to it. Next the patches start to enlarge and swell up, turning into ugly bulbs. The hands turn to claws, and the face is so deformed as to be unrecognizable. Now that I am nearing the final stages, I cannot close my eyelids anymore. Tears and saliva flow without my control. Six of the nails on my hands have fallen off, and one is on its way. Oddly enough, I still have my hair. I guess I should consider that lucky.

I heard that in Europe lepers are kept outside the city walls. Here they let us live in the city as long as we carry a bell to warn other people of our presence. We are also allowed to beg, which is a good thing, because otherwise we would probably starve. Begging is one of only two ways to survive. The other is praying. Not because God pays special attention to lepers but because for some strange reason people think He does. Hence, as much as they despise us, the townspeople also respect us. They hire us to pray for the sick, the crippled, and the elderly. They pay and feed us well, hoping to squeeze out of our mouths a few extra prayers. On the streets, lepers might be treated worse than dogs, but in places where death and despair loom large, we are the sultans.

Whenever I am hired to pray, I bow my head and make incomprehensible sounds in Arabic, pretending to be absorbed in prayer. Pretend is all I can do, for I don't think God hears me. I have no reason to believe He does.

Though it is less profitable, I find begging much easier than praying. At least I am not deceiving anyone. Friday is the best day of the week to beg, except when it is Ramadan, in which case the whole month is quite lucrative. The last day of Ramadan is by far the best time to make money. That is when even the hopeless penny-pinchers race to give alms, keen to compensate for all their sins, past and present. Once a year, people don't turn away from beggars. To the contrary, they specifically look for one, the more miserable the better. So profound is their need to show off how generous and charitable they are, not only do they race to give us alms, but for that single day they almost love us.

Today could be a very profitable day, too, since Rumi is giving one of his Friday sermons. The mosque is already packed. Those who can't find a seat inside are lining up in the courtyard. The afternoon is the perfect occasion for panhandlers and pickpockets. And just like me, they are all present here, scattered within the crowd.

I sat down right across from the entrance of the mosque with my back to a maple tree. There was a dank smell of rain in the air, mixed with the sweet, faint tang coming from the orchards far away. I put my mendicant bowl in front of me. Unlike many others in this business, I never have to openly ask for alms. A leper doesn't need to whine and implore, making up stories about how wretched his life is or how poor his health. Giving people a glimpse of my face has the effect of a thousand words. So I simply uncovered my face and sat back.

In the next hour, a few coins were dropped into my bowl. All were chipped copper. I yearned for a gold coin, with symbols of sun, lion, and crescent. Since the late Aladdin Keykubad had loosened the rules on currency, coins issued by the beys of Aleppo, the Fatimid rulers in

Cairo, and the caliph of Baghdad, not to mention the Italian florin, were all pronounced valid. The rulers of Konya accepted them all, and so did the town's beggars.

Together with the coins, a few dry leaves fell on my lap. The maple tree was shedding its reddish gold leaves, and as a gusty wind blew, quite a number of these made it into my bowl, as if the tree were giving me alms. Suddenly I realized that the maple tree and I had something in common. A tree shedding its leaves in autumn resembled a man shedding his limbs in the final stages of leprosy.

I was a naked tree. My skin, my organs, my face falling apart. Every day another part of my body abandoned me. And for me, unlike the maple tree, there would be no spring in which I would blossom. What I lost, I lost forever. When people looked at me, they didn't see who I was but what I was missing. Whenever they placed a coin in my bowl, they did so with amazing speed and avoided any eye contact, as if my gaze were contagious. In their eyes I was worse than a thief or a murderer. As much as they disapproved of such outlaws, they didn't treat them as if they were invisible. When it came to me, however, all they saw was death staring them in the face. That's what scared them—to recognize that death could be this close and this ugly.

Suddenly there was a great commotion in the background. I heard somebody yell, "He is coming! He is coming!"

Sure enough, there was Rumi, riding a horse as white as milk, wearing an exquisite amber caftan embroidered with golden leaves and baby pearls, erect and proud, wise and noble, followed by a throng of admirers. Radiating an air of charisma and confidence, he looked less like a scholar than a ruler—the sultan of the wind, the fire, the water, and the earth. Even his horse stood tall and firm, as if aware of the distinction of the man he carried.

I pocketed the coins in my bowl, wrapped my head so as to leave half of my face in the open, and entered the mosque. Inside, it was so packed it seemed impossible to breathe, let alone find a seat. But the one good thing about being a leper was that no matter how crowded a place, I could always find a seat, since nobody wanted to sit next to me.

"Brothers," Rumi said, his voice rising high, sweeping low. "The vastness of the universe makes us feel small, even inconsequential. Some of you might be asking, 'What meaning could I, in my limitedness, possibly have for God?' This, I believe, is a question that has occurred to many from time to time. In today's sermon I want to generate some specific answers to that."

Rumi's two sons were in the front row—the handsome one, Sultan Walad, who everyone said resembled his late mother, and the young one, Aladdin, with an animated face but curiously furtive eyes. I could see that both were proud of their father.

"The children of Adam were honored with knowledge so great that neither the mountains nor the heavens could shoulder it," Rumi continued. "That is why it says in the Qur'an, *Truly We offered the trust to the heavens and the earth and the mountains, but they refused to bear it because they were afraid of it. Only man took it up.* Having been given such an honorable position, human beings should not aim any lower than what God had intended."

Pronouncing his vowels in that strange way only the educated are capable of, Rumi talked about God, assuring us that He dwelled not on a distant throne in the sky but very close to each and every one of us. What brought us even closer to God, he said, was none other than suffering.

"Your hand opens and closes all the time. If it did not, you would be paralyzed. Your deepest presence is in every small contracting and expanding. The two are as beautifully balanced and coordinated as the wings of a bird."

At first I liked what he said. It warmed my heart to think of joy and sorrow as dependent on each other as a bird's wings. But almost instantly I felt a wave of resentment rise up in my throat. What did Rumi know about suffering? As the son of an eminent man and heir to a wealthy, prominent family, life had always been good to him. I knew he had lost his first wife, but I didn't believe he had ever experienced real misfortune. Born with a silver spoon in his mouth, raised in distinguished circles, tutored by the best scholars, and always loved, pampered, and admired—how dare he preach on suffering?

With a sinking heart, I realized that the contrast between Rumi and me couldn't be greater. Why was God so unfair? To me He had given poverty, sickness, and misery. To Rumi riches, success, and wisdom. With his flawless reputation and royal demeanor, he hardly belonged to this world, at least not to this city. I had to cover my face if I didn't want people to be revolted by the sight of me, while he shone in public like a precious gem. I wondered how he would fare if he were in my shoes? Had it ever occurred to him that even someone as perfect and privileged as he could someday tumble and fall? Had he ever contemplated how it would feel to be an outcast, even for one day? Would he still be the great Rumi if he had been given the life I was given?

With each new question, my resentment rose, sweeping away whatever admiration I might otherwise have had for him. Bitter and petulant, I stood up and pushed my way out. Several people in the audience eyed me curiously, wondering why I was leaving a sermon that so many others were dying to attend.

Shams

KONYA, OCTOBER 17, 1244

Beholden to the peasant who dropped me off at the town center, I found myself and my horse a place to stay. The Inn of Sugar Vendors seemed just what I needed. Of the four rooms I was shown, I chose the one with the fewest possessions, which consisted of a sleeping mat with a moldy blanket, an oil lamp that was sputtering its last, a sun-dried brick that I could use as a pillow, and a good view of the whole town up to the base of the surrounding hills.

Having thus settled down, I roamed the streets, amazed at the mixture of religions, customs, and languages permeating the air. I ran into Gypsy musicians, Arab travelers, Christian pilgrims, Jewish merchants, Buddhist priests, Frankish troubadours, Persian artists, Chinese acrobats, Indian snake charmers, Zoroastrian magicians, and Greek philosophers. In the slave market, I saw concubines with skin white as milk and hefty, dark eunuchs who had seen such atrocities that they had lost their ability to speak. In the bazaar I came across traveling barbers with bloodletting devices, fortune-tellers with crystal balls, and magicians who swallowed fire. There were pilgrims on their way to Jerusalem and vagrants who I suspected were runaway soldiers from the last Crusades. I heard people speak Venetian, Frankish, Saxon, Greek, Persian, Turkish, Kurdish, Armenian, Hebrew, and several other dialects I couldn't even distinguish. Despite their seemingly endless differences, all of these people gave off a similar air of incompleteness, of the works in progress that they were, each an unfinished masterwork.

The whole city was a Tower of Babel. Everything was constantly shifting, splitting, coming to light, transpiring, thriving, dissolving, decomposing, and dying. Amid this chaos I stood in a place of unperturbed silence and serenity, utterly indifferent to the world and yet at the same time feeling a burning love for all the people struggling and suffering in it. As I watched the people around me, I recalled another golden rule: *It's easy to love a perfect God, unblemished and infallible that He is. What is far more difficult is to love fellow human beings with all their imperfections and defects. Remember, one can only know what one is capable of loving. There is no wisdom without love. Unless we learn to love God's creation, we can neither truly love nor truly know God.*

I roamed the narrow alleys where artisans of all ages toiled in their small, dingy stores. In every place I visited, I overheard the townspeople talk about Rumi. How did it feel, I wondered, to be this popular? How did it affect his nafs? My mind busy with these questions, I strolled in the opposite direction from the mosque where Rumi was preaching. Gradually the surroundings began to change. As I moved northward, the houses became more dilapidated, the garden walls falling down, and the children more raucous and unruly. The smells changed, too, getting heavier, more garlicky and spicy. Finally I stepped into a street where three odors loomed in the air: sweat, perfume, and lust. I had reached the seamy side of town.

There was a ramshackle house atop the steep cobbled street, the walls supported by bamboo pillars, the roof of thatched grass. In front of the house, a group of women sat chatting. When they saw me approach, they eyed me curiously, looking half amused. Beside them was a garden with roses of every color and shade imaginable and the most amazing smell. I wondered who tended to them.

I didn't have to wait too long to learn the answer. No sooner had I reached the garden than the entrance door of the house was flung open and a woman dashed out. She was heavy-jowled, tall, and enormously fat. When she squinted, the way she did now, her eyes were lost in rolls of flesh. She had a thin, dark mustache and thick sideburns. It took me a while to comprehend that she was both man and woman.

"What do you want?" the hermaphrodite asked suspiciously. Her face was in constant flux: One moment it looked like the face of a woman; then the tide came back, replacing it with the face of a man.

I introduced myself and asked her name, but she ignored my question.

"This is no place for you," she said, waving her hands as if I were a fly she'd like to chase away.

"Why not?"

"Don't you see this place is a brothel? Don't you dervishes take an oath to stay away from lust? People think I wallow in sin here, but I give my alms and close my doors in the month of Ramadan. And now I'm saving you. Stay away from us. This is the filthiest corner in town."

"Filth is inside, not outside," I objected. "Thus says the rule."

"What are you talking about?" she croaked.

"It is one of the forty rules," I tried to explain. *"Real filth is the one inside. The rest simply washes off. There is only one type of dirt that cannot be cleansed with pure waters, and that is the stain of hatred and bigotry contaminating the soul. You can purify your body through abstinence and fasting, but only love will purify your heart."*

The hermaphrodite was having none of it. "You dervishes are out of your minds. I've got all sorts of customers here. But a dervish? When frogs grow beards! If I let you linger, God will raze this place to the ground and put a curse on us for seducing a man of faith."

I couldn't help chuckling. "Where do you get these ridiculous ideas? Do you think God is an angry, moody patriarch watching us from the skies above so that He can rain stones and frogs on our heads the moment we err?"

The patron pulled at the ends of her thin mustache, giving me an annoyed look that verged on meanness.

"Don't worry, I'm not here to visit your brothel," I assured her. "I was just admiring your rose garden."

"Oh, that"—the hermaphrodite shrugged dismissively—"is the creation of one of my girls, Desert Rose."

With that, the patron gestured to a young woman sitting among the harlots ahead of us. Delicate chin, pearl-luster skin, and dark almond eyes clouded with worry. She was heartbreakingly beautiful. As I looked at her, I had a sense she would not be staying there much longer.

I dropped my voice to a whisper so that only the patron could hear me. "That girl is a good girl. One day soon she'll embark on a spiritual journey to find God. She'll abandon this place forever. When that day comes, do not try to stop her."

The hermaphrodite looked at me flabbergasted before she burst out, "What the hell are you talking about? Nobody is telling me what to do with my girls! You better get the hell out of here. Or else I'm calling Jackal Head!"

"Who's that?" I asked.

"Believe me, you wouldn't want to know," the hermaphrodite said, shaking her finger to emphasize her point.

Hearing the name of this stranger made me shiver slightly, but I didn't dwell on it. "Anyway, I'm leaving," I said. "But I'll come back, so don't be surprised next time you see me around. I'm not one of those pious types who spend their whole lives hunched on prayer rugs while their eyes and hearts remain closed to the outside world. They read the Qur'an only on the surface. But I read the Qur'an in the budding flowers and migrating birds. I read the Breathing Qur'an secreted in human beings."

"You mean you read people?" The patron laughed a halfhearted laugh. "What kind of nonsense is that?"

"Every man is an open book, each and every one of us a walking Qur'an. The quest for God is ingrained in the hearts of all, be it a prostitute or a saint. Love exists within each of us from the moment we are born and waits to be discovered from then on. That is what one of the forty rules is all about: *The whole universe is contained within a single human being—you. Everything that you see around, including the things you might not be fond of and even the people you despise or abhor, is present within you in varying degrees. Therefore, do not look for Sheitan outside yourself either. The devil is not an extraordinary force that attacks from without. It is an ordinary voice within. If you get to know yourself fully, facing with honesty and hardness both your dark and bright sides, you will arrive at a supreme form of consciousness. When a person knows himself or herself, he or she knows God.*"

Crossing her arms above her chest, the hermaphrodite leaned forward and squinted at me menacingly.

"A dervish who preaches to harlots!" she grunted. "I warn you, I'm not going to let you badger anyone around here with your silly ideas. You better stay away from my brothel! Because if you don't, I swear to God, Jackal Head will cut off that sharp tongue of yours and I'll eat it with pleasure."

Ella

NORTHAMPTON, MAY 28, 2008

Befitting her general mood, Ella woke up sad. But not sad as in weepy and unhappy, only sad as in unwilling to smile and take things lightly. She felt as though she had reached a milestone she was not prepared for. As she was brewing coffee in the kitchen, she took her list of resolutions out of the drawer and scanned through it.

Ten Things to Do Before Turning Forty

1. Improve your time management, be better organized, and be determined to make the most of your time. Buy a new day planner. (Accomplished)
2. Add mineral supplements and antioxidants to your diet. (Accomplished)
3. Take action for fewer wrinkles. Try alpha hydroxy products, and start using the new L'Oréal cream. (Accomplished)
4. Change the upholstery, buy new plants, get new cushions. (Accomplished)
5. Evaluate your life, values, and beliefs. (Half accomplished)
6. Eliminate meat from your diet, make a healthy menu every week, and start giving your body the respect it deserves. (Half accomplished)
7. Start reading Rumi's poems. (Accomplished)
8. Take the kids to a Broadway musical. (Accomplished)

9. Start writing a cookbook. (Unaccomplished)
10. Open your heart to love!!!

Ella stood still, her eyes fixed on the tenth item on her list, not knowing whether to put a check next to it or not. She didn't even know what she'd meant when she wrote that. What was she thinking? "It must be the effect of *Sweet Blasphemy*," she murmured to herself. Lately she found herself frequently thinking about love.

Dear Aziz,

Today is my birthday! I feel like I have reached a milestone in my life. They say turning forty is a defining moment, especially for women. They also say that forty is the new thirty (and sixty is the new forty), but as much as I'd like to believe all that, it sounds too far-fetched to me. I mean, who are we kidding? Forty is forty! I guess now I'll have "more" of everything—more knowledge, more wisdom, and of course more wrinkles and gray hair.

Birthdays have always made me happy, but this morning I woke up with heaviness in my chest, asking questions too large for someone who hadn't even had her morning coffee yet. I kept wondering, is the way I've lived my life the way I want to continue from now on?

And then a fearful feeling came over me. What if both a yes and a no might generate equally disastrous consequences? So I found another answer: maybe!

Warm wishes,
Ella

P.S. Sorry I couldn't write a more cheerful e-mail. I don't know why I'm down in the dumps today. I can't give you a reason. (That is, other than turning forty. I guess this is what they call midlife crisis.)

Dear Ella,

Happy birthday! Forty is a most beautiful age for both men and women. Did you know that in mystic thought forty symbolizes the ascent from one level to a higher one and spiritual awakening? When we mourn we mourn for forty days. When a baby is born it takes forty days for him to get ready to start life on earth. And when we are in love we need to wait for forty days to be sure of our feelings.

The Flood of Noah lasted forty days, and while the waters destroyed life, they also washed all impurity away and enabled human beings to make a new, fresh start. In Islamic mysticism there are forty degrees between man and God. Likewise, there are four basic stages of consciousness and ten degrees in each, making forty levels in total. Jesus went into the wilderness for forty days and nights. Muhammad was forty years old when he received the call to become a prophet. Buddha meditated under a linden tree for forty days. Not to mention the forty rules of Shams.

You receive a new mission at forty, a new lease on life! You have reached a most auspicious number. Congratulations! And don't worry about getting old. There are no wrinkles or gray hair strong enough to defy the power of forty!

Warmly,
Aziz

Desert Rose the Harlot

KONYA, OCTOBER 17, 1244

Brothels have existed since the beginning of time. And so have women like me. But there is something that amazes me: Why is it that although people say they hate seeing women prostitute themselves, the same people make life hard for a prostitute who wants to repent and start life anew? It is as if they are telling us they are sorry that we have fallen so low, but now that we are where we are, we should stay there forever. I don't know why this is. All I know is, some people feed on the miseries of others and they don't like it when there is one less miserable person on the face of the earth. But no matter what they say or do, I am going to walk out of this place one day.

This morning I woke up bursting with a desire to listen to the great Rumi preach. Had I told the patron the truth and asked permission, she would have made fun of me. "Since when do whores go to mosques?" she would have said, laughing so hard her round face would have turned crimson.

That's why I lied. After that hairless dervish left, the patron looked so preoccupied I sensed it was the right time to go and talk. She is always more approachable when distracted. I told her I needed to go to the bazaar to run some errands. She believed me. After nine years of my working like a dog for her, she does.

"Only on one condition," she said. "Sesame is coming with you."

That wasn't a problem. I liked Sesame. A big, hefty man with the mind of a child, he was reliable and honest to the point of simplicity. How he survived in such a cruel world was a mystery to me. Nobody knew what his real name was, perhaps not even himself. We had named him so because of his infatuation with sesame halva. When a harlot from the brothel needed to go out, Sesame accompanied her like a silent shadow. He was the best guard I could have wished for.

The two of us took the dusty road winding through the orchards. When we reached the first intersection, I asked Sesame to wait for me, and I disappeared behind a bush where I had hidden a bag full of men's clothes.

It was harder than I thought to dress up as a man. Wrapping long scarves around my breasts, I flattened my chest. Then I put on baggy trousers, a cotton vest, a long maroon robe, and a turban. Finally I covered half my face with a scarf, hoping to resemble an Arab traveler.

When I walked back toward him, Sesame flinched, looking puzzled.

"Let's go," I urged him, and when he didn't budge, I uncovered my face. "My dear, haven't you recognized me?"

"Desert Rose, is that you?" Sesame exclaimed, putting one hand on his mouth like a child in awe. "Why did you dress up like that?"

"Can you keep a secret?"

Sesame nodded, his eyes widening with excitement.

"All right," I whispered. "We are going to a mosque. But don't tell the patron."

Sesame's bottom lip quivered. "No, no. We were going to the bazaar."

"Yes, dear, later. First we are going to listen to the great Rumi."

Sesame panicked slightly, as I knew he would. The change in plans was unsettling to him. "Please, this means a lot to me," I begged. "If you agree and promise not to tell anyone about it, I'll buy you a huge chunk of halva."

"Halva." Sesame clucked his tongue with delight, as if the word alone had left a sweet taste in his mouth.

And with sweet expectation, we set off toward the mosque where Rumi was going to speak.

I was born in a small village near Nicaea. My mother always said to me, "You were born in the right place, but I am afraid it was under the wrong star." The times were bad, unpredictable. From one year to the next, nothing remained the same. First there were rumors of the Crusaders coming back. We heard terrible stories about the atrocities they committed in

Constantinople, ransacking the mansions, demolishing the icons inside chapels and churches. Next we heard about Seljuk attacks. And before the tales of terror of the Seljuk army faded, those of the ruthless Mongols started. The name and the face of the enemy changed, but the fear of being destroyed by outsiders remained as steady as snow on Mount Ida.

My parents were bakers and good Christians. One of my earliest memories is the smell of bread out of the oven. We weren't rich. Even as a child, I knew that. But we weren't poor either. I had seen the stare in the eyes of the poor when they came to the bakery begging for crumbs. Every night before going to sleep, I thanked the Lord for not sending me to bed hungry. It felt like talking to a friend. For back then God was my friend.

When I was seven, my mother became pregnant. Looking back today, I suspect she might have had several miscarriages before that, but I didn't know anything about such things. I was so innocent that if anyone asked me how babies were made, I would have said God kneaded them out of soft, sweet dough.

But the bread baby that God kneaded for my mother must have been enormous, because before long her belly swelled up, big and tight. Mother had become so huge she could barely move. The midwife said her body was retaining water, but that didn't sound like a bad thing to me.

What neither my mother nor the midwife knew was, there wasn't one baby but three. All were boys. My brothers had waged a war inside my mother's body. One of the triplets had strangled his brother with his umbilical cord, and as if to take revenge, the dead baby had blocked the passage, thus preventing the others from coming out. For four days my mother remained in labor. Night and day we listened to her screams until we heard her no more.

Unable to save my mother, the midwife did her best to save my brothers. Taking a pair of scissors, she cut my mom's belly open, but in the end only one baby survived. This is how my brother was born. My father never forgave him, and when the baby was baptized, he did not attend the ceremony.

With my mother gone and my father turned into a sullen, bitter man, life was never the same. Things rapidly deteriorated at the bakery. We lost our customers. Afraid of becoming poor and having to beg someday, I started to hide bread rolls under my bed, where they would get dry and stale. But it was my brother who really suffered. I at least had been loved and taken good care of in the past. He never had any of that. It broke my heart to see him being mistreated, and yet a part of me was relieved, even grateful, that it wasn't I who had become the target of my father's fury. I wish I had protected my brother. Everything would be different then, and I wouldn't be in a brothel in Konya today. Life is so strange.

A year later my father remarried. The only difference in my brother's life was that whereas before it was my father who ill-treated him, now it was my father and his new wife who did so. He started to run away from home, only to come back with the worst habits and the wrong friends. One day my father beat him so badly he almost killed him. After that, the boy changed. There was a cold, cruel stare in his eyes that wasn't there before. I knew he had something in mind, but it never occurred to me what a horrible plan he was brewing. I wish I had known. I wish I could have prevented the tragedy.

Then, one morning in spring, my father and stepmother were found dead, killed with rat poison. As soon as the incident became public, everyone suspected my brother. When the guards started asking questions, he ran away in panic. I never saw him again. And just like that, I was alone in the world. Unable to stay at home where I still sensed my mother's smell, unable to work at the bakery where disturbing memories hovered in the air, I decided to go to Constantinople to stay with an old spinster aunt who had now become my closest relative. I was thirteen.

I took a carriage to Constantinople. I was the youngest passenger on board and the only one traveling alone. A few hours on the road, we were stopped by a gang of robbers. They took everything—suitcases, clothes, boots, belts, and jewelry, even the driver's sausages. Having nothing to give them, I stood aside quietly, certain that they would do me no harm. But just when they were about to leave, the gang leader turned to me and asked, "Are you a virgin, dainty thing?"

I blushed and refused to answer such an improper question. Little did I know that my blushing was the answer he wanted.

"Let's go!" the gang leader shouted. "Take the horses and the girl!"

While I resisted them in tears, none of the other passengers even tried to help me. The robbers took me to a thick, dense forest, where I was surprised to see they had created a whole village. There were women and children. Ducks, goats, and pigs were all over the place. It looked like an idyllic village, except it was inhabited by criminals.

Soon I understood why the gang leader had asked me if I was a virgin. The chief of the village was severely ill with nervous fever. He had been in bed for a long time, with red spots all over his body, trying countless treatments to no avail. Recently someone had convinced him that if he slept with a virgin, his illness would be transmitted to her and he would be clean and cured.

There are things in my life I don't want to remember. My time in the forest is one of them. Even today, whenever the forest comes to my mind, I think of the pine trees and only the pine trees. I preferred sitting alone under those trees to the company of the women in the village, most of whom were the wives or daughters of the robbers. There were also a number of harlots who had come there on their own. I couldn't understand for the life of me why they didn't run away. I was determined to do so.

There were carriages crossing the forest, most of them belonging to the nobility. It was a mystery to me why they were not robbed, until I realized that some carriage drivers bribed the robbers before passing through the forest and in return got the right to travel safely. Once I figured out how things worked, I made my own arrangement. After stopping a carriage heading to the big city, I pleaded with the driver to take me with him. He asked too much money, although he knew I had none. I paid him the only way I knew how.

Only long after I arrived in Constantinople would I comprehend why the harlots in the forest would never run away. The city was worse. It was ruthless. I never looked for my old aunt. Now that I was fallen, I knew a proper lady like her wouldn't want me. I was on my own. It didn't take the city long to crush my spirits and ruin my body. Suddenly I was in another world altogether—a world of malice, rape, brutality, and disease. I had successive abortions until I was damaged so badly that I stopped having periods and could no longer conceive.

I saw things on those streets for which I have no words. After I left the city, I traveled with soldiers, performers, and Gypsies, serving the needs of all. Then a man called Jackal Head found me and brought me to this brothel in Konya. The patron wasn't interested in where I came from as long as I was in good shape. She was delighted to learn I couldn't have babies and would not cause her any problems in that respect. To refer to my barrenness, she named me "Desert," and to embellish that name somewhat, she added "Rose," which was fine with me, as I adored roses.

Which is how I think of faith—like a hidden rose garden where I once roamed and inhaled its perfumed smells but can no longer enter. I want God to be my friend again. With that longing I am circling that garden, searching for an entrance, hoping to find a gate that will let me in.

When Sesame and I reached the mosque, I couldn't believe my eyes. Men of all ages and professions occupied every corner, even the place in the back that would normally be reserved for women. I was about to give up and leave when I noticed a beggar relinquish his seat and inch his way out. Thanking my lucky stars, I wriggled into his space, leaving Sesame outside.

This is how I found myself listening to the great Rumi in a mosque full of men. I didn't even want to think what could happen if they found out there was a woman amid them, let alone a harlot. Chasing off all dark thoughts, I gave my full attention to the sermon.

"God created suffering so that joy might appear through its opposite," Rumi said. "Things become manifest through opposites. Since God has no opposite, He remains hidden."

As the preacher talked, his voice rose and swelled like a mountain stream fed by the melting snow. "Look at the abasement of the earth and the exaltation of the heavens. Know that all the states of the world are like this: flooding and drought, peace and war. Whatever happens, do not forget, nothing God has created is in vain, whether wrath or forbearance, honesty or guile."

Sitting there, I saw that everything served a purpose. My mother's pregnancy and the war in her womb, my brother's incurable loneliness, even the murder of my father and stepmother, my dreadful days in the forest, and every brutality I saw on the streets of Constantinople—they each contributed, in their own way, to my story. Behind all hardships was a larger scheme. I couldn't make it out clearly, but I could feel it with my whole heart. Listening to Rumi in a packed mosque on that afternoon, I felt a cloud of tranquillity descend over me, as delightful and soothing as the sight of my mother baking bread.

Hasan the Beggar

KONYA, OCTOBER 17, 1244

Bristling with irritation, I sat under the maple tree. I continued to be angry at Rumi for his flamboyant speech on suffering—a subject he clearly knew little about. The shadow of the minaret inched its way across the street. Half dozing, half eyeing the passersby, I was about to fall asleep when I caught sight of a dervish I had never seen before. Dressed in black rags, holding a large staff in his hand, with no facial hair and a tiny silver earring in one ear, he looked so different that I couldn't help fixing my gaze upon him.

As his eyes scanned left and right, it didn't take the dervish long to notice me. Instead of ignoring my presence, the way people who saw me for the first time always did, he put his right hand on his heart and greeted me as if we were two old friends. I was so stunned I looked around just to make sure he wasn't greeting someone else. But there was only me and the maple tree. Dazed, confused, I nonetheless put my hand on my heart and greeted him back.

Slowly the dervish walked toward me. I lowered my gaze, expecting him to leave a copper coin in my bowl or hand me a piece of bread. But instead he knelt down to my eye level.

"*Selamun aleykum,* beggar," he said.

"*Aleykum selam,* dervish," I responded. My voice sounded hoarse and strange to me. It had been such a long time since I'd felt the need to speak to anyone that I had almost forgotten what my voice sounded like.

He introduced himself as Shams of Tabriz and asked my name.

I laughed. "What does a man like me need a name for?"

"Everybody has a name," he objected. "God has countless names. Of those, only ninety-nine are known to us. If God has so many names, how can a human being who is the very reflection of Him go around without a name?"

I didn't know how to respond to that and so didn't even try. Instead I conceded, "I had a wife and a mother once. They used to call me Hasan."

"Hasan it is, then." The dervish nodded. Then, to my surprise, he gave me a silver mirror. "Keep it," he said. "A good man in Baghdad gave it to me, but you need it more than I do. It will remind you that you bear God within you."

Before I found the chance to say anything in return, a commotion broke out in the background. The first thing that came to my mind was that a pickpocket had been caught in the mosque. But when the shouts grew louder and fiercer, I knew that it had to be something bigger. No pickpocket would create such an uproar.

We found out soon enough. A woman, a known prostitute, had been found in the mosque dressed up as a man. A group of people were shoving her out, chanting, "Lash the deceiver! Lash the whore!"

In this state the angry mob reached the street. I caught sight of the young woman in men's clothing. Her face was pale as death and her almond eyes terrified. I had seen many lynchings before. It never ceased to amaze me how dramatically people changed when they joined a mob. Ordinary men with no history of violence—artisans, vendors, or peddlers—turned aggressive to the point of murder when they banded together. Lynchings were common and ended with the corpses put on display to deter others.

"Poor woman," I muttered to Shams of Tabriz, but when I turned to him for a response, there was no one standing there.

I caught sight of the dervish darting toward the mob, like a flaming arrow shot straight up into the sky. I jumped to my feet and rushed to catch up with him.

When he reached the head of the procession, Shams raised his staff like a flag and yelled at the top of his voice, "Stop it, people! Halt!"

Baffled, and suddenly silent, the men stared at him in wonder.

"You should all be ashamed of yourselves!" Shams of Tabriz shouted as he struck the ground with his staff. "Thirty men against one woman. Is that fair?"

"She doesn't deserve fairness," said a square-faced, burly man with a lazy eye, who seemed to have proclaimed himself the leader of this impromptu group. I recognized him instantly. He was a security guard named Baybars, a man all the beggars in town knew well for his cruelty and rapacity.

"This woman here dressed up as a man and sneaked into the mosque to deceive good Muslims," Baybars said.

"Are you telling me you want to punish a person for going into a mosque? Is that a crime?" Shams of Tabriz asked, his voice dripping with scorn.

The question created a momentary lull. Apparently nobody had thought of it that way.

"She is a whore!" yelled another man, who looked so enraged that his face had turned a dark scarlet color. "She has no place in a holy mosque!"

That seemed enough to inflame the group again. "Whore! Whore!" a few people at the back chanted in unison. "Let's get the whore!"

As if that were an order, a young lad leaped forward and grabbed the woman's turban, yanking it forcefully. The turban came loose, and the woman's long blond hair, bright as sunflowers, fell down in graceful waves. We all held our breath, astonished by her youth and beauty.

Shams must have recognized the mixed feelings in the air, for he reproached them without skipping a beat: "You have to make up your minds, brothers. Do you really despise this woman, or do you in fact desire her?"

With that, the dervish caught the harlot's hand and pulled her toward him, away from the young lad and the mob. She hid behind him, like a little girl hiding behind her mother's skirts.

"You are making a big mistake," the leader of the group said, raising his voice above the murmur of the crowd. "You are a stranger in this town and don't know our ways. Stay out of this matter."

Someone else chimed in. "What kind of a dervish are you anyway? Don't you have anything better to do than to defend the interests of a whore?"

Shams of Tabriz was quiet for a moment, as if considering the questions. He displayed no temper, remaining invariably tranquil. Then he said, "But how did you notice her in the first place? You go to a mosque but pay more attention to the people around you than to God? If you were the good believers you claim to be, you would not have noticed this woman even if she were naked. Now, go back to the sermon and do a better job this time."

An awkward silence descended on the entire street. Leaves skittered along the sidewalk, and for a moment they were the only things that moved.

"Come on, you lot! Off you go, back to the sermon." Shams of Tabriz waved his staff, shooing the men away like flies.

They did not all turn and walk away, but they *did* take a few steps back, swaying unsteadily, puzzled as to what to do next. A few of them were looking in the direction of the mosque as if considering returning. It was exactly then that the harlot mustered the courage to get out from behind the dervish. Fast as a rabbit, she took to her heels, her long hair flying every which way while she scurried into the closest side street.

Only two men attempted to chase her. But Shams of Tabriz blocked their path, swinging his staff under their feet with such suddenness and force that they tumbled over and fell down. A few passersby laughed at the sight, and so did I.

Embarrassed and stupefied, the two men managed to get to their feet again, but by that time the harlot had long vanished and the dervish was walking away, his work here done.

Suleiman the Drunk

KONYA, OCTOBER 17, 1244

Before the commotion I was snoozing peacefully with my back to the tavern wall, and then the racket outside made me nearly jump out of my skin.

"What's going on?" I screamed as my eyes snapped open. "Did the Mongols attack us?"

There was a ripple of laughter. I turned around and found several other customers making fun of me. Dirty bastards!

"Don't you worry, old drunk!" yelled Hristos, the tavern owner. "No Mongols coming after you. It's Rumi passing by with an army of admirers."

I went to the window and looked out. Sure enough, there they were—an excited procession of disciples and admirers repeatedly chanting, "God is great! God is great!" In the middle of it all was the erect figure of Rumi, mounted on a white horse, radiating strength and confidence. I opened the window, ducked my head out, and watched them. Moving at a pace no faster than a snail's, the procession came very near. In fact, some of the crowd were so close that I could easily have touched a few heads. Suddenly I had a brilliant idea. I was going to snatch off some people's turbans!

I grabbed the wooden back scratcher that belongs to Hristos. Holding the window open with one hand and the scratcher in the other, I leaned forward, managing to reach the turban of a man in the crowd. I was just about to pull the turban off when another man inadvertently looked up and saw me.

"Selamun aleykum," I saluted, smiling from ear to ear.

"A Muslim in a tavern! Shame on you!" the man roared. "Don't you know wine is the handiwork of Sheitan?"

I opened my mouth to answer, but before I could make a sound, something sharp whizzed by my head. I realized in sheer horror that it was a stone. If I hadn't ducked at the last second, it would have cracked my skull. Instead it had shot through the open window, landing on the table of the Persian merchant sitting behind me. Too tipsy to comprehend what had happened, the merchant held the stone in his hand, examining it as if it were an obscure message from the skies.

"Suleiman, close that window and go back to your table!" Hristos bellowed, his voice hoarse with worry.

"Did you see what happened?" I said as I staggered back toward my table. "Someone hurled a stone at me. They could have killed me!"

Hristos raised an eyebrow. "I'm sorry, but what were you expecting? Don't you know there are people who don't want to see a Muslim in a tavern? And here you are displaying yourself, reeking of alcohol, your nose glowing like a red lantern."

"S-so what?" I stuttered. "Am I not a human being?"

Hristos patted me on the shoulder as if to say, *There, there.*

"You know, this is exactly why I abhor religion. All sorts of them! Religious people are so confident of having God by their side that they think they are superior to everyone else," I said.

Hristos did not respond. He was a religious man, but also a skilled tavern owner who knew how to soothe an incensed customer. He brought me another carafe of red wine and watched me as I guzzled it. Outside, a wild wind blew, slamming shut the windows and scattering dry leaves left and right. For a moment we stood still, listening carefully, as if there were a melody to be heard.

"I don't understand why wine was forbidden in this world but promised in heaven," I said. "If it's as bad as they claim, why would they serve it in paradise?"

"Questions, questions . . ." Hristos murmured as he threw his hands up. "You are always full of questions. Do you have to question everything?"

"Of course I do. That's why we were given a brain, don't you think?"

"Suleiman, I have known you for a long time. You are not just any customer to me. You are my friend. And I worry about you."

"I'll be fine—" I said, but Hristos interrupted me.

"You are a good man, but your tongue is as sharp as a dagger. That's what worries me. There are all sorts of people in Konya. And it's no secret that some of them don't think highly of a Muslim who has taken to drink. You need to learn to be careful in public. Hide your ways, and watch what you say."

I grinned. "May we top off this speech with a poem from Khayyám?"

Hristos heaved a sigh, but the Persian merchant who had overheard me exclaimed cheerfully, "Yes, we want a poem from Khayyám."

Other customers joined in, giving me a big round of applause. Motivated and slightly provoked, I jumped onto a table and began to recite:

"Did God set grapes a-growing, do you think,
And at the same time make it a sin to drink?"

The Persian merchant yelled, "Of course not! That wouldn't make any sense!"

"Give thanks to Him who foreordained it thus—
Surely He loves to hear the glasses clink!"

If there was one thing these many years of drinking had taught me, it was that different people drank differently. I knew people who drank gallons every night, and all they did was get merry, sing songs, and then doze off. But then there were others who turned into monsters with a few drops. If the same drink made some merry and tipsy and others wicked and aggressive, shouldn't we hold the drinkers responsible instead of the drink?

"Drink! for you know not whence you came, nor why;
Drink! for you know not why you go, nor where."

Another round of applause followed. Even Hristos joined the excitement. In the Jewish quarter of Konya, in a tavern owned by a Christian, we, a mixed bunch of wine lovers of all faiths, raised our glasses and toasted together, hard though it was to believe, to a God who could love and forgive us even when we ourselves clearly failed to do so.

Ella

NORTHAMPTON, MAY 31, 2008

"Better safe than sorry," said the Web site. "Check his shirts for lipstick stains, see if he comes home smelling of unfamiliar perfumes."

This was the first time Ella Rubinstein had taken an online test, titled "How to Tell If Your Husband Is Cheating on You!" Although she found the questions tacky, by now she knew that life itself could occasionally feel like one big cliché.

In spite of her final test score, Ella didn't want to confront David on this matter. She still had not asked him where he'd been on the nights he hadn't come home. These days she spent most of her time reading *Sweet Blasphemy,* using the novel as an excuse to cover up her silence. Her mind was so distracted that it was taking her longer than usual to finish the book. Still, she was enjoying the story, and with every new rule of Shams's she mulled her life over.

When the children were around, she acted normal. *They* acted normal. However, the moment she and David were alone, she caught her husband looking at her curiously, as if wondering what kind of wife would avoid asking her husband where he'd spent the night. But the truth was that Ella didn't want a piece of information she wouldn't know how to handle. The less she knew about her husband's flings, the less they would occupy her mind, she thought. It was true what they say about ignorance. It was bliss.

The only time that bliss had been disrupted was last Christmas, when a survey from a local hotel arrived in their mailbox, addressed directly to David. Customer service wanted to know whether he was happy with his stays. Ella left the letter on the table, on top of a pile of mail, and that evening she watched him take the letter out of the opened envelope and read it.

"Ah, a guest evaluation form! The last thing I needed," David said, managing a half smile for her. "We held a dental conference there last year. They must have included all the participants on their customer list."

She believed him. At least the part of her that didn't like to rock the boat did. The other part of her was cynical and distrustful. It was that same part that the next day found the hotel's number and dialed it, just to hear what she already knew: Neither this year nor the one before had they ever hosted a dental conference.

Deep inside, Ella blamed herself. She hadn't aged well, and she'd gained considerable weight over the last six years. With every new pound, her sexual drive had declined a bit further. The cooking classes rendered it more difficult to shed the extra pounds, though there were women in her group who cooked more often, and better, and still remained half her size.

When she looked back at her life, she realized that rebellion had never suited her. She had never smoked weed with boys behind closed doors, gotten kicked out of bars, used morning-after pills, thrown fits, or lied to her mother. Never cut class. Never had teen sex. All around her, girls her age were having abortions or putting their out-of-wedlock babies up for adoption, while she observed their stories as though watching a TV program on famine in Ethiopia. It saddened Ella that such tragedies were unfolding in the world, but the truth was that she never saw herself as sharing the same universe with those unfortunate ones.

She had never been a party girl, not even as a teenager. She preferred to sit at home and read a good book on a Friday night rather than whoop it up with strangers at some wild party.

"Why can't you be like Ella?" the mothers in the neighborhood asked their daughters. "See, she never gets herself in trouble."

While their mothers adored her, the kids themselves saw her as a nerd with no sense of humor. No wonder she wasn't very popular in high school. Once a classmate told her, "You know what your problem is? You take life so seriously. You're fucking boring!"

She listened carefully and said she would think about that.

Even her hairstyle hadn't changed much over the years—long, straight, honey-blond hair that she pulled into an unrelenting bun or braided down her back. She wore little makeup, just a touch of reddish brown lipstick and a moss green eyeliner, which according to her daughter did more to hide than to bring out the gray-blue of her eyes. In any event, she never managed to draw two perfectly curved lines with the eyeliner and often went out with the line on one eyelid looking thicker than that on the other.

Ella suspected that there must be something wrong with her. She was either too intrusive and pushy (with regard to Jeannette's marriage plans) or too passive and docile (with regard to her husband's flings). There was an Ella-the-control-freak and an Ella-the-hopelessly-meek. She could never tell which one was about to emerge, or when.

And then there was a third Ella, observing everything quietly, waiting for her time to come. It was this Ella who told her she was calm to the point of numbness but that underneath there was a strangled self, harboring a fast freshet of anger and rebellion. If she kept going like this, the third Ella warned, she was bound to explode someday. It was just a matter of time.

Contemplating these issues on the last day of May, Ella did something she hadn't done in a long while. She prayed. She asked God to either provide her with a love that would absorb her whole being or else make her tough and careless enough not to mind the absence of love in her life.

"Whichever one You choose, please be quick," she added as an afterthought. "You might have forgotten, but I'm already forty. And as You can see, I don't carry my years well."

Desert Rose the Harlot

KONYA, OCTOBER 17, 1244

Breathless, I ran and ran along the narrow alley, unable to look back. My lungs burning, my chest pounding, when I finally reached the busy bazaar, I dodged behind a wall, almost collapsing. Only then could I muster the courage to look behind me. To my great surprise and relief, there was only one person following me: Sesame. He stopped beside me, out of breath, his hands dangling limply at his sides, his expression bewildered and vexed, unable to comprehend why all of a sudden I had started running like crazy through the streets of Konya.

Everything had happened so fast that it was only in the bazaar that I could put the pieces together. One minute I was sitting in the mosque, absorbed in the sermon, drinking in Rumi's pearls of wisdom. In my trance I failed to notice that the lad next to me had accidentally stepped on the ends of the scarf covering my face. Before I knew it, the scarf came loose and my turban slid aside, exposing my face and a bit of my hair. I fixed the scarf swiftly and continued listening to Rumi, confident that nobody had noticed anything. But when I raised my eyes again, I saw a young man in the front row looking at me intently. Square face, lazy eye, sharp nose, sneering mouth. I recognized him. He was Baybars.

Baybars was one of those pesky customers none of the girls in the brothel wanted to sleep with. Some men have a way of wanting to sleep with prostitutes and yet at the same time insulting them. He was such a man. Always cracking lewd jokes, he had a terrible temper. Once he beat a girl so badly that even the boss, who loved money more than anything, had to ask him to leave and never come back. But he kept returning. At least for a few more months. Then, for some reason unbeknownst to me, he stopped visiting the brothel, and we didn't hear from him again. Now there he was, sitting in the front row, having grown a full beard like a devout man but still with the same fierce sparkle in his eyes.

I averted my gaze. But it was too late. He had recognized me.

Baybars whispered something to the man next to him, and then the two of them turned around and stared at me. Next they pointed me out to someone else, and one after another all the men in that row stared in my direction. I felt my face blush and my heart race, but I couldn't budge. Instead I clung to the childish hope that if I stayed still and closed my eyes, the darkness would engulf us all, leaving nothing to worry about.

When I dared to open my eyes again, Baybars was pushing his way through the crowd toward me. I made a dash for the door, but it was impossible to escape, surrounded as I was by a thick sea of people. In a flash Baybars had reached me, so menacingly close I could smell his breath. Grabbing me by the arm, he said between clenched teeth, "What is a harlot doing here? Don't you have any shame?"

"Please . . . please, let me go," I stammered, but I don't think he even heard me.

His friends joined him. Tough, scary, confident, disdainful fellows, reeking of anger and vinegar, raining insults on me. Everyone around turned to see what the commotion was about, and a few people tsk-tsked disapprovingly, but nobody intervened. My body as listless as a lump of dough, I meekly let them push me toward the exit. Once we reached the street, I hoped, Sesame would come to my aid, and if worst came to worst, I would run away. But no sooner had we stepped into the street than the men grew more belligerent and aggressive. I realized in horror that in the mosque, out of respect for the preacher and the community, they had been careful not to raise their voices or shove me around, but outside on the street there was nothing to stop them.

I had been through harder things in my life, and yet I doubt if I had ever felt so dejected before. After years of hesitation, today I had taken a step toward God, and how had He responded? By kicking me out of His house!

"I should never have gone there," I said to Sesame, my voice cracking like thin ice. "They're right, you know. A harlot has no place in a mosque or a church or in any of His houses."

"Don't say that!"

When I turned around to see who had said this, I couldn't believe my eyes. It was him, the wandering hairless dervish. Sesame broke into a wide smile, delighted to see him again. I lurched forward to kiss his hands, but he stopped me midway. "Please don't."

"But how can I thank you? I owe you so much," I beseeched.

He shrugged and looked uninterested. "You owe me nothing," he said. "We are indebted to no other than Him."

He introduced himself as Shams of Tabriz and then said the strangest thing ever: "Some people start life with a perfectly glowing aura but then lose color and fade. You seem to be one of them. Once your aura was whiter than lilies with specks of yellow and pink, but it faded over time. Now it is a pale brown. Don't you miss your original colors? Wouldn't you like to unite with your essence?"

I looked at him, feeling utterly lost in his words.

"Your aura has lost its shine because all these years you have convinced yourself that you are dirty inside and out."

"I *am* dirty," I said, biting my lip. "Don't you know what I do for a living?"

"Allow me to tell you a story," Shams said. And this is what he told me:

One day a prostitute passed by a street dog. The animal was panting under the hot sun, thirsty and helpless. The prostitute immediately took off her shoe and filled it with water from the nearest well for the dog. Then she went on her way. The next day she ran into a Sufi who was a man of great wisdom. As soon as he saw her, he kissed her hands. She was shocked. But he told her that her kindness toward the dog had been so genuine that all her sins had been pardoned there and then.

I understood what Shams of Tabriz was trying to tell me, but something inside me refused to believe him. So I said, "Let me assure you, even if I fed all the dogs in Konya, it wouldn't be enough for my redemption."

"You cannot know that; only God can. Besides, what makes you think any of those men who pushed you out of the mosque today are closer to God?"

"Even if they are not closer to God," I replied, unconvinced, "who will tell them that? Will you?"

But the dervish shook his head. "No, that's not the way the system works. It is *you* who needs to tell it to them."

"Do you think they would listen to me? Those men hate me."

"They will listen," he said determinedly. "Because there is no such thing as 'them,' just as there is no 'I.' All you need to do is keep in mind how everything and everyone in this universe is interconnected. We are not hundreds and thousands of different beings. We are all One."

I waited for him to explain, but instead he continued: "It's one of the forty rules. *If you want to change the way others treat you, you should first change the way you treat yourself. Unless you learn to love yourself, fully and sincerely, there is no way you can be loved. Once you achieve that stage, however, be thankful for every thorn that others might throw at you. It is a sign that you will soon be showered in roses.*" He paused briefly and then added, "How can you blame others for disrespecting you when you think of yourself as unworthy of respect?"

I stood there unable to say a word as I felt my grip on what was real slip away. I thought about all the men I had slept with—the way they smelled, the way their callused hands felt, the way they cried when they came. . . . I had seen nice boys turn into monsters and monsters turn into nice boys. Once I had a customer who had the habit of spitting on prostitutes while he had sex with them. "Dirty," he would say as he spit into my mouth and all over my face. "You dirty whore."

And here was this dervish telling me I was cleaner than fresh spring-water. It felt like a tasteless joke, but when I forced myself to laugh, the sound didn't pass through my throat, and I ended up suppressing a sob.

"The past is a whirlpool. If you let it dominate your present moment, it will suck you in," said Shams as if he had read my thoughts. "Time is just an illusion. What you need is to live this very moment. That is all that matters."

Upon saying that, he took out a silk handkerchief from the inside pocket of his robe. "Keep it," he said. "A good man in Baghdad gave it to me, but you need it more than I do. It will remind you that your heart is pure and that you bear God within you."

With that, the dervish grabbed his staff and stood up, ready to go. "Just walk out of that brothel."

"Where? How? I have no place to go."

"That's not a problem," Shams said, his eyes gleaming. *"Fret not where the road will take you. Instead concentrate on the first step. That's the hardest part and that's what you are responsible for. Once you take that step let everything do what it naturally does and the rest will follow. Do not go with the flow. Be the flow."*

I nodded. I didn't need to ask in order to understand that this, too, was one of the rules.

Suleiman the Drunk

KONYA, OCTOBER 17, 1244

Before midnight I downed my last drink and left the tavern.

"Remember what I said. Watch your tongue," Hristos cautioned as he waved good-bye.

I nodded, feeling fortunate to have a friend who cared about me. But as soon as I stepped into the dark, empty street, I was seized by a kind of exhaustion such as I had never felt before. I wished I had taken a bottle of wine with me. I could have used a drink.

As I tottered with my boots clacking on the broken cobblestones, the sight of the men in Rumi's procession crossed my mind. It pained me to recall the flicker of loathing in their eyes. If there was one thing I hated most in the world, it was prudishness. I had been reprimanded by prim and proper people so many times that even the memory of them was enough to send a shiver down my spine.

Struggling with these thoughts, I turned a corner and entered a side street. It was darker here because of the massive trees towering above. As if that weren't enough, the moon suddenly hid behind a cloud, shrouding me in thick, dense darkness. Otherwise I would have noticed the two security guards approaching me.

"Selamun aleykum," I chimed, my voice coming out too merrily in the attempt to hide my anxiety.

But the guards didn't return my greeting. Instead they asked me what I was doing out on the streets at this late hour.

"Just walking," I mumbled.

We stood face-to-face, anchored in an awkward silence pierced only by the howling of dogs far away. One of the men took a step toward me and sniffed the air. "It stinks around here," he blurted out.

"Yeah, it reeks of wine," the other guard confirmed.

I decided to treat the situation lightly. "Don't worry yourselves. The stench is only metaphorical. Since it is only metaphorical wine that we Muslims are allowed to drink, the smell must also be metaphorical."

"What the hell is he raving about?" the first guard grumbled.

Just then the moon came out from behind the cloud, covering us with its soft, pallid light. I could now see the man facing me. He had a square face with a protruding chin, ice blue eyes, and a sharp nose. He could have been handsome were it not for his lazy eye and the permanent scowl on his face.

"What are you doing on the streets at this hour?" the man repeated. "Where are you coming from, and where are you going?"

I couldn't help it. "These are profound questions, son. If I knew the answers, I would have solved the mystery of our purpose in this world."

"Are you making fun of me, you filth?" the guard demanded, frowning, and before I knew what was happening, he took out a whip, cracking it in the air.

His gestures were so dramatically exaggerated that I chuckled. The next thing he did was to bring the whip down on my chest. The strike was so sudden that I lost my balance and fell.

"Perhaps this will teach you some manners," the guard retorted as he passed his whip from one hand to the other. "Don't you know drinking is a major sin?"

Even when I felt the warmth of my own blood, even as my head swirled in a sea of pain, I still couldn't believe I had been lashed in the middle of the street by a man young enough to be my son.

"Then go ahead and punish me," I retorted. "If God's paradise is reserved for people of your kind, I'd rather burn in hell anyhow."

In a fit of rage, the young guard started to whip me with all his might. I covered my face with my hands, but it didn't help much. A merry old song popped into my mind, forcing its way past my bloodied lips. Determined not to show my misery, I sang louder and louder with every crack of the whip:

"Kiss me, my beloved, peel my heart down to the core,

Your lips are as sweet as cherry wine, pour me some more."

My sarcasm drove the guard into a deeper rage. The louder I sang, the harder he hit. I would never have guessed there could be so much anger piled up inside one man.

"That's enough, Baybars!" I heard the other guard yell in panic. "Stop it, man!"

As suddenly as it had started, the lashing stopped. I wanted to have the last word, say something powerful and blunt, but the blood in my mouth muffled my voice. My stomach churned, and before I knew it, I vomited.

"You are a wreck," Baybars reprimanded. "You have only yourself to blame for what I did to you."

They turned their backs on me and strode off into the night.

I don't know how long I lay there. It could have been no more than a few minutes or the whole night. Time lost its weight, and so did everything else. The moon hid behind the clouds, leaving me not only without its light but also without a sense of who I was. Soon I was floating in limbo between life and death and not caring where I would end up. Then the numbness started to wear off, and every bruise, every welt, every cut on my body ached madly, washing me with wave after wave of pain. My head was wobbly, my limbs sore. In that state I moaned like a wounded animal.

I must have blacked out. When I opened my eyes, my *salwar* was drenched in urine and every limb of my body hurt dreadfully. I was praying to God either to numb me or to provide me with drink when I heard footsteps approaching. My heart skipped a beat. It could be a street urchin or a robber, even a murderer. But then I thought, what did I have to fear? I had reached a point where nothing the night could bring was scary anymore.

Out of the shadows walked a tall, slender dervish with no hair. He knelt down beside me and helped me sit up. He introduced himself as Shams of Tabriz and asked my name.

"Suleiman the drunk of Konya at your service," I said as I plucked a loose tooth from my mouth. "Nice to meet you."

"You are bleeding," Shams murmured as he started to wipe the blood off my face. "Not only on the outside, but inside as well."

Upon saying that, he took out a silver flask from the pocket of his robe. "Apply this ointment to your wounds," he said. "A good man in Baghdad gave it to me, but you need it more than I do. However, you should know that the wound inside you is deeper, and that is the one you should worry about. This will remind you that you bear God within you."

"Thank you," I heard myself stutter, touched by his kindness. "That security guard . . . he whipped me. He said I deserved it."

As soon as I uttered those words, I was struck by the childish whining in my voice and my need for comfort and compassion.

Shams of Tabriz shook his head. "They had no right to do that. Every individual is self-sufficient in his search for the divine. There is a rule regarding this: *We were all created in His image, and yet we were each created different and unique. No two people are alike. No two hearts beat to the same rhythm. If God had wanted everyone to be the same, He would have made it so. Therefore, disrespecting differences and imposing your thoughts on others is tantamount to disrespecting God's holy scheme.*"

"That sounds good," I said, amazing myself by the ease in my voice. "But don't you Sufis ever doubt anything about Him?"

Shams of Tabriz smiled a tired smile. "We do, and doubts are good. It means you are alive and searching."

He spoke in a lilting tone, exactly as if he were reciting from a book.

"Besides, one does not become a believer overnight. He thinks he is a believer; then something happens in his life and he becomes an unbeliever; after that, he becomes a believer again, and then an unbeliever again, and so on. Until we reach a certain stage, we constantly waver. This is the only way forward. At each new step, we come closer to the Truth."

"If Hristos heard you talk like this, he would tell you to watch your tongue," I said. "He says not every word is fit for every ear."

"Well, he's got a point." Shams of Tabriz let out a brief laugh as he jumped to his feet. "Come on, let me take you home. We need to tend to your wounds and make sure you get some sleep."

He helped me get on my feet, but I could hardly walk. Without hesitation the dervish lifted me as though I weighed nothing and took me on his back.

"I warn you, I stink," I mumbled in shame.

"That's all right, Suleiman, don't worry."

In this way, never minding the blood, urine, or stench, the dervish carried me along the narrow streets of Konya. We passed by houses and shacks plunged in deep slumber. Dogs barked at us, loudly and ferociously, from behind the garden walls, informing everyone of our presence.

"I have always been curious about the mention of wine in Sufi poetry," I said. "Is it real or metaphorical wine that the Sufis praise?"

"What difference does it make, my friend?" Shams of Tabriz asked before he dropped me off in front of my house. "There is a rule that explains this: *When a true lover of God goes into a tavern, the tavern becomes his chamber of prayer, but when a wine bibber goes into the same chamber, it becomes his tavern. In everything we do, it is our hearts that make the difference, not our outer appearances. Sufis do not judge other people on how they look or who they are. When a Sufi stares at someone, he keeps both eyes closed and instead opens a third eye—the eye that sees the inner realm.*"

Alone in my house after this long and exhausting night, I pondered what had transpired. As miserable as I felt, somewhere deep inside me there was a blissful tranquillity. For a fleeting moment, I caught a glimpse of it and yearned to remain there forever. At that moment I knew there was a God after all, and He loved me.

Though I was sore, sore all over, strangely enough I was not hurting anymore.

Ella

NORTHAMPTON, JUNE 3, 2008

Beach Boys tunes streaming through their open windows, university students drove past, their faces sporting early-summer tans. Ella watched, numb to their happiness, as her mind reverted to the events of the past few days. First she had found Spirit dead in the kitchen, and although she'd told herself many times to be ready for this moment, she was seized by not only a profound grief but also a sense of vulnerability and loneliness, as if losing her dog had the effect of throwing her out into the world all by herself. Then she found out that Orly was suffering from bulimia and that almost everyone in her class knew about it. This brought a wave of guilt to Ella, leading her to have doubts about her relationship with her younger daughter and to question her record as a mother. Guilt was not a new element in Ella's repertoire of feelings, but this loss of confidence in her mothering was.

During this time Ella started exchanging multiple e-mails with Aziz Z. Zahara every day. Two, three, sometimes up to five. She wrote to him about everything, and, to her surprise, he was always prompt to respond. How he could find the time or even an Internet connection to check his e-mails while traveling in remote places was beyond Ella. But it didn't take her long to become addicted to his words. Soon she was checking her e-mail at every opportunity—first thing in the morning and then again after breakfast, when she came back from her morning walk and while she was making lunch, before she went out to run errands and even during them, by stopping at Internet cafés. While she was watching her favorite TV shows, chopping tomatoes at the Fusion Cooking Club, talking on the phone with her friends, or listening to her twins rant about school and homework, she kept her laptop on and her mailbox open. When there were no new messages from Aziz, she reread the old ones. And every time she received a new message from him, she couldn't help breaking into a smile, half gleeful, half embarrassed by what was taking place. For something *was* taking place.

Soon exchanging e-mails with Aziz made Ella feel that she was somehow breaking away from her staid and tranquil life. From a woman with lots of dull grays and browns on her life's canvas, she was turning into a woman with a secret color—a bright, tantalizing red. And she loved it.

Aziz was no man for small pleasantries. To him, people who had not made their heart their primary guide to life, who could not open up to love and follow its path the way a sunflower follows the sun, were not really alive. (Ella wondered if this might put her on his list of inanimate objects.) Aziz didn't write about the weather or the latest movie he had seen. He wrote about other things, deeper things, like life and death, and above all love. Ella was not used to expressing her feelings on such issues, especially to a stranger, but perhaps it took a stranger to make a woman like her speak her mind.

If there was a trace of flirtation in their exchange, Ella thought, it was an innocent one that might do them both good. They could flirt with each other, positioning themselves in distant corners within the infinite maze of cyberspace. Thanks to this exchange, she hoped to regain a portion of the sense of worth she had lost during her marriage. Aziz was that rare type of man a woman could love without losing her self-respect. And perhaps he, too, could find something pleasing in being the center of attention of a middle-aged American woman. Cyberspace both magnified and mellowed offline behaviors, providing an opportunity to flirt without guilt (which she didn't want because she already had too much) and an adventure without risks (which she did want because she never had any). It was like nibbling on forbidden delicacies without having to worry about the extra calories—there were no consequences.

So maybe it was blasphemy for a married woman with children to write intimate e-mails to a stranger, but given the platonic nature of their relationship, Ella deduced, it was sweet blasphemy.

Ella

NORTHAMPTON, JUNE 5, 2008

Beloved Aziz,

In one of your earlier e-mails, you said the idea that we could control the course of our lives through rational choices was as absurd as a fish trying to control the ocean in which it swam. I thought about your next sentence a lot: "The idea of a Knowing Self has generated not only false expectations but also disappointments in places where life does not match our expectations."

And now it's time for me to confess: I'm a bit of a control freak myself. At least that's what people who know me best will tell you. Until recently I was a very strict mom. I had a lot of rules (and believe me, they're not as nice as your Sufi rules!), and there was no bargaining with me. Once my eldest daughter accused me of adopting the strategy of a guerrilla. She said I dug into their lives and from my trench I tried to capture every errant thought or desire that they might have!

Remember the song "Que Será, Será"? Well, I guess it has never been my song. "What will be, will be" has never sat right with me; I just can't go with the flow. I know you're a religious person, but I'm not. Though as a family we celebrate the Sabbath every so often, personally I don't even remember the last time I prayed. (Oops, I do now. In my kitchen just two days ago, but that doesn't count, because it was more like complaining to a higher Self.)

There was a time back in college when I got hooked on Eastern spirituality and did some reading on Buddhism and Taoism. I had even made plans with an eccentric girlfriend to spend a month at an ashram in India, but that phase of my life didn't last long. As inviting as the mystic teachings were, I thought they were too compliant and inapplicable to modern life. Since then I haven't changed my mind.

I hope my aversion to religion won't offend you. Please see it as a confession long overdue from someone who cares about you.

Warmly,
Ella

Dear guerrilla Ella,

Your e-mail found me as I was getting ready to leave Amsterdam for Malawi. I have been assigned to take pictures of the people in a village where AIDS is rampant and most children are orphans.

Now, if everything goes well, I'll be back in four days. Can I hope so? Yes. Can I control it? No! All I can do is take my laptop with me, try to find a good Internet connection, and hope that I will live another day. The rest is not in my hands. And this is what the Sufis call the fifth element—the void. The inexplicable and uncontrollable divine element that we as human beings cannot comprehend and yet should always be aware of. I don't believe in "inaction" if by that you mean doing nothing at all and showing no deep interest in life. But I do believe in respecting the fifth element.

I believe we each make a covenant with God. I know that I did. When I became a Sufi, I promised God to do my part to the best of my ability and leave the rest to Him and Him only. I accepted the fact that there are things beyond my limits. I can see only some parts, like floating fragments from a movie, but the bigger scheme is beyond my comprehension.

Now, you think I am a religious man. But I am not.

I am spiritual, which is different. Religiosity and spirituality are not the same thing, and I believe that the gap between the two has never been greater than it is today. When I look at the world, I see a deepening quandary. On the one hand, we believe in the freedom and power of the individual regardless of God, government, or society. In many ways human beings are becoming more self-centered and the world is becoming more materialistic. On the other hand, humanity as a whole is becoming more spiritual. After relying on reason for so long, we seem to have reached a point where we acknowledge the limits of the mind.

Today, just as in medieval times, there is an explosion of interest in spirituality. More and more people in the West are trying to carve out a space for spirituality in the midst of their busy lives. But though they intend well, their methods are often inadequate. Spirituality is not yet another dressing for the same old dish. It is not something we can add to our life without making major changes there.

I know you like to cook. Did you know that Shams says the world is a huge cauldron and something big is cooking in it? We don't know what yet. Everything we do, feel, or think is an ingredient in that mixture. We need to ask ourselves what we are adding to the cauldron. Are we adding resentments, animosities, anger, and violence? Or are we adding love and harmony?

How about you, dear Ella? What ingredients do you think you are putting in the collective stew of humanity? Whenever I think about you, the ingredient I add is a big smile.

With love,
Aziz

PART THREE

Wind

THE THINGS THAT SHIFT, EVOLVE, AND CHALLENGE

The Zealot

KONYA, OCTOBER 19, 1244

Below my open window, dogs were barking and growling. I propped myself up in bed, suspecting they must have noticed a robber trying to break in to a house, or some dirty drunk passing by. Decent people cannot sleep in peace anymore. There is debauchery and lechery everywhere. It wasn't always like this. This town was a safer place until a few years ago. Moral corruption is no different from a ghastly disease that comes without warning and spreads fast, infecting the rich and the poor, the old and the young alike. Such is the state of our town today. If it weren't for my position at the madrassa, I would hardly leave my house.

Thank God there are people who put the interests of the community before their own and work day and night to enforce order. People like my young nephew, Baybars. My wife and I are proud of him. It is comforting to know that at this late hour, when villains, criminals, and drunks go on a rampage, Baybars and his fellow security guards patrol the town to protect us.

Upon my brother's early death, I became the primary guardian for Baybars. Young, adamant, he started working as a security guard six months ago. Gossipmongers claimed that it was thanks to my position as a madrassa teacher that he was able to get the job. Nonsense! Baybars is strong and brave enough to qualify for the job. He would also have made an excellent soldier. He wanted to go to Jerusalem to fight against the Crusaders, but my wife and I thought it was time for him to settle down and start a family.

"We need you here, son," I said. "There is so much to fight against here, too."

Indeed there was. Just this morning I told my wife we were living in difficult times. It is no coincidence that every day we hear of a new tragedy. If the Mongols have been this victorious, if the Christians could succeed in furthering their cause, if town after town, village after village is sacked by the enemies of Islam, it is because of the people who are Muslims in name only. When people lose hold of the rope of God, they are bound to go astray. The Mongols were sent as a punishment for our sins. If not the Mongols, it would have been an earthquake, a famine, or a flood. How many more calamities do we have to experience for the sinners in this town to get the message and repent their ways? Next I fear stones will rain down from above. One day soon we might all be wiped out, walking in the footsteps of the residents of Sodom and Gomorrah.

And these Sufis, they are such a bad influence. How dare they call themselves Muslims when they say things no Muslim should even think of? It boils my blood to hear them utter the name of the Prophet, peace be upon him, to promote their silly views. They claim that following a war campaign, the Prophet Muhammad had announced that his people were henceforth abandoning the small jihad for the greater jihad—the struggle against one's own self. Sufis argue that ever since then the nafs is the only adversary a Muslim should be warring against. Sounds nice, but how is that going to help to fight the enemies of Islam? I wonder.

The Sufis go as far as claiming that the sharia is merely a stage on the way. What stage, I say, what are they speaking of? As if that weren't alarming enough, they argue that an enlightened person cannot be bound by the rules of early stages. And since they like to think of themselves as having already reached a supreme level, they use this as a poor excuse to disregard the rules of the sharia. Drinking, dancing, music, poetry, and painting seem more vital to them than religious duties. They keep preaching that since there is no hierarchy in Islam, everyone is entitled to his own personal quest for God. It all sounds inoffensive and harmless, but after one wades through the boring verbosity, one discovers that there is a sinister side to their message: that there is no need to pay attention to religious authorities!

As far as the Sufis are concerned, the holy Qur'an is replete with obscure symbols and layered allusions, each of which ought to be interpreted in a mystic way. So they examine how every word vibrates to a number, study the hidden meaning of numbers, and look out for veiled references in the text, doing everything in their power to avoid reading God's message, plain and clear.

Some Sufis even say that human beings are the Speaking Qur'an. If this isn't sheer blasphemy, I don't know what is. Then there are the wandering dervishes, another troubled category of misfits. Qalandaris, Haydaris, Camiis—they're known under all sorts of names. I'd say they are the worst. What good could come out of a man who cannot settle down? If a man has no sense of belonging, he can drift in every direction, like a dry leaf in the wind. The perfect victim for Sheitan.

Philosophers are no better than the Sufis. They ruminate and cogitate as if their limited minds could grasp the incomprehensibility of the universe! There is a story that is indicative of the conspiracy between the philosophers and the Sufis.

A philosopher met a dervish one day, and they instantly hit it off. The two talked for days on end, completing each other's sentences.

Finally, when they parted company, the philosopher reported of the conversation, "All that I know, he sees."

Next the Sufi gave his account: "All that I see, he knows."

So the Sufi thinks he *sees,* and the philosopher thinks he *knows.* In my opinion they see nothing and know nothing. Don't they realize that as simple, limited, and ultimately mortal human beings, we are not expected to know more than we should? The most a human being is capable of attaining is a mere smattering of information about the Almighty. That's all. Our task is not to interpret God's teachings but to obey them.

When Baybars comes home, we will talk about these matters. It has become a habit, our small ritual. Every night after his shift, he eats the soup and flatbread that my wife serves him, and we engage in conversation about the state of things. It pleases me to see what a good appetite he has. He needs to be strong. A young, principled guy like him has much work to do in this ungodly town.

Shams

KONYA, OCTOBER 30, 1244

Before I met Rumi, just one night prior, I sat on my balcony at the Inn of Sugar Vendors. My heart rejoiced at the magnificence of the universe God had created in His image, so that everywhere we turned, we could both seek and find Him. And yet human beings rarely did that.

I recalled the individuals I had met—the beggar, the prostitute, and the drunk. Ordinary people who suffered from a common malady: separation from the One. These were the kind of people that the scholars failed to see while sitting in their ivory towers. I wondered if Rumi was any different. If not, I made a note to myself that I should be a conduit between him and the underbelly of society.

The town had finally gone to sleep. It was that time of night when even the nocturnal animals are reluctant to disturb the reigning peace. It always made me both immensely sad and elated to listen to a town sleep, wondering what sorts of stories were being lived behind closed doors, what sorts of stories I could have lived had I chosen another path. But I hadn't made any choice. If anything, the path had chosen me.

I remembered a tale. *A wandering dervish arrived in a town where the natives didn't trust strangers. "Go away!" they shouted at him. "No one knows you here!"*

The dervish calmly responded, "Yes, but I know myself, and believe me, it would have been much worse if it were the other way round."

As long as I knew myself, I would be all right. Whosoever knows himself, knows the One.

The moon showered me with its warm glow. A light rain, as delicate as a silk scarf, began to fall on the town. I thanked God for this blessed moment and left myself in His hands. The fragility and brevity of life struck me once again, and I recalled another rule: *Life is a temporary loan, and this world is nothing but a sketchy imitation of Reality. Only children would mistake a toy for the real thing. And yet human beings either become infatuated with the toy or disrespectfully break it and throw it aside. In this life stay away from all kinds of extremities, for they will destroy your inner balance.*

Sufis do not go to extremes. A Sufi always remains mild and moderate.

Tomorrow morning I will go to the big mosque and listen to Rumi. He can be as great a preacher as everyone says, but in the end the breadth and scope of every speaker are determined by those of his audience. Rumi's words might be like a wild garden, full of teasels, herbs, spruces, and shrubs, but it is always up to the visitor to pick his fancy. While pretty flowers are instantly plucked, few people pay attention to plants with thorns and prickles. But the truth is, great medicines are often made from these.

Isn't it the same with the garden of love? How can love be worthy of its name if one selects solely the pretty things and leaves out the hardships? It is easy to enjoy the good and dislike the bad. Anybody can do that. The real challenge is to love the good and the bad together, not because you need to take the rough with the smooth but because you need to go beyond such descriptions and accept love in its entirety.

There is only one more day before I meet my companion. I cannot sleep.

Oh, Rumi! The king of the realm of words and meanings!

Will you know me when you see me?

See me!

Rumi

KONYA, OCTOBER 31, 1244

Blessed is this day, for I have met Shams of Tabriz. On this last day of October, the air has a new chill and the winds blow stronger, announcing the departure of autumn.

This afternoon the mosque was packed, as usual. While preaching to large crowds, I always take care to neither forget nor remember my audience. And there is only one way of doing this: to imagine the crowd as one single person. Hundreds of people listen to me every week, but I always talk to one person alone—the one who hears my words echo in his heart and who knows me like no other.

When I walked out of the mosque afterward, I found my horse readied for me. The animal's mane had been braided with strands of gold and tiny silver bells. I enjoyed listening to the tinkling of the bells at every step, but with so many people blocking the way it was impossible to proceed very fast. In a measured pace, we passed by shabby stores and houses with thatched roofs. The calls of the petitioners mingled with the cries of children and the shouts of beggars eager to earn a few coins. Most of these people wanted me to pray for them; some simply wished to walk close to me. But there were others who had come with bigger expectations, asking me to heal them of a terminal illness or an evil spell. These were the ones who worried me. How could they not see that, neither a prophet nor a sage, I was incapable of performing miracles?

As we turned a corner and approached the Inn of Sugar Vendors, I noticed a wandering holy man push his way through the crowd, strutting directly toward me and regarding me with piercing eyes. His movements were deft and focused, and he exuded an aura of self-sufficient competence. He had no hair. No beard. No eyebrows. And though his face was as open as a man's face could ever be, his expression was inscrutable.

But it wasn't his appearance that intrigued me. Over the years I had seen wandering dervishes of all sorts pass through Konya in their quest for God. With striking tattoos, multiple earrings and nose rings, most of these people enjoyed their reputation for unruly behavior. They either wore their hair very long or shaved it off completely. Some Qalandaris even had their tongues and nipples pierced. So when I saw the dervish for the first time, it wasn't his outer shell that startled me. It was, I dare to say, his gaze.

His black eyes blazing at me sharper than daggers, he stood in the middle of the street and raised his arms high and wide, as if he wanted to halt not only the procession but also the flow of time. I felt a jolt run through my body, like a sudden intuition. My horse got nervous and started to snort loudly, jerking its head up and down. I tried to calm it, but it got so skittish that I, too, felt nervous.

Before my eyes the dervish approached my horse, which was shying and dancing about, and whispered something inaudible to it. The animal started to breathe heavily, but when the dervish waved his hand in a final gesture, it instantly quieted down. A wave of excitement rippled through the crowd, and I heard someone mutter, "That's black magic!"

Oblivious to his surroundings, the dervish eyed me curiously. "O great scholar of East and West, I have heard so much about you. I came here today to ask you a question, if I may?"

"Go ahead," I said under my breath.

"Well, you need to get down from your horse first and be on the same level with me."

I was so stunned to hear this that I couldn't speak for a moment. The people around me seemed equally taken aback. No one had ever dared to address me like this before.

I felt my face burn and my stomach turn with irritation, but I managed to control my annoyance and dismounted my horse. The dervish had already turned his back and was walking away.

"Hey, wait, please!" I yelled as I caught up with him. "I want to hear your question."

He stopped and turned around, smiling at me for the first time. "All right, do tell me, please, which of the two is greater, do you think: the Prophet Muhammad or the Sufi Bistami?"

"What kind of a question is that?" I said. "How can you compare our venerated Prophet, may peace be upon him, the last in the line of prophets, with an infamous mystic?"

A curious crowd had gathered around us, but the dervish didn't seem to mind the audience. Still studying my face carefully, he insisted, "Please think about it. Didn't the Prophet say, 'Forgive me, God, I couldn't know Thee as I should have,' while Bistami pronounced, 'Glory be to me, I carry God inside my cloak'? If one man feels so small in relation to God while another man claims to carry God inside, which of the two is greater?"

My heart pulsed in my throat. The question didn't seem so absurd anymore. In fact, it felt as if a veil had been lifted and what awaited me underneath was an intriguing puzzle. A furtive smile, like a passing breeze, crossed the lips of the dervish. Now I knew he was not some crazy lunatic. He was a man with a question—a question I hadn't thought about before.

"I see what you are trying to say," I began, not wanting him to hear so much as a quaver in my voice. "I'll compare the two statements and tell you why, even though Bistami's statement sounds higher, it is in fact the other way round."

"I am all ears," the dervish said.

"You see, God's love is an endless ocean, and human beings strive to get as much water as they can out of it. But at the end of the day, how much water we each get depends on the size of our cups. Some people have barrels, some buckets, while some others have only got bowls."

As I spoke, I watched the dervish's expression change from subtle scorn to open acknowledgment and from there into the soft smile of someone recognizing his own thoughts in the words of another.

"Bistami's container was relatively small, and his thirst was quenched after a mouthful. He was happy in the stage he was at. It was wonderful that he recognized the divine in himself, but even then there still remains a distinction between God and Self. Unity is not achieved. As for the Prophet, he was the Elect of God and had a much bigger cup to fill. This is why God asked him in the Qur'an, *Have we not opened up your heart?* His heart thus widened, his cup immense, it was thirst upon thirst for him.

No wonder he said, 'We do not know You as we should,' although he certainly knew Him as no other did."

Breaking into a good-natured grin, the dervish nodded and thanked me. He then placed his hand on his heart in a gesture of gratitude and stayed like that for a few seconds. When our eyes met again, I noticed that a trace of gentleness had crept into his gaze.

I stared past the dervish into the pearl gray landscape that was typical of our town at this time of the year. A few dry leaves skittered around our feet. The dervish looked at me with renewed interest, and in the dying light of the setting sun, for a split second, I could swear that I saw an amber aura around him.

He bowed to me respectfully. And I bowed to him. I don't know how long we stood like that, the sky hanging violet above our heads. After a while the crowd around us began to stir nervously, having watched our exchange with an astonishment that verged on disapproval. They had never seen me bow to anyone before, and the fact that I had done so for a simple wandering Sufi had come as a shock to some people, including my closest disciples.

The dervish must have sensed the censure in the air.

"I'd better go now and leave you to your admirers," he said, his voice dwindling to a velvety timbre, almost a whisper.

"Wait," I objected. "Don't go, please. Stay!"

I glimpsed a trace of thoughtfulness in his face, a wistful pucker of the lips, as if he wanted to say more but simply couldn't or wouldn't. And in that moment, in that pause, I heard the question he hadn't asked me.

And how about you, great preacher? Tell me, how big is your cup?

Then there was nothing else to say. We ran out of words. I took a step toward the dervish, getting so close I could see the flecks of gold in his black eyes. Suddenly I was overcome with a strange feeling, as if I had lived this moment before. Not once, but more than a dozen times. I started to remember bits and pieces. A tall, slender man with a veil on his face, his fingers aflame. And then I knew. The dervish who stood across from me was no other than the man I had been seeing in my dreams.

I knew that I had found my companion. But instead of feeling ecstatic with joy, as I always thought I would be, I was seized by cold dread.

Ella

NORTHAMPTON, JUNE 8, 2008

Beleaguered by questions and lacking answers, Ella found that there were many things that surprised her about her correspondence with Aziz, particularly the fact that it was happening. The two of them were so different in every respect that she wondered what they could possibly have in common to e-mail each other about so frequently.

Aziz was like a jigsaw puzzle she aimed to complete piece by piece. With every new e-mail from him, another piece of that puzzle fell into place. Ella had yet to see the entire picture, but by now she had discovered a few things about the man she'd been corresponding with.

She had learned from his blog that Aziz was a professional photographer and an avid globe-trotter who found navigating his way through the farthest corners of the world as natural and easy as taking a stroll around the neighborhood park. A relentless nomad at heart, he had been everywhere, equally at home in Siberia, Shanghai, Calcutta, and Casablanca. Traveling with only a backpack and a reed flute, he had made friends in places Ella couldn't even find on the map. Uncompromising border guards, the impossibility of getting a visa from hostile governments, waterborne parasitic diseases, intestinal disorders due to contaminated food, the danger of being mugged, clashes between government troops and rebels—nothing could hold him back from traveling east and west, north and south.

Ella thought Aziz was a gushing waterfall. Where she feared to step, he surged full blast. Where she hesitated and worried before acting, he acted first and worried later, if he ever worried at all. He had an animated personality, too much idealism and passion for one body. He wore many hats and he wore them well.

Ella saw herself as a liberal, opinionated Democrat, a nonpracticing Jew, and an aspiring vegetarian who was determined to cut all sorts of meat from her meals one day. She separated issues into clear-cut categories, organizing her world pretty much as she organized her house, neat and tidy. Her mind operated with two mutually exclusive and equally lengthy lists: the things she liked versus the things she hated.

Though she was by no means an atheist and enjoyed performing a few rituals every now and then, Ella believed that the major problem consuming the world today, just as in the past, was religion. With their unparalleled arrogance and self-proclaimed belief in the supremacy of their ways, religious people got on her nerves. Fanatics of all persuasions were unbearable, but deep inside she thought that fanatics of Islam were the worst.

Aziz, however, was a spiritual man who took matters of religion and faith seriously, stayed away from all contemporary politics, and didn't "hate" anything or anyone. A die-hard meat eater, he said he would never refuse a plate of well-cooked shish kebab. He had converted to Islam from atheism in the mid-1970s, as he jokingly put it, "sometime after Kareem Abdul-Jabbar and before Cat Stevens." Ever since then he had shared bread with hundreds of mystics from every country and religion, and he declared them "brothers and sisters along the path."

A committed pacifist with strong humanitarian views, Aziz believed that all religious wars were in essence a "linguistic problem." Language, he said, did more to hide than reveal the Truth, and as a result people constantly misunderstood and misjudged one another. In a world beset with mistranslations, there was no use in being resolute about any topic, because it might as well be that even our strongest convictions were caused by a simple misunderstanding. In general, one shouldn't be too rigid about anything because "to live meant to constantly shift colors."

Aziz and Ella lived in different time zones. Literally and metaphorically. For her, time primarily meant the future. She spent a considerable part of her days obsessing over plans for the next year, the next month, the next day, or even the next minute. Even for things as trivial as shopping or replacing a broken chair, Ella planned every detail in advance and went around with meticulous schedules and to-do lists in her bag.

For Aziz, on the other hand, time centered on this very moment, and anything other than now was an illusion. For the same reason, he believed that love had nothing to do with "plans for tomorrow" or "memories of yesterday." Love could only be here and now. One of his earlier e-mails to her had ended with this note: "I am a Sufi, the child of the present moment."

"What a bizarre thing to say," Ella wrote him back, "to a woman who has always put too much thought into the past and even more thought into the future but somehow never even touched the present moment."

Aladdin

KONYA, DECEMBER 16, 1244

By the fates I wasn't there when the dervish crossed my father's path. I had gone deer hunting with several friends and came back only the next day. By then my father's encounter with Shams of Tabriz was the talk of the town. Who was this dervish, people gossiped, and how come an erudite man like Rumi had taken him seriously, to the point of bowing down to him?

Ever since I was a boy, I had watched people kneel in front of my father and had never imagined that it could be any other way—that is, unless the other person was a king or a grand vizier. So I refused to believe half the things I heard and didn't let the gossip get under my skin, until I arrived home and Kerra, my stepmother, who never lies and never exaggerates, confirmed the whole story. Yes, it was true, a wandering dervish named Shams of Tabriz had challenged my father in public, and, what's more, he was now staying in our house.

Who was this stranger who had plummeted into our lives like a mysterious rock hurled from the sky? Eager to see him with my own eyes, I asked Kerra, "So where is this man?"

"Be quiet," Kerra whispered, a little nervously. "Your father and the dervish are in the library."

We could hear the far hum of their voices, though it was impossible to make out what they were talking about. I headed in that direction, but Kerra stopped me.

"I am afraid you will have to wait. They asked not to be disturbed."

For the whole day, they didn't come out of the library. Neither the next day nor the one following. What could they possibly be talking about? What could someone like my father and a simple sage have in common?

A week passed, then another. Every morning Kerra prepared breakfast and left it on a tray in front of their door. No matter what delicacies she prepared for them, they refused it all, content with only a slice of bread in the morning and a glass of goat's milk in the evening.

Perturbed, jittery, I was grabbed by an ill mood during this period. At various hours throughout the day, I tried every hole and crack in the door to peep inside the library. Never minding what would happen if they suddenly opened the door and found me eavesdropping there, I spent a lot of time hunched over, trying to comprehend what they were talking about. But all I could hear was a low murmuring. I couldn't see much either. The room was shadowy, on account of the curtains being half closed. Without much to see or hear, I allowed my mind busily to fill in the silences, fabricating the conversations they must be having.

Once Kerra found me with my ear to the door, but she didn't say anything. By this time she was more desperate than I to learn what was going on. Women can't help their curiosity; it is in their nature.

But it was a different story when my brother, Sultan Walad, caught me eavesdropping. He gave me a burning look, his face turning sour.

"You have no right to spy on other people, especially not on your father," he reprimanded.

I shrugged. "Honestly, brother, doesn't it bother you that our father spends his time with a stranger? It has been more than a month now. Father has brushed his family aside. Doesn't that upset you?"

"Our father hasn't brushed anyone aside," my brother said. "He found a very good friend in Shams of Tabriz. Instead of nagging and complaining like a whining schoolboy, you should be happy for our father. If you truly love him, that is."

That was the sort of thing only my brother could say. I was used to his peculiarities, so I did not take umbrage at his scathing remarks. Always the nice boy, he was the darling of the family and the neighborhood, my father's favorite son.

Exactly forty days after my father and the dervish had cloistered themselves in the library, something strange happened. I was crouched at the door again, eavesdropping on a thicker silence than usual, when all of a sudden I heard the dervish speak up.

"It has been forty days since we retreated here. Every day we discussed another of The Forty Rules of the Religion of Love. Now that we are done, I think we'd better go out. Your absence might have upset your family."

My father objected. "Don't worry. My wife and sons are mature enough to understand that I might need to spend some time away from them."

"Well, I don't know anything about your wife, but your two boys are as different as night and day," Shams responded. "The older one walks in your footsteps, but the younger one, I am afraid, marches to a different drummer altogether. His heart is darkened with resentment and envy."

My cheeks burned with anger. How could he say such awful things about me when we hadn't even met?

"He thinks I don't know him, but I do," said the dervish a little while later. "While he was crouching with his ear to the door, watching me through peepholes, I was watching him, too."

I felt a sudden chill pass across me as every hair on my arms stood on end. Without giving it another thought, I thrust the door open and stomped into the room. My father's eyes widened with incomprehension, but it didn't take long for his shock to be replaced by anger.

"Aladdin, have you lost your mind? How dare you disturb us like this!" my father thundered.

Ignoring that question, I pointed at Shams and exclaimed, "Why don't you first ask him how he dares to talk about me like that?"

My father didn't say a word. He just looked at me and drew in a deep breath, as if my presence were a heavy burden on his shoulders.

"Please, Father, Kerra misses you. And so do your students. How can you turn your back on all your loved ones for a lousy dervish?"

As soon as those words came out of my mouth, I regretted them, but it was too late. My father stared at me with disappointment in his eyes. I had never seen him like this before.

"Aladdin, do something for me. Get out of here—this minute," my father said. "Go into a quiet place and think about what you did. Do not talk to me until you have looked inside and recognized your mistake."

"But, Father—"

"Just get out!" my father repeated, turning away from me.

With a sinking heart, I left the room, my palms wet, my knees trembling.

At that moment it dawned upon me that in some incomprehensible way our lives had changed, and nothing would be the same again. Since the death of my mother eight years ago, this was the second time I had felt abandoned by a parent.

Rumi

KONYA, DECEMBER 18, 1244

B*atın Allah—the hidden face of God. Open my mind so I may see the Truth.*

When Shams of Tabriz asked me that question about the Prophet Muhammad and the Sufi Bistami, I felt as though we were the only two people left on the face of the earth. In front of us extended the seven stages on the Path to Truth—seven *maqamat* every soul had to go through in order to attain Oneness.

The first stage is the *Depraved Nafs,* the most primitive and common state of being, when the soul is entrapped in worldly pursuits. Most human beings are stuck there, struggling and suffering in the service of their baser selves but always holding others responsible for their continuing unhappiness.

If and when a person becomes aware of the soul's abased situation, by starting to work on himself, he can move to the next stage, which in a way is the opposite of the previous one. Instead of blaming other people all the time, the person who has reached this stage blames himself, sometimes to the point of self-effacement. Herein the self becomes the *Accusing Nafs* and thus starts the journey toward inner purification.

In the third stage, the person is more mature and the self has evolved into the *Inspired Nafs*. It is only at this level, and not anytime before, that one can experience the true meaning of the word "surrender" and roam the Valley of Knowledge. Anyone who has made it this far will possess and display patience, perseverance, wisdom, and humility. The world will feel new and full of inspiration. Nevertheless, many of the people who reach the third level feel an urge to dwell here, losing the will or the courage to go further. That is why, as beautiful and blessed as it is, the third stage is a trap for the one who aims higher.

Those who manage to go further reach the Valley of Wisdom and come to know the *Serene Nafs*. Here one's sense of self is not what it used to be, having altered into a high level of consciousness. Generosity, gratitude, and an unwavering sense of contentment regardless of the hardships in life are the main characteristics accompanying anyone who has arrived here. Beyond that lies the Valley of Unity. Those who are here will be pleased with whatever situation God places them in. Mundane matters make no difference to them, as they have achieved the *Pleased Nafs*.

In the next stage, the *Pleasing Nafs,* one becomes a lantern to humanity, radiating energy to everyone who asks for it, teaching and illuminating like a true master. Sometimes such a person can also have healing powers. Wherever he goes, he will make a big difference in other people's lives. In everything he does and aspires to do, his main goal is to serve God through serving others.

Finally, in the seventh stage, one attains the *Purified Nafs* and becomes *Insan-i Kâmil*, a perfect human being. But nobody knows much about that state, and even if a few ever did, they wouldn't speak of it.

The stages along the path are easy to summarize, difficult to experience. Adding to the obstacles that appear along the way is the fact that there is no guarantee of continuous progress. The route from the first to the last stage is by no means linear. There is always the danger of tumbling back into earlier stages, sometimes even from a superior stage all the way down to the first one. Given the many traps along the way, it is no wonder that in every century only a few people manage to reach the final stages.

So when Shams asked me that question, it wasn't simply a comparison that he was after. He wanted me to consider how far I was willing to go to efface my personality in order to be absorbed in God. There was a second question hidden within his first question.

"How about you, great preacher?" he was asking me. "Of the seven stages, which stage are you at? And do you think you have the heart to go further, till the very end? Tell me, how big is your cup?"

Kerra

KONYA, DECEMBER 18, 1244

Bemoaning my fate does me no good, I know. Yet I cannot help but wish that I were more knowledgeable in religion, history, and philosophy and all the things Rumi and Shams must be talking about day and night. There are times I want to rebel against having been created a woman. When you are born a girl, you are taught how to cook and clean, wash dirty clothes, mend old socks, make butter and cheese, and feed babies. Some women are also taught the art of love and making themselves attractive to men. But that's about it. Nobody gives women books to open their eyes.

In the first year of our marriage, I used to sneak into Rumi's library at every opportunity. I would sit there amid the books he loved so much, breathing in their dusty, moldy smells, wondering what mysteries they hid inside. I knew how much Rumi adored his books, most of which had been handed down to him by his late father, Baha' al-Din. Of those, he was particularly fond of the *Ma'arif.* Many nights he would stay awake until dawn reading it, although I suspected he knew the whole text by heart.

"Even if they paid me sacks of gold, I would never exchange my father's books," Rumi used to say. "Each of these books is a priceless legacy from my ancestors. I took them from my father, and I will pass them on to my sons."

I learned the hard way just how much his books meant to him. Still in our first year of marriage, while I was alone at home one day, it occurred to me to dust the library. I took out all the books from the shelves and wiped their covers with a piece of velvet dabbed in rosewater. The locals believe that there is a kind of juvenile djinn by the name of Kebikec who takes a twisted pleasure in destroying books. In order to ward him off, it is the custom to write a note of warning inside each book: *"Stand thou still, Kebikec, stay away from this book!"* How was I to know that it wasn't only Kebikec who was supposed to stay away from my husband's books, but me as well?

That afternoon I dusted and cleaned every book in the library. As I kept working, I read from Ghazzali's *Vivification of the Religious Sciences.* Only when I heard a dry, distant voice behind me did I realize how much time I had spent there.

"Kerra, what do you think you are doing here?"

It was Rumi, or someone who resembled him—the voice was harsher in tone, sterner in expression. In all our eight years of marriage, that was the only time he'd spoken to me like that.

"I am cleaning," I muttered, my voice weak. "I wanted to make it a surprise."

Rumi responded, "I understand, but please do not touch my books again. In fact, I'd rather you did not enter this room at all."

After that day I stayed away from the library even when there was no one at home. I understood and accepted that the world of books was not and never had been, nor ever would be, for me.

But when Shams of Tabriz came to our house, and he and my husband locked themselves in the library for forty days, I felt an old resentment boil up inside me. A wound that I didn't even know I had began to bleed.

Kimya

KONYA, DECEMBER 20, 1244

Born to simple peasants in a valley by the Taurus Mountains, I was twelve the year Rumi adopted me. My real parents were people who worked hard and aged before their time. We lived in a small house, and my sister and I shared the same room with the ghosts of our dead siblings, five children all lost to simple diseases. I was the only one in the house who could see the ghosts. It frightened my sister and made my mother cry each time I mentioned what the little spirits were doing. I tried to explain, to no avail, that they didn't need to be frightened or worried, since none of my dead siblings looked scary or unhappy. This I could never make my family understand.

One day a hermit passed by our village. Seeing how exhausted he was, my father invited him to spend the night in our house. That evening, as we all sat by the fireplace and grilled goat cheese, the hermit told us enchanting stories from faraway lands. While his voice droned on, I closed my eyes, traveling with him to the deserts of Arabia, Bedouin tents in North Africa, and a sea of the bluest water, called the Mediterranean. I found a seashell there on the beach, big and coiled, and put it in my pocket. I was planning to walk the beach from one end to the other, but a sharp, repulsive smell stopped me midway.

When I opened my eyes, I found myself lying on the floor with everyone in the house around me, looking worried. My mother was holding my head with one hand, and in her other hand was half an onion, which she was forcing me to smell.

"She is back!" My sister clapped her hands with glee.

"Thank God!" My mother heaved a sigh. Then she turned to the hermit, explaining, "Ever since she was a little girl, Kimya has been having fainting spells. It happens all the time."

In the morning the hermit thanked us for our hospitality and bade us farewell.

Before he left, however, he said to my father, "Your daughter Kimya is an unusual child. She is very gifted. It would be a pity if such gifts went unappreciated. You should send her to a school—"

"What would a girl need an education for?" my mother exclaimed. "Where did you hear such a thing? She should stay by my side and weave carpets until she gets married. She's a talented carpet weaver, you know."

But the hermit didn't waver. "Well, she could make an even better scholar someday. Obviously, God has not disfavored your daughter for being a girl and has bestowed many gifts upon her. Do you claim to know better than God?" he asked. "If there are no schools available, send her to a scholar to receive the education she deserves."

My mother shook her head. But I could see that my father was of a different mind. Knowing his love for education and knowledge, and his appreciation of my abilities, it didn't surprise me to hear him ask, "We don't know of any scholars. Where am I going to find one?"

It was then that the hermit uttered the name that would change my life. He said, "I know a wonderful scholar in Konya named Mawlana Jalal ad-Din Rumi. He might be glad to teach a girl like Kimya. Take her to him. You won't regret it."

When the hermit was gone, my mother threw her arms up. "I am pregnant. Soon there will be another mouth to feed in this house. I need help. A girl doesn't need books. She needs to learn housework and child care."

I would have much preferred it if my mother had opposed my going away for other reasons. Had she said she would miss me and couldn't bear to give me to another family, even if for a temporary period, I might have chosen to stay. But she said none of this. In any case, my father was convinced that the hermit had a point, and within a few days so was I.

Shortly after, my father and I traveled to Konya. We waited for Rumi outside the madrassa where he taught. When he walked out, I was too embarrassed to look up at him. Instead I looked at his hands. His fingers were long, supple, and slender, more like an artisan's than a scholar's. My father shoved me toward him.

"My daughter is very gifted. But I am a simple man, and so is my wife. We have been told you are the most learned man in the region. Would you be willing to teach her?"

Even without looking at his face, I could sense that Rumi wasn't surprised. He must have been used to such requests. While he and my father engaged in a conversation, I walked toward the yard, where I saw several boys but no girls. But on the way back, I was pleasantly surprised when I spotted a young woman standing in a corner by herself, her round face still and white as if carved of marble. I waved at her. She looked stunned, but after a brief hesitation she returned my wave.

"Hello, little girl, can you see me?" she asked.

When I nodded, the woman broke into a smile, clapping her hands. "That's wonderful! No one else can."

We walked back toward my father and Rumi. I thought they would stop talking when they noticed her, but she was right—they couldn't see her.

"Come here, Kimya," said Rumi. "Your father informs me you love to study. Tell me, what is it in books that you like so much?"

I swallowed hard, unable to answer, paralyzed.

"Come on my dear," my father said, sounding disappointed.

I wanted to answer correctly, with a response that would make my father proud of me, except I didn't know what that was. In my anxiety the only sound that came out of my mouth was a desperate gasp.

My father and I would have gone back to our village empty-handed had the young woman not intervened then. She held my hand and said, "Just tell the truth about yourself. It's going to be fine, I promise."

Feeling better, I turned to Rumi and said, "I'd be honored to study the Qur'an with you, Master. I'm not afraid of hard work."

Rumi's face brightened up. "That's very good," he said, yet then he paused as if he had just remembered a nasty detail. "But you are a girl. Even if we study intensely and make good progress, you'll soon get married and have children. Years of education will be of no use."

Now I didn't know what to say and felt disheartened, almost guilty. My father, too, seemed troubled, suddenly inspecting his shoes. Once again it was the young woman who came to my help. "Tell him his wife always wanted to have a little girl and now she would be happy to see him educate one."

Rumi laughed when I conveyed the message. "So I see you have visited my house and talked to my wife. But let me assure you, Kerra doesn't get involved in my teaching responsibilities."

Slowly, forlornly, the young woman shook her head and whispered in my ear, "Tell him you were not talking about Kerra, his second wife. You were talking about Gevher, the mother of his two sons."

"I was talking about Gevher," I said, pronouncing the name carefully. "The mother of your sons."

Rumi's face turned pale. "Gevher is dead, my child," he said dryly. "But what do you know about my late wife? Is this a tasteless joke?"

My father stepped in. "I'm sure she didn't mean ill, Master. I can assure you Kimya is a serious child. She never disrespects her elders."

I realized I had to tell the truth. "Your late wife is here. She is holding my hand and encouraging me to speak. She has dark brown almond eyes, pretty freckles, and she wears a long yellow robe. . . ."

I paused as I noticed the young woman gesture to her slippers. "She wants me to tell you about her slippers. They are made of bright orange silk and embroidered with small red flowers. They are very pretty."

"I brought her those slippers from Damascus," Rumi said, his eyes filling with tears. "She loved them."

Upon saying that, the scholar lapsed into silence, scratching his beard, his expression solemn and distant. But when he spoke again, his voice was gentle and friendly, without a trace of gloom.

"Now I understand why everyone thinks your daughter is gifted," Rumi said to my father. "Let's go to my house. We can talk about her future over dinner. I'm sure she'll make an excellent student. Better than many boys."

Rumi then turned to me and asked, "Will you tell this to Gevher?"

"There is no need, Master. She has heard you," I said. "She says she needs to go now. But she is always watching you with love."

Rumi smiled warmly. So did my father. There was now an easiness hanging in the air that hadn't been there before. At that moment, I knew my encounter with Rumi was going to have far-reaching consequences.

I had never been close to my mother, but as if to compensate for her lack, God was giving me two fathers, my real father and my adopted father.

That is how I arrived in Rumi's house eight years ago, a timid child hungry for knowledge. Kerra was loving and compassionate, more so than my own mother, and Rumi's sons were welcoming, especially his elder son, who in time became a big brother to me.

In the end the hermit was right. As much as I missed my father and siblings, there hasn't been a single moment when I regretted coming to Konya and joining Rumi's family. I spent many happy days under this roof.

That is, until Shams of Tabriz came. His presence changed everything.

Ella

NORTHAMPTON, JUNE 9, 2008

Being one who had never enjoyed solitude, Ella found she preferred it lately. Immersed in putting the final touches to her editorial report on *Sweet Blasphemy,* she had asked Michelle for another week to turn it in. She could have finished earlier, but she did not want to. The task gave her an excuse to retreat into her mind and shun family duties and long-awaited marital confrontations. This week, for the first time, she skipped the Fusion Cooking Club, unwilling to cook and chat with fifteen women who had similar lives at a time when she wasn't sure what to do with hers. She called in sick at the last minute.

Ella treated her communication with Aziz as a secret, of which suddenly she had way too many. Aziz didn't know she was not only reading his novel but also writing a report on it; the literary agency didn't know she was secretly flirting with the author of the book she was assigned to report on; and her children and husband did not know anything regarding what the novel was about, the author, or the flirtation. In the span of a few weeks, she had converted from a woman whose life was as transparent as the skin of a newborn baby into a woman wallowing in secrets and lies. What surprised her even more than this change was seeing that it did not disturb her in the least. It was as if she were waiting, confidently and patiently, for something momentous to happen. This irrational expectation was part of the charm of her new mood, for despite all the secrets, charming it was.

By this time e-mails weren't enough. It was Ella who first called Aziz. Now, despite the five-hour time difference, they talked on the phone almost every day. Aziz had told her that her voice was soft and fragile. When she laughed, her laughter came in ripples, punctuated by short gasps, as if she weren't sure how much more to laugh. It was the laughter of a woman who had never learned not to pay too much attention to the judgments of others.

"Just go with the flow," he said. "Let go!"

But the flow around her was unsteady and disruptive as several things were happening in her house at this time. Avi had started taking private classes in mathematics, and Orly was now seeing a counselor for her eating disorder. This morning she had eaten half an omelet—her first substantial food in months—and though she had instantly inquired how many calories there were in it, it was a small miracle that she hadn't felt guilty and punished herself by throwing up afterward. Meanwhile Jeannette had set off a bombshell by announcing her breakup with Scott. She had offered no explanation other than the fact that they both needed space. Ella wondered if "space" was a code for a new love, given that neither Jeannette nor Scott had lost any time in finding someone new.

The speed with which human relations materialized and dissipated amazed Ella more than ever, and yet she tried not to pass judgment on other people anymore. If there was one thing she had learned from her correspondence with Aziz, it was that the more she remained calm and composed, the more her children shared with her. Once she had stopped running after them, they had stopped running away from her. Somehow things were working more smoothly and closer to her liking than in the times when she had tirelessly tried to help and repair.

And to think she was doing nothing to achieve this result! Instead of seeing her role in the house as some sort of glue, the invisible yet central bond that held everyone together, she had become a silent spectator. She watched events unfold and days waft by, not necessarily coldly or indifferently but with visible detachment. She had discovered that once she accepted that she didn't have to stress herself about things she had no control over, another self emerged from inside—one who was wiser, calmer, and far more sensible.

"The fifth element," she muttered to herself several times during the day. "Just accept the void!"

It didn't take long for her husband to notice there was something strange about her, something so not Ella. Was this why all of a sudden he wanted to spend more time with her? He came home earlier these days, and Ella suspected he had not been seeing other women for a while.

"Honey, are you all right?" David asked repeatedly.

"I am right as rain," she answered, smiling back each time. It was as if her withdrawal into a calm, private space of her own stripped away the polite decorum behind which her marriage had slept undisturbed for many years. Now that the pretenses between them were gone, she could see their defects and mistakes in all their nakedness. She had stopped pretending. And she had a feeling David was about to do the same.

Over breakfasts and dinners, they talked about the day's events in composed, adult voices, as though discussing the annual return on their stock investments. Then they remained silent, acknowledging the blunt fact that they didn't have much else to talk about. Not anymore.

Sometimes she caught her husband looking at her intently, waiting for her to say something, almost anything. Ella sensed if she asked him about his affairs, he would gladly have come clean. But she wasn't sure she wanted to know.

In the past she used to feign ignorance in order not to rock the boat of her marriage. Now, however, she stopped acting as if she didn't know what he'd been doing when he was away. She made it clear that she *did* know and that she was uninterested. It was precisely this new aloofness that scared her husband. Ella could understand him, because deep inside it scared her, too.

A month ago if David had taken even a tiny step to improve their marriage, she would have felt grateful. Any attempt on his part would have delighted her. Not anymore. Now she suspected that her life wasn't real enough. How had she arrived at this point? How had the fulfilled mother of three discovered her own despondency? More important, if she *was* unhappy, as she once told Jeannette she was, why was she not doing the things unhappy people did all the time? No crying on the bathroom floor, no sobbing into the kitchen sink, no melancholic long walks away from the house, no throwing things at the walls . . . nothing.

A strange calm had descended upon Ella. She felt more stable than she'd ever been, even as she was swiftly gliding away from the life she'd known. In the morning she looked into the mirror long and hard to see if there was a visible change in her face. Did she look younger? Prettier? Or perhaps more full of life? She couldn't see any difference. Nothing had changed, and yet nothing was the same anymore.

Kerra

KONYA, MAY 5, 1245

Branches that once sagged under the weight of snow are now blossoming outside our window, and still Shams of Tabriz is with us. During this time I have watched my husband turn into a different man, every day drifting a bit further from me and his family. In the beginning I thought they would soon get bored with each other, but no such thing occurred. If anything, they have become more attached. When together, either they are strangely silent or they talk in an incessant murmur interspersed with peals of laughter, making me wonder why they never run out of words. After each conversation with Shams, Rumi walks around a transformed man, detached and absorbed, as if intoxicated by a substance I can neither taste nor see.

The bond that unites them is a nest for two, where there is no room for a third person. They nod, smile, chuckle, or frown in the same way and at the same time, exchanging long, meaningful glances between words. Even their moods seem to depend on each other. Some days they are calmer than a lullaby, eating nothing, saying nothing, whereas other days they whirl around with such euphoria that they both resemble madmen. Either way, I cannot recognize my husband anymore. The man I have been married to for more than eight years now, the man whose children I have raised as if they were my own and with whom I had a baby, has turned into a stranger. The only time I feel close to him is when he is in deep sleep. Many nights over the past weeks, I have lain awake listening to the rhythm of his breathing, feeling the soft whisper of his breath on my skin and the comfort of his heart beating in my ear, just to remind myself that he is still the man I married.

I keep telling myself that this is a temporary stage. Shams will leave someday. He is a wandering dervish, after all. Rumi will stay here with me. He belongs to this town and to his students. I need do nothing except wait. But patience doesn't come easily, and it's getting harder with each passing day. When I feel too despondent, I try to recall the old days—especially the time when Rumi stood by me despite all odds.

"Kerra is a Christian. Even if she converts to Islam, she'll never be one of us," people had gossiped when they first got wind of our impending marriage. "A leading scholar of Islam should not marry a woman outside his faith."

But Rumi took no notice of them. Neither then nor later on. For that reason I will always be grateful to him.

Anatolia is made up of a mixture of religions, peoples, and cuisines. If we can eat the same food, sing the same sad songs, believe in the same superstitions, and dream the same dreams at night, why shouldn't we be able to live together? I have known Christian babies with Muslim names and Muslim babies fed by Christian milk mothers. Ours is an ever-liquid world where everything flows and mixes. If there is a frontier between Christianity and Islam, it has to be more flexible than scholars on both sides think it is.

Because I am the wife of a famous scholar, people expect me to think highly of scholars, but the truth is, I don't. Scholars know a lot, that's for sure, but is too much knowledge any good when it comes to matters of faith? They always speak such big words that it is hard to follow what they are saying. Muslim scholars criticize Christianity for accepting the Trinity, and Christian scholars criticize Islam for seeing the Qur'an as a perfect book. They make it sound as if the two religions are a world apart. But if you ask me, when it comes to the basics, ordinary Christians and ordinary Muslims have more in common with each other than with their own scholars.

They say that the hardest thing for a Muslim converting to Christianity is to accept the Trinity. And the hardest thing for a Christian converting to Islam is said to be letting go of the Trinity. In the Qur'an, Jesus says, *Surely I am a servant of God; He has given me the Book and made me a prophet.*

Yet for me the idea that Jesus was not a son of God but a servant of God wasn't that hard to believe. What I found much harder to do was to abandon Mary. I haven't told this to anyone, not even to Rumi, but sometimes I yearn to see Mary's kind brown eyes. Her gaze always had a soothing effect on me.

The truth is, ever since Shams of Tabriz came to our house, I have been so distressed and confused that I find myself longing for Mary more than ever. Like a fever running wild through my veins, my need to pray to Mary comes back with a force I can hardly control. At times like these, guilt consumes me, as if I am cheating on my new religion.

Nobody knows this. Not even my neighbor Safiya, who is my confidante in all other matters. She wouldn't understand. I wish I could share it with my husband, but I cannot see how. He has been so detached; I am afraid of distancing him even more. Rumi used to be everything to me. Now he is a stranger. I never knew it was possible to live with someone under the same roof, sleep in the same bed, and still feel that he was not really there.

Shams of Tabriz

KONYA, JUNE 12, 1245

Befuddled believer! If every Ramadan one fasts in the name of God and every Eid one sacrifices a sheep or a goat as an atonement for his sins, if all his life one strives to make the pilgrimage to Mecca and five times a day kneels on a prayer rug but at the same time has no room for love in his heart, what is the use of all this trouble? Faith is only a word if there is no love at its center, so flaccid and lifeless, vague and hollow—not anything you could truly feel.

Do they think God resides in Mecca or Medina? Or in some local mosque somewhere? How can they imagine that God could be confined to limited space when He openly says, *Neither My heaven nor My earth embraces Me, but the heart of My believing servant does embrace Me.*

Pity the fool who thinks the boundaries of his mortal mind are the boundaries of God the Almighty. Pity the ignorant who assume they can negotiate and settle debts with God. Do such people think God is a grocer who attempts to weigh our virtues and our wrongdoings on two separate scales? Is He a clerk meticulously writing down our sins in His accounting book so as to make us pay Him back someday? Is this their notion of Oneness?

Neither a grocer nor a clerk, my God is a magnificent God. A living God! Why would I want a dead God? Alive He is. His name is al-Hayy—the Ever-Living. Why would I wallow in endless fears and anxieties, always restricted by prohibitions and limitations? Infinitely compassionate He is. The name is al-Wadud. All-Praiseworthy He is. I praise Him with all my words and deeds, as naturally and effortlessly as I breathe. The name is al-Hamid. How can I ever spread gossip and slander if I know deep down in my heart that God hears and sees it all? His name is al-Başir. Beautiful beyond all dreams and hopes.

Al-Jamal, al-Kayyum, al-Rahman, al-Rahim. Through famine and flood, dry and athirst, I will sing and dance for Him till my knees buckle, my body collapses, and my heart stops pounding. I will smash my nafs to smithereens, until I am no more than a particle of nothingness, the wayfarer of pure emptiness, the dust of the dust in His great architecture. Gratefully, joyously, and relentlessly, I commend His splendor and generosity. I thank Him for all the things He has both given and denied me, for only He knows what is best for me.

Recalling another rule on my list, I felt a fresh wave of happiness and hope. *The human being has a unique place among God's creation. "I breathed into him of My Spirit," God says. Each and every one of us without exception is designed to be God's delegate on earth. Ask yourself, just how often do you behave like a delegate, if you ever do so? Remember, it falls upon each of us to discover the divine spirit inside and live by it.*

Instead of losing themselves in the Love of God and waging a war against their ego, religious zealots fight other people, generating wave after wave of fear. Looking at the whole universe with fear-tinted eyes, it is no wonder that they see a plethora of things to be afraid of. Wherever there is an earthquake, drought, or any other calamity, they take it as a sign of Divine Wrath—as if God does not openly say, *My compassion outweighs My wrath.* Always resentful of somebody for this or that, they seem to expect God the Almighty to step in on their behalf and take their pitiful revenges. Their life is a state of uninterrupted bitterness and hostility, a discontentment so vast it follows them wherever they go, like a black cloud, darkening both their past and their future.

There is such a thing in faith as not being able to see the forest for the trees. The totality of religion is far greater and deeper than the sum of its component parts. Individual rules need to be read in the light of the whole. And the whole is concealed in the essence.

Instead of searching for the essence of the Qur'an and embracing it as a whole, however, the bigots single out a specific verse or two, giving priority to the divine commands that they deem to be in tune with their fearful minds. They keep reminding everyone that on the Day of Judgment all human beings will be forced to walk the Bridge of Sirat, thinner than a hair, sharper than a razor. Unable to cross the bridge, the sinful will tumble into the pits of hell underneath, where they will suffer forever. Those who have led a virtuous life will make it to the other end of the bridge, where they will be rewarded with exotic fruits, sweet waters, and virgins. This, in a nutshell, is their notion of afterlife. So great is their obsession with horrors and rewards, flames and fruits, angels and demons, that in their itch to reach a future that will justify who they are today they forget about God! Don't they know one of the forty rules? *Hell is in the here and now. So is heaven. Quit worrying about hell or dreaming about heaven, as they are both present inside this very moment. Every time we fall in love, we ascend to heaven. Every time we hate, envy, or fight someone, we tumble straight into the fires of hell.* This is what Rule Number Twenty-five is about.

Is there a worse hell than the torment a man suffers when he knows deep down in his conscience that he has done something wrong, awfully wrong? Ask that man. He will tell you what hell is. Is there a better paradise than the bliss that descends upon a man at those rare moments in life when the bolts of the universe fly open and he feels in possession of all the secrets of eternity and fully united with God? Ask that man. He will tell you what heaven is.

Why worry so much about the aftermath, an imaginary future, when this very moment is the only time we can truly and fully experience both the presence and the absence of God in our lives? Motivated by neither the fear of punishment in hell nor the desire to be rewarded in heaven, Sufis love God simply because they love Him, pure and easy, untainted and nonnegotiable.

Love is the reason. Love is the goal.

And when you love God so much, when you love each and every one of His creations because of Him and thanks to Him, superfluous divisions melt into thin air. From that point on, there can be no "I" anymore. All you amount to is a zero so big it covers your whole being.

The other day Rumi and I were contemplating these issues when all of a sudden he closed his eyes and uttered the following lines:

"Not Christian or Jew or Muslim, not Hindu, Buddhist, Sufi or zen. Not any religion or cultural system. I am not of the East, nor of the West. . . .
My place is placeless, a trace of the traceless."

Rumi thinks he can never be a poet. But there is a poet in him. And a fabulous one! Now that poet is being revealed.

Yes, Rumi is right. He is neither of the East nor of the West. He belongs in the Kingdom of Love. He belongs to the Beloved.

Ella

NORTHAMPTON, JUNE 12, 2008

By now Ella had finished reading *Sweet Blasphemy* and was putting the final touches on her editorial report. Although she was dying to discuss the details of his novel with Aziz, her sense of professionalism stopped her. It wouldn't be right. Not before she was done with the assignment. She hadn't even told Aziz that after reading his novel she had bought a copy of Rumi's poems and was now reading at least a few poems every night before going to sleep. She had so neatly separated her work on the novel from her exchange with the author. But on the twelfth of June, something happened that blurred the line between the two forever.

Up until that day, Ella had never seen a picture of Aziz. There being no photos of him on his Web site, she had no idea what he looked like. In the beginning she had enjoyed the mystery of writing to a man with no face. But over time her curiosity began to get the best of her, and the need to put a face to his messages tugged at her. He had never asked for a picture of her, which she found odd, really odd.

So, out of the blue, she sent him a picture of herself. There she was, out on the porch with dear Spirit, wearing a skimpy cerulean dress that slightly revealed her curves. She was smiling in the picture—a half-pleased, half-troubled smile. Her fingers firmly grasped the dog's collar, as if trying to derive some strength from him. Above them the sky was a patchwork of grays and purples. It wasn't one of her best pictures, but there was something spiritual, almost otherworldly, in this one. Or so she hoped. Ella sent it as an e-mail attachment and then simply waited. It was her way of asking Aziz to send her his photo.

He did.

When Ella saw the picture Aziz sent her, she thought it must have been taken somewhere in the Far East, not that she had ever been there. In the picture, Aziz was surrounded by more than a dozen dark-haired native children of every age. Dressed in a black shirt and black trousers, he had a lean build, a sharp nose, high cheekbones, and long, dark, wavy hair falling to his shoulders. His eyes were two emeralds brimming with energy and something else that Ella recognized as compassion. He wore a single earring and a necklace with an intricate shape that Ella couldn't make out. In the background was a silvery lake surrounded by tall grass, and in one corner loomed the shadow of something or someone that was outside the frame.

As she inspected the man in the picture, taking in every detail, Ella had a feeling she recognized him from somewhere. As bizarre as it felt, she could swear she had seen him before.

And suddenly she knew.

Shams of Tabriz bore more than a passing resemblance to Aziz Z. Zahara. He looked exactly the way Shams was described in the manuscript before he headed to Konya to meet Rumi. Ella wondered if Aziz had deliberately based his character's looks on himself. As a writer, he might have wanted to create his central character in his own image, just as God had created human beings in His image.

As she considered this, another possibility arose. Could it be that the real Shams of Tabriz had looked just as he was described in the book, in which case it could only mean that there was a surprising resemblance between two men almost eight hundred years apart? Could it be that the resemblance was beyond the control and perhaps even the knowledge of the author? The more thought Ella put into this dilemma, the more strongly she suspected that Shams of Tabriz and Aziz Z. Zahara could be connected in a way that went beyond a simple literary gimmick.

The discovery had two unexpected impacts on Ella. First, she felt the need to go back to *Sweet Blasphemy* and read the novel again, with a different eye, not for the sake of the story this time but to find the author hidden in its central character, to find the Aziz in Shams of Tabriz.

Second, she became more intrigued by Aziz's personality. Who was he? What was his story? In an earlier e-mail, he had told her he was

Scottish, but then why did he have an Eastern name—Aziz? Was it his real name? Or was it his Sufi name? And by the way, what did it mean to be a Sufi?

There was something else that occupied her mind: the very first, almost imperceptible signs of desire. It had been such a long time since she'd last felt it that it took her a few extra seconds to recognize the feeling. But it was there. Strong, prodding, and disobedient. She realized that she desired the man in the picture and wondered what it would be like to kiss him.

The feeling was so unexpected and embarrassing that she quickly turned off her laptop, as though the man in the picture could otherwise suck her in.

Baybars the Warrior

KONYA, JULY 10, 1245

"Baybars, my son, trust no one," my uncle says, "because the world is getting more corrupt each day." He claims that the only time when things were different was during the Golden Age, when the Prophet Muhammad, peace be upon him, was duly in charge. Since his death everything has been going downhill. But if you ask me, anyplace where there are more than two people is bound to become a battleground. Even at the time of the Prophet, people had their share of hostilities, didn't they? War is the core of life. The lion eats the deer, and vultures reduce to bare bones what remains of the carcass. Nature is cruel. On land, in sea or air, for every creature without exception, there is only one way to survive: to be shrewder and stronger than your worst enemy. To stay alive you need to fight. It's as simple as that.

And fight we must. Even the most naïve can see there is no other way in this day and age. Things took a nasty turn five years ago when a hundred Mongol diplomats sent out by Genghis Khan to negotiate for peace were all slaughtered. After that, Genghis Khan turned into a fireball of fury, declaring war against Islam. How and why the diplomats were killed, nobody could say. Some people suspected that it was Genghis Khan himself who had his own diplomats killed, so that he could start this massive war campaign in the first place. It could be true. One never knows. But I *do* know that in five years the Mongols devastated the whole Khorasan area, causing destruction and death everywhere they galloped. And two years ago they defeated the Seljuk forces at Kosedag, turning the sultan into a tribute-paying vassal. The only reason the Mongols didn't wipe us out is that it is more profitable for them to keep us under their yoke.

Wars might be present since time immemorial, at least since Cain killed his brother Abel, but the Mongol army is like nothing we have seen before. Specialized in more ways than one, they use a vast array of weapons, each designed for a specific purpose. Every Mongol soldier is heavily armored, with a mace, an ax, a saber, and a spear. On top of that, they have arrows that can penetrate armor, set whole villages ablaze, poison their victims, or pierce the hardest bones in the human body. They even have whistling arrows, which they use to send signals from one battalion to another. With such well-developed warfare skills and no God to fear, the Mongols attack and annihilate every city, town, and village on their way. Even ancient cities like Bukhara have been turned into heaps of rubble. And it is not only the Mongols. We need to get Jerusalem back from the Crusaders, not to mention the pressure from the Byzantines and the rivalry between Shiites and Sunnis. When surrounded by cold-blooded enemies on all sides, how can we afford to be peaceful?

This is why people like Rumi get on my nerves. I don't care how highly everyone thinks of him. For me he is a coward who spreads nothing but cowardice. He might have been a good scholar in the past, but nowadays he is clearly under the influence of that heretic Shams. At a time when the enemies of Islam are looming large, what does Rumi preach? Peace! Passivity! Submission!

Brother, stand the pain. Escape the poison
Of your impulses. The sky will bow to your beauty
If you do. . . . That way a thorn expands to a rose.
A particular glows with the universal.

Rumi preaches submissiveness, turning Muslims into a flock of sheep, meek and timid. He says for every prophet there is a community of followers and for every community there is an appointed time. Other than "love," his favorite words seem to be "patience," "balance," and "tolerance." If it were up to him, we would all just sit in our houses and wait to be slaughtered by our enemies or be stricken by some other calamity. And I am sure he would then come and briefly examine the wreck, calling it *baraqa.* There are people who have heard him say, "When school and mosque and minaret get torn down, then dervishes can begin their community." Now, what kind of talk is that?

And when you come to think of it, the only reason Rumi ended up in this city is that decades ago his family left Afghanistan seeking refuge in Anatolia. Many other powerful and wealthy people at the time had received an open invitation from the sultan of Seljuks, among them Rumi's father. Thus sheltered and privileged and always showered with attention and approval, Rumi's family left the bedlam of Afghanistan for the tranquil orchards of Konya. It's easy to preach tolerance when you have a history like that!

The other day I heard a story that Shams of Tabriz told a group of people in the bazaar. He said that Ali, the Prophet's successor and companion, was fighting with an infidel on a battlefield. Ali was about to thrust his sword into the other man's heart when all of a sudden the infidel raised his head and spit at him. Ali immediately dropped his sword, took a deep breath, and walked away. The infidel was stunned. He ran after Ali and asked him why he was letting him go.

"Because I'm very angry at you," said Ali.

"Then why don't you kill me?" the infidel asked. "I don't understand."

Ali explained, "When you spit in my face, I got very angry. My pride was provoked, yearning for revenge. If I kill you now, I'll be following my worse instincts. And that would be a huge mistake."

So Ali set the man free. The infidel was so touched that he became Ali's friend and follower, and in time he converted to Islam of his own free will.

This, apparently, is the kind of story Shams of Tabriz likes to tell. And what is his message? Let the infidels spit in your face! I say, over my dead body! Infidel or not, nobody can spit in the face of Baybars the Warrior.

Ella

NORTHAMPTON, JUNE 13, 2008

Beloved Aziz,

You're going to think I'm crazy, but there's something I've been meaning to ask you: Are you Shams?

Or is it the other way round? Is Shams you?

Yours sincerely,

Ella

Dear Ella,

Shams is the person who was responsible for the transformation of Rumi from a local cleric to a world-famous poet and mystic.

Master Sameed used to say to me, "Even if there might be a Shams equivalent in some people, what matters is, where are the Rumis to see it?"

Warm regards,

Aziz

Dear Aziz,

Who is Master Sameed?

Best,

Ella

Beloved Ella,

It's a long story. Do you really want to know?

Warmly,

Aziz

Dear Aziz,

I have plenty of time.

Love,

Ella

Rumi

KONYA, AUGUST 2, 1245

Bountiful is your life, full and complete. Or so you think, until someone comes along and makes you realize what you have been missing all this time. Like a mirror that reflects what is absent rather than present, he shows you the void in your soul—the void you have resisted seeing. That person can be a lover, a friend, or a spiritual master. Sometimes it can be a child to look after. What matters is to find the soul that will complete yours. All the prophets have given the same advice: Find the one who will be your mirror! For me that mirror is Shams of Tabriz. Until he came and forced me to look deep into the crannies of my soul, I had not faced the fundamental truth about myself: that though successful and prosperous outside, I was lonely and unfulfilled inside.

It's as if for years on end you compile a personal dictionary. In it you give your definition of every concept that matters to you, such as "truth," "happiness," or "beauty." At every major turning point in life, you refer to this dictionary, hardly ever feeling the need to question its premises. Then one day a stranger comes and snatches your precious dictionary and throws it away.

"All your definitions need to be redefined," he says. "It's time for you to unlearn everything you know."

And you, for some reason unbeknownst to your mind but obvious to your heart, instead of raising objections or getting cross with him, gladly comply. This is what Shams has done to me. Our friendship has taught me so much. But more than that, he has taught me to unlearn everything I knew.

When you love someone this much, you expect everyone around you to feel the same way, sharing your joy and euphoria. And when that doesn't happen, you feel surprised, then offended and betrayed.

How could I possibly make my family and friends see what I see? How could I describe the indescribable? Shams is my Sea of Mercy and Grace. He is my Sun of Truth and Faith. I call him the King of Kings of Spirit. He is my fountain of life and my tall cypress tree, majestic and evergreen. His companionship is like the fourth reading of the Qur'an—a journey that can only be experienced from within but never grasped from the outside.

Unfortunately, most people make their evaluations based on images and hearsay. To them Shams is an eccentric dervish. They think he behaves bizarrely and speaks blasphemy, that he is utterly unpredictable and unreliable. To me, however, he is the epitome of Love that moves the whole universe, at times retreating into the background and holding every piece together, at times exploding in bursts. An encounter of this kind happens once in a lifetime. Once in thirty-eight years.

Ever since Shams came into our lives, people have been asking me what it is in him that I find so special. But there is no way I can answer them. At the end of the day, those who ask this question are the ones who won't understand it, and as for those who *do* understand, they don't ask such things.

The quandary I find myself in reminds me of the story of Layla and Harun ar-Rashid, the famous Abbasid emperor. Upon hearing that a Bedouin poet named Qays had fallen hopelessly in love with Layla and lost his mind for her, and was therefore named Majnun—the madman—the emperor became very curious about the woman who had caused such misery.

This Layla must be a very special creature, he thought. *A woman far superior to all other women. Perhaps she is an enchantress unequaled in beauty and charm.*

Excited, intrigued, he played every trick in the book to find a way to see Layla with his own eyes.

Finally one day they brought Layla to the emperor's palace. When she took off her veil, Harun ar-Rashid was disillusioned. Not that Layla was ugly, crippled, or old. But she wasn't extraordinarily attractive either. She was a human being with ordinary human needs and several defects, a simple woman, like countless others.

The emperor did not hide his disappointment. "Are you the one Majnun has been crazy about? Why, you look so ordinary. What is so special about you?"

Layla broke into a smile. "Yes, I am Layla. But you are not Majnun," she answered. "You have to see me with the eyes of Majnun. Otherwise you could never solve this mystery called love."

How can I explain the same mystery to my family, friends, or students? How can I make them understand that for them to grasp what is so special about Shams of Tabriz, they have to start looking at him with the eyes of Majnun?

Is there a way to grasp what love means without becoming a lover first?

Love cannot be explained. It can only be experienced.

Love cannot be explained, yet it explains all.

Kimya

KONYA, AUGUST 17, 1245

Breathlessly I wait for a summons, but Rumi doesn't have time to study with me anymore. As much as I miss our lessons and feel neglected, I am not upset with him. Maybe it's because I love Rumi too much to get cross with him. Or maybe it's because I can understand better than anyone else how he feels, for deep inside I, too, am swept up by the bewildering current that is Shams of Tabriz.

Rumi's eyes follow Shams the way a sunflower follows the sun. Their love for each other is so visible and intense, and what they have is so rare, that one can't help feeling despondent around them, seized by the realization that a bond of such magnitude is missing in one's own life. Not everyone in the house can tolerate this, starting with Aladdin. So many times I've caught him looking daggers at Shams. Kerra, too, is ill at ease, but she never says anything and I never ask. We are all sitting on a powder keg. Strangely, Shams of Tabriz, the man who is responsible for all the tension, either is unaware of the situation or simply doesn't care.

Part of me is bitter at Shams for taking Rumi away from us. Another part of me, however, is dying to get to know him better. I have been struggling with these mixed feelings for some time now, but today, I am afraid, I might have given myself away.

Late in the afternoon, I took out the Qur'an hanging on the wall, determined to study it on my own. In the past, Rumi and I had always followed the order in which the verses were handed down to us, but now that there was nobody guiding me and our lives had been turned topsy-turvy, I saw no harm in reading without an order. So I haphazardly opened a page and put my finger on the first verse that came up. It turned out to be al-Nisa, the one verse in the whole book that has troubled me the most. With its unpromising teachings on women, I found the Nisa hard to understand and harder to accept. As I stood there reading the verse one more time, it occurred to me to ask for help. Rumi might be skipping our lessons, but there was no reason I couldn't ask him questions. So I grabbed my Qur'an and went to his room.

To my surprise, instead of Rumi I found Shams there, sitting by the window with a rosary in his hand, the dying light of the setting sun caressing his face. He looked so handsome I had to avert my eyes.

"I'm sorry," I said quickly. "I was looking for Mawlana. I'll come later."

"Why the rush? Stay," Shams said. "You seem to have come here to ask something. Perhaps I could be of help."

I saw no reason not to share it with him. "Well, there is this verse in the Qur'an that I find a bit hard to understand," I said tentatively.

Shams murmured, as if talking to himself, "The Qur'an is like a shy bride. She'll open her veil only if she sees that the onlooker is soft and compassionate at heart." Then he squared his shoulders and asked, "Which verse is it?"

"Al-Nisa," I said. "There are some parts in it where men are said to be superior to women. It even says men can beat their wives. . . . "

"Is that so?" Shams asked with such exaggerated interest that I couldn't be sure whether he was serious or teasing me. After a momentary silence, he broke into a soft smile and out of memory recited the verse.

"Men are the maintainers of women because Allah has made some of them to excel others and because they spend out of their property; the good women are therefore obedient, guarding the unseen as Allah has guarded; and (as to) those on whose part you fear desertion, admonish them, and leave them alone in the sleeping-places and beat them; then if they obey you, do not seek a way against them; surely Allah is High, Great."

When he finished, Shams closed his eyes and recited the same verse, this time in a different translation.

"Men are the support of women as God gives some more means than others, and because they spend of their wealth (to provide for them). So women who are virtuous are obedient to God and guard the hidden as God has guarded it. As for

women you feel are averse, talk to them suasively; then leave them alone in bed (without molesting them) and go to bed with them (when they are willing). If they open out to you, do not seek an excuse for blaming them. Surely God is sublime and great.

"Do you see any difference between the two?" Shams asked.

"Yes I do," I said. "Their whole texture is different. The former sounds as if it gives consent to married men to beat their wives, whereas the latter advises them to simply walk away. I think that is a big difference. Why is that?"

"Why is that? Why is that?" Shams echoed several times, as if enjoying the question. "Tell me something, Kimya. Have you ever gone swimming in a river?"

I nodded as a childhood memory returned to me. The cold, thirst-quenching streams of the Taurus Mountains crossed my mind. Of the younger girl who had spent many happy afternoons in those streams with her sister and her friends, there was now little left behind. I turned my face away as I didn't want Shams to see the tears in my eyes.

"When you look at a river from a distance, Kimya, you might think there is only one watercourse. But if you dive into the water, you'll realize there is more than one river. The river conceals various currents, all of them flowing in harmony and yet completely separate from one another."

Upon saying that, Shams of Tabriz approached me and held my chin between his two fingers, forcing me to look directly into his deep, dark, soulful eyes. My heart skipped a beat. I couldn't even breathe.

"The Qur'an is a gushing river," he said. "Those who look at it from a distance see only one river. But for those swimming in it, there are four currents. Like different types of fish, some of us swim closer to the surface while some others swim in deep waters down below."

"I'm afraid I don't understand," I said, although I was beginning to.

"Those who like to swim close to the surface are content with the outer meaning of the Qur'an. Many people are like that. They take the verses too literally. No wonder when they read a verse like the Nisa, they arrive at the conclusion that men are held superior to women. Because that is exactly what they want to see."

"How about the other currents?" I asked.

Shams sighed softly, and I couldn't help noticing his mouth, as mysterious and inviting as a secret garden.

"There are three more currents. The second one is deeper than the first, but still close to the surface. As your awareness expands, so does your grasp of the Qur'an. But for that to happen, you need to take the plunge."

Listening to him, I felt both empty and fulfilled at the same time. "What happens when you take the plunge?" I asked cautiously.

"The third undercurrent is the esoteric, *batini,* reading. If you read the Nisa with your inner eye open, you'll see that the verse is not about women and men but about *womanhood* and *manhood.* And each and every one of us, including you and me, has both femininity and masculinity in us, in varying degrees and shades. Only when we learn to embrace both can we attain harmonious Oneness."

"Are you telling me that I have manliness inside me?"

"Oh, yes, definitely. And I have a female side, too."

I couldn't help but chuckle. "And Rumi? How about him?"

Shams smiled fleetingly. "Every man has a degree of womanliness inside."

"Even the ones who are manly men?"

"Especially those, my dear," Shams said, garnishing his words with a wink and dropping his voice to a whisper, as if sharing a secret.

I stifled a giggle, feeling like a little girl. That was the impact of having Shams so close. He was a strange man, his voice oddly charming, his hands lithe and muscular, and his stare like a crease of sunlight, making everything that it fell upon look more intense and alive. Next to him I felt my youth in all its fullness, and yet somewhere inside me a maternal instinct sprawled, exuding the thick, milky scent of motherhood. I wanted to protect him. How or from what, I could not tell.

Shams put his hand on my shoulder, his face so close to mine that I could feel the warmth of his breath. There was now a new, dreamy gaze to his eyes. He held me captive with his touch, caressing my cheeks, his fingertips as warm as a flame against my skin. I was flabbergasted. Now his finger moved down, reaching my bottom lip. Baffled and giddy, I closed my eyes, feeling a lifetime's worth of excitement welling up in my stomach. But no sooner had he touched my lips than Shams drew his hand back.

"You should go now, dear Kimya," Shams murmured, making my name sound like a sad word.

I walked out, my head dizzy and my cheeks flushed.

Only after I went to my room, reclined on my back on the sleeping mat, and stared up at the ceiling, wondering how it would feel to be kissed by Shams, did it dawn upon me that I had forgotten to ask him about the fourth undercurrent in the stream—the deeper reading of the Qur'an. What was it? How could one ever achieve that kind of depth?

And what happened to those who took the plunge?

Sultan Walad

KONYA, SEPTEMBER 4, 1245

Being his older brother, I have always worried for Aladdin, but never as much as I do now. He has always had a quick temper, even as a toddler, but lately he is more quarrelsome and easily incensed. Ready to squabble over almost anything, no matter how senseless or small, he is so petulant these days that even the children on the street take fright when they see him coming. Only seventeen, he has creases around his eyes from frowning and squinting too much. Just this morning I noticed a new wrinkle next to his mouth from holding it in a tight line all the time.

I was busy writing on sheepskin parchment when I heard a faint rattling sound behind me. It was Aladdin, his lips set in a tense scowl. God knows how long he had been standing there like that, watching me with a strained look in his brown eyes. He asked me what I was doing.

"I'm copying an old lecture of our father's," I said. "It's good to have an extra copy of every one of them."

"What's the use of it?" Aladdin exhaled loudly. "Father has stopped giving lectures or sermons. In case you haven't noticed, he doesn't teach at the madrassa either. Don't you see he has thrust aside all his responsibilities?"

"This is a temporary situation," I said. "He'll soon start teaching again."

"You are only fooling yourself. Don't you see that our father doesn't have time for anything or anyone other than Shams? Isn't that funny? The man is supposed to be a wandering dervish, but he has taken root in our house."

Aladdin emitted a mirthless laugh, waiting for me to agree with him, but when I said nothing, he started pacing the room. Even without looking at him, I could feel the angry blaze in his eyes.

"People are gossiping," Aladdin went on morosely. "They are all asking the same question: How can a respected scholar let himself be manipulated by a heretic? Our father's reputation is like ice melting under the sun. If he doesn't get a hold of himself soon, he might never be able to find students again in this town. Nobody would want him as a teacher. And I wouldn't blame them."

I placed the parchment aside and looked at my brother. He was only a boy, really, although his every gesture and expression said he felt on the edge of manhood. He had changed a lot since last year, and I was beginning to suspect he could be in love. Just who the girl could be, I didn't know, and his close friends wouldn't tell me.

"Brother, I realize you don't like Shams, but he is a guest in our house and we ought to respect him. Don't listen to what others say. Honestly, we shouldn't make a fuss about this."

As soon as these words came from my mouth, I regretted my patronizing tone. But it was too late. Like bone-dry wood, Aladdin easily catches fire.

"A fuss?!" Aladdin snorted. "Is that what you call this calamity that has befallen us? How can you be so blind?"

I took out another parchment, caressing its delicate surface. It always gave me tremendous pleasure to reproduce my father's words and to think that in doing so I was helping them to last longer. Even after a hundred years passed, people could read my father's teachings and be inspired by them. To play a role in this transmission, however small a role it might be, made me proud.

Still complaining, Aladdin stood next to me and glanced at my work, his eyes brooding and bitter. For a fleeting moment, I saw a longing in his eyes and recognized the face of a boy in need of his father's love. With a plunging heart, I realized it wasn't Shams he was truly angry at. It was my father.

Aladdin was angry at my father for not loving him enough and for being who he was. My father could be distinguished and famous, but he had also been utterly helpless in the face of the death that had taken our mother at such a tender age.

"They say Shams put a spell on our father," Aladdin said. "They say he was sent by the Assassins."

"The Assassins!" I protested. "That is nonsense."

The Assassins were a sect famous for their meticulous killing methods and extensive use of poisonous substances. Targeting influential people, they murdered their victims in public, so as to plant fear and panic in people's hearts. They had gone as far as leaving a poisoned cake in Saladin's tent with a note that said *You are in our hands*. And Saladin, this great commandeer of Islam who had fought bravely against the Christian Crusaders and recaptured Jerusalem, had not dared to fight against the Assassins, preferring to make peace with them. How could people think Shams could be linked with this sect of terror?

I put my hand on Aladdin's shoulder and forced him to look at me. "Besides, don't you know the sect is not what it used to be? They are barely more than a name now."

Aladdin briefly considered this possibility. "Yes, but they say there were three very loyal commandeers of Hassan Sabbah. They left the castle of Alamut, pledging to spread terror and trouble wherever they went. People suspect that Shams is their leader."

I was starting to lose patience. "God help me! And could you please tell me why a Hashshashin would want to kill our father?"

"Because they hate influential people and love to create chaos, that's why," Aladdin responded. So agitated was he by his conspiracy theories that red blotches had formed on his cheeks.

I knew I had to handle this more carefully. "Look, people say all sorts of things all the time," I said. "You can't take these awful rumors seriously. Clear your mind of spiteful thoughts. They are poisoning you."

Aladdin groaned resentfully, but I continued nonetheless. "You might not like Shams personally. You do not have to. But for Father's sake you ought to show him some respect."

Aladdin looked at me with bitterness and contempt. I understood that my younger brother was not only cross with our father and infuriated at Shams. He was also disappointed in me. He saw my appreciation of Shams as a sign of weakness. Perhaps he thought that in order to earn my father's favor, I was being subservient and spineless. It was only a suspicion on my part, but one that hurt me deeply.

Still, I could not get angry at him, and even if I did, my anger would not last very long. He was my little brother. To me he would always be that boy running after street cats, getting his feet dirty in rain puddles, and nibbling slices of bread topped with yogurt all day long. I couldn't help seeing in his face the boy he once had been, a bit on the plump side and a tad short for his age, the boy who took the news of the death of his mother without shedding a tear. All he did was to look down at his feet as if suddenly ashamed of his shoes and purse his bottom lip until its color was gone. Neither a word nor a sob had come out of his mouth. I wish he would have cried.

"Do you remember the time you got into a fight with some neighboring kids?" I asked. "You came home crying, with a bloody nose. What did our mother tell you then?"

Aladdin's eyes first narrowed and then grew in recognition, but he didn't say anything.

"She told you that whenever you got angry with someone, you should replace the face of that person in your mind with the face of someone you love. Have you tried replacing Shams's face with our mother's face? Perhaps you could find something to like in him."

A furtive smile, as swift and timid as a passing cloud, hovered over Aladdin's lips, and I was amazed at how much it softened his expression.

"Perhaps I could," he said, all anger draining out of his voice now.

My heart melted. I gave my brother a hug, unsure of what else to say. As he hugged me back, I felt confident that he would repair his relationship with Shams and the harmony in our house would soon be restored.

Given the course of events that followed, I couldn't have been more mistaken.

Kerra

KONYA, OCTOBER 22, 1245

Beyond the closed door, Shams and Rumi were talking fervently about God knows what the other day. I knocked and entered without waiting for a response, carrying a tray with a plate of halva. Normally Shams doesn't say anything when I am around, as if my presence forces him into silence. And he never comments upon my cooking skills. He eats very little anyhow. Sometimes I have the impression it makes no difference to him whether I serve a fabulous dinner or dry bread. But this time as soon as he took a bite from my halva, his eyes lit up.

"This is delicious, Kerra. How did you make it?" he asked.

I don't know what came over me. Instead of seeing the compliment for what it was, I heard myself retort, "Why are you asking? Even if I told you how, you couldn't make it."

Shams locked a level gaze into my eyes and nodded slightly, as if he agreed with what I'd said. I waited for him to say something in return, but he just stood there, mute and calm.

In a little while, I left the room and returned to the kitchen, thinking the incident was left behind. And I probably would not have remembered it again, had it not been for what transpired this morning.

I was churning butter by the hearth in the kitchen when I heard strange voices out in the courtyard. I rushed outside, only to witness the craziest scene ever. There were books everyplace, piled up in rickety towers, and still more books floating inside the fountain. From all the ink dissolving in it, the water in the fountain had turned a vivid blue.

With Rumi standing right there, Shams picked a book from the pile—*The Collected Poems of al-Mutanabbi*—eyed it with a grim expression, and tossed it into the water. No sooner had the book submerged than he reached for another. This time it was Attar's *The Book of Secrets.*

I gasped in horror. One by one, he was destroying Rumi's favorite books! The next to be hurled into the water was *The Divine Sciences* by Rumi's father. Knowing how much Rumi adored his father and doted upon this old manuscript, I looked at him, expecting him to explode.

Instead I found Rumi standing aside, his face pale as wax, his hands trembling. I couldn't understand for the life of me why he didn't say anything. The man who once had reprimanded me for just dusting his books was now watching a lunatic destroy his entire library, and yet he didn't even utter a word. It wasn't fair. If Rumi wasn't going to intervene, I would.

"What are you doing?" I asked Shams. "These books have no other copies. They are very valuable. Why are you throwing them into the water? Have you lost your mind?"

Instead of an answer, Shams cocked his head toward Rumi. "Is that what you think, too?" he asked.

Rumi pursed his lips and smiled faintly but remained silent.

"Why don't you say anything?" I yelled at my husband.

At this, Rumi approached me and held my hand tightly. "Calm down, Kerra, please. I trust in Shams."

Giving me a glance over his shoulder, relaxed and confident, Shams rolled up his sleeves and started to pull the books out of the water. To my amazement, every single book he took out was as dry as a bone.

"Is this magic? How did you do that?" I asked.

"But why are you asking?" Shams said. "Even if I told you how, you couldn't do it."

Trembling with anger, choking back sobs, I ran to the kitchen, which has become my sanctuary these days. And there, amid pots and pans, stacks of herbs and spices, I sat down and cried my heart out.

Rumi

KONYA, DECEMBER 1245

Bent on praying the morning prayer together in the open air, Shams and I left the house shortly after dawn. We rode our horses for a while, through meadows and valleys and across ice-cold streams, enjoying the breeze on our faces. Scarecrows in wheat fields greeted us with an eerie poise, and newly washed clothes in front of a farmhouse fluttered madly in the breeze as we passed by, pointing in all directions into the semidarkness.

On the way back, Shams pulled at the reins of his horse and pointed to a massive oak tree outside the town. Together we sat under the tree, the sky hanging above our heads in shades of purple. Shams placed his cloak on the ground, and as calls to prayer echoed from mosques near and far, we prayed there together.

"When I first came to Konya, I sat under this tree," Shams said. He smiled at a distant memory, but then grew pensive and said, "A peasant gave me a ride. He was a great admirer of yours. He told me your sermons cured sadness."

"They used to call me the Wizard of Words," I said. "But it all feels so far away now. I don't want to give sermons anymore. I feel like I am done."

"You *are* the Wizard of Words," Shams said determinedly. "But instead of a preaching mind, you have a chanting heart now."

I didn't know what he meant by that, and I didn't ask. The dawn had erased what remained of the night before, turning the sky into a blameless orange. Far ahead of us, the town was waking up, crows were diving into vegetable gardens to peck at whatever they could steal, doors were screeching, donkeys braying, and stoves burning as everyone got ready for a brand-new day.

"People everywhere are struggling on their own for fulfillment, but without any guidance as to how to achieve it," murmured Shams with a shake of his head. "Your words help them. And I'll do everything in my power to help *you*. I am your servant."

"Don't say that," I protested. "You are my friend."

Oblivious to my objection, Shams continued. "My only concern is the shell you have been living in. As a famous preacher, you have been surrounded by fawning admirers. But how well do you know common people? Drunks, beggars, thieves, prostitutes, gamblers—the most inconsolable and the most downtrodden. Can we love all of God's creatures? It is a difficult test, and one that only a few can pass."

As he kept speaking, I saw gentleness and concern in his face, and something else that looked almost like maternal compassion.

"You are right," I conceded. "I have always lived a protected life. I don't even know how ordinary people live."

Shams picked up a lump of soil, and as he crumbled it between his fingers, he added softly, "If we can embrace the universe as a whole, with all its differences and contradictions, everything will melt into One."

With this, Shams picked up a dead branch and drew a large circle around the oak tree. When he was done, he raised his arms toward the sky, as if wishing to be pulled up by an invisible rope, and uttered the ninety-nine names of God. At the same time, he began to whirl inside the circle, first slowly and tenderly but then accelerating steadily, like a late-afternoon breeze. Soon he was whirling with the speed and might of gusty winds. So captivating was his frenzy that I couldn't help but feel as if the whole universe—the earth, the stars, and the moon—spun with him. I watched this most unusual dance, letting the energy it radiated envelop my soul and body.

Finally Shams slowed down to a halt, his chest rising and falling with every ragged breath, his face white, his voice suddenly deep, as if coming from a distant place. *"The universe is one being. Everything and everyone is interconnected through an invisible web of stories. Whether we are aware of it or not, we are all in a silent conversation. Do no harm. Practice compassion. And do not gossip behind anyone's back—not even a seemingly innocent remark! The words that come out of our mouths do not vanish but are perpetually stored in infinite space, and they will come back to us in due time. One man's pain will hurt us all. One man's joy will make everyone smile,"* he murmured. "This is what one of the forty rules reminds us."

Then he turned his inquisitive gaze to me. There was a shadow of despair in the bottomless depths of his eyes, a wave of sorrow that I had never seen in him before.

"One day you will be known as the Voice of Love," Shams remarked. "East and West, people who have never seen your face will be inspired by your voice."

"How is that going to happen?" I asked incredulously.

"Through your words," Shams answered. "But I am not talking about lectures or sermons. I am talking about poetry."

"Poetry?" My voice cracked. "I don't write poetry. I am a scholar."

This elicited a subtle smile from Shams. "You, my friend, are one of the finest poets the world will ever come to know."

I was about to protest, but the determined look in Shams's eyes stopped me. Besides, I didn't feel like arguing. "Even so, whatever needs to be done, we will do it together. We will walk on this path together."

Shams nodded absently and lapsed into an eerie silence, gazing at the fading colors in the horizon. When he finally spoke, he uttered those ominous words that have never left me, scarring my soul permanently: "As much as I would love to join you, I'm afraid you will have to do it alone."

"What do you mean? Where are you going?" I asked.

With a wistful pucker of the lips, Shams lowered his gaze. "It is not in my hands."

A sudden wind blew in our direction, and the weather turned chilly, as if warning us that the fall would soon be over. It began to rain out of the clear blue sky, in light, warm drops, as faint and delicate as the touch of butterflies. And that was the first time the thought of Shams's leaving me hit me like a sharp pain in the chest.

Sultan Walad

KONYA, DECEMBER 1245

Banter to some, but it pains me to hear the gossip. How can people be so disdainful and scornful with regard to things they know so little about? It is queer, if not frightening, how out of touch with truth people are! They don't understand the depth of the bond between my father and Shams. Apparently they haven't read the Qur'an. Because if they had, they would know that there are similar stories of spiritual companionship, such as the story of Moses and Khidr.

It is in the verse al-Kahf, clear and plain. Moses was an exemplary man, great enough to become a prophet someday, as well as a legendary commander and lawmaker. But there was a time when he sorely needed a spiritual companion to open his third eye. And that companion was no other than Khidr, the Comforter of the Distressed and Dejected.

Khidr said to Moses, "I am a lifelong traveler. God has assigned me to roam the world and do what needs to be done. You say you want to join me in my journeys, but if you follow me, you must not question anything I do. Can you bear to accompany me without questioning? Can you trust me fully?"

"Yes, I can," Moses assured him. "Let me come with you. I promise, I won't ask you any questions."

So they set out on the road, visiting various towns on the way. But when he witnessed Khidr perform senseless actions, like killing a young boy or sinking a boat, Moses could not hold his tongue. "Why did you do those awful things?" he asked desperately.

"What happened to your promise?" Khidr asked back. "Did I not tell you that you can ask me no questions?"

Each time Moses apologized, promising not to ask anything, and each time he broke his promise. In the end, Khidr explained the reason behind each and every one of his actions. Slowly but surely, Moses understood that things that can seem malicious or unfortunate are often a blessing in disguise, whereas things that might seem pleasant can be harmful in the long run. His brief companionship with Khidr was to be the most eye-opening experience in his life.

As in this parable, there are friendships in this world that seem incomprehensible to ordinary people but are in fact conduits to deeper wisdom and insight. This is how I regard Shams's presence in my father's life.

But I know that other people don't see it in the same way, and I am worried. Unfortunately, Shams does not make it easy for people to like him. Sitting at the gate of the seminary in an embarrassing and threatening manner, he stops and interrogates everyone who wants to go in to talk to my father.

"What do you want to see the great Mawlana for?" he asks. "What did you bring as a gift?"

Not knowing what to say, people stammer and falter, even apologize. And Shams sends them away.

Some of these visitors return in a few days with presents, carrying dried fruits, silver dirhams, silk carpets, or newborn lambs. But seeing these goods annoys Shams even more. His black eyes aglow, his face glittering with fervor, he chases them away again.

One day a man got so upset with Shams he shouted, "What gives you the right to block Mawlana's door? You keep asking everyone what they are bringing! How about you? What did *you* bring him?"

"I brought myself," Shams said, just loud enough to be heard. "I sacrificed my head for him."

The man trudged off, mumbling something under his breath, looking more confused than enraged.

The same day I asked Shams if it didn't trouble him that he was so widely misunderstood and underappreciated. Scarcely able to contain my apprehension, I pointed out that he had gained many enemies lately.

Shams looked at me blankly, as if he had no idea what I was talking about. "But I have no enemies," he said with a shrug. "The lovers of God can have critics and even rivals, but they cannot have enemies."

"Yes, but you quarrel with people," I objected.

Shams bristled with fervor. "I don't quarrel with them, I quarrel with their inflated sense of themselves. That's different."

Then he added softly, "It is one of the forty rules: *This world is like a snowy mountain that echoes your voice. Whatever you speak, good or evil, will somehow come back to you. Therefore, if there is someone who harbors ill thoughts about you, saying similarly bad things about him will only make matters worse. You will be locked in a vicious circle of malevolent energy. Instead for forty days and nights say and think nice things about that person. Everything will be different at the end of forty days, because you will be different inside.*"

"But people are saying all sorts of things about you. They even say for two men to be so fond of each other there has to be an unspeakable bond between them," I said, my voice failing me toward the end.

Upon hearing this, Shams put his hand on my arm and smiled his usual calming smile. He then told me a story.

Two men were traveling from one town to another. They came to a stream that had risen due to heavy rainfall. Just when they were about to cross the water, they noticed a young, beautiful woman standing there all alone, in need of help. One of the men immediately went to her side. He picked the woman up and carried her in his arms across the stream. Then he dropped her there, waved good-bye, and the two men went their way.

During the rest of the trip, the second traveler was unusually silent and sullen, not responding to his friend's questions. After several hours of sulking, unable to keep silent anymore, he said, "Why did you touch that woman? She could have seduced you! Men and women cannot come into contact like that!"

The first man responded calmly, "My friend, I carried the woman across the stream, and that is where I left her. It is you who have been carrying her ever since."

"Some people are like that," Shams said. "They carry their own fears and biases on their shoulders, crushed under all that weight. If you hear of anyone who cannot comprehend the depth of the bond between your father and me, tell him to wash his mind!"

Ella

NORTHAMPTON, JUNE 15, 2008

Beloved Ella,

You asked me how I became a Sufi. It didn't happen overnight.

I was born Craig Richardson in Kinlochbervie, a remote harbor in the Highlands of Scotland. Whenever I think about the past, I fondly remember the fishing boats, their nets heavy with fish and strands of seaweed dangling like green snakes, sandpipers scurrying along the shore pecking at worms, ragwort plants growing in the most unexpected places, and the smell of the sea in the background, sharp and salty. That smell, as well as those of the mountains and lochs, and the dreary tranquillity of life in postwar Europe composed the background against which my childhood was set.

While the world tumbled heavily into the 1960s and became the scene of student demonstrations, hijackings, and revolutions, I was cut off from it all in my quiet, green corner. My father owned a secondhand-book store, and my mother raised sheep that produced high-quality wool. As a child I had a touch of both the loneliness of a shepherd and the introspectiveness of a bookseller. Many days I would climb an old tree and gaze out at the scenery, convinced that I would spend my whole life there. Every now and then, my heart would constrict with a longing for adventures, but I liked Kinlochbervie and was happy with the predictability of my life. How could I know that God had other plans for me?

Shortly after I turned twenty, I discovered the two things that would change my life forever. The first was a professional camera. I enrolled in a photography class, not knowing that what I saw as a simple hobby would become a lifelong passion. The second was love—a Dutch woman who was touring Europe with friends. Her name was Margot.

She was eight years my elder, beautiful, tall, and remarkably headstrong. Margot regarded herself as a bohemian, an idealist, a radical, a bisexual, a leftist, an individualist anarchist, a multiculturalist, a human-rights advocate, a counterculture activist, an ecofeminist—labels I couldn't even define should one ask me what they meant. But I had early on observed that she was one more thing: a pendulum woman. Capable of swinging from extreme joy to extreme depression in the span of a few minutes, Margot had unpredictability written all over her. Always furious at what she construed as "the hypocrisy of the bourgeois lifestyle," she questioned every detail in life, waging battles against society. To this day it is still a mystery to me why I did not run away from her. But I didn't. Instead I let myself get sucked into the whirling vortex of her animated personality. I was head over heels in love.

She was an impossible combination, full of revolutionary ideas, unbridled courage, and creativity, yet as fragile as a crystal flower. I promised myself to stay by her side and protect her not only from the outside world but also from herself. Did she ever love me as much as I loved her? I don't think so. But I know she did love me in her own self-centered and self-destructive way.

This is how I ended up in Amsterdam at the age of twenty. We got married there. Margot dedicated her time to helping refugees who had found themselves in Europe for political or humanitarian reasons. Working for an organization that specialized in immigrants' needs, she helped traumatized people from the most troubled corners of the world find their feet in Holland. She was their guardian angel. Families from Indonesia, Somalia, Argentina, and Palestine named their daughters after her.

As for me, I wasn't interested in greater causes, being too busy working my way up the corporate ladder. After graduating from business school, I started working for an international firm. The fact that Margot didn't care about my status or salary made me yearn even more for the trinkets of success. Hungry for power, I wanted to make my mark on the world.

I had our life completely planned out. In two years we would start having children. Two little girls completed my picture of an ideal family. I was confident of the future that awaited us. After all, we lived in one of the safest places on earth, not in one of those troubled countries that kept pumping immigrants into the European continent like a broken faucet. We were young, healthy, and in love. Nothing could go wrong. It is hard to believe I am fifty-four years old now and Margot is no longer alive.

She was the healthy one. A staunch vegan at a time when the word hadn't been coined, she ate only healthy things, exercised routinely, stayed away from drugs. Her angelic face brimmed with health, her body was always thin, brisk, and angular. She took such good care of herself that despite the age difference between us, I looked older than she did.

She died a most unexpected and simple death. One night, on her way back from a visit to a famous Russian journalist who had applied for asylum, her car broke down in the middle of the highway. And she, who always abided by the rules, did something completely out of her character. Instead of putting on the flashers and waiting for help, she got out of the car and decided to walk to the next village. Wearing a taupe trench coat with dark trousers, she didn't have a flashlight or anything that would make her more noticeable. A vehicle hit her—a trailer from Yugoslavia. The driver said he never saw her. So completely had Margot melted into the night.

I was a boy once. Love opened up my eyes to a more fulfilled life. After I lost the woman I loved, I metamorphosed drastically. Neither a boy nor an adult, I became a trapped animal. This stage of my life I call my encounter with the letter *S* in the word "Sufi."

I hope I haven't bored you with such a long letter.

Love,
Aziz

Desert Rose the Harlot

KONYA, JANUARY 1246

Barricading me in since the disgrace I caused at the mosque, the patron doesn't let me go anywhere. I am grounded forever. But it doesn't upset me. The truth is, I haven't been feeling much of anything lately.

Every morning the face that greets me in the mirror looks paler. I don't comb my hair or pinch my cheeks to redden them anymore. The other girls constantly complain about my bad looks, saying that it keeps the customers away. They may be right. Which is why I was quite surprised when the other day I was told that a particular client insisted on seeing me.

To my horror, it turned out to be Baybars.

As soon as we were alone in the room, I asked, "What is a security guard like you doing here?"

"Well, my coming to a brothel is no more bizarre than a harlot going to a mosque," he said, his voice heavy with insinuation.

"I am sure you would have loved to lynch me that day," I said. "I owe my life to Shams of Tabriz."

"Don't mention that revolting name. That guy is a heretic!"

"No, he is not!" I don't know what came over me, but I heard myself say, "Since that day Shams of Tabriz has come to see me many times."

"Hah! A dervish in a brothel!" Baybars snorted. "Why am I not surprised?"

"It's not like that," I said. "It's not like that at all."

I had never told this to anyone else before and had no idea why I was telling Baybars now, but Shams had been visiting me every week for the past several months. How he managed to sneak inside without being seen by the others, especially by the patron, was beyond my comprehension. Anyone else would assume that it was with the aid of black magic. But I knew it wasn't that. He was a good man, Shams. A man of faith. And he had special talents. Other than my mother back in my childhood, Shams was the only person who treated me with unconditional compassion. He had taught me not to be despondent, no matter what. Whenever I told him there was no way someone like me could shed the past, he would remind me of one of his rules: *The past is an interpretation. The future is an illusion. The world does not move through time as if it were a straight line, proceeding from the past to the future. Instead time moves through and within us, in endless spirals.*

Eternity does not mean infinite time, but simply timelessness.

If you want to experience eternal illumination, put the past and the future out of your mind and remain within the present moment.

Shams always told me, "You see, the present moment is all there is and all that there ever will be. When you grasp this truth, you'll have nothing to fear anymore. Then you can walk out of this brothel for good."

Baybars was watching my face carefully. When he looked at me, his right eye looked off to the side. It felt as if there were another person in the room with us, someone I couldn't see. He scared me.

Realizing that it would be best not to talk about Shams anymore, I served him a pitcher of beer, which he drank in a hurry.

"So what is *your* specialty?" Baybars asked after he guzzled his second beer. "Don't you girls each have a talent? Can you belly dance?"

I told him I didn't have such talents and whatever gift I had in the past was gone now, as I was suffering from an unknown illness. The boss would have killed me if she heard me say such things to a client, but I didn't care. The truth was, I secretly hoped Baybars would spend the night with another girl.

But, to my disappointment, Baybars shrugged and said he didn't care. Then he took out his pouch, spilled a reddish brown substance from it into his palm, and popped it into his mouth, chewing slowly. "Do you want some?" he asked.

I shook my head. I knew what it was.

"You don't know what you are missing." He grinned as he reclined on the bed, drifting away from his own body into a stupor of cannabis.

That evening, high on beer and cannabis, Baybars bragged about the terrible things he had seen on the battlefields. Even though Genghis Khan was dead and his flesh decomposed, his ghost still accompanied the Mongol armies, Baybars said. Egged on by the ghost, the Mongol army was attacking caravans, plundering villages, and massacring women and men alike. He told me about the veil of silence, as soft and peaceful as a blanket on a cold winter night, that descended upon a battlefield after hundreds had been killed and wounded, and dozens more were about to give up their last breath.

"The silence that follows a massive disaster is the most peaceful sound you can hear on the surface of the world," he said, his voice slurring.

"It sounds so sad," I murmured.

Suddenly he had no more words inside him. There was nothing else to talk about. Grabbing my arm, he pushed me onto the bed and pulled off my robe. His eyes were bloodshot, his voice hoarse, and his smell was a repugnant mixture of cannabis, sweat, and hunger. He entered me in one harsh, abrasive thrust. I tried to move aside and relax my thighs to lessen the pain, but he pressed both hands on my bosom with such force that it was impossible to budge. He kept rocking back and forth even long after he came inside me, like a string puppet that was manipulated by unseen hands and could not possibly stop. Clearly dissatisfied, he kept moving with such roughness that I feared he was going to get hard again, but then suddenly it all came to an end. Still on top of me, he looked at my face with pure hatred, as if the body that had aroused him a moment ago now disgusted him.

"Put something on," he ordered as he rolled aside.

I put on my robe, watching out of the corner of my eye as he popped more cannabis into his mouth. "From now on, I want you to be my mistress," he said with his jaw jutting out.

It wasn't all that uncommon for clients to come up with such demands. I knew how to handle these delicate situations, giving the client the false impression that I would love to be his mistress and serve solely him, but for that to happen he had to spend a lot of money and make the patron happy first. But today I didn't feel like pretending.

"I can't be your mistress," I said. "I am going to leave this place very soon."

Baybars guffawed as if this were the funniest thing he had ever heard. "You can't do that," he said with certainty.

I knew I shouldn't be quarreling with him, but I couldn't help it. "You and I are not that different. We both have done things in the past that we deeply regret. But you have been made a security guard, thanks to your uncle's position. I have no uncle backing me, you see."

Baybars's face became wooden, and his eyes, cold and distant up till now, suddenly widened with fury. Dashing forward, he grabbed me by the hair. "I was nice to you, wasn't I?" he growled. "Who do you think you are?"

I opened my mouth to say something, but a sharp stab of pain silenced me. Baybars punched me in the face and pushed me against the wall.

It wasn't the first time. I had been beaten by clients before but never this badly.

I fell on the floor, and then Baybars started to kick me hard in the ribs and legs while hurling insults at me. It was then and there that I had the strangest experience. As I cringed in pain, my body crushed under the weight of each blow, my soul—or what felt like it—separated from my body, turning itself into a kite, light and free.

Soon I was floating in the ether. As if thrown into a peaceful vacuum where there was nothing to resist and nowhere to go, I simply hovered. I passed over recently harvested wheat fields, where the wind fluttered the head scarves of peasant girls and at night, fireflies glinted here and there like fairy lights. It felt like falling, except falling upward into the bottomless sky.

Was I dying? If this was what death was like, it wasn't terrifying at all. My worries diminished. I had tumbled into a place of absolute lightness and purity, a magic zone where nothing could pull me down. And suddenly I realized I was facing my worst dread and, to my surprise, it wasn't frightful. Wasn't it because of the fear of being harmed that I had been scared to leave the brothel all this time? If I could manage not to be scared of death, I realized with an expanding heart, I could leave this rat hole.

Shams of Tabriz was right. The only filth was the filth inside. I shut my eyes and imagined this other me, pristine and penitent and looking much younger, walking out of the brothel and into a new life. Glowing with youth and confidence, this was what my face would have looked like if only I'd experienced security and love in my life. The vision was so alluring and so very real, despite the blood before my eyes and the throbbing in my ribs, that I couldn't help smiling.

Kimya

KONYA, JANUARY 1246

Blushing and sweating slightly, I mustered the courage to talk to Shams of Tabriz. I had been meaning to ask him about the deepest reading of the Qur'an, but for weeks I hadn't had a chance. Though we lived under the same roof, our paths never crossed. But this morning as I was sweeping the courtyard, Shams appeared next to me, alone and in the mood to chat. And this time not only did I manage to talk with him longer, but I also managed to look him in the eye.

"How is it going, dear Kimya?" he asked jovially.

I couldn't help noticing that Shams looked dazed, as if he had just woken up from sleep, or else another vision. I knew he had been having visions, lately more often than ever, and by now I had learned to read the signs. Each time he had a vision, his face became pale and his eyes dreamy.

"A storm is impending," Shams murmured, squinting at the sky, where grayish flakes swirled, heralding the first snow of the year.

This seemed the right time to ask him the question I had been holding inside. "Remember when you told me that we all understood the Qur'an in accordance with the depth of our insight?" I said carefully. "Ever since then I have been meaning to ask you about the fourth level."

Now Shams turned toward me, his gaze raking my face. I liked it when he stared at me so attentively. I thought he was his handsomest at times like this, his lips pursed, his forehead slightly creased.

"The fourth level is unspeakable," he said. "There is a stage after which language fails us. When you step into the zone of love, you won't need language."

"I wish I could step into the zone of love someday," I blurted, but then instantly felt embarrassed. "I mean, so that I could read the Qur'an with deeper insight."

An odd little smile etched Shams's mouth. "If you have it in you, I am sure you will. You'll dive into the fourth current, and then you'll be the stream."

I had forgotten this mixed feeling that only Shams was capable of stirring in me. Next to him I felt both like a child learning life anew and like a woman ready to nurture life inside my womb.

"What do you mean, 'if you have it in you'?" I asked. "You mean, like destiny?"

"Yes, that's right." Shams nodded.

"But what does destiny mean?"

"I cannot tell you what destiny is. All I can tell you is what it isn't. In fact, there is another rule regarding this question. *Destiny doesn't mean that your life has been strictly predetermined. Therefore, to leave everything to fate and to not actively contribute to the music of the universe is a sign of sheer ignorance.*

"The music of the universe is all-pervading and it is composed on forty different levels.

"Your destiny is the level where you will play your tune. You might not change your instrument but how well to play is entirely in your hands."

I must have given him a befuddled look, for Shams felt the need to explain. He placed his hand on mine, gently squeezing. With dark, deep eyes glinting he said, "Allow me to tell you a story."

And here is what he told me:

One day a young woman asked a dervish what fate was about. "Come with me," the dervish said. "Let's take a look at the world together." Soon they ran into a procession. A killer was being taken to the plaza to be hanged. The dervish asked, "That man will be executed. But is that because somebody gave him the money with which he bought his murder weapon? Or is it because nobody stopped him while he was committing the crime? Or is it because someone caught him afterward? Where is the cause and effect in this case?"

I interjected, cutting his story short, and said, "That man is going to be hanged because what he did was awful. He is paying for what he did. There is the cause and there, too, the effect. There are good things and bad things, and a difference between the two."

"Ah, sweet Kimya," Shams replied, in a small voice as if he suddenly felt tired. "You like distinctions because you think they make life easier. What if things are not that clear all the time?"

"But God wants us to be clear. Otherwise there would be no notions of haram or halal. There would be no hell and heaven. Imagine if you could not scare people with hell or encourage them with heaven. The world would be a whole lot worse."

Snowflakes skittered in the wind, and Shams leaned forward to pull my shawl tighter. For a passing moment, I stood frozen, inhaling his smell. It was a mixture of sandalwood and soft amber with a faint, crisp tang underneath, like the smell of earth after the rain. I felt a warm glow in the pit of my stomach and a wave of desire between my legs. How embarrassing it was—and yet, oddly, not embarrassing at all.

"In love, boundaries are blurred," said Shams, staring at me half compassionately, half concernedly.

Was he talking about the Love of God or the love between a woman and a man? Could he be referring to us? Was there such a thing as "us"?

Unaware of my thoughts, Shams continued. "I don't care about haram or halal. I'd rather extinguish the fire in hell and burn heaven, so that people could start loving God for no other reason than love."

"You shouldn't go around saying such things. People are mean. Not everyone would understand," I said, not realizing that I would have to think more about this warning before its full implications could sink in.

Shams smiled a brave, almost valiant smile. I allowed him to hold me captive, his palm feeling hot and heavy against mine.

"Perhaps you are right, but don't you think that gives me all the more reason to speak my mind? Besides, narrow-minded people are deaf anyhow. To their sealed ears, whatever I say is sheer blasphemy."

"Whereas to me everything you say is only sweet!"

Shams looked at me with a disbelief that verged on astonishment. But I was more shocked than he was. How could I have said such a thing? Had I taken leave of my senses? I must have been possessed by a djinn or something.

"I'm sorry, I'd better go now," I said as I jumped to my feet.

My cheeks burning with shame, my heart pounding with all the things we had said and left unsaid, I scampered out of the courtyard back into the house. But even as I ran, I knew that a threshold had been crossed. After this moment I could not ignore the truth that I had known all along: I was in love with Shams of Tabriz.

Shams

KONYA, JANUARY 1246

Bad-mouthing one another is second nature to many people. I heard the rumors about me. Ever since I came to Konya, there have been so many of them. It doesn't surprise me. Although it clearly says in the Qur'an that slandering is one of the gravest sins ever, most people make hardly any effort to avoid it. They always condemn those who drink wine, or are on the lookout for adulterous women to stone, but when it comes to gossiping, which is a far more serious sin in the eyes of God, they take no notice of any wrongdoing.

All of this reminds me of a story.

One day a man came running to a Sufi and said, panting, "Hey, they are carrying trays, look over there!"

The Sufi answered calmly, "What is it to us? Is it any of my business?"

"But they are taking those trays to your house!" the man exclaimed.

"Then is it any of your business?" the Sufi said.

Unfortunately, people always watch the trays of others. Instead of minding their own business, they pass judgment on other people. It never ceases to amaze me the things they fabricate! Their imagination knows no limits when it comes to suspicion and slander.

Apparently there are people in this town who believe that I am the secret commander of the Assassins. Some go so far as to claim that I am the son of the last Ismaili imam of Alamut. They say I am so skilled in black magic and witchcraft that whomever I curse will die on the spot. Some others even make the outrageous accusation that I have put a spell on Rumi. Just to make sure he doesn't break the spell, I force him to drink snake soup every day at dawn!

When I hear such nonsense, I laugh and walk away. What else is there to do? What harm comes to a dervish from the sourness of others? If the whole world were swallowed by the sea, what would it matter to a duck?

Nevertheless, I can see that the people around me are worried, particularly Sultan Walad. He is such a bright young man I am sure someday soon he will become his father's right-hand man. And then there is Kimya, sweet Kimya. . . . She, too, seems concerned. But the worst thing about the gossip is that Rumi gets his share of vilification. Unlike me, he isn't used to being bad-mouthed by others. It torments me to see him distressed over the words of ignorant people. Mawlana has immense beauty inside. I, on the other hand, have both beauty and ugliness. It is easier for me to deal with the ugliness of others than it is for him. But how can an erudite scholar who is used to having serious conversations and logical conclusions handle the claptrap of ignorant people?

No wonder the Prophet Muhammad said, "In this world take pity on three kinds of people. The rich man who has lost his fortune, the well-respected man who has lost his respectability, and the wise man who is surrounded by ignorants."

And yet I can't help thinking that there could be some good for Rumi in all this. Slander is a hurtful, albeit necessary, element in Rumi's inner transformation. His whole life he has been admired, respected, and imitated, having a reputation beyond reproach. He doesn't know how it feels to be misunderstood and criticized by others. Nor has he been pestered by the sort of vulnerability and loneliness that one feels from time to time. His ego has not been bruised, not even slightly damaged, by other people. But he needs that. As hurtful as it is, being slandered is ultimately good for one on the path. It is Rule Number Thirty: *The true Sufi is such that even when he is unjustly accused, attacked, and condemned from all sides, he patiently endures, uttering not a single bad word about any of his critics. A Sufi never apportions blame. How can there be opponents or rivals or even "others" when there is no "self" in the first place?*

How can there be anyone to blame when there is only One?

Ella

NORTHAMPTON, JUNE 17, 2008

Beloved Ella,

You were kind enough to ask me to tell you more. Frankly, I do not find it easy to write about this period of my life for it brings back unwanted memories. But here it is:

After Margot's death my life underwent a dramatic change. Losing myself in a circle of addicts, becoming a regular at all-night parties and dance clubs in an Amsterdam I had never known before, I looked for comfort and compassion in all the wrong places. I became a night creature, befriended the wrong people, woke up in strangers' beds, and lost more than twenty-five pounds in just a few months.

The first time I sniffed heroin, I threw up and got so sick I couldn't keep my head up the whole day. My body had rejected the drug. It was a sign but I was in no state to see it. Before I knew it, I had replaced sniffing with injections. Marijuana, hashish, acid, cocaine—I tried whatever I could get my hands on. It didn't take me long to make a mess of myself, mentally and physically. Everything I did, I did to stay high.

And when high I planned spectacular ways to kill myself. I even tried hemlock, in the manner of Socrates, but either its poison didn't have an effect on me or the dark herb I bought at the back door of a Chinese takeout was some ordinary plant. Perhaps they sold me some kind of green tea and had a laugh at my expense. Many mornings I woke up in unfamiliar places with someone new by my side, but with the same emptiness eating me up inside. Women took care of me. Some were younger than me, others much older. I lived in their houses, slept in their beds, stayed in their weekend cottages, ate the food they cooked, wore their husbands' clothes, shopped with their credit cards, and refused to give them even a speck of the love they demanded and no doubt deserved.

The life I had chosen quickly took its toll. I lost my job, I lost my friends, and finally I lost the apartment Margot and I had spent many happy days in. When it became apparent that I couldn't bear this lifestyle anymore, I stayed in squat houses where everything was collective. I spent more than fifteen months at one squat house in Rotterdam. There were no doors in the building, neither outside nor inside, not even in the bathroom. We shared everything. Our songs, dreams, pocket money, drugs, food, beds . . . Everything but the pain.

Years into a life of drugs and debauchery, I hit rock bottom, a shadow of the man I used to be. As I was washing my face one morning, I stared into the mirror. I had never seen anybody so young who was so drained and sad. I went back to bed and cried like a child. The same day I rummaged through the boxes where I kept Margot's belongings. Her books, clothes, records, hairpins, notes, pictures—one by one, I bade farewell to every keepsake. Then I put them back in boxes and gave them away to the children of the immigrants she cared so deeply about. It was 1977.

With the help of God-sent connections, I found a job at a well-known travel magazine as a photographer. This is how I embarked on a journey to North Africa with a canvas suitcase and a framed picture of Margot, running away from the man I had become.

Then a British anthropologist I met in the Saharan Atlas gave me an idea. He asked me if I had ever considered being the first Western photographer to sneak into the holiest cities of Islam. I didn't know what he was talking about. He said there was a Saudi law that strictly forbade non-Muslims from entering Mecca and Medina. No Christians or Jews were allowed, unless one found a way to break in to the city and take pictures. If caught, you could go to jail, or even worse. I was all ears. The thrill of trespassing into forbidden territory, achieving what no one else had accomplished before, the surge of adrenaline, not to mention the fame and money that would come at the end . . . I was attracted to the idea like a bee drawn to a pot of honey.

The anthropologist said I could not do this alone and needed a connection. He suggested checking the Sufi brotherhoods in the area. You never know, they might agree to help, he said.

I didn't know anything about Sufism, and I couldn't have cared less. As long as they offered to help, I was happy to meet the Sufis. To me they were just a means to an end. But then, at the time, so was everyone and everything else.

Life is odd, Ella. In the end I never made it to Mecca or Medina. Not then, not later. Not even after I converted to Islam. Destiny took me on a different route altogether, one of unexpected twists and turns, each of which changed me so profoundly and irrevocably that after a while the original destination lost its significance. Though motivated by purely materialistic reasons at the outset, when the journey came to an end, I was a transformed man.

As for the Sufis, who could have known that what I had initially seen as a means to an end would very soon become an end in itself? This part of my life I call my encounter with the letter *u* in the word "Sufi."

Love,
Aziz

Desert Rose the Harlot

KONYA, FEBRUARY 1246

Bitter and bleak, the day I left the brothel was the coldest day in forty years. The narrow, serpentine streets glistened with fresh snow, and sharp pendants of ice hung from the roofs of the houses and the minarets of the mosques in dangerous beauty. By midafternoon the chill had become so severe there were frozen cats on the streets with whiskers turned into thin threads of ice, and several ramshackle houses collapsed under the weight of the snow. After the street cats, Konya's homeless suffered the most. There were half a dozen frozen bodies—all curled up in the fetal position with beatific smiles on their faces, as if expecting to be reborn into a better and warmer life.

Late in the afternoon, when everyone was taking a nap before the hustle of the evening began, I sneaked out of my room. I took no more than a few simple clothes, leaving behind all the silk garments and accessories I used to wear for special customers. Whatever was earned in the brothel had to stay in the brothel.

Halfway down the stairs, I saw Magnolia standing at the main door, chewing the brown leaves she was addicted to. Older than all the other girls in the brothel, lately she had been complaining about sudden burning heat. At night I heard her toss and turn in bed. It was no secret that her womanhood was drying up. Younger girls jokingly said they envied Magnolia, since she would not have to worry about having periods, pregnancies, or terminations anymore and could sleep with a man every single day of the month, but we all knew that an aged prostitute had little chance of survival.

As soon as I saw Magnolia standing there, I knew I had only two options: either return to my room and forget about running away or walk through that door and bear the consequences. My heart chose the latter.

"Hey, Magnolia, are you feeling better?" I said, adopting what I hoped was a relaxed and casual tone of voice.

Magnolia's face brightened but then darkened again as she noticed the bag in my hand. There was no point in lying. She knew that the patron had forbidden me to leave my room, never mind leaving the brothel.

"Are you leaving?" Magnolia gasped as if the question scared her.

I didn't say anything. Now it was her turn to make a choice. She could either stop me in my tracks and alert everyone to my plan or simply let me go. Magnolia stared at me, her expression grave and embittered.

"Go back to your room, Desert Rose," she said. "The patron will send Jackal Head after you. Don't you know what he did to . . . ?"

But she didn't finish her sentence. That was one of the unwritten rules in the brothel: We didn't bring up the stories of the unfortunate girls who had worked here before us and had met a premature end, and on those rare occasions when we did mention them, we took care not to utter their names. There was no point in disturbing them in their graves. They had already led tough lives; it was better to let them rest.

"Even if you manage to escape, how are you going to make a living?" Magnolia insisted. "You will starve to death."

What I saw in Magnolia's eyes was fear—not the fear that I could fail and be punished by the patron but the fear that I might succeed. I was going to do the one thing she had always dreamed about and yet never dared to carry out, and now she both respected and hated me for my audacity. I felt a momentary pang of doubt and would have gone back had the voice of Shams of Tabriz not kept echoing in my head.

"Let me go, Magnolia," I said. "I'm not staying here another day."

After being beaten by Baybars and looking death in the face, I felt that something within me had changed irreversibly. It was as if I had no more fear left inside me. One way or another, I didn't care. I was determined to dedicate what remained of my life to God. Whether this would be for a single day or for many more years to come did not matter. Shams of Tabriz had said that faith and love turned human beings into heroes because they removed all the fear and anxiety from their hearts. I was beginning to understand what he meant.

And the strange thing is, Magnolia understood it, too. She gave me a long, painful look and slowly moved aside, opening the way out for me.

Ella

NORTHAMPTON, JUNE 19, 2008

Beloved Ella,

Thank you for being so compassionate. I'm glad you like my story and that you think about it a lot. I am not used to talking about my past with anyone, and it strangely makes me lighter to share all this with you.

I spent the summer of 1977 with a group of Sufis in Morocco. My room was white, small, and simple. It had just the bare necessities: a sleeping mat, an oil lamp, an amber rosary, a potted flower by the window, an evil-eye charm, and a walnut desk with a book of Rumi's poetry in the drawer. There was no telephone, no television, no clock, and no electricity. I didn't mind. Having lived in squat houses for years, I couldn't see why I shouldn't survive in a dervish lodge.

On my first evening, Master Sameed came to my room to check on me. He said I was more than welcome to stay with them until ready to leave for Mecca. But there was one condition: no drugs!

I remember feeling my face burn, like a child caught with his hand in the biscuit tin. How did they know? Had they been rummaging through my suitcase while I was out? I'll never forget what the master said next: "We don't need to look through your belongings to know you are using drugs, Brother Craig. You have the eyes of an addict."

And the funny thing is, Ella, until that day I had never thought of myself in those terms. I was so sure that I was in control and that drugs helped me with my problems. "Numbing the pain is not the same as healing it," Master Sameed said. "When the anesthesia wears off, the pain is still there."

I knew he was right. With conceited determination I handed them all the drugs I carried with me, even my sleeping pills. But soon it became apparent that my determination was not strong enough to pull me through what was to come. During the four months I stayed in that small lodge, I broke my promise and strayed badly on more than a dozen occasions. For one who chose intoxication over sobriety, it wasn't hard to find drugs, even as a foreigner. One night I came to the lodge dead drunk and found all the doors bolted from inside. I had to sleep in the garden. The next day Master Sameed asked nothing, and I offered no apologies.

Apart from these shaming incidents, I managed to get along fine with the Sufis, enjoying the calm that settled on the lodge in the evenings. Being there felt peculiar but oddly peaceful, and though I was no stranger to living under the same roof with many people, I found something there I had never experienced before: inner peace.

On the surface we lived a collective life where everyone ate, drank, and performed the same activities at the same time, but underneath we were expected and encouraged to remain alone and look within. On the Sufi path, first you discover the art of being alone amid the crowd. Next you discover the crowd within your solitude—the voices inside you.

While I waited for the Sufis in Morocco to safely sneak me into Mecca and Medina, I read extensively on Sufi philosophy and poetry, at first out of boredom and lack of anything better to do, then with growing interest. Like a man who had not realized how thirsty he was until he took his first sip of water, I found that my encounter with Sufism made me yearn for more. Of all the books I read that long summer, it was the collected poems of Rumi that had the most impact on me.

Three months later, out of the blue, Master Sameed said I reminded him of someone—a wandering dervish by the name of Shams of Tabriz. He said that some people regarded Shams as a brazen heretic, but if you asked Rumi, he was the moon and the sun.

I was intrigued. But it was more than simple curiosity. As I listened to Master Sameed tell me more about Shams, I felt a shiver down my spine, an odd feeling of déjà vu.

Now, you are going to think I'm crazy. But I swear to God, at that moment I heard a rustle of silk in the background, first far off, then drawing nearer, and I saw the shadow of someone who wasn't there. Perhaps it was the evening breeze moving across the branches, or maybe it was a pair of angel wings. Either way, I suddenly knew that I didn't need to go anywhere. Not anymore. I was sick and tired of always longing to be somewhere else, somewhere beyond, always in a rush despite myself.

I was already where I wanted to be. All I needed was to stay and look within. This new part of my life I call my encounter with the letter *f* in the word "Sufi."

Love,

Aziz

Shams

KONYA, FEBRUARY 1246

Boding well to be an eventful day, the morning proceeded faster than usual, and the sky hung low and gray. Late in the afternoon, I found Rumi in his room sitting by the window, his forehead creased in contemplation, his fingers moving restlessly over rosary beads. The room was dim on account of the heavy velvet curtains being half closed, and there was a strange wedge of daylight that fell upon the spot where Rumi sat, giving the whole scene a dreamy quality. I couldn't help but wonder whether Rumi would see the real intention behind what I was about to ask him to do, or would he be shocked and upset?

As I stood there absorbing the serenity of the moment, but also feeling slightly nervous, I had a glimpse of a vision. I saw Rumi, a much older and frailer version of himself, clad in a dark green robe and sitting in exactly the same spot, looking more compassionate and generous than ever, but with a permanent scar on his heart in the shape of me. I understood two things at once: That Rumi would spend his old age here in this house. And that the wound left by my absence would never heal. Tears pricked in my eyes.

"Are you all right? You look pale," said Rumi.

I forced myself to smile, but the burden of what I was planning to say next weighed heavily on my shoulders. My voice came out a bit cranky and less forceful than I intended. "Not really. I am very thirsty, and there is nothing in this house to quench my thirst."

"Would you like me to ask Kerra what she can do about it?" Rumi asked.

"No, because what I need is not in the kitchen. It is in the tavern. I am in the mood to get drunk, you see."

I pretended not to notice the shadow of incomprehension that crossed Rumi's face, and I continued. "Instead of going to the kitchen for water, would you go to the tavern for wine?"

"You mean, you want me to get you wine?" Rumi asked, pronouncing the last word cautiously, as if afraid of breaking it.

"That's right. I'd so much appreciate it if you would get us some wine. Two bottles would be enough, one for you, one for me. But do me a favor, please. When you go to the tavern, don't just simply get the bottles and come back. Stay there for a while. Talk to the people. I'll be waiting here for you. No need to rush."

Rumi gave me a look that was half irritated, half bewildered. I recalled the face of the novice in Baghdad who had wanted to accompany me but cared too much about his reputation to take the plunge. His concern for the opinions of others had held him back. Now I wondered if his reputation was going to hold Rumi back, too.

But to my great relief, Rumi stood up and nodded.

"I have never been to a tavern before and have never consumed wine. I don't think drinking is the right thing to do. But I trust you fully, because I trust the love between us. There must be a reason you have asked me to do such a thing. I need to find out what that reason is. I'll go and bring us wine."

With that, he said good-bye and walked out.

As soon as he was out of the room, I fell to the ground in a state of profound ecstasy. Grabbing the amber rosary Rumi had left behind, I thanked God over and over again for giving me a true companion and prayed that his beautiful soul would never sober up from the drunkenness of Divine Love.

PART FOUR

Fire

THE THINGS THAT DAMAGE,
DEVASTATE, AND DESTROY

Suleiman the Drunk

KONYA, FEBRUARY 1246

Beguiled by wine, I have had many crazy delusions when drunk, but seeing the great Rumi enter the tavern door was really wild, even for me. I pinched myself, but the vision didn't vanish.

"Hey, Hristos, what did you serve me, man?" I yelled. "That last bottle of wine must have been some mighty booze. You'd never guess what I'm seeing right now."

"Hush, you idiot," whispered someone from behind me.

I looked around to see who was trying to quiet me and was stunned to find every man in the tavern, including Hristos, gawking at the door. The whole place had plunged into an eerie silence, and even the tavern dog, Saqui, seemed perplexed as he lay with his floppy ears glued to the floor. The Persian rug merchant stopped singing those awful melodies he called songs. Instead he swayed on his feet, holding his chin up with the overstated seriousness of a drunk who was trying to appear to be otherwise.

It was Hristos who broke the silence. "Welcome to my tavern, Mawlana," he said, his voice dripping with politeness. "It is an honor to see you under this roof. How may I help you?"

I blinked repeatedly as it finally dawned on me that it really was Rumi standing there.

"Thank you," Rumi said with a large but flat smile. "I'd like to get some wine."

Poor Hristos was so surprised to hear this that his jaw dropped. When he could move again, he ushered Rumi to the first available table, which happened to be next to mine!

"Selamun aleykum," Rumi greeted me as soon as he sat down.

I greeted him back and uttered a few pleasantries, but I am not sure the words came out right. With his tranquil expression, expensive robe, and elegant dark brown caftan, Rumi looked totally out of place.

I leaned forward and, dropping my voice to a whisper, said, "Would it be terribly rude if I ask what a man like you is doing here?"

"I'm going through a Sufi trial," Rumi said, winking at me as if we were best friends. "I've been sent here by Shams so that I could have my reputation ruined."

"And is that a good thing?" I asked.

Rumi laughed. "Well, it depends on how you look at it. Sometimes it is necessary to destroy all attachments in order to win over your self. If we are too attached to our family, our position in society, even our local school or mosque, to the extent that they stand in the way of Union with God, we need to tear those attachments down."

I wasn't sure I was following him correctly, but somehow this explanation made perfect sense to my addled mind. I had always suspected that these Sufis were a crazy, colorful bunch capable of all kinds of eccentricities.

Now it was Rumi's turn to lean forward and ask in the same whispery tone, "Would it be terribly rude if I asked you how you got that scar on your face?"

"It's not a very interesting story, I'm afraid," I said. "I was walking home late at night, and I bumped into this security guard who beat the crap out of me."

"But why?" asked Rumi, looking genuinely concerned.

"Because I had drunk wine," I said, pointing to the bottle that Hristos had just placed in front of Rumi.

Rumi shook his head. At first he seemed entirely befuddled, as if he didn't believe that such things could happen, but soon his lips twisted into a friendly smile. And just like that, we continued to talk. Over bread and goat cheese, we conversed about faith and friendship and other things in life that I thought I had long forgotten but was now delighted to rake up from my heart.

Shortly after sunset Rumi rose to leave. Everyone in the tavern stood to bid him farewell. It was quite a scene.

"You cannot leave without telling us why wine has been forbidden," I said.

Hristos ran to my side with a frown, worried that my question might annoy his prestigious customer. "Hush, Suleiman. Why do you have to ask such things?"

"No, seriously," I insisted, staring at Rumi. "You have seen us. We are not evil people, but that is what they say about us all the time. You tell me, what is so wrong with drinking wine, provided we behave ourselves and don't harm anyone?"

Despite an open window in the corner, the air inside the tavern had become musty and smoky, and suffused with anticipation. I could see that everyone was curious to hear the answer. Pensive, kind, sober, Rumi walked toward me, and here is what he said:

"If the wine drinker
Has a deep gentleness in him,
He will show that,
When drunk.
But if he has hidden anger and arrogance,
Those appear,
And since most people do,
Wine is forbidden to everyone."

There was a brief lull as we all contemplated these words.

"My friends, wine is not an innocent drink," Rumi addressed us in a renewed voice, so commanding and yet so composed and solid, "because it brings out the worst in us. I believe it is better for us to abstain from drinking. That said, we cannot blame alcohol for what *we* are responsible for. It is our own arrogance and anger that we should be working on. That is more urgent. At the end of the day whoever wants to drink will drink and whoever wants to stay away from wine will stay away. We have no right to impose our ways on others. There is no compulsion in religion."

This elicited heartened nods from some customers. I, for my part, preferred to raise my glass in my belief that no piece of wisdom should go untoasted.

"You are a good man with a great heart," I said. "No matter what people say about what you did today, and I'm sure they are going to say plenty, I think as a preacher it was very brave of you to come to the tavern and talk with us without judgment."

Rumi gave me a friendly look. Then he grabbed the wine bottles he had left untouched and walked out into the evening breeze.

Aladdin

KONYA, FEBRUARY 1246

Besieged with anticipation, for the last three weeks I have been waiting to find the right moment to ask my father for Kimya's hand in marriage. I have spent many hours talking to him in my imagination, rephrasing the same sentences over and over, searching for a better way of expressing myself. I had an answer ready for every possible objection he could come up with. If he said that Kimya and I were like sister and brother, I would remind him that we were not bound by blood. Knowing how much my father loved Kimya, I was also planning to say that if he let us get married, she would not have to go and live anywhere else and could stay with us all her life. I had everything worked out in my mind, except I couldn't find a moment alone with my father.

But then this evening I ran into him in the worst way possible. I was about to leave the house to meet with my friends when the door creaked open and in walked my father holding a bottle in each hand.

I stood still, agape. "Father, what is it that you are carrying?" I asked.

"Oh, that!" my father responded without the slightest trace of embarrassment. "It's wine, my son."

"Is that so?" I exclaimed. "Is this what has become of the great Mawlana? An old man blasted on wine?"

"Watch your tongue," came a sulky voice from behind me.

It was Shams. Staring into my face without so much as a blink, he said, "That is no way to talk to your father. I'm the one who asked him to go to the tavern."

"Why am I not surprised?" I couldn't help smirking.

If Shams was offended by my words, he didn't show it. "Aladdin, we can talk about this," he said flatly. "That is, if you don't let your anger blur your vision."

Then he cocked his head to one side and told me I had to soften my heart.

"It's one of the rules," he said. *"If you want to strengthen your faith, you will need to soften inside. For your faith to be rock solid, your heart needs to be as soft as a feather. Through an illness, accident, loss, or fright, one way or another, we all are faced with incidents that teach us how to become less selfish and judgmental, and more compassionate and generous. Yet some of us learn the lesson and manage to become milder, while some others end up becoming even harsher than before. The only way to get closer to Truth is to expand your heart so that it will encompass all humanity and still have room for more Love."*

"You stay out of this," I said. "I'm not taking orders from drunken dervishes. Unlike my father, that is."

"Aladdin, shame on you," my father broke in.

I felt an instant and potent pang of guilt, but it was too late. So many resentments I thought I had left behind came flooding back to me.

"I have no doubt you hate me as much as you say you do," Shams proclaimed, "but I don't think you have stopped loving your father even for a minute. Don't you see you are hurting him?"

"Don't you see you are ruining our lives?" I shot back.

That was when my father lunged forward, his mouth set in a grim line, his right hand raised above his head. I thought he was going to slap me, but when he didn't, when he wouldn't, I felt even more uneasy.

"You shame me," my father said without looking at my face.

My eyes welled with tears. I turned my head aside and suddenly came face-to-face with Kimya. How long had she been standing there watching us from a corner with fearful eyes? How much of this squabble had she heard?

The shame of being humiliated by my father in front of the girl I wanted to marry churned in my stomach, leaving a bad taste in my mouth. It felt like the room was spinning all around me, threatening to collapse.

Unable to stay there a moment longer, I grabbed my coat, pushed Shams aside, and dashed out of the house, away from Kimya, away from all of them.

Shams

KONYA, FEBRUARY 1246

Bottles of wine stood between us, loaded with the smells of hot earth, wild herbs, and dark berries. After Aladdin was gone, Rumi was so sad he couldn't talk for a while. He and I stepped out into the snow-covered courtyard. It was one of those bleak February evenings when the air felt heavy with a peculiar stillness. We stood there watching the clouds move, listening to a world that offered us nothing but silence. The wind brought us a whiff of the forests from afar, fragrant and musky, and for a moment I believe we both wanted to leave this town for good.

Then I took one of the bottles of wine. I knelt beside a climbing rose tree that stood thorny and bare in the snow, and I started to pour the wine on the soil beneath it. Rumi's face brightened as he smiled his half-thoughtful, half-excited smile.

Slowly, stunningly, the bare rose tree came alive, its bark softening like human skin. It produced a single rose in front of our eyes. As I kept pouring the wine under the tree, the rose revealed a lovely warm shade of orange.

Next I took the second bottle and poured it in the same way. The rose's orangey color turned into a bright crimson tone, glowing with life. Now there remained only a glassful of wine at the bottom of the bottle. I poured that into a glass, drank half of it, and the remaining half I offered to Rumi.

He took the glass with trembling hands, responding to my gesture with a beaming reciprocity of kindness and equanimity, this man who had never touched alcohol in his life.

"Religious rules and prohibitions are important," he said. "But they should not be turned into unquestionable taboos. It is with such awareness that I drink the wine you offer me today, believing with all my heart that there is a sobriety beyond the drunkenness of love."

Just as Rumi was about to take the glass to his lips, I snatched it back and flung it to the ground. The wine spilled on the snow, like drops of blood.

"Don't drink it," I said, no longer feeling the need to continue with this trial.

"If you weren't going to ask me to drink this wine, why did you send me to the tavern in the first place?" Rumi asked, his tone not so much curious as compassionate.

"You know why," I said, smiling. "Spiritual growth is about the totality of our consciousness, not about obsessing over particular aspects. Rule Number Thirty-two: *Nothing should stand between yourself and God. Not imams, priests, rabbis, or any other custodians of moral or religious leadership. Not spiritual masters, not even your faith. Believe in your values and your rules, but never lord them over others. If you keep breaking other people's hearts, whatever religious duty you perform is no good.*

"Stay away from all sorts of idolatry, for they will blur your vision. Let God and only God be your guide. Learn the Truth, my friend, but be careful not to make a fetish out of your truths."

I had always admired Rumi's personality and known that his compassion, endless and extraordinary, was what I lacked in life. But today my admiration for him had grown by leaps and bounds.

This world was full of people obsessed with wealth, recognition, or power. The more signs of success they earned, the more they seemed to be in need of them. Greedy and covetous, they rendered worldly possessions their *qibla,* always looking in that direction, unaware of becoming the servants of the things they hungered after. That was a common pattern. It happened all the time. But it was rare, as rare as rubies, for a man who had already made his way up, a man who had plenty of gold, fame, and authority, to renounce his position all of a sudden one day and endanger his reputation for an inner journey, one that nobody could tell where or how it would end. Rumi was that rare ruby.

"God wants us to be modest and unpretentious," I said.

"And He wants to be *known,*" Rumi added softly. "He wants us to know Him with every fiber of our being. That is why it is better to be watchful and sober than to be drunk and dizzy."

I agreed. Until it turned dark and cold, we sat in the courtyard with a single red rose between us. There was, beneath the chill of the evening, the scent of something fresh and sweet. The Wine of Love made our heads spin gently, and I realized with glee and gratitude that the wind no longer whispered despair.

Ella

NORTHAMPTON, JUNE 24, 2008

"Baby, there's a new Thai place in town," David said. "They say it's good. Why don't we go there tonight? Just the two of us."

The last thing Ella wanted to do on this Tuesday was go out for dinner with her husband. But David was so insistent that she couldn't say no.

The Silver Moon was a small restaurant with stylish lamps, leather booths, black napkins, and so many mirrors hung low on every wall that the customers felt as if they were dining with their own reflections. It didn't take Ella long to feel out of place there. But it wasn't the restaurant that had made her feel this way. It was her husband. She had glimpsed in David's eyes an unusual glitter. Something wasn't normal. He looked pensive—worried, even. What disturbed her most was that he had stuttered a few times. Ella knew that for his childhood speech impediment to surface, David had to be very distressed.

A young waitress dressed in a traditional outfit came to take their orders. David asked for chili basil scallops, and Ella decided on the vegetables and tofu in coconut sauce, staying true to her fortieth-birthday decision to refrain from eating meat. They also ordered wine.

They talked about the sophisticated decor for a few minutes, discussing the effect of black napkins versus white napkins. Then there was silence. Twenty years of marriage, twenty years of sleeping in the same bed, sharing the same shower, eating the same food, raising three kids . . . and what it all added up to was silence. Or so Ella thought.

"I see you've been reading Rumi," David remarked.

Ella nodded, though with some surprise. She didn't know what surprised her more: to hear that David knew about Rumi or that he cared about what she read.

"I started reading his poetry to help me to write my report on *Sweet Blasphemy,* but then I became interested in it, and now I'm reading it for myself," Ella said by way of explanation.

David grew distracted by a wine stain on the tablecloth, then sighed with a valedictory expression on his face. "Ella, I know what's going on," he said. "I know everything."

"What are you talking about?" Ella asked, although she wasn't sure she wanted to hear the answer.

"About . . . about your affair . . ." David stammered. "I'm aware of it."

Ella looked at her husband, flabbergasted. In the glow of the candle that the waitress had just lit for them, David's face showed pure despair.

"My *affair*?!" Ella blurted out, quicker and louder than she intended. She instantly noticed the couple at the next table turning in their direction. Embarrassed, she dropped her voice to a whisper and repeated, "What affair?"

"I'm not stupid," David said. "I checked your e-mail account and read your messages with that man."

"You did what?" Ella exclaimed.

Ignoring the question, his face contorted with the weight of what he was about to announce, David said, "I don't blame you, Ella. I deserve it. I neglected you, and you looked for compassion elsewhere."

Ella lowered her gaze to her glass. The wine had a charming color—a deep, dark ruby. For a second she thought she glimpsed specks of iridescent sparkle on its surface, like a trail of lights guiding her. And perhaps there *was* a trail. It all felt surreal.

Now David paused, deciding how best, or whether, to reveal what he had in mind. "I'm ready to forgive you and leave this behind," he finally remarked.

There were many things Ella wanted to say at that moment, poignant and mocking, tense and dramatic, but she chose the easiest one. With gleaming eyes, she asked, "What about *your* affairs? Are you also going to leave them behind?"

The waitress arrived then with their orders. Ella and David sat back and watched her leave the plates on the table and refill the glasses with exaggerated politeness. When she finally left, David flicked his eyes up toward Ella and asked, "So is this what this was about? Was it for revenge?"

"No," Ella said, shaking her head in disappointment. "This is not about revenge. It never was."

"Then what *is* it about?"

Ella clasped her hands, feeling as if everything and everyone in the restaurant—the customers, the waiters, the cooks, and even the tropical fish in the fish tank—had stopped to hear what she was going to say.

"It is about love," she said at last. "I love Aziz."

Ella expected her husband to roll with laughter. But when she finally found the courage to look him in the eye, there was only horror on his face, quickly replaced by the expression of someone who was trying to solve a problem with minimal damage. Suddenly she had a moment of clarity. "Love" was a serious word, loaded and quite unusual, for her—a woman who had said so many negative things about love in the past.

"We have three kids," David said, his voice trailing off.

"Yes, and I love them very much," Ella said with a slump in her shoulders. "But I also love Aziz—"

"Stop using that word," David interjected. He took a big gulp from his glass before he spoke again. "I made major mistakes, but I never stopped loving you, Ella. And I have never loved anyone else. We can both learn from our mistakes. For my part I can promise you that the same thing won't happen again. You don't need to go out and look for love anymore."

"I didn't go out and seek love," Ella muttered, more to herself than to him. "Rumi says we don't need to hunt for love outside ourselves. All we need to do is to eliminate the barriers inside that keep us away from love."

"Oh, my God! What's come over you? This isn't you! Stop being so romantic, will you? Come back to your old self," David snapped, then added, "Please!"

Ella furrowed her brow and inspected her nails as if there were something about them troubling her. In truth, she'd remembered another moment in time when she herself had said virtually the same words to her daughter. She felt as if a circle had been completed. Nodding her head slowly, she put her napkin aside.

"Can we please go now?" she said. "I'm not hungry."

That night they slept in separate beds. And early in the morning, the first thing Ella did was write a letter to Aziz.

The Zealot

KONYA, FEBRUARY 1246

"Batten down the hatches! Sheikh Yassin! Sheikh Yassin! Did you hear the scandal?" Abdullah, the father of one of my students, exclaimed as he approached me on the street. "Rumi was seen in a tavern in the Jewish quarter yesterday!"

"Yes, I heard about that," I said, "but I wasn't surprised. The man has a Christian wife, and his best friend is a heretic. What did you expect?"

Abdullah nodded gravely. "I guess you are right. We should have seen it coming."

A number of passersby gathered around us, overhearing our conversation. Somebody suggested that Rumi should not be allowed to preach in the Great Mosque anymore. Not until he apologized publicly. I agreed. Being late for my class in the madrassa, I then left them to their talk and hurried off.

I had always suspected that Rumi had a dark side ready to float up to the surface someday. But even I hadn't expected him to take to the bottle. It was utterly disgusting. People say Shams is the primary reason for the downfall of Rumi, and if he weren't around, Rumi would go back to normal. But I hold a different view. Not that I doubt that Shams is an evil man—he is—or that he doesn't have a bad influence on Rumi—he does—but the question is, why hasn't Shams led other scholars astray, such as me? At the end of the day, those two are alike in more ways than people are willing to recognize.

There are people who heard Shams remark, "A scholar lives on the marks of a pen. A Sufi loves and lives on footprints!" Now, what does that mean? Apparently Shams thinks scholars hide in ivory towers, while Sufis immerse themselves in real life. But Rumi, too, is a scholar, isn't he? Or does he not consider himself one of us anymore?

Should Shams enter my classroom, I would chase him away like a fly, never giving him the opportunity to sputter gibberish in my presence. Why can't Rumi do the same? There must be something wrong with him. The man has a Christian wife, for starters. I don't care if she has converted to Islam. It is in her blood and in the blood of her child. Unfortunately, the townspeople don't take the threat of Christianity as seriously as they should, and they assume that we can live side by side. To those who are naïve enough to believe that, I always say, "Can water and oil ever mix? That is the extent to which Muslims and Christians can!"

Having a Christian for a wife and being notoriously soft toward minorities, Rumi was already an undependable man in my eyes, but when Shams of Tabriz started living under his roof, he totally deviated from the right path. As I tell my students every day, one needs to be alert against Sheitan. And Shams is the devil incarnate. I am sure it was his idea to send Rumi to the tavern. God knows how he convinced him. But isn't beguiling righteous people into sacrilege what Sheitan excels at?

I understood Shams's evil side right from the start. How dare he compare the Prophet Muhammad, may peace be upon him, with that irreligious Sufi Bistami? Wasn't it Bistami who pronounced, "Look at me! How great is my glory!" Wasn't it he who then said, "I saw the Kaaba walking around *me*"? The man went as far as stating, "I am the smith of my own self." If this is not blasphemy, then what is? Such is the level of the man Shams quotes with respect. For just like Bistami, he, too, is a heretic.

The only good news is that the townspeople are waking up to the truth. Finally! Shams's critics increase with each passing day. And the things they say! Even I am appalled sometimes. In the bathhouses and teahouses, in the wheat fields and orchards, people tear him apart.

I reached the madrassa later than usual, my mind heavy with these thoughts. As soon as I opened the door to my classroom, I sensed there was something unusual. My students were sitting in a perfect line, pale and oddly silent, as if they had all seen a ghost.

Then I understood why. Sitting there by the open window with his back resting against the wall, his hairless face lit with an arrogant smile, was none other than Shams of Tabriz.

"*Selamun aleykum,* Sheikh Yassin," he said, staring hard at me across the room.

I hesitated, not knowing whether to greet him, and decided not to. Instead I turned to my students and inquired, "What is this man doing here? Why did you let him in?"

Dazed and uneasy, none of the students dared to answer. It was Shams himself who shattered the silence.

His tone insolent, his gaze unwavering, he said to me, "Don't scold them, Sheikh Yassin. It was my idea. You see, I was in the neighborhood and said to myself, 'Why don't I stop by the madrassa and visit the one person in this town who hates me most?' "

Husam the Student

KONYA, FEBRUARY 1246

Bright-eyed and bushy-tailed, we were all sitting on the floor in the classroom when the door opened and in walked Shams of Tabriz. Everyone was stunned. Having heard so many bad and bizarre things about him, mostly from our teacher, I, too, couldn't help but cringe upon seeing him in our classroom in the flesh. He, however, seemed relaxed and friendly. After greeting us all, he said he had come to have a word with Sheikh Yassin.

"Our teacher doesn't like to have strangers in the classroom. Perhaps you should talk to him some other time," I said, hoping to avoid a nasty encounter.

"Thanks for your concern, young man, but sometimes nasty encounters are not only inevitable, they are necessary," Shams answered, as if he had read my thoughts. "Don't you worry, though. It won't take too long."

Irshad, sitting next to me, muttered between clenched teeth, "Look at his nerve! He is the devil incarnate."

I nodded, though I wasn't sure Shams looked like the devil to me. Set against him as I was, I couldn't help liking his forthrightness and audacity.

A few minutes later, Sheikh Yassin entered through the door, his brow furrowed in contemplation. He had taken no more than a few steps inside when he stopped and blinked distractedly in the direction of the uninvited visitor.

"What is this man doing here? Why did you let him in?"

My friends and I exchanged shocked glances and frightened

whispers, but before anyone could muster the courage to say anything, Shams blurted out that he had been in the neighborhood and had decided to visit the one person in Konya who hated him most!

I heard several students cough tautly and saw Irshad draw in a sharp breath. The tension between the two men was so thick that the air in the classroom could be cut with a knife.

"I don't know what you are doing here, but I have better things to do than talk to you," Sheikh Yassin reprimanded. "Now, why don't you take your leave, so that we can get on with our studies?"

"You say you won't talk to me, but you have been talking *about* me," Shams remarked. "You have constantly spoken ill of me and Rumi, and of all the mystics along the Sufi path."

Sheikh Yassin sniffed through his big, bony nose and narrowed his mouth to a pout, as if he had something sour on his tongue. "As I said, I have nothing to talk with you about. I already know what I need to know. I have my opinions."

Shams now turned to us with a swift, sardonic glance. "A man with many opinions but no questions! There's something so wrong with that."

"Really?" Sheikh Yassin looked amused and animated. "Then why don't we ask the students which of the two they'd rather be: the wise man who knows the answers or the perplexed man who has nothing but questions?"

All of my friends sided with Sheikh Yassin, but I sensed that many did so less out of sincere agreement than to get favors from the teacher. I chose to remain silent.

"One who thinks he has all the answers is the most ignorant," Shams said with a dismissive shrug, and turned to our teacher. "But since you are so good with answers, may I ask you a question?"

That was when I started to worry about where this conversation was heading. But there was nothing I could do to prevent the escalating tension.

"Since you claim I am the devil's servant, could you kindly tell us what exactly your notion of Sheitan is?" asked Shams.

"Certainly," Sheikh Yassin said, never missing an opportunity to preach. "Our religion, which is the last and the best of Abrahamic religions, tells us it was Sheitan who caused Adam and Eve to be expelled from heaven. As the children of fallen parents, we all need to be alert, because Sheitan comes in many forms. Sometimes he comes in the form of a gambler who invites us to gamble, sometimes a beautiful young woman who tries to seduce us. . . . Sheitan can come in the least expected forms, like that of a wandering dervish."

As if expecting this remark, Shams smiled knowingly. "I see what you mean. It must be a huge relief, and an easy way out, to think the devil is always outside of us."

"What do you mean?" Sheikh Yassin asked.

"Well, if Sheitan is as wicked and indomitable as you are saying he is, then we human beings have no reason to blame ourselves for our wrongdoings. Whatever good happens we'll attribute to God, and all the bad things in life we'll simply attribute to Sheitan. In either case we'll be exempt from all criticism and self-examination. How easy that is!"

Still talking, Shams started to pace the room, his voice rising with each word. "But let's for one moment imagine there is no Sheitan. No demons waiting to burn us in scorching cauldrons. All these bloodcurdling images were designed to show us something, but then they became clichés and lost their original message."

"And what might that message be?" Sheikh Yassin asked wearily, crossing his arms on his chest.

"Ah, so you do have questions after all," Shams said. "The message is that the torment a person can inflict upon himself is endless. Hell is inside us, and so is heaven. The Qur'an says human beings are the most dignified. We are higher than the highest, but also lower than the lowest. If we could grasp the full meaning of this, we would stop looking for Sheitan outside and instead focus on ourselves. What we need is sincere self-examination. Not being on the watch for the faults of others."

"You go and examine yourself, and *inshallah* someday you will redeem yourself," Sheikh Yassin answered, "but a proper scholar has to keep an eye on his community."

"Then allow me to tell you a story," Shams said, with such graciousness that we couldn't be sure whether he was sincere or mocking.

And here is what he told us:

Four merchants were praying in a mosque when they saw the muezzin enter. The first merchant stopped his prayer and asked, "Muezzin! Has the prayer been called? Or do we still have time?"

The second merchant stopped praying and turned to his friend. "Hey, you spoke while you were praying. Your prayer is now void. You need to start anew!"

Upon hearing this, the third merchant interjected, "Why do you blame him, you idiot? You should have minded your own prayer. Now yours is void, too."

The fourth merchant broke into a smile and said loudly, "Look at them! All three have messed up. Thank God I'm not one of the misguided."

After telling this story, Shams stood facing the classroom and asked, "So what do you think? Which of the merchants' prayers, in your opinion, were invalid?"

There was a brief stirring in the classroom as we discussed the answer among ourselves. Finally someone at the back said, "The second, the third, and the fourth merchants' prayers were void. But the first merchant is innocent, because all he wanted was to consult the muezzin."

"Yes, but he shouldn't have abandoned his prayer like that," Irshad interposed. "It is obvious that all the merchants were wrong, except the fourth one, who was just talking to himself."

I averted my gaze, disagreeing with both answers but determined to keep my mouth shut. I had a feeling my views might not be welcome.

But no sooner had this thought crossed my mind than Shams of Tabriz pointed at me and asked, "And you over there! What do *you* think?"

I swallowed hard before I could find my voice. "If these merchants made a mistake, it is not because they spoke during prayer," I said, "but because instead of minding their own business and connecting with God, they were more interested in what was going on around them. However, if we pass judgment on them, I am afraid we'll be making the same crucial mistake."

"So what is your answer?" Sheikh Yassin asked, suddenly interested in the conversation.

"My answer is, all four merchants have erred for a similar reason, and yet none of them can be said to be in the wrong, because at the end of the day, it is not up to us to judge them."

Shams of Tabriz took a step toward me and looked at me with such affection and kindness that I felt like a little boy savoring the unconditional love of a parent. He asked my name, and when I told him, he remarked, "Your friend Husam here has a Sufi heart."

I blushed up to my ears when I heard this. There was no doubt I would be scolded by Sheikh Yassin after the class and mocked and ridiculed by my friends. But all my worries quickly evaporated. I sat straight and smiled at Shams. He gave me a wink in return and, still smiling, continued to explain.

"The Sufi says, 'I should mind my inner encounter with God rather than judging other people.' An orthodox scholar, however, is always on the lookout for the mistakes of others. But don't forget, students, most of the time he who complains about others is himself at fault."

"Stop confusing the minds of my students!" Sheikh Yassin broke in. "As scholars we cannot afford to be uninterested in what others are doing. People ask us many questions and expect to be answered duly, so that they can live their religion fully and properly. They ask us if their ablutions need to be redone should their noses bleed or if it is okay to fast while traveling and so on. The Shafi, Hanefi, Hanbali, and Maliki teachings differ from one another when it comes to these matters. Each school of law has its own set of meticulous answers that must be studied and learned."

"That's good, but don't get so attached to nominal distinctions." Shams sighed. "The logos of God is complete. Don't reach for details at the expense of the whole."

"Details?" Sheikh Yassin echoed incredulously. "Believers take rules seriously. And we scholars guide them in their endeavor."

"Keep guiding—that is, as long as you don't forget that your guidance is limited and there is no word above the word of God," Shams said, and then he added, "But try not to preach to those who have attained enlightenment. They derive a different pleasure in the verses of the Qur'an and so do not require the guidance of a sheikh."

Upon hearing this, Sheikh Yassin got so furious that his withered cheeks flushed waves of crimson and his Adam's apple jutted out sharply. "There is nothing temporary in the guidance we provide," he said. "The sharia constitutes the rules and regulations that every Muslim should consult from cradle to grave."

"The sharia is only a boat that sails in the ocean of Truth. The true seeker of God will sooner or later abandon the vessel and plunge into the sea."

"So that sharks might eat him up," Sheikh Yassin retorted, chuckling. "That's what happens to the one who refuses to be guided."

A few students joined in the chuckle, but the rest of us sat quietly, feeling increasingly uncomfortable. The class was coming to an end, and I couldn't see how this conversation could conclude on a positive note.

Shams of Tabriz must have felt the same gloom, for he looked pensive now, almost forlorn. He closed his eyes as if suddenly tired of so much talk, a move so subtle as to be almost imperceptible.

"In all my travels, I have come to know many sheikhs," Shams said. "While some were sincere men, others were condescending, and they didn't know anything about Islam. I wouldn't trade the dust off of the old shoes of a real lover of God for the heads of today's sheikhs. Even shadow players who display images behind curtains are better than they are, because at least they admit that what they provide is mere illusion."

"That's enough! I think we've heard enough of your forked tongue," Sheikh Yassin announced. "Now, get out of my classroom!"

"Don't worry, I was about to leave," Shams said roguishly, and then he turned toward us. "What you witnessed here today is an old debate that extends back to the time of the Prophet Muhammad, may peace be upon him," he remarked. "But the debate is not only germane to the history of Islam. It is present in the heart of every Abrahamic religion. This is the conflict between the scholar and the mystic, between the mind and the heart."

Shams paused briefly to let us feel the full impact of his words. I felt his stare fall upon me, and it was almost like sharing a secret—entrance into an untold, unwritten brotherhood.

Then he added, "In the end, neither your teacher nor I can know more than God allows us to know. We all play our parts. Only one thing matters, though. That the light of the sun isn't overshadowed by the blindness of the eye of the denier, the one who refuses to see."

With that, Shams of Tabriz placed his right hand on his heart and bade farewell to us all, including Sheikh Yassin, who stood aside, grim and unresponsive. The dervish walked out and shut the door behind him, leaving us swathed in a silence so profound that we could not talk or fidget for a long while.

It was Irshad who pulled me out of my trance. I noticed he was staring at me with something akin to disapproval. Only then did I realize that my right hand was resting on my heart in salute to a Truth that it had recognized.

Baybars the Warrior

KONYA, MAY 1246

Bloody but unbowed. I couldn't believe my ears when I heard that Shams had found the nerve to confront my uncle in front of his students. Doesn't this man have any decency? How I wished I had been in the madrassa when he arrived. I would have kicked him out before he even had the chance to open that wicked mouth of his. But I wasn't there, and it seems that he and my uncle had a long conversation, which the students have been blabbering about ever since. I take their words with a grain of salt, though, since their accounts are inconsistent and give too much credit to that rotten dervish.

I feel very nervous tonight. It is all because of that harlot Desert Rose. I can't rid my mind of her. She reminds me of jewelry boxes with secret compartments. You think you own her, but unless you have the keys, she remains locked up and unreachable even when you hold her in your arms.

It is her surrendering that troubles me most. I keep asking myself why she didn't resist my fits. How come she just lay there on the floor under my feet, listless as a dirty old rug? Had she hit me back or screamed for help, I would have stopped hitting her. But she lay motionless, her eyes bulging, her mouth shut, as if determined to take it passively, come what may. Did she really not care at all whether I killed her?

I have been trying hard not to go to the brothel again, but today I gave in to the need to see her. On the way there, I kept wondering how she would react upon seeing me. In case she complained about me and things got nasty, I was going to bribe or threaten that fat patron of hers.

I had everything worked out in my mind and was ready for every possibility, except for the possibility of her having run away.

"What do you mean, Desert Rose is not here?" I burst out. "Where is she?"

"Forget about that harlot," the patron said, popping a lokum into her mouth and sucking the syrup off of her finger. Seeing how upset I was, she added in a softer voice, "Why don't you take a look at the other girls, Baybars?"

"I don't want your cheap whores, you fat hag. I need to see Desert Rose, and I need to see her now."

The hermaphrodite raised her dark, pointed eyebrows at this form of address but didn't dare to argue with me. Her voice dwindled to a whisper, as if ashamed of what she was about to say. "She is gone. Apparently she ran away while everyone was sleeping."

It was too absurd to be even laughable. "Since when do whores walk out of their brothels?" I asked. "You find her now!"

The patron looked at me as if she were seeing, really seeing me, for the first time. "Who are you to give me orders?" she hissed, as her small, defiant eyes, so unlike those of Desert Rose, blazed back at me.

"I am a security guard who has an uncle in high places. I can shut this den down and put you all out on the street," I said as I reached over to the bowl on her lap and plucked out a lokum. It was soft and chewy.

I wiped my sticky fingers on the patron's silk scarf. Her face became livid with rage, but she did not dare to pick a fight.

"Why are you blaming me?" she said. "Blame that dervish. He is the one who convinced Desert Rose to leave the brothel and find God."

For a moment I couldn't understand who she was talking about, but then it dawned upon me it was no other than Shams of Tabriz that she meant.

First disrespecting my uncle in front of his students, and now this. Clearly that heretic didn't know his boundaries.

Ella

NORTHAMPTON, JUNE 26, 2008

Beloved Aziz,

I decided to write you a letter this time. You know, the old-fashioned way, with ink, a perfumed paper, a matching envelope, and a stamp. I am going to mail it to Amsterdam this afternoon. I need to do this right away because if I delay in mailing my letter, I am afraid I will never be able to do it.

First you meet someone—someone who is completely different from everyone around you. Someone who sees everything in a different light and forces you to shift, change your angle of vision, observe everything anew, within and without. You think you can keep a safe distance from him. You think you can navigate your way through this beautiful storm until you realize, much too suddenly, you are thrust out into the open and in fact you control nothing.

I cannot tell when exactly I became captivated by your words. All I know is, our correspondence has been changing me. Right from the start. Chances are I will regret saying this. But having spent my whole life regretting the things I failed to do, I see no harm in doing something regrettable for a change.

Ever since I "met" you through your novel and your e-mails, you have dominated my thoughts. Every time I read an e-mail from you, I feel something inside me swirl and realize that I have not known such contentment and excitement in a long while. Throughout the day you are on my mind all the time. I talk to you silently, wondering how you would respond to my daily life. When I go to a nice restaurant, I want to go there with you. When I see anything of interest, I am saddened by not being able to show it to you. The other day my younger daughter asked me if I had done something with my hair. My hair is the same as always! But it's true that I look different, because I feel different.

Then I remind myself that we haven't even met yet. And that brings me back to reality. And the reality is that I don't know what to do with you. I have finished reading your novel and turned in my report. (Oh, yes, I was writing an editorial report on it. There were times when I wanted to share my views with you, or at least send you the report I gave the literary agent, but I thought that wouldn't be right. Although I can't share with you the details of my report, you should know that I absolutely loved your book. Thank you for the pleasure. Your words will stay with me always.)

Anyway, Sweet Blasphemy has nothing to do with my decision to write this letter, or perhaps it has everything to do with it. What has compelled me is this thing between us, whatever it is, and its overwhelming impact upon me is eluding my control. It has become more serious than I can handle. I first loved your imagination and your stories, and then I realized I love the man behind the stories.

Now I don't know what to do with you.

As I said, I need to send this letter immediately. If not, I will have to tear it into a dozen bits. I will act as if there is nothing new in my life, nothing unusual.

Yes, I could do what I always do and pretend that everything is normal.

I could pretend if it weren't for this sweet ache in my heart . . .

With love,
Ella

Kerra

KONYA, MAY 1246

Baptism of fire. I don't know how to deal with this situation. This morning, out of nowhere, a woman came asking for Shams of Tabriz. I told her to come back later, as he wasn't at home, but she said she had nowhere to go and would rather wait in the courtyard. That was when I got suspicious and started to inquire into who she was and where she came from. She fell to her knees and opened her veil, showing a face scarred and swollen from many beatings. Despite her bruises and cuts, she was very pretty and so lithe. Amid tears and sobs, and in a surprisingly articulate way, she confirmed what I had already suspected. She was a harlot from the brothel.

"But I have abandoned that awful place," she said. "I went to the public bath and washed myself forty times with forty prayers. I took an oath to stay away from men. From now on, my life is dedicated to God."

Not knowing what to say, I stared into her wounded eyes and wondered how she, young and fragile as she was, had found the courage to abandon the only life she knew. I didn't want to see a fallen woman anywhere near my house, but there was something about her that broke my heart, a kind of simplicity, almost innocence, I had never seen in anyone before. Her brown eyes reminded me of Mother Mary's eyes. I couldn't bring myself to shoo her away. I let her wait in the courtyard. That was the most I could do. She sat there by the wall, staring into space as motionless as a marble statue.

An hour later, when Shams and Rumi returned from their walk, I rushed to tell them about the unexpected visitor.

"Did you say there was a harlot in our courtyard?" Rumi asked, sounding puzzled.

"Yes, and she says she has left the brothel to find God."

"Oh, that must be Desert Rose," Shams exclaimed, his tone not so much surprised as pleased. "Why did you keep her outside? Bring her in!"

"But what will our neighbors say if they learn we have a girl of ill-repute under our roof?" I objected, my voice cracking with the tension.

"Aren't we all living under the same roof anyhow?" Shams said, pointing to the sky above. "Kings and beggars, virgins and harlots, all are under the same sky!"

How could I argue with Shams? He always had a ready answer for everything.

I ushered the harlot into the house, praying that the inquisitive eyes of the neighbors would not fall upon us. No sooner had Desert Rose entered the room than she ran to kiss the hands of Shams, sobbing.

"I am so glad you are here." Shams beamed as if talking to an old friend. "You won't go back to that place ever again. That stage of your life is completely over. May God make your journey toward Truth a fruitful one!"

Desert Rose commenced to cry harder. "But the patron will never leave me in peace. She will send Jackal Head after me. You don't know how—"

"Clear your mind, child," Shams interrupted. "Remember another rule: *While everyone in this world strives to get somewhere and become someone, only to leave it all behind after death, you aim for the supreme stage of nothingness. Live this life as light and empty as the number zero. We are no different from a pot. It is not the decorations outside but the emptiness inside that holds us straight. Just like that, it is not what we aspire to achieve but the consciousness of nothingness that keeps us going.*"

Late in the evening, I showed Desert Rose the bed where she would sleep. And when she fell asleep immediately, I returned to the main room, where I found Rumi and Shams talking.

"You should come to our performance," Shams said when he saw me coming.

"What performance?" I asked.

"A spiritual dance, Kerra, the likes of which you have never seen."

I looked at my husband in astonishment. What was going on? What dance were they talking about?

"Mawlana, you are a respected scholar, not an entertainer. What will people think of you?" I asked, feeling my face growing hot.

"Don't you worry," Rumi said. "Shams and I have been talking about this for a long time. We want to introduce the dance of the whirling dervishes. It is called the *sema.* Whoever yearns for Divine Love is more than welcome to join us."

My head started to ache madly, but the pain was slight compared to the torment in my heart.

"What if people don't like it? Not everyone thinks highly of dance," I said to Shams, hoping this would have the effect of stopping whatever he was about to say next. "At least consider putting off this performance for a while."

"Not everyone thinks highly of God," Shams said without missing a beat. "Are we going to put off believing in Him, too?"

And that was the end of the argument. There were no more words to exchange, and the sound of the wind filled the house, bursting through the slats in the walls and pounding in my ears.

Sultan Walad

KONYA, JUNE 1246

"Beauty is in the eye of the beholder," Shams kept saying. "Everybody will watch the same dance, but each will see it differently. So why worry? Some will like it, some won't."

Yet on the evening of the *sema,* I told Shams I was worried that nobody would show up.

"Don't worry," he said forcefully. "The townspeople might not like me, they might not even be fond of your father anymore, but they cannot possibly ignore us. Their curiosity will bring them here."

And just so, on the evening of the performance, I found the open-air hall packed. There were merchants, blacksmiths, carpenters, peasants, stonecutters, dye makers, medicine vendors, guild masters, clerks, potters, bakers, mourners, soothsayers, rat catchers, perfume sellers—even Sheikh Yassin had come with a group of students. Women were sitting in the rear.

I was relieved to see the sovereign Kaykhusraw sitting with his advisers in the front row. That a man of such a high rank supported my father would keep tongues quiet.

It took a long time for the members of the audience to settle down, and even after they had, the noise inside didn't fully subside and there remained a murmur of heated gossip. In my itch to sit next to someone who would not speak ill of Shams, I sat next to Suleiman the Drunk. The man reeked of wine, but I didn't mind.

My legs were jumpy, my palms sweaty, and though the air was warm enough for us to take off our cloaks, my teeth chattered. This performance was so important for my father's declining reputation. I prayed to God, but since I didn't know what exactly to ask for, other than things turning out all right, my prayer sounded too lame.

Shortly there came a sound, first from far away, and then it drew nearer. It was so captivating and moving that all held their breath, listening.

"What kind of an instrument is this?" Suleiman whispered with a mixture of awe and delight.

"It is called the *ney*," I said, remembering a conversation between my father and Shams. "And its sound is the sigh of the lover for the beloved."

When the *ney* abated, my father appeared onstage. With measured, soft steps, he approached and greeted the audience. Six dervishes followed him, all my father's disciples, all wearing long white garments with large skirts. They crossed their hands on their chests, bowing in front of my father to get his blessing. Then the music started, and, one by one, the dervishes began to spin, first slowly, then with breathtaking speed, their skirts opening up like lotus flowers.

It was quite a scene. I couldn't help but smile with pride and joy. Out of the corner of my eye, I checked the reaction of the audience. Even the nastiest gossipers were watching the performance with visible admiration.

The dervishes whirled and whirled for what seemed like an eternity. Then the music rose, the sound of a *rebab* from behind a curtain catching up with the *ney* and the drums. And that was when Shams of Tabriz entered the stage, like the wild desert wind. Wearing a darker robe than everyone else and looking taller, he was also spinning faster. His hands were wide open toward the sky, as was his face, like a sunflower in search of the sun.

I heard many people in the audience gasp with awe. Even those who hated Shams of Tabriz seemed to have fallen under the spell of the moment. I glanced at my father. While Shams spun in a frenzy and the disciples whirled more slowly in their orbits, my father remained as still as an old oak tree, wise and calm, his lips constantly moving in prayer.

Finally the music slowed down. All at once the dervishes stopped whirling, each lotus flower closing up into itself. With a tender salute, my father blessed everyone onstage and in the audience, and for a moment it was as if we were all connected in perfect harmony. A thick, sudden silence ensued. Nobody knew how to react. Nobody had seen anything like this before.

My father's voice pierced the silence. "This, my friends, is called the *sema*—the dance of the whirling dervishes. From this day on, dervishes of every age will dance the *sema*. One hand pointed up to the sky, the other hand pointing down to earth, every speck of love we receive from God, we pledge to distribute to the people."

The audience smiled and mumbled in agreement. There was a warm, friendly commotion all over the hall. I was so touched by seeing this affirming response that tears welled up in my eyes. At long last my father and Shams were beginning to receive the respect and love that they most certainly deserved.

The evening could have ended on that warm note and I could have gone home a happy man, feeling confident that things were improving, had it not been for what happened next, ruining everything.

Suleiman the Drunk

KONYA, JUNE 1246

Blood and thunder! What an unforgettable evening! I still have not recovered from its effects. And of all the things that I have witnessed tonight, the most startling was the finale.

After the *sema,* the great Kaykhusraw II stood up, his eyes ranging round the room imperiously. In consummate smugness he approached the stage, and after giving a great whoop of laughter, he said, "Congratulations, dervishes! I was impressed by your performance."

Rumi gracefully thanked him, and all the dervishes onstage did the same. Then the musicians stood up together and greeted the sovereign with ultimate respect. His face brimming with satisfaction, Kaykhusraw signaled to one of his guards, who immediately handed him a velvet pouch. Kaykhusraw bounced the pouch in his palm several times to show how heavy it was with golden coins and then flung it onto the stage. People around me sighed and applauded. So deeply were we moved by the generosity of our ruler.

Content and confident, Kaykhusraw turned to leave. But no sooner had he taken a step toward the exit than the very pouch he'd flung on the stage was tossed back at him. The coins landed under his feet, jingling like a new bride's bracelets. Everything had happened so fast that for a full minute we all stood still and perplexed, unable to make sense of what was going on. But no doubt the one who was most shocked was Kaykhusraw himself. The insult was so obvious and definitely too personal to be forgivable. He looked over his shoulder with unbelieving eyes to see who could have done such a horrible thing.

It was Shams of Tabriz. All heads turned toward him as he stood onstage arms akimbo, his eyes wild and bloodshot.

"We don't dance for money," he boomed in a deep voice. "The *sema* is a spiritual dance performed for love and love alone. So take back your gold, sovereign! Your money is no good here!"

A dreadful silence descended upon the hall. Rumi's elder son looked so shaken that all the blood had been drained from his young face. Nobody dared to make a sound. Without a sigh, without a gasp, we all held our breaths. As if the skies had been waiting for this signal, it started to rain, sharp and stinging. The raindrops drowned everything and everyone in their steady sound.

"Let's go!" Kaykhusraw yelled to his men.

His cheeks wobbling with humiliation, his lips quivering uncontrollably, and his shoulders visibly slumped, the sovereign headed for the exit. His many guards and servants scurried behind him one by one, stomping on the spilled coins on the floor with their heavy boots. People rushed to scoop up the coins, pushing and pulling one another.

As soon as the sovereign had left, a murmur of disapproval and disappointment rippled through the audience.

"Who does he think he is!" some people burst out.

"How dare he insult our ruler?" others joined in. "What if Kaykhusraw makes the whole town pay the price now?"

A group of people stood up, shaking their heads in disbelief, and stalked toward the exit in a clear sign of protest. At the head of the protesters were Sheikh Yassin and his students. To my great surprise, I noticed among them two of Rumi's old disciples—and his own son Aladdin.

Aladdin

KONYA, JUNE 1246

By Allah, I had never been so embarrassed in my life. As if it weren't shameful enough to see my own father in cahoots with a heretic, I had to suffer the mortification of watching him lead a dance performance. How could he disgrace himself like that in front of the whole town? On top of this, I was utterly appalled when I heard there was among the audience a harlot from the brothel. As I sat there wondering how much more madness and destruction my father's love for Shams could cause us all, for the first time in my life I wished to be the son of another man.

To me the entire performance was sheer sacrilege. But what happened afterward was far beyond the pale. How could that insolent man find the nerve to pour scorn on our ruler? He is very lucky that Kaykhusraw didn't have him arrested on the spot and sent to the gallows.

When I saw Sheikh Yassin walk out after Kaykhusraw, I knew I had to do the same. The last thing I wanted was for the townspeople to think that I was on the side of a heretic. Everyone had to see once and for all that, unlike my brother, I wasn't my father's puppet.

That night I didn't go home. I stayed at Irshad's house with a few friends. Overcome with emotion, we talked about the day's events and discussed at great length what to do.

"That man is a terrible influence on your father," said Irshad tautly. "And now he has brought a prostitute into your house. You need to clean your family's name, Aladdin."

As I stood listening to the things they said, my face burning with a scalding shame, one thing was clear to me: Shams had brought us nothing but misery.

In unison we reached the conclusion that Shams had to leave this town—if not willingly, then by force.

The next day I went back home determined to talk to Shams of Tabriz man to man. I found him alone in the courtyard, playing the *ney*, his head bowed, his eyes closed, his back turned to me. Fully immersed in his music, he hadn't noticed my presence. I approached as quiet as a mouse, taking the opportunity to observe him and get to know my enemy better.

After what seemed like several minutes, the music stopped. Shams raised his head slightly, and without looking in my direction, he mumbled flatly, as if talking to himself, "*Selamun aleykum,* Aladdin, were you looking for me?"

I didn't say a word. Knowing of his ability to see through closed doors, it didn't surprise me that he had eyes in the back of his head.

"So did you enjoy the performance yesterday?" Shams asked, now turning his face toward mine.

"I thought it was disgraceful," I answered at once. "Let's get something straight, shall we? I don't like you. I never have. And I'm not going to let you ruin my father's reputation any more than you have already."

A spark flickered in his eyes as Shams put his *ney* aside and said, "Is that what this is about? If Rumi's reputation is ruined, people won't look up to you as the son of an eminent man anymore. Does that scare you?"

Determined not to let him get under my skin, I ignored his mordant remarks. Still, it was a while before I could say anything.

"Why don't you go and leave us in peace? We were so good before you came," I shot back. "My father is a respected scholar and a family man. You two have nothing in common."

His neck craned forward, his brow furrowed in mighty concentration, Shams drew in a deep breath. Suddenly he looked old and vulnerable. It flashed through my mind that I could slug him, beat him to a pulp, before anyone could run to his rescue. The thought was so dreadful and malevolent, and yet frighteningly seducing, that I had to avert my eyes.

When I stared back at him, I found Shams inspecting me, his gaze avid, bright. Could he be reading my mind? A creepy feeling got hold of me, spreading from my hands to my feet, as if I were being pricked by a thousand needles, and my knees felt wobbly, unwilling to carry me. It must have been black magic. I had no doubt that Shams excelled in the darkest forms of sorcery.

"You are scared of me, Aladdin," Shams said after a pause. "You know who you remind me of? The cross-eyed assistant!"

"What are you talking about?" I said.

"It's a story. Do you like stories?"

I shrugged. "I have no time for them."

A flicker of condescension crossed Shams's lips. "A man who has no time for stories is a man who has no time for God," he said. "Don't you know that God is the best storyteller?"

And without waiting for me to say anything, he told me this story:

Once there was an artisan who had a bitter assistant, who was cross-eyed to boot. This assistant always saw double. One day the artisan asked him to bring a jar of honey from storage. The assistant came back empty-handed. "But, Master, there are two jars of honey there," he complained. "Which one do you want me to bring?" Knowing his assistant too well, the artisan said, "Why don't you break one of the jars and bring me the other one?"

Alas, the assistant was too shallow to understand the wisdom behind these words. He did as told. He broke one of the jars and was very surprised to see the other one break, too.

"What are you trying to tell me?" I asked. To display my temper in front of Shams was a mistake, but I couldn't help it. "You and your stories! Damn it! Can't you ever talk straight?"

"But it is so clear, Aladdin. I am telling you that like the cross-eyed assistant you see dualities everywhere," Shams said. "Your father and I are one. If you break me, you'll break him as well."

"You and my father have nothing in common," I riposted. "If I break the second jar, I'll set the first one free."

I was so full of rage and resentment that I didn't consider the ramifications of my words. Not then. Not until much later.

Not until it was too late.

Shams

KONYA, JUNE 1246

By and large, the narrow-minded say that dancing is sacrilege. They think God gave us music—not only the music we make with our voices and instruments but the music underlying all forms of life, and then He forbade our listening to it. Don't they see that all nature is singing? Everything in this universe moves with a rhythm—the pumping of the heart, the flaps of a bird's wings, the wind on a stormy night, a blacksmith working iron, or the sounds an unborn baby is surrounded with inside the womb. . . . Everything partakes, passionately and spontaneously, in one magnificent melody. The dance of the whirling dervishes is a link in that perpetual chain. Just as a drop of seawater carries within it the entire ocean, our dance both reflects and shrouds the secrets of the cosmos.

Hours before the performance, Rumi and I retreated into a quiet room to meditate. The six dervishes who were going to whirl in the evening joined us. Together we performed our ablutions and prayed. Then we donned our costumes. Earlier we had talked at great length about what the proper attire should be and had chosen simple fabric and colors of the earth. The honey-colored hat symbolized the tombstone, the long white skirt the shroud, and the black cloak the grave. Our dance projected how Sufis discard the entire Self, like shedding a piece of old skin.

Before leaving the hall for the stage, Rumi recited a poem:

"The gnostic has escaped from the five senses
And the six directions and makes you aware of what is beyond them."

With those feelings we were ready. First came the sound of the *ney*. Then Rumi entered the stage in his capacity as *semazenbashi*. One by one, the dervishes followed him, their heads bowed in modesty. The last to appear had to be the sheikh. As firmly as I resisted the suggestion, Rumi insisted on my performing that part tonight.

The *hafiz* chanted a verse from the Qur'an: *There are certainly Signs on earth for people with certainty; and in yourselves as well. Do you not see?*

Then started the *kudüm* accompanying the piercing sound of *ney* and *rebab*.

Listen to the reed and the tale it tells,
how it sings of separation:
Ever since they cut me from the reed bed,
my wail has caused men and women to weep.

Giving himself over to the hands of God, the first dervish started to whirl, the hems of his skirts gently swishing with a separate life of their own. We all joined in and whirled until there remained around us nothing but Oneness. Whatever we received from the skies, we passed on to the earth, from God to people. Each and every one of us became a link connecting the Lover to the Beloved. When the music ceased, we jointly bowed to the essential forces of the universe: fire, wind, earth, and water, and the fifth element, the void.

I don't regret what transpired between me and Kaykhusraw at the end of the performance. But I am sorry for putting Rumi in a difficult position. As a man who has always enjoyed privilege and protection, he has never before felt estranged from a ruler. Now he has at least a smattering of insight into something that average people experience all the time—the deep, vast rift between the ruling elite and the masses.

And with that, I suppose I am nearing the end of my time in Konya.

Every true love and friendship is a story of unexpected transformation. If we are the same person before and after we loved, that means we haven't loved enough.

With the initiation of poetry, music, and dance, a huge part of Rumi's transformation is complete. Once a rigid scholar who disliked poetry and a preacher who enjoyed the sound of his own voice as he lectured others, Rumi is now turning into a poet himself, becoming the voice of pure emptiness, though he might not have realized this fully yet. As for me, I, too, have changed and am changing. I am moving from being into nothingness. From one season to another, one stage to the next, from life to death.

Our friendship was a blessing, a gift from God. We thrived, rejoiced, bloomed, and basked in each other's company, savoring absolute fullness and felicity.

I remembered what Baba Zaman once told me. For the silk to prosper, the silkworm had to die. Sitting there all alone in the whirling hall after everyone had left and the hubbub had died away, I knew that my time with Rumi was coming to an end. Through our companionship Rumi and I had experienced an exceptional beauty and learned what it was like to encounter infinity through two mirrors reflecting each other endlessly. But the old maxim still applies: Where there is love, there is bound to be heartache.

Ella

NORTHAMPTON, JUNE 29, 2008

Beyond wildest dreams, Aziz said, strange things happened to people when they were ready for the unusual and the unexpected. But not a single bone in Ella's body was ready for the one strange thing that happened this week: Aziz Z. Zahara came to Boston to see her.

It was Sunday evening. The Rubinsteins had just sat down to eat when Ella noticed a text message on her cell phone. Assuming that it must be from someone at the Fusion Cooking Club, she didn't hurry to check it. Instead she served the evening's specialty: honey-roasted duck with sautéed potatoes and caramelized onions on a bed of brown rice. When she placed the duck on the table, everyone perked up. Even Jeannette, who was depressed after seeing Scott with his new girlfriend and realizing she still loved him, seemed ravenous.

It was a long, languid dinner, peppered with good wine and the usual talk. Ella was fully engaged with every conversation at the table. With her husband she discussed having the gazebo repainted a bright blue, with Jeannette she chatted about her busy schedule at college, and with the twins she talked about renting some new DVDs, including the latest *Pirates of the Caribbean.* Only after she had placed the dirty dishes in the dishwasher and served the white chocolate crème brûlée did it occur to her to check the message on her cell phone.

> Hi, Ella, I'm in Boston on an assignment for Smithsonian magazine. Just got off the plane. Would you like to meet? I'm staying at the Onyx and would love to see you, Aziz

Ella put the phone away and took her place at the dinner table for dessert, feeling slightly dizzy.

"You got a message?" David asked, raising his head from his plate.

"Yes, it's from Michelle," Ella answered without a moment's hesitation.

Turning his anguished face away, David dabbed his mouth and then, with amazing slowness and precision, folded his napkin into a perfect square. "I see," he said when he was done.

Ella knew that her husband didn't believe her, not in the least, and yet she also felt she had to stick with her story, not to convince her husband or deceive her children but for herself, to make it possible for her to take that one step from her house to Aziz's hotel. So she continued, measuring each word. "She called to tell me there's going to be a meeting tomorrow morning at the agency to discuss next year's catalog. She wants me to join them."

"Well, you should go, then," said David with a flicker in his eyes that indicated he, too, was in on the game. "Why don't I give you a ride in the morning, and we could go there together? I could reschedule a few appointments."

Ella stared at her husband, aghast. What was he trying to do? Did he want to make a scene in front of the kids?

"That'd be lovely," she said, forcing herself to smile. "But we're going to need to leave the house before seven A.M. Michelle says she wants to talk to me in private before the others join in."

"Oh, forget it, then," Orly chimed in, knowing how much her father detested waking up early. "Daddy could never get up in time!"

Now Ella and David looked at each other, locking into a level gaze over the heads of their children, each waiting for the other one to make the first move.

"That's true," David conceded finally.

Ella nodded with relief, though she felt a slight flush of shame at her audacity, because at that moment she had another idea, a bolder one.

"Yes, it is awfully early. In fact," she said, "why don't I go *now*?"

The thought of going to Boston tomorrow morning and having breakfast with Aziz was enough to make her heart beat faster. Yet she wanted to see Aziz right away, now rather than tomorrow, which all of a sudden felt too far away. It was almost a two-hour drive from her house to Boston, but she didn't mind. He had come all the way from Amsterdam for her. She could certainly drive two hours.

"I could be in Boston before ten tonight. And tomorrow I could be at the agency early enough to see Michelle before the meeting."

A shadow of agony crossed David's face. It seemed an eternity before he could say anything. In that long moment, his eyes were the eyes of a man who had neither the strength nor the emotion left in him to stop his wife from going to another man.

"I can drive to Boston tonight, and stay in our apartment," Ella said, seemingly to her children but in truth only to David. That was her way of assuring her husband there would be no physical contact between her and whomever he assumed she was going to meet.

David rose from his chair with a glass of wine in his hand. Giving a sweeping gesture in the direction of the door, he smiled at Ella with assurance and added, a bit too eagerly, "All right, honey, if that's what you want, you should go now."

"But, Mom, I thought you were going to help me with math this evening," Avi objected.

Ella felt her face burn. "I know, dear. Why don't we do that tomorrow?"

"Oh, let her go." Orly turned to her brother teasingly. "You don't need your mama by your side all the time. When are you going to grow up?"

Avi frowned but said nothing further, Orly was supportive, Jeannette didn't care one way or the other, and just like that, Ella grabbed her cell phone and dashed upstairs. As soon as she closed the bedroom door, she threw herself onto the bed and text-messaged Aziz.

I can't believe you're here. I'll be at the Onyx in two hours.

She stared at her phone in growing panic as she watched her message being sent. What was she doing? But there was no time to think. If she was going to regret this evening, which she suspected she might, she could regret it later. Now she needed to hurry. It took her twenty minutes to jump into the shower, blow-dry her hair, brush her teeth, choose a dress, take it off, try another dress, then another, comb her hair, put on some makeup, look for the small earrings Grandma Ruth had given her on her eighteenth birthday, and change her dress again.

Taking in a deep breath, she put on some perfume. Eternity by Calvin Klein. The bottle had been waiting in the bathroom cabinet for ages. David had never been fond of perfume. He said women should smell like women, not like vanilla beans or cinnamon sticks. But European men might have a different take on this, Ella assumed. Wasn't perfume a big thing in Europe?

When she was done, she inspected the woman in the mirror. Why hadn't he told her he was coming? If she'd known, she would have gone to a hairdresser, gotten a manicure, had a facial, and perhaps tried a new hairstyle. What if Aziz didn't like her? What if there was no chemistry between them and he regretted coming all the way to Boston?

All at once she came to her senses. Why did she want to change her looks? What difference would it make whether there was chemistry between them or not? Any adventure with this man was bound to be ephemeral. She had a family. She had a life. Her past was here, and so was her future. Annoyed with herself for indulging in such unlikely scenarios, she closed down her mind, which always proved easier.

At a quarter to eight, Ella kissed her children good night and left the house. David was nowhere to be seen.

As she walked toward her car, jingling the keys to the apartment in Boston in her hand, her mind was still numb, but her heart raced.

PART FIVE

The Void

THE THINGS THAT ARE PRESENT
THROUGH THEIR ABSENCE

Sultan Walad

KONYA, JULY 1246

Breathing with difficulty and barely able to stand straight, my father came to my room, looking like a shadow of the man he used to be. There were bags under his eyes, dark and ominous, as if he had stayed awake all night. But what surprised me most was that his beard had gone white.

"My son, help me," he said in a voice that didn't sound like him.

I ran to him and grabbed his arm. "Anything, Father, just ask for it."

He was silent for a minute, as though crushed under the weight of what he was going to say next. "Shams is gone. He has left me."

For the briefest of moments, I was awash with confusion and a strange sense of relief, but of that I said nothing. Sad and shocked though I was, it also occurred to me that this could be for the best. Wouldn't life be easier and more tranquil now? My father had gained many enemies lately, all because of Shams. I wanted things to get back to how they were before he came. Could Aladdin be right? Weren't we all better off without Shams?

"Don't forget how much he means to me," my father said as if he sensed my thoughts. "He and I are one. The same moon has a bright and a dark side. Shams is my unruly side."

I nodded, feeling ashamed. My heart sank. My father didn't have to say more. I had never seen so much suffering in a man's eyes. My tongue felt heavy in my mouth. I couldn't speak for a while.

"I want you to find Shams—that is, of course, if he wants to be found. Bring him back. Tell him how my heart aches." My father's voice dropped to a whisper. "Tell him his absence is killing me."

I promised him I would bring Shams back. His hand gripped mine and squeezed it with such gratitude that I had to avert my gaze, for I didn't want him to see the indecision in my eyes.

I spent the whole week roaming the streets of Konya, hoping to trace the footsteps of Shams. By this time everyone in town had heard he had disappeared, and there was much speculation as to his whereabouts. I met a leper who loved Shams immensely. He directed me to many desperate and unfortunate people whom the wandering dervish had helped. I never knew there were so many who loved Shams, since they were the kind of people who had been invisible to me till now.

One evening I came home feeling tired and disoriented. Kerra brought me a bowl of rice pudding, fragrant with the essence of roses. She sat down next to me and watched me eat, her smile framed by crescents of anguish. I couldn't help noticing how much she had aged this past year.

"I heard you were trying to bring Shams back. Do you know where he has gone?" she asked.

"There are rumors he might have gone to Damascus. But I also heard people say he headed to Isfahan, Cairo, or even Tabriz, the city of his birth. We need to check them all. I'll go to Damascus. Some of my father's disciples will go to the other three cities."

A solemn expression crossed Kerra's face, and she murmured, as though thinking aloud, "Mawlana is writing verses. They are beautiful. Shams's absence is turning him into a poet."

Dropping her gaze to the Persian carpet, her cheeks moist, her round mouth pouting, Kerra sighed, and then she recited the following:

"I have seen the king with a face of Glory
He who is the eye and the sun of heaven"

There was something in the air now that wasn't there a moment ago. I could see that Kerra was torn deep inside. One had only to look at her face to understand how it pained her to watch her husband suffer. She was ready to do anything in her power just to see him smile again. And yet she was equally relieved, almost glad, to have finally gotten rid of Shams.

"What if I cannot find him?" I heard myself ask.

"Then there won't be much to do. We will continue with our lives as before," she remarked, a sparkle of hope flickering in her eyes.

At that moment I understood in all clarity and beyond doubt what she insinuated. I didn't have to find Shams of Tabriz. I didn't even have to go to Damascus. I could leave Konya tomorrow, wander for a while, find myself a nice roadside inn to stay at, and come back a few weeks later, pretending to have looked for Shams everywhere. My father would trust my word, and the subject would be dropped forever. Perhaps that would be best, not only for Kerra and Aladdin, who had always been suspicious of Shams, but also for my father's students and disciples, and even for me.

"Kerra," I said, "what shall I do?"

And this woman who had converted to Islam to marry my father, who had been a wonderful mother to me and my brother, and who loved her husband so much she memorized the poems he wrote for someone else, gave me a pained look and said nothing. Suddenly she had no more words inside her.

I had to find the answer for myself.

Rumi

KONYA, AUGUST 1246

Barren is the world, devoid of sun, since Shams is gone. This city is a sad, cold place, and my soul is empty. I can't sleep at night, and during the day I only wander around. I am here and I am not here—a ghost among people. I can't help feeling cross at everyone. How can they go on living their lives as if nothing has changed? How can life be the same without Shams of Tabriz?

Every day from dusk to dawn, I sit in the library on my own and think of nothing but Shams. I remember what he, with a touch of harshness in his voice, had once told me: "Someday you will be the voice of love."

I don't know about that, but it is true that I find silence painful these days. Words give me openings to break through the darkness in my heart. This was what Shams had wanted all along, wasn't it? To make a poet out of me!

Life is about perfection. Every incident that happens, no matter how colossal or small, and every hardship that we endure is an aspect of a divine plan that works to that end. Struggle is intrinsic to being human. That is why it says in the Qur'an, *Certainly we will show Our ways to those who struggle on Our way.* There is no such thing as coincidence in God's scheme. And it was no coincidence that Shams of Tabriz crossed my path on that day in October almost two years ago.

"I didn't come to you because of the wind," Shams had said.

And then he had told me a story.

Once there was a Sufi master who was so knowledgeable that he had been given the breath of Jesus. He had only one student, and he was quite happy with what he was given. But his disciple was of a different mind. In his desire to see everyone else marvel at the powers of his master, he kept begging him to take on more followers.

"All right," the master finally agreed. "If it will make you happy, I'll do as you say."

They went to the market that day. In one of the stalls, there were bird-shaped candies. As soon as the master blew upon them, the birds came alive and flew away with the wind. Speechless, the townspeople immediately gathered around him with admiration. From that day on, everyone in town was singing the master's praises. Soon there were so many followers and admirers around him that his old disciple couldn't see him much anymore.

"Oh, Master, I was wrong. It was much better in the old days," the disciple moaned forlornly. "Do something. Make them all go away, please."

"All right. If it will make you happy, I'll shoo them away."

The next day while he was preaching, the master broke wind. His followers were appalled. One by one, they turned and walked away from him. Only his old disciple remained.

"Why didn't you leave with the others?" the master asked.

And the disciple answered, "I didn't come to you because of the first wind, nor would I leave you because of the last."

Everything Shams did, he did for my perfection. This is what the townspeople could never understand. Shams deliberately fanned the flames of gossip, touched raw nerves, and spoke words that sounded like blasphemy to ordinary ears, shocking and provoking people, even those who loved him. He threw my books into water, forcing me to unlearn all that I knew. Though everyone had heard that he was critical of sheikhs and scholars, very few people knew how capable of *tafsir* he was. Shams had deep knowledge in alchemy, astrology, astronomy, theology, philosophy, and logic, but he kept his knowledge hidden from ignorant eyes. Though he was a *faqih,* he acted as if he were a *faqir.*

He opened our doors to a prostitute and made us share our food with her. He sent me to the tavern and encouraged me to talk to drunks. Once he made me beg across from the mosque where I used to preach, forcing me to put myself in the shoes of a leper beggar. He cut me off first from my admirers, then from the ruling elite, bringing me in touch with the common people. Thanks to him I came to know persons I would have otherwise never met. In his belief that all idols that stood between the individual and God had to be demolished, including fame, wealth, rank, and even religion, Shams cut loose all the moorings that tied me to life as I knew it. Wherever he saw any kind of mental boundary, a prejudice or a taboo, he took the bull by the horns and confronted it.

For him I went through trial and tests, states and stages, each of which made me look more deranged in the eyes of even my most loyal followers. Before, I had plenty of admirers; now I have gotten rid of the need for an audience. Blow after blow, Shams managed to ruin my reputation. Because of him I learned the value of madness and have come to know the taste of loneliness, helplessness, slander, seclusion, and, finally, heartbreak.

Whatever you see as profitable, flee from it!
Drink poison and pour away the water of life!
Abandon security and stay in frightful places!
Throw away reputation, become disgraced and shameless!

At the end of the day, aren't we are all put on trial? Every day, every passing minute, God asks us, *Do you remember the covenant we made before you were sent to this world? Do you understand your role in revealing My treasure?*

Most of the time, we are not ready to answer these questions. They are too frightening. But God is patient. He asks again and again.

And if this heartache, too, is part of a trial, my only wish is to find Shams at the end of it. My books, sermons, family, wealth, or name—I am ready to give up anything and everything, just to see his face one more time.

The other day Kerra said I was turning into a poet, almost despite myself. Though I have never thought highly of poets, I wasn't surprised to hear that. At any other time, I might have objected to what she said, but not anymore.

My mouth is spewing out lines of verse, constantly and involuntarily, and, listening to them, one might conclude that I am becoming a poet indeed. The Sultan of Language! But the truth, insofar as I am able to tell, is that the poems do not belong to me. I am only a vehicle for letters that are placed in my mouth. Like a pen that writes down the words it is ordered to inscribe or a flute that plays the notes blown into it, I, too, am simply doing my part.

Marvelous sun of Tabriz! Where are you?

Shams

DAMASCUS, APRIL 1247

By the time spring was in full swing in Damascus, and ten months had passed since my departure from Konya, Sultan Walad found me. Under a clear blue sky, I was playing chess with a Christian hermit named Francis. He was a man whose inner balance did not tilt easily, a man who knew the meaning of submission. And since Islam means the inner peace that comes from submission, to me Francis was more Muslim than many who claim to be so. For it is one of the forty rules: *Submission does not mean being weak or passive. It leads to neither fatalism nor capitulation. Just the opposite. True power resides in submission—a power that comes from within. Those who submit to the divine essence of life will live in unperturbed tranquillity and peace even when the whole wide world goes through turbulence after turbulence.*

I moved my vizier in order to force Francis's king to shift position. With a quick and brave decision, he moved his rook. I had begun to suspect I was going to lose this game when I lifted my head and came eye to eye with Sultan Walad.

"Nice to see you," I said. "So you have decided to look for me after all."

He gave me a rueful smile, then turned somber, surprised to hear that I was aware of the internal struggle he had been through. But being the honest man that he was, he didn't deny the truth.

"I spent some time wandering around instead of looking for you. But after a while I couldn't do it anymore. I couldn't bring myself to lie to my father. I came to Damascus and started looking for you, but you weren't easy to find."

"You are an honest man and a good son," I said. "One day soon you'll be a great companion to your father."

Sultan Walad shook his head dolefully. "You are the only companion he needs. I want you to come back to Konya with me. My father needs you."

Many things churned in my brain upon hearing this invitation, and none of them were clear at first. My *nafs* reacted with fear at the idea of going back to a place where I was clearly unwelcome.

Don't listen to him. You are done with your mission. You don't have to return to Konya. Remember what Baba Zaman told you. It's way too dangerous. If you go back to that town you will never come out again.

I wanted to keep traveling the world, meet new people and see new cities. I had liked Damascus, too, and could easily stay there until the next winter. Traveling to a new place often engendered a dreadful sense of loneliness and sadness in the soul of a man. But with God by my side, I was content and fulfilled in my solitude.

Yet I knew too well that my heart was in Konya. I missed Rumi so much that it was too painful even to utter his name. At the end of the day, what difference would it make which city I stayed in, as long as Rumi was not beside me? Wherever he lived, there was my *qibla*.

I moved my king on the chessboard. Francis's eyes flew open as he detected the fatal position. But in chess, just as in life, there were moves that you made for the sake of winning and there were moves you made because they were the right thing to do.

"Please come with me," implored Sultan Walad, interrupting my thoughts. "The people who gossiped about you and treated you badly are remorseful. Everything will be better this time, I promise."

My boy, you can't make such promises, I wanted to tell him. *Nobody can!*

But instead I nodded and said, "I would like to watch the sunset in Damascus one more time. Tomorrow we can leave for Konya."

"Really? Thank you!" Sultan Walad beamed with relief. "You don't know how much this will mean to my father."

I then turned to Francis, who was patiently waiting for me to return to the game. When he had my full attention, an impish smile crept along his mouth.

"Watch out, my friend," he said, his voice triumphant. "Checkmate."

Kimya

KONYA, MAY 1247

Bearing a mysterious gaze in his eyes and a distance in his demeanor that he'd never had before, Shams of Tabriz came back into my life. He seems to have changed a lot. His hair long enough to fall into his eyes, his skin tanned under the Damascus sun, he looks younger and more handsome. But there is something else in him, a change I cannot quite put my finger on. As bright and reckless as ever his black eyes might be, there is now a new glimmer to them. I can't help suspecting he has the eyes of a man who has seen it all and doesn't want to struggle anymore.

But I think a deeper transformation has been taking place in Rumi. I had thought all his worries would diminish when Shams came back, but that doesn't seem to be the case. On the day Shams returned, Rumi greeted him outside the city walls with flowers. But when the joy of the first days somewhat abated, Rumi became even more anxious and withdrawn than before. I think I know the reason. Having lost Shams once, he is afraid of losing him again. I can understand as no one else can, because I, too, am afraid of losing him.

The only person I share my feelings with is Gevher, Rumi's late wife. Well, she is not technically a *person,* but I don't call her a ghost either. Less dreamy and distant than most of the ghosts I have known, she has been moving like a slow flow of water around me ever since I came to this house. Although we converse about everything, lately there is only one topic between us: Shams.

"Rumi looks so distressed. I wish I could help him," I said to Gevher today.

"Perhaps you could. There is something occupying his mind these days, but he hasn't shared it with anyone yet," Gevher said mysteriously.

"What is it?" I inquired.

"Rumi thinks if Shams gets married and starts a family, the townspeople would be less set against him. There would be less gossip, and Shams would not have to leave again."

My heart skipped a beat. Shams getting married! But to whom?

Gevher gave me a sidelong look and said, "Rumi has been wondering if *you* would like to marry Shams."

I was stunned. Not that this was the first time the thought of marriage had crossed my mind. Now fifteen, I knew I had reached the age to marry, but I also knew that girls who got married changed forever. A new gaze came to their eyes, and they took on a new demeanor, to such an extent that people started to treat them differently. Even little children could tell the difference between a married woman and an unmarried one.

Gevher smiled tenderly and held my hand. She had noticed that it was the getting-married part that worried me, not getting married to Shams.

The next day, in the afternoon, I went to see Rumi and found him immersed in a book titled *Tahafut al-Tahafut*.

"Tell me, Kimya," he said lovingly, "what can I do for you?"

"When my father brought me to you, you had told him that a girl would not make as good a student as a boy because she would have to marry and raise her children, do you remember that?"

"Of course, I remember," he answered, his hazel eyes filled with curiosity.

"That day I promised myself never to get married, so that I could remain your student forever," I said, my voice dwindling under the weight of what I was planning to say next. "But perhaps it is possible to get married and not have to leave this house. I mean, if I get married to someone who lives here . . ."

"Are you telling me you want to marry Aladdin?" Rumi asked.

"Aladdin?" I repeated in shock. But what made him think I wanted to marry Aladdin? He was like a brother to me.

Rumi must have detected my surprise. "Some time ago Aladdin came to me and asked for your hand," he said.

I gasped. I knew it wasn't proper for a girl to ask too many questions on such matters, but I was dying to learn more. "And what did you say, Master?"

"I told him I would have to ask you first," Rumi said.

"Master . . ." I said, my voice trailing off. "I came here to tell you I want to marry Shams of Tabriz."

Rumi gave me a look that bordered on disbelief. "Are you sure about this?"

"It could be good in many ways," I said, as inside me the need to say more wrestled with the regret of having said too much. "Shams would be part of our family, and he wouldn't ever have to leave again."

"So is that why you want to marry him? To help him stay here?" asked Rumi.

"No," I said. "I mean, yes, but that's not all. . . . I believe Shams is my destiny."

This was as close as I could get to confessing to anyone that I loved Shams of Tabriz.

The first to hear about the marriage was Kerra. In stunned silence she greeted the news with a broken smile, but as soon as we were alone in the house, she started to ask me questions. "Are you sure this is what you want to do? You are not doing this to help Rumi, are you?" she said. "You are so young! Don't you think you should marry someone closer to your own age?"

"Shams says in love all boundaries are blurred," I told her.

Kerra sighed loudly. "My child, I wish things were that simple," she remarked, tucking a lock of gray hair into her scarf. "Shams is a wandering dervish, an unruly man. Men like him aren't used to domestic life, and they don't make good husbands."

"That's all right, he can change," I concluded firmly. "I will give him so much love and happiness he will have to change. He will learn how to be a good husband and a good father."

That was the end of our talk. Whatever it was that she saw on my face, Kerra had no more objections to raise.

I slept peacefully that night, feeling exultant and determined. Little did I know that I was making the most common and the most painful mistake women have made all throughout the ages: to naïvely think that with their love they can change the men they love.

Kerra

KONYA, MAY 1247

Broaching a subject as deep and delicate as love is like trying to capture a gusty wind. You can feel the harm the wind is about to cause, but there is no way to slow it down. After a while I didn't ask Kimya any other questions, not because I was convinced by her answers but because I saw in her eyes a woman in love. I stopped questioning this marriage, accepting it as one of those odd things in life I had no control over.

The month of Ramadan went by so fast and busy, I didn't have time to dwell on this matter again. Eid fell on Sunday. Four days later we married Kimya to Shams.

The evening before the wedding, something happened that changed my entire mood. I was alone in the kitchen, sitting in front of a floured board and a rolling pin, preparing flatbread for the guests. All of a sudden, without thinking what I was doing, I started molding a shape out of a ball of dough. I sculpted a small, soft Mother Mary. My Mother Mary. With the help of a knife, I carved her long robe and her face, calm and compassionate. So absorbed was I in this that I didn't notice someone standing behind me.

"What is it that you are making, Kerra?"

My heart jumped inside my chest. When I turned around, I saw Shams standing by the door, watching me with inquisitive eyes. It occurred to me to hide the dough, but it was too late. Shams approached the tray and looked at the figure.

"Is that Mary?" he asked, and when I didn't answer, he turned to me with a beaming countenance. "Why, she is beautiful. Do you miss Mary?"

"I converted long ago. I am a Muslim woman," I answered curtly.

But Shams continued to talk as if he hadn't heard me. "Perhaps you wonder why Islam doesn't have a female figure like Mary. There is Aisha, for sure, and certainly Fatima, but you might think it is not the same."

I felt uneasy, not knowing what to say.

"May I tell you a story?" Shams asked.

And this is what he told me:

Once there were four travelers, a Greek, an Arab, a Persian, and a Turk. Upon reaching a small town, they decided to get something to eat. As they had limited money they had only one choice to make. Each said he had the best food in the world in mind. When asked what that was, the Persian answered "angoor," the Greek said "staphalion," the Arab asked for "aneb," and the Turk demanded "üzüm." Unable to understand one another's language, they began to argue.

They kept quarreling among themselves, feeling more resentful and bitter with every passing minute, until a Sufi who happened to pass by interrupted them. With the money collected the Sufi bought a bunch of grapes. He then put the grapes in a container and pressed hard. He made the travelers drink the juice and threw away the skin, because what mattered was the essence of the fruit, not its outer form.

"Christians, Jews, and Muslims are like those travelers. While they quarrel about the outer form, the Sufi is after the essence," Shams said, giving me a smile that conveyed such excitement that it was hard not to be carried away by it.

"What I am trying to say is, there is no reason for you to miss Mother Mary, because you don't need to abandon her in the first place. As a Muslim woman, you can still feel attached to her."

"I . . . I don't think that would be right," I stammered.

"I don't see why not. Religions are like rivers: They all flow to the same sea. Mother Mary stands for compassion, mercy, affection, and unconditional love. She is both personal and universal. As a Muslim woman, you can keep liking her and even name your daughter Mary."

"I don't have a daughter," I said.

"You will have one."

"You think so?"

"I know so."

I felt excited to hear such words, but before long the excitement was washed away by another feeling: solidarity. Sharing an unusual moment of serenity and harmony, we looked at the figure of Mother Mary together. My heart warmed to Shams, and for the first time since he'd come to our house, I was able to see what Rumi saw in him: a man with a big heart.

Still, I doubted he would make a good husband for Kimya.

Ella

BOSTON, JUNE 29, 2008

By the time Ella got to the hotel, she was so tense she couldn't think properly. There was a group of Japanese tourists in the lobby, all of whom appeared to be in their seventies and sported the same haircut. She crossed the lobby, scanning the paintings on the walls, so as not to have to look in the eyes of the people around her. But it didn't take long for her curiosity to defeat her timidity. And the moment her gaze slid toward the meeting area, she saw him, watching her.

He was wearing a khaki button-down shirt and dark corduroy trousers, and had a two-day stubble that she thought made him quite attractive. His curly chestnut hair fell over his green eyes, giving him an air of confidence and mischief all at once. Wiry and thin, light and lithe, he was very different from David in his expensive tailor-made suits. He spoke with a Scottish brogue, which she found charming, and smiled with an ease of manner, looking genuinely happy and excited to see her. And Ella couldn't help asking herself what harm there could be in having a cup of coffee with him.

Later on, she would not be able to remember how one cup of coffee became several cups, or how the conversation took on an increasingly intimate tone, or how at some point he planted a kiss on her fingertip, just as she would not be able to explain why she didn't do anything to stop him. After a while nothing seemed to matter as long as he kept talking and she could let her gaze linger on the small dimple at the corner of his mouth, wondering what it would be like to kiss him there. It was half past eleven o'clock in the evening. She was in a hotel with a man she didn't know anything about, aside from some e-mails and phone calls and the novel he'd written.

"So you're here for *Smithsonian* magazine?" Ella asked.

"Actually, I'm here for you," Aziz answered. "After reading your letter, I wanted to come and see you."

Still, there were possible exit routes off this fast-moving highway. Up to a certain moment, it remained possible to pretend that everything was just on friendly terms—the e-mails, the phone calls, even the glances. A bit flirtatious and playful, perhaps, but nothing more than that. She could have drawn a line. That is, until he asked, "Ella, would you like to come to my room?"

If this was a game they were both playing, that was when it got serious. His question made everything far too real, as if a mantle had been lifted and the truth, the naked truth that had been there all along, now looked them squarely in the face. Ella felt something stir in her stomach, a bubbling discomfort that she recognized as panic, but she did not turn him down. This was the most impulsive decision she had made in her life, and yet at the same time it felt as if the decision had already been made for her. All she needed to do was to accept it.

Room 608 was pleasantly decorated in hues of black, red, gray, and beige. It was warm and spacious. She tried to remember the last time she'd stayed in a hotel. A trip to Montreal with her husband and children a long time ago popped into her mind. After that, they had spent all their vacations at their house in Rhode Island, and she'd had no reason to stay in a place where the towels were changed daily and breakfast was prepared by others. Being in a hotel room felt like being in a different country. And perhaps she was. Already she could feel the frivolous freedom one could enjoy only in a city where everyone was a complete stranger.

But as soon as she walked into the room, her nervousness came back. No matter how tasteful the decor or how spacious the room, the king-size bed was clearly at its center. Standing next to it made her feel awkward and guilty. She started struggling with internal questions, getting nowhere. Would they make love now? Should they? If they did, how could she look her husband in the eye afterward? But David never had any difficulty looking *her* in the eye despite his many flings, did he? And what would Aziz think of her body? What if he didn't like it? Shouldn't she be thinking about her children now? Were they asleep or awake watching TV at this hour? If they learned what she was about to do, would they ever forgive her?

Sensing her unease, Aziz held her hand and moved her toward an armchair in the corner, away from the bed.

"Hush," he whispered. "It's so crowded inside your mind. Too many voices."

"I wish we had met earlier," Ella heard herself say.

"There is no such thing as early or late in life," Aziz said. "Everything happens at the right time."

"Do you really believe that?"

He smiled and brushed a cloud of hair out of his eyes. Then he opened a suitcase and brought out the tapestry he'd bought in Guatemala and a small box that turned out to be a necklace of turquoise and red coral beads with a silver whirling dervish.

Ella let him put the necklace around her neck. Where his fingers touched her skin, she felt warm. "Am I what you expected?" she asked.

"I already love you." Aziz smiled.

"But you don't even know me!"

"I don't have to know to love."

Ella sighed. "This is crazy."

Aziz reached around and pulled out the pin holding her bun, letting her hair loose. Then he gently moved her onto the bed. Slowly, tenderly, and in ever-growing circles, he moved his palms up from her feet toward her ankles and from there toward her belly. All the while his lips muttered words that sounded like a secret ancient code to Ella. Suddenly she understood. He was praying. While his hands caressed every inch of her body, his eyes remained firmly closed and his lips prayed for her. It was the most spiritual thing she had ever experienced. And although she kept her clothes on, and so did he, and although there was nothing carnal about it, it was the sexiest feeling she had ever experienced.

All at once her palms, her elbows, her shoulders, her whole body began to tingle with a strange energy. She was possessed by so magnificent a desire that she felt as though she were floating on warm, wavy waters where all she could do was surrender and smile. She sensed a living presence around him, then around her, as if they were both being showered in a drizzle of light.

She, too, closed her eyes now, drifting in a wild river without holding on to anything. There might be a waterfall at the end for all she knew, but even if she could have stopped, she wasn't sure she wanted to.

Ella felt a burning between her legs when his hands reached her belly, drawing a circle there. She felt insecure about her body, her hips and thighs and the shape of her breasts, which were far from perfect after three kids and all these years, but the anxiety came and went. Feeling buoyant, almost protected, she drifted into a state of bliss. And just like that, she realized she could love this man. She could love him so much.

With that feeling she put her arms around Aziz, pulling him toward her, ready to go further. But he snapped his eyes open, kissed her on the tip of her nose, and pulled away.

"You don't want me?" Ella asked, amazed by the fragility of her voice.

"I don't want to do anything that would make you unhappy afterward."

Half of her felt like crying; the other half was elated. A strange feeling of lightness took hold of her. She was entirely confused, but, to her great surprise, for once it felt okay to be confused.

At half past one in the morning, Ella opened the door to her apartment in Boston. She lay on the leather couch, unwilling to sleep in the master bed. Not because she knew that her husband had been sleeping there with other women, but because somehow it felt better like this, as if this house didn't belong to her any more than a hotel room, as if she were a guest here and her true self were waiting elsewhere.

Shams

KONYA, MAY 1247

Beautiful bride, don't you cry
Say bye to your mom, bye to dad
You will hear the birds sing tomorrow
Though it will never be the same. . . .

On our wedding night, I slipped out into the courtyard and sat there for a while, listening to an old Anatolian song pour from the house amid the many other sounds. Laughter, music, gossip. Female musicians played in the women's section. I stood there thinking and chanting, shivering and feeling numb, all at the same time. I pondered the lyrics of the song. Why was it that women always sang sad songs on wedding nights? Sufis associated death with weddings and celebrated the day they died as their union with God. Women, too, associated weddings with death, though for entirely different reasons. Even when they were happily getting married, a wave of sadness descended upon them. In every wedding celebration, there was mourning for the virgin who was soon to become a wife and a mother.

After the guests left, I returned to the house and meditated in a quiet corner. Then I went to the room where Kimya was waiting for me. I found her sitting on the bed, wearing a white robe adorned with golden threads, her hair braided into a multitude of plaits, each of which was ornamented with beads. It was impossible to see her expression, as her face was covered with thick, red tulle. Except for a candle that flickered by the window, the room was without light. The mirror on the wall had been covered by a velvet cloth, as it was deemed to be bad luck for a young bride to see her reflection on her wedding night. Beside our bed there was a pomegranate and a knife, so that we could eat the fruit and have as many children as the seeds inside.

Kerra had told me all about the local customs, reminding me to give the bride a necklace with gold coins upon opening her veil. But I never had gold coins in my life and did not want to greet my bride with coins borrowed from someone else. So when I lifted Kimya's veil, all I did was to give her a comb made of tortoiseshell and plant a small kiss on her lips. She smiled. And for a second I felt as shy as a lost little boy.

"You are beautiful," I said.

She blushed. But then she squared her shoulders, doing her best to look more tranquil and mature than she could ever be.

"I am your wife now," she said.

Then she pointed toward the beautiful carpet on the floor, which she had crafted on her own and with great care as part of her dowry. Exuberant colors, sharp contrasts. As soon as I saw it I knew that every knot and every pattern on the carpet was about me. Kimya had been weaving her dreams.

I kissed her again. The warmth of her lips sent waves of desire across my entire body. She smelled of jasmine and wildflowers. Stretching out beside her, I inhaled her smell and touched her breasts, so small and firm. All I wanted was to enter her and get lost inside her. She offered herself to me the way a rosebud opens to the rain.

I pulled away. "I'm sorry, Kimya. I can't do this."

She looked at me, still and stunned, forgetting to breathe. The disappointment in her eyes was too much to bear. I jumped to my feet.

"I need to go," I said.

"You cannot go now," Kimya said in a voice that didn't sound like her. "What will people say if you leave the room now? They will know that this marriage was not consummated. And they'll think it was because of me."

"What do you mean?" I murmured, half to myself, because I knew what she was suggesting.

Averting her eyes, she mumbled something incomprehensible, and then she said quietly, "They'll think I wasn't a virgin. I'll have to live in shame."

It made my blood boil that society imposed such ridiculous rules on its individuals. These codes of honor had less to do with the harmony God created than with the order human beings wanted to sustain.

"That's nonsense. People should mind their own business," I objected, but I knew that Kimya was right.

With one quick move, I grabbed the knife beside the pomegranate. I glimpsed a trace of panic in Kimya's face, slowly replaced by the expression of someone who recognized a sad situation and accepted it. Without hesitation I cut my left palm. My blood dripped on our bedsheet, leaving dark crimson stains.

"Just give them this sheet. This will shut their mouths, and your name will remain pure and clean, the way it should be."

"Wait, please! Don't go," Kimya beseeched. She rose to her feet, but, not knowing what to do next, she repeated once again, "I am your wife now."

In that moment I understood what a terrible mistake I had made by marrying her. My head throbbing with pain, I walked out of the room into the night. A man like me should never have gotten married. I wasn't intended for the settled life. I saw this clearly. What saddened me was the cost of this knowledge.

I felt a strong need to run away from everything, not only from this house, this marriage, this town, but also from this body I had been given. Yet the thought of seeing Rumi the next morning held me anchored here. I couldn't abandon him again.

I was trapped.

Aladdin

KONYA, MAY 1247

Being forced into a decision that I knew I would deeply regret later, I remained silent and did not openly object to this marriage. But on the day Kimya was going to be married to Shams, I woke up with a pain such as I had never felt before. I sat up in bed gasping for breath like a drowning man, and then, annoyed with myself for wallowing in self-pity I slapped my face again and again. A strangled sigh escaped my lips. And it was that sound that made me realize I wasn't my father's son anymore.

I had no mother. No father. No brother. And no Kimya. I was all alone in the world. What little remained of my respect for my father had disappeared overnight. Kimya was like a daughter to him. I thought he cared about her. But apparently the only person he really cared about was Shams of Tabriz. How could he marry Kimya to a man like him? Anyone could see that Shams would make a terrible husband. The more I thought about it, the clearer it became that just to make Shams safe, my father had sacrificed Kimya's happiness—and along with it mine.

I spent the whole day struggling with these thoughts while having to watch the preparations. The house was spruced up, and the bedroom where the newlyweds would sleep was cleansed with rosewater to ward off evil spirits. But they forgot the biggest evil! How were they going to fend off Shams?

By late afternoon I couldn't stand it anymore. Determined not to be part of a celebration that meant only torture for me, I headed for the door.

"Aladdin, wait! Where are you going?" My brother's voice came from behind me, loud and sharp.

"I am going to stay at Irshad's house tonight," I said without looking at him.

"Have you gone crazy? How can you not stay for the wedding? If our father hears this it will break his heart."

I could feel rage rising from the pit of my stomach. "How about the hearts our father is breaking?"

"What are you talking about?"

"Don't you get it? Our father arranged this marriage just to please Shams and make sure he doesn't run away again! He offered Kimya to him on a silver tray."

My brother pursed his lips, looking hurt. "I know what you are thinking, but you are wrong. You think this is a forced marriage," he said, "whereas it was Kimya who wanted to marry Shams."

"As if she had a choice in the matter," I snapped.

"Oh, God! Don't you understand?" my brother exclaimed, lifting both palms up as though asking help from God. "She is in love with Shams."

"Don't say that again. That is not true." My voice cracked like thawing ice.

"My brother," Sultan Walad said, "please don't let your feelings veil your eyes. You are jealous. But even jealousy can be used in a constructive way and serve a higher purpose. Even disbelief can be positive. It is one of the rules. Rule Number Thirty-five: *In this world, it is not similarities or regularities that take us a step forward, but blunt opposites. And all the opposites in the universe are present within each and every one of us. Therefore the believer needs to meet the unbeliever residing within. And the nonbeliever should get to know the silent faithful in him. Until the day one reaches the stage of Insan-i Kâmil, the perfect human being, faith is a gradual process and one that necessitates its seeming opposite: disbelief.*

That was the last straw for me.

"Look here, I'm sick of all this syrupy Sufi talk. Besides, why should I listen to you? It's all your fault! You could have left Shams in Damascus. Why did you bring him back? If things get messy, and I am sure they will, you are the one who is responsible."

My brother gnawed the insides of his mouth with a look that verged on fearfulness. I realized in that instant that for the first time in our lives he was frightened of me and the things I was capable of doing. It was a bizarre feeling, but strangely comforting.

As I walked to Irshad's house, taking the side streets that reeked of foul smells so that nobody would see me cry, I could think of only one thing: Shams and Kimya sharing the same bed. The thought of him taking her wedding dress off and touching her milky skin with his rough, ugly hands was revolting. My stomach was tied in knots.

I knew that a line had been crossed. Somebody had to do something.

Kimya

KONYA, DECEMBER 1247

Bride and groom—that is what we were supposed to be. It has been seven months since we got married. All this time he hasn't slept with me as my husband even once. Hard as I try to hide the truth from people, I can't help suspecting they know it. Sometimes I fear that my shame is visible on my face. Like writing on my forehead, it is the first thing that anyone who looks at me notices. While I am talking to neighbors on the street, working in the orchards, or bartering with the vendors in the bazaar, it takes people, even strangers, only a glance to see that I am a married woman but still a virgin.

Not that Shams never comes to my room. He does. Each time he wants to visit me in the evening, he asks me beforehand if it is all right. And each time I give the same answer.

"Of course it is," I say. "You are my husband."

Then all day long I wait for him with bated breath, hoping and praying that this time our marriage will be consummated. But when he finally knocks on my door, all he wants to do is sit and talk. He also enjoys reading together. We have read *Layla and Majnun*, *Farhad and Shirin*, *Yusuf and Zuleikha*, *The Rose and the Nightingale*—stories of lovers who have loved each other against all odds. Despite the strength and determination of their main characters, I find these stories depressing. Perhaps it is because deep inside I know that I will never taste love of such proportions.

When not reading stories, Shams talks about the Forty Rules of the Itinerant Mystics of Islam—the basic principles of the religion of love.

Once he put his head on my lap as he was explaining a rule. He slowly closed his eyes, and as his voice trailed off into a whisper, he fell asleep. My fingers combed through his long hair, and my lips kissed his forehead. It seemed an eternity before he opened his eyes. Pulling me down toward himself, he kissed me softly. It was the most blissful moment we ever had together. But that was it. To this day his body is an unknown continent to me, as is my body to him.

During these seven months, I, too, have been to his room several times. But each time I visit him unannounced, my heart constricts with anxiety as I can never tell how he will receive me. It is impossible to predict Shams's moods. Sometimes he is so warm and loving that I forget all my sorrow, but then at other times he can be extremely grumpy. Once he slammed his door in my face, yelling that he wanted to be left alone. I have learned not to take any offense, just as I have learned not to bother him when he is in deep meditation.

For months on end after the wedding, I pretended to be content, perhaps less with others than with myself. I forced myself to see Shams not as a husband but as almost everything else: a friend, a soul mate, a master, a companion, even a son. Depending on the day, depending on his mood, I thought of him as one or the other, dressing him up in a different costume in my imagination.

And for a while it worked. Without expecting much, I began to look forward to our conversations. It pleased me immensely that he appreciated my thoughts and encouraged me to think more widely. I learned so many things from him, and in time, I realized, I, too, could teach him a few things such as the joys of family life, which he had never tasted before. To this day I believe I can make him laugh as no one else could.

But it wasn't enough. Whatever I did, I could not rid my mind of the thought that he didn't love me. I had no doubt that he liked me and meant me well. But this wasn't anything even close to love. So harrowing was this thought that it was eating me up inside, gnawing at my body and soul. I became detached from the people around me, friends and neighbors alike. I now preferred to stay in my room and talk with dead people. Unlike the living, the dead never judged.

Other than the dead, the only friend I had was Desert Rose.

United in our desire to stay away from the eyes of others, we had become close friends. She is a Sufi now. She leads a solitary life, having left the brothel behind her. Once I told her I envied her courage and determination to start life anew.

She shook her head and said, "But I have not started life anew. The only thing I did was to die before death."

Today I went to see Desert Rose for an entirely different reason. I had planned to maintain my composure and talk to her calmly, but as soon as I entered, I started choking back sobs.

"Kimya, are you all right?" she asked.

"I am not feeling well," I confessed. "I think I need your help."

"Certainly," she said. "What can I do for you?"

"It is about Shams. . . . He doesn't come near me . . . I mean, not in that way," I stuttered halfway through but managed to finish my sentence. "I want to make myself attractive to him. I want you to teach me how."

Desert Rose exhaled, almost a sigh. "I took an oath, Kimya," she said, a weary note slipping into her voice. "I promised God to stay clean and pure and not even *think* anymore about the ways a woman could give pleasure to a man."

"But you are not going to break your oath. You are just going to help me," I pleaded. "I am the one who needs to learn how to make Shams happy."

"Shams is an enlightened man," Desert Rose said, lowering her voice a notch, as if afraid of being heard. "I don't think this is the right way to approach him."

"But he is a *man,* isn't he?" I reasoned. "Aren't all men the sons of Adam and bound by the flesh? Enlightened or not, we all have been given a body. Even Shams has a body, doesn't he?"

"Yes, but . . . " Desert Rose grabbed her *tàsbih* and started to finger the beads one at a time, her head tilted in contemplation.

"Oh, please," I begged. "You are the only one I can confide in. It has been seven months. Every morning I wake up with the same heaviness in my chest, every night I go to sleep in tears. It can't go on like this. I need to seduce my husband!"

Desert Rose said nothing. I took off my scarf, grabbed her head, and forced her to look at me. I said, "Tell me the truth. Am I so ugly?"

"Of course not, Kimya. You are a beautiful young woman."

"Then help me. Teach me the way to a man's heart," I insisted.

"The way to a man's heart can sometimes take a woman far away from herself, my dear," Desert Rose said ominously.

"I don't care," I said. "I am ready to go as far as it takes."

Desert Rose

KONYA, DECEMBER 1247

Bursting into tears, she kept begging me to help, her face swollen, her chest heaving harder and faster, until I finally told her I would lend a hand. Even as I comforted her, deep inside I knew it was hopeless, I knew I should never have yielded to her demands. Still, I wonder how could I not have seen this tragedy coming? Torn with guilt, I keep asking myself again and again, how could I have been so naïve and not seen that things would take such a terrible turn?

But the day she came to me crying for help, there was no way I could turn her down.

"Teach me, please," she begged me, her hands demurely folded in her lap, like the good girl she was raised to be. Hers was a voice that no longer had a reason to hope yet was hopeful all the same.

What harm could there be in this? I thought as my heart lurched in compassion. It was her husband she wanted to seduce, for God's sake. Not a stranger! She had only one motive: love. How could this lead to anything incorrect? Her passion might be too strong, but it was halal, wasn't it? A halal passion!

Something inside me sensed a trap, but since it was God who set it, I saw no harm in walking right in. This is how I decided to help Kimya, this village girl whose only notion of beauty was applying henna to her hands.

I taught her how to make herself more attractive and good-looking. She was an avid student, eager to learn. I showed her how to take long perfumed baths, soften her skin with scented oils and ointments, and apply masks of milk and honey. I gave her amber beads to braid in her hair so that her head would have a sweet, lasting smell. Lavender, chamomile, rosemary, thyme, lily, marjoram, and olive oil—I told her how to apply each and which incenses to burn at night. Then I showed her how to whiten her teeth, paint her nails and toes with henna, apply kohl on her eyes and eyebrows, redden her lips and cheeks, how to make her hair look lush and silky and her breasts bigger and rounder. Together we went to a store in the bazaar I knew too well from the past. There we bought her silk robes and silk undergarments, the likes of which she had never seen or touched before.

Then I taught her how to dance in front of a man, how to use this body God had given her. After two weeks of preparation, she was ready.

That afternoon I prepared Kimya for Shams of Tabriz, the way a shepherd prepares a sacrificial lamb. First she took a warm bath, scrubbing her skin with soapy cloths and anointing her hair with oils. Then I helped her to get dressed in clothes that a woman could wear only for her husband, and even for him only once or twice in a lifetime. I had chosen a cherry-colored sheath and a pink robe gilded with hyacinths, of the sort that would reveal the shape of her breasts. Lastly we applied lots and lots of paint on her face. With a string of pearls across her forehead added as a final touch, she looked so pretty that I couldn't take my eyes off her.

When we were done, Kimya didn't look like an inexperienced, timid girl anymore, but a woman burning with love and passion. A woman ready to make a bold move for the man she loved and, if necessary, to pay a price. As I stood inspecting her, I remembered the verse of Joseph and Zuleikha in the Holy Qur'an.

Just like Kimya, Zuleikha, too, had been consumed by a desire for a man who did not respond to her overtures. When the ladies in the city had maliciously gossiped about her, Zuleikha had invited them all to a banquet. *She gave each of them a knife: and she said (to Joseph), "Come out before them." When they saw him, they did extol him, and (in their amazement) cut their hands: they said, "God preserve us! No mortal is this! This is none other than a noble angel."*

Who could blame Zuleikha for desiring Joseph so much?

"How do I look?" Kimya asked anxiously before she put on her veil, ready to step out the door and onto the street.

"You look exquisite," I said. "Your husband will not only make love to you tonight, he'll come back tomorrow asking for more."

Kimya blushed so hard her cheeks turned rosy red. I laughed, and after a brief pause she joined me, her laughter warming me like sunshine.

I meant what I'd said, as I felt confident that she would be able to attract Shams, the way a flower rich with nectar attracts a bee. And yet when our eyes met just before she opened the door, I saw that a trace of doubt had crept into her gaze. Suddenly I had a bad feeling in the pit of my stomach, almost a premonition that something terrible was going to happen.

But I didn't stop her. I should have known better. I should have seen it coming. For as long as I live, I will never forgive myself.

Kimya

KONYA, DECEMBER 1247

Bold, boisterous, and intelligent, Shams of Tabriz knows a great deal about love. But there is one thing he doesn't know anything about: the pain of unrequited love.

The evening Desert Rose dressed me, I was full of excitement and an audacity I didn't know I had in me. The soft rustle of the silk dress against my body, the scent of my perfume, the taste of rose petals on my tongue—it all made me feel awkward, but also unusually brave. Back at home I caught my reflection on a pane of glass. My body was neither rotund nor milky, and my bosom not as ample as I would have liked, but I still thought I looked pretty.

I waited until I was sure everyone in the house had gone to sleep. Then I wrapped myself in a long, thick shawl and tiptoed to Shams's room.

"Kimya, I wasn't expecting you," he said as soon as he opened his door.

"I had to see you," I said and stepped inside without waiting for him to invite me in. "Could you please close the door?"

Shams looked puzzled, but he did as told.

When we were alone in the room, it took me a few seconds to muster my courage. I turned my back to him, took a deep breath, and then, in one quick move, removed my shawl and slid my robe off. Almost instantly I felt the weight of my husband's surprised eyes on my back, from my neck down to my feet. Wherever his gaze touched felt warm. But that warmth, whether it was real or imagined in my excitement, was quickly replaced by the coldness of the silence that descended upon the room. My chest rising and falling with apprehension, I stood in front of Shams as naked and inviting as the houris in paradise are said to be.

In the pregnant silence, we stood listening to the wind outside, howling, raging, and wailing through the city.

"What do you think you are doing?" he asked coldly.

It was quite an effort to find my voice, but I managed to say, "I want you."

Shams of Tabriz walked a half circle around me and stood right in front of me, forcing me to look him in the eye. My knees buckled beneath me, but I didn't budge. Instead I took a step toward him and pressed my body against his, squirming ever so slightly, offering him my warmth, the way Desert Rose had taught me. I caressed his chest and whispered soft words of love. I drank in his fragrance as I moved my fingers up and down his muscular back.

As if he had touched a burning stove, Shams jerked away. "You think you want me, you think you do, but all you want is to indulge your vanity."

I put my arms around his neck and kissed him, ever so hard. I pushed my tongue into his mouth and began flicking it back and forth, as I remembered what Desert Rose had told me: "Men love to suck their wives' tongues, Kimya. They all do."

His lips tasted like blackberries, sweet and sour, but just as quickly as I thought a swirl of pleasure pulled us together, Shams stopped me and pushed me away.

"I am disappointed in you, Kimya," Shams said. "Now, could you please leave me?"

As harsh as his words sounded, not a trace of feeling grazed his face. No anger. Not even the slightest irritation. And I couldn't tell which hurt me the most: the sharpness of his words or the blankness on his face.

I had never felt so humiliated in my life. I bent down to take my robe, but my hands were trembling so hard I couldn't hold the slippery, delicate fabric. Instead I grabbed my shawl and wrapped it around myself. Sobbing, gasping, and still half naked, I ran out of the room and away from him, away from this love that I now understood existed only in my imagination.

I never saw Shams again. After that day I never left my room. I spent all my time lying on my bed, lacking not so much the energy as the will to go out. A week passed, then another, and then I stopped counting the days. All strength was drained from my body, ebbing away bit by bit. Only my palms felt alive. They remembered the feel of Shams's hands and the warmth of his skin.

I never knew that death had a smell. A strong odor, like pickled ginger and broken pine needles, pungent and bitter, but not necessarily bad. I came to know it only when it started to waft around my room, enveloping me like thick, wet fog. I started running a high fever, slipping into delirium. People came to see me. Neighbors and friends. Kerra waited by one side of my bed, her eyes swollen, her face ashen. Gevher stood on the other side, smiling her soft, dimpled smile.

"Goddamn that heretic," said Safiya. "This poor girl has fallen sick of heartbreak. All because of him!"

I tried to force a sound, but it didn't make it past my throat.

"How can you say such things? Is he God?" Kerra said, trying to help. "How can you attribute such powers to a mortal man?"

But they didn't listen to Kerra, and I was in no state to convince anyone of anything. In any case, I soon realized that whatever I said or didn't say, the outcome would be much the same. People who didn't like Shams had found another reason in my illness to hate him, whereas I could not dislike him even if I wanted to.

Before long I drifted into a state of nothingness, where all colors melted into white and all sounds dissolved into a perpetual drone. I could not distinguish people's faces anymore and could not hear spoken words beyond a distant hum in the background.

I don't know if Shams of Tabriz ever came to my room to see me. Perhaps he never did. Perhaps he wanted to see me but the women in the room would not let him in. Or perhaps he did come after all, and sat by my bed, played me the *ney* for hours, held my hand, and prayed for my soul. I'd like to believe that.

Nonetheless, one way or the other, it didn't matter anymore. I was neither angry nor cross with him. How could I be, when I was flowing in a stream of pure awareness?

There was so much kindness and compassion in God and an explanation for everything. A perfect system of love behind it all. Ten days after I visited Shams's room clad in silk and perfumed tulles, ten days after I fell ill, I plunged into a river of pure nonexistence. There I swam to my heart's content, finally sensing that this must be what the deepest reading of the Qur'an feels like—a drop in infinity!

And it was flowing waters that carried me from life to death.

Ella

BOSTON, JULY 3, 2008

Boston had never been this colorful and vibrant, Ella thought. Had she been blind to the city's beauty all this time? Aziz spent five days in Boston. Every day Ella drove from Northampton to Boston to see him. They had tasty, modest lunches in Little Italy, visited the Museum of Fine Arts, took long walks on Boston Common and the Waterfront, watched the whales in the aquarium, and had coffee after coffee in the busy, small cafés of Harvard Square. They talked endlessly on subjects as diverse as the curiosities of local cuisines, different meditation techniques, aboriginal art, gothic novels, bird-watching, gardening, growing perfect tomatoes, and the interpretation of dreams, constantly interrupting and completing each other's sentences. Ella didn't remember ever talking so much with anyone.

When they were outside on the street, they took care not to touch each other, but that proved to get increasingly difficult. Small peccadilloes became exciting, and Ella started looking forward to a brush of their hands. Goaded by a strange courage she never knew she had in her, in restaurants and on the streets Ella held Aziz's hand, kissed his lips. Not only did she not *mind* being seen, it felt as if a part of her *longed* to be seen. Several times they returned to the hotel together, and on each occasion they came very close to making love, but they never did.

The morning of the day Aziz was going to fly back to Amsterdam, they were in his room, his suitcase standing between them like a nasty reminder of the parting to come.

"There's something I need to tell you," Ella said. "I've been thinking about this for too long."

Aziz raised one eyebrow, acknowledging the sudden shift in Ella's tone. Then he said carefully, "There's something I need to tell you, too."

"Okay, you go first."

"No, you go first."

Still smiling her half smile, Ella lowered her gaze, contemplating what to say and how to say it. Finally she started. "Before you came to Boston, David and I went out one evening and had a long talk. He asked me about you. Apparently he read our e-mails without my knowledge. I was incredibly angry at him for that, but I didn't deny the truth. About us, I mean."

Now Ella raised her eyes with apprehension to see how Aziz would react to what she was about to reveal. "To make a long story short, I told my husband that I loved another man."

Outside on the street, the sirens of several fire trucks broke the usual sounds of the city. Ella was distracted momentarily, but then she was able to finish. "It sounds crazy, I know, but I've been thinking this over very carefully. I want to come with you to Amsterdam."

Aziz walked to the window and looked down at the hurrying and bustle outside. There was smoke coming out of one of the buildings in the distance—a thick black cloud hovering in the air. He silently prayed for the people who lived there. When he started to speak, it sounded as if he were addressing the entire city.

"I would love to take you to Amsterdam with me, but I cannot promise you a future there."

"What do you mean?" Ella asked nervously.

At this, Aziz walked back, sat by her side, put his hand on hers, and as he caressed it absentmindedly, said, "When you first wrote to me, it happened to be a very strange time in my life."

"You mean there is someone else in your life . . . ?"

"No, sweetheart, no." Aziz smiled a little, and then the smile faded. "It's nothing like that. I once wrote to you about the three stages in my life, remember? Those were the first three letters in the word 'Sufi.' You never asked me about the fourth stage, and hard as I tried, I couldn't bring myself to tell you. My encounter with the letter *i*. Would you like to listen to it now?"

"Yes," Ella said, although she feared anything and everything that could disrupt this moment. "Yes, I would."

In a hotel room on that day in July, a few hours prior to his flight back to Amsterdam, Aziz told Ella how he had become a Sufi in 1977, adopting a new name for himself and also, as he had hoped, a new destiny. Ever since then he had traveled the world as a photographer by profession, a wandering dervish at heart. He had made close friends on six continents, people who saw him as part of their family. Though he hadn't married again, he had become the foster father of two orphans in Eastern Europe. Never taking off the necklace in the shape of the sun that he wore to remind him of Shams of Tabriz, Aziz had lived life by traveling, reading, and teaching in the footsteps of Sufi dervishes, encountering signs of God everywhere and in everything.

Then, two years ago, he learned about his sickness.

It started with a lump in his armpit, which apparently he was late to notice. The lump turned out to be a malignant melanoma, a fatal form of skin cancer. The doctors said it didn't look good, but they had to run several tests before giving him a more definite diagnosis. A week later they returned with bad news: The melanoma had spread to his internal organs and invaded his lungs.

At the time he was fifty-two. He was told he would not make it past fifty-five.

Ella moved her lips to say something, but the words did not come out and her mouth felt bone dry. Two tears rolled down her cheeks, which she quickly wiped off.

Aziz kept speaking, his tone firm and urgent. He said thus commenced a new, and in some ways a more productive, phase in his life. There were still places he wanted to see, and the first thing he did was find a way to get to them all. He established a Sufi foundation in Amsterdam with worldwide connections. As an amateur *ney* player, he gave concerts with Sufi musicians in Indonesia, Pakistan, and Egypt and even made an album with a group of Jewish and Muslim mystics in Córdoba, Spain.

He went back to Morocco and visited the lodge where he had met real Sufis for the first time in his life. Master Sameed was long dead, and Aziz prayed and meditated by his grave, contemplating on the trajectory his life had followed.

"Then I retreated to write the novel I had always wanted to write but, in my laziness or lack of courage, had postponed endlessly," said Aziz with a wink. "You know, it was one of those things I had wanted to do for a long time. I named the book *Sweet Blasphemy* and sent it to a literary agency in America, not expecting much and at the same time feeling open to all possibilities. A week later I received an intriguing e-mail from a mystery woman in Boston."

Ella couldn't help but smile. A weak smile of respectful compassion, tender and pained.

Aziz said ever since that moment nothing had been the same. From a man getting ready to die, he had turned into a man falling in love at a most unexpected time. Suddenly all the pieces that he thought he'd long ago put into place had to be moved. Spirituality, life, family, mortality, faith, and love—he found himself rethinking their meanings again and not wanting to die.

This new and final stage of his life he called his encounter with the letter *i* in the word "Sufi." And he said so far this stage had proved to be much more difficult than all the earlier ones, because it had come at a time when he thought he'd worked through most, if not all, of his inner conflicts, a time when he thought he was spiritually mature and fulfilled.

"In Sufism you learn how to die before death. I have gone through each of those stages, step by step. Then, just when I start to think I've got it all neatly sorted, here comes this woman out of nowhere. She writes to me, and I write back. After each e-mail I start waiting for her answer with bated breath. Words become more precious than ever. The whole world turns into a blank screen, waiting to be written upon. And I realize I want to get to know this person. I need more time with her. Suddenly my life is not enough anymore. I realize I am scared of death, and one part of me is ready to rebel against the God I have revered and submitted to."

"But we *will* have time. . . . " Ella said when she found her voice.

"My doctors tell me I have sixteen months," Aziz said, lightly but firmly. "They might be wrong. Or they might be right. I cannot know.

You see, Ella, all I can give you is the present moment. That is all *I* have. But the truth is, no one has more than that. It is just that we like to pretend we do."

Ella peered down at her feet, leaning sideways, as if part of her were about to fall down and part of her resisted. She started to cry.

"Don't, please. I wanted you to come with me to Amsterdam more than anything. I wanted to say, 'Let's travel the world together. Let's see distant lands, get to know other people and admire God's composition together.' "

"That would be nice," Ella said sniffing, like a child offered some bright-colored toy in the midst of her wailing.

Aziz's face darkened. He looked away from her toward the window.

"But I was afraid to ask you. I was even afraid to touch you, let alone make love. How could I ask you to be with me and abandon your family when I had no future to offer you?"

Cringing at his question, Ella said, "Why are we being so pessimistic? You can fight this illness. You can do it for me. For *us*."

"Why do we have to *fight* everything?" Aziz wanted to know. "We're always talking about fighting inflation, fighting AIDS, fighting cancer, fighting corruption, fighting terrorism, even fighting extra pounds. . . . Don't we have any other way of dealing with things?"

"I'm not a Sufi," Ella croaked impatiently, her voice sounding like the voice of someone else, someone older.

At that moment many thoughts crossed her mind: the death of her father, the pain of losing a loved one to suicide, the years and years of resentment and regret that followed, sifting through every little bit of memory of the one who is dead, wondering if things could have been any different had those details been shuffled differently somewhere.

"I know you're not a Sufi." Aziz smiled. "And you don't have to be one. Just be Rumi. That's all I'm asking of you."

"What do you mean?" she asked.

"Some time ago you asked me if I was Shams, remember? You said I reminded you of him. As happy as I was to hear that, I cannot be Shams. I think he was way beyond and above me. But you can be Rumi. If you let love take hold of you and change you, at first through its presence, then through its absence—"

"I'm not a poet," Ella said this time.

"Rumi wasn't a poet either. But he was transformed into one."

"Don't you get it? I'm just a housewife, for God's sake, a mother of three," Ella exclaimed, breathing in huge gulps.

"We're all what we are," murmured Aziz. "And we're all subject to change. It is a journey from here to there. You can make that journey. And if you are brave enough and if I am brave enough, we can go to Konya together in the end. That is where I want to die."

Ella gasped. "Stop talking like that!"

Aziz watched her for a moment, and then his eyes dropped. There was a new expression on his face now, a distance in his tone, as if he were swiftly drifting away, like a dry leaf at the mercy of the wind.

"Or else," he said slowly, "go home, Ella. Go back to your children and your house. You decide, love. Whatever you choose, I will respect your decision."

Suleiman the Drunk

KONYA, MARCH 1248

Blood, sweat, and tears. Outsiders think drinkers are lazy people who have nothing else to do. Little do they know that drinking increasing amounts of wine every day requires a lot of effort. We carry the weight of the world on our shoulders.

Tired and petulant, I was dozing with my head on the table, having a not-so-pleasant dream. There was a big, black bull, angry as hell, chasing me on unfamiliar streets. I ran away from the animal without a clue as to what I had done wrong to stir him up, knocking over stalls and smashing merchandise, drawing the anger of all the vendors in the bazaar. Still running, I entered a thoroughfare that turned out to be a dead-end street. And there I bumped into a mammoth egg, bigger than a house. Suddenly the egg started to hatch, and out came the ugliest baby bird ever, wet and noisy. I tried to get out of the street, but the mother bird appeared in the sky, glaring down at me as if I had been responsible for the ugliness of her baby. Just as the bird began to descend, its sharp beak and even sharper claws pointed at me, I woke up.

I opened my eyes and realized that I had fallen asleep on a table by the window. Though my mouth tasted like rusty nails and I was dying to have a drink, I felt too tired to even move. So I kept resting my heavy head on the table, sinking ever deeper into my stupor and listening to the usual sounds in the tavern.

I heard a heated argument rising and falling like the buzz of swarming bees. It came from the men sitting at the next table, and though I briefly considered the possibility of turning my head to see who they were, I did not move a muscle. And that is when I overheard that ominous word: murder.

At first I dismissed their talk as drunken ravings. One hears all sorts of things in a tavern and in time learns not to take every spoken word seriously. But there was something in their tone too menacing and potent to disregard, so I pricked my ears and listened. My jaw dropped open when it finally dawned upon me that they were serious. But even deeper was my shock when I understood who it was that they wanted to kill: Shams of Tabriz.

As soon as they left the table, I stopped feigning sleep and jumped to my feet.

"Hristos, come here! Be quick!" I yelled in panic.

"What is it this time?" Hristos came running. "Why are you so distressed?"

But I couldn't tell. Not even him. All of a sudden, everyone looked suspicious. What if there were more people involved in this conspiracy against Shams? I had to keep my mouth shut and my eyes wide open.

"Nothing! I'm hungry, that's all," I said. "Could you please bring me some soup? Make it with a lot of garlic. I need to sober up!"

Hristos stared at me quizzically, but, being used to my moodiness, he did not ask me any more questions. In a few minutes, he brought me a bowl of goat-intestine soup, spicy and scorching, which I ate in haste, my tongue burning. Having sobered up sufficiently, I dashed into the street to warn Shams of Tabriz.

First I tried Rumi's house. He wasn't there. Then I went to the mosque, the madrassa, the teahouse, the bakery, the *hamam*. . . . I looked in every store and cellar on the street of artisans. I even checked the old Gypsy woman's tent among the ruins, in case he had gone there to get rid of a sore tooth or a bad spell. I looked for him everywhere, my anxiety growing with every passing minute. Fear began to gnaw at me. What if it was too late? What if they had already killed him?

Hours later, not knowing where else to look, I made my way back to the tavern, downhearted and exhausted. And just like magic, only a few steps away from the tavern door, I bumped right into him.

"Hello, Suleiman. You look preoccupied," Shams said, smiling.

"Oh, my God! You're alive!" I exclaimed, and ran to his arms.

When he managed to pull away from my embrace, Shams stared at me, looking quite amused. "Of course I'm alive! Do I look like a ghost to you?"

I smiled, but not for long. My head ached so much that at any other time I would have downed a few bottles to get drunk as quickly as possible and doze off.

"What is it, my friend? Is everything all right?" Shams asked suspiciously.

I swallowed hard. What if he didn't believe me when I told him about the plot? What if he thought I'd been hallucinating under the influence of wine? And perhaps I was. Even I couldn't be sure.

"They're planning to kill you," I said. "I have no idea who they are. I couldn't see their faces. You see, I was sleeping. . . . But I didn't dream this. I mean, I did have a dream, but it wasn't like this. And I wasn't drunk. Well, I had drunk a few glasses, but I wasn't—"

Shams put his hand on my shoulder. "Calm down, my friend. I understand."

"You do?"

"Yes. Now, go back to the tavern, and don't you worry about me."

"No, no! I'm not going anywhere. And neither are you," I objected. "These people are serious. You need to be careful. You cannot go back to Rumi's house. That is the first place they will look for you."

Oblivious to my panic, Shams stayed silent.

"Listen, dervish, my house is small and a bit stuffy. But if you don't mind that, you can stay with me as long as you want."

"Thank you for your concern," Shams murmured. "But nothing happens outside of God's will. It is one of the rules: *This world is erected upon the principle of reciprocity. Neither a drop of kindness nor a speck of evil will remain unreciprocated. Fear not the plots, deceptions, or tricks of other people. If somebody is setting a trap, remember, so is God. He is the biggest plotter. Not even a leaf stirs outside God's knowledge. Simply and fully believe in that. Whatever God does, He does beautifully.*"

Having said that, Shams gave me a wink and waved good-bye. I watched him thread his way rapidly through the muddy street in the direction of Rumi's house, despite my warnings.

The Killer

KONYA, MARCH 1248

Bastards! Idiots! I told them not to come with me. I explained to them that I always work alone and hate to see clients meddling in my affairs. But they insisted, reasoning that since the dervish had supernatural powers, they had to see him dead with their own eyes.

"All right," I conceded in the end. "But make sure you don't get anywhere near me until everything is over."

They agreed. There were three of them now. The two men I knew from the earlier meeting and a new guy who sounded just as young and tense as the others. They all had their faces wrapped in black scarves. As if I cared about discovering their identities!

After midnight I was outside Rumi's house. I jumped over the stone wall into the courtyard and hid myself behind a bush. My clients had assured me that Shams of Tabriz had the habit of meditating in the courtyard every night, before or after performing his ablutions. All I had to do was wait.

It was a windy night, unusually chilly for this time of the year. The sword felt heavy and cold in my palm, the two coral beads that embellished its handle rough under my fingers. Just in case, I had also brought with me a small sheathed dagger.

There was a pale blue haze around the moon. A few nocturnal animals hooted and howled from afar. I caught the sweet whiff of roses in the wind buffeting the trees. Strangely, the smell made me uneasy. Even before I reached the house, I hadn't been in the best of moods. But now it was worse. As I stood there, wrapped by that overly sweet odor, I couldn't help but feel a strong urge to drop the entire plan and leave this spooky place at once.

But I stayed, true to my word. I didn't know how much time had passed. My eyelids began to feel heavy, and I kept yawning despite myself. As the wind's fury intensified, for some reason unbeknownst to me my mind kept raking up memories, dark and vexing, of all the men I had killed. My apprehension surprised me. It usually didn't make me nervous to remember the past. Pensive and withdrawn, perhaps, even sullen from time to time, but never nervous.

I whistled a few songs to boost my spirits, and when that didn't help, I fixed my gaze on the back door of the house and whispered, "Come on, Shams. Don't make me wait here too long. Come out into the courtyard."

No sound. No movement. Nothing.

All of a sudden, it began to rain. From where I stood, I could see over the slanted walls of the courtyard. Soon the downpour was so hard that the streets turned into rushing rivers and I was completely soaked.

"Damn it," I said. "Damn! Damn!"

I was considering giving up for the night when I heard a sharp sound over the clatter of rain on the roofs and roads. There was someone in the courtyard.

It was Shams of Tabriz. Holding an oil lamp in his hand, he walked in my direction and stopped only a few steps away from the bush where I was hiding.

"It is a lovely night, isn't it?" he asked.

Scarcely able to contain my confusion, I gasped. Was there someone else next to him, or was he talking to himself? Did he know I was here? Could he possibly be aware of my presence? My mind was boiling with questions.

Then another thought occurred to me. How could the lamp in his hand keep burning despite the mighty wind and the heavy rain? And as soon as this question crossed my mind, I felt a shiver down my spine.

I remembered the rumors about Shams. He so excelled in black magic, people said, that he could turn anyone into a braying donkey or a blind bat by simply tying a piece of string from that person's clothes and uttering his evil incantations. Though I had never believed in such nonsense and wasn't going to start doing so now, as I stood watching the flame of Shams's lamp flicker under the heavy rain, I couldn't stay still, I was trembling so.

"Years ago I had a master in Tabriz," Shams said as he put the lamp on the ground, thus taking it out of my eyesight. "He is the one who taught me there was a time for everything. It is one of the last rules."

What rules was he talking about? What cryptic talk was this? I had to decide quickly whether I should come out of the bush now or wait until he turned his back to me—except he never did. If he knew I was here, there was no point in hiding. In case he didn't, though, I had to measure well when to come out.

But then, as if to deepen my confusion, I noticed the silhouettes of the three men waiting under a covering outside the garden wall shift restlessly. They must have been wondering why I hadn't moved to kill the dervish.

"It is Rule Number Thirty-seven," Shams continued. *"God is a meticulous clockmaker. So precise is His order that everything on earth happens in its own time. Neither a minute late nor a minute early. And for everyone without exception, the clock works accurately. For each there is a time to love and a time to die."*

In that moment I understood that he was talking to me. He knew I was here. He had known it even before he stepped out into the courtyard. My heart started to race. I felt as if all around me the air were being sucked away. There was no use in hiding anymore. And just like that, I stood up and walked out from behind the bush. The rain stopped as abruptly as it had started, plunging everything into silence. We stood face-to-face, the killer and the victim, and despite the strangeness of the situation everything seemed natural, almost peaceful.

I pulled out my sword and swung it with all my might. The dervish dodged the blow with a swiftness I did not expect from a man of his size. I was about to swing again when suddenly a rush of movement swirled in the darkness and six men appeared out of nowhere, attacking the dervish with clubs and spears. Apparently the three young men had brought friends. The ensuing battle was so intense that they all toppled to the ground, rolling around, regaining footing, and falling again, breaking spear after spear into splinters.

I stood watching, shocked and furious. Never before had I been reduced to playing witness to a murder I was paid to commit. I was so angry at the three young men for their insolence that I could easily have let the dervish go and fought them instead.

But before long, one of the men started to yell hysterically. "Help! Help us, Jackal Head! He is going to kill us."

Fast as lightning I threw my sword aside, pulled my dagger out of my belt, and dashed forward. The seven of us knocked the dervish to the ground, and in one swift move I stabbed him in the heart. A single hoarse cry came out of his mouth, his voice breaking at its peak. He didn't stir again, nor did he breathe.

Together we lifted his body, which was strangely light, and dumped him into the well. Gasping loudly for air, we each then took a step back and waited to hear the sound of his body hitting the water.

It never came.

"What the hell is going on?" said one of the men. "Didn't he fall in?"

"Of course he did," another said. "How could he not?"

They were panicking. So was I.

"Maybe he got caught on a hook on the wall," the third man suggested.

The suggestion made sense. It took the burden of finding an explanation off our shoulders, and we gladly embraced it, though we all knew there were no hooks on the walls of wells.

I don't know how long we waited there, avoiding one another's eyes. A cool breeze crossed the courtyard, sprinkling thin, brown willow leaves around our feet. High in the sky above, the dark blue of the morning was just beginning to break into violet. We might have stayed there until long into the day had the back door of the house not opened and a man walked out. I recognized him instantly. It was Mawlana.

"Where are you?" he yelled, his voice heavy with concern. "Are you there, Shams?"

At the mention of his name, all seven of us took to our heels. The six men jumped over the garden walls and disappeared into the night. I remained behind, searching for my dagger, which I found under a bush, covered with mud. I knew I should not linger there, not even a second, but I couldn't resist the temptation of looking back.

And when I did, I saw Rumi stagger into the courtyard and then suddenly lurch to his left, toward the well, as if guided by an intuition. He leaned forward, peered down, and stood like that for a moment, his eyes adjusting to the semidarkness inside the well. Then he pulled back, fell to his knees, pounded his chest, and let out a terrifying scream.

"They killed him! They killed my Shams!"

I jumped over the wall and, leaving behind the dagger with the blood of the dervish on it, ran as I had never run before.

Ella

NORTHAMPTON, AUGUST 12, 2008

Balmy and sunny, it was an ordinary day in August. A day like any other. Ella woke up early in the morning, prepared breakfast for her husband and children, watched them leave for work and chess and tennis clubs, went back to her kitchen, opened her cookbook, and chose the day's menu:

Spinach Soup with Creamy Mushroom Mash
Mussels with Mustard Mayonnaise
Seared Scallops with Tarragon-Butter Sauce
Garden Salad with Cranberries
Zucchini Rice Gratin
Rhubarb and Vanilla Cream Lattice Pie

It took her all afternoon to cook the dishes. When she was done, she took out her best china. She set the table, folded the napkins, and arranged the flowers. She set the oven timer for forty minutes, so that the gratin could be warm by seven o'clock. She prepared the croutons, put the dressing in the salad, rich and oily, just as Avi preferred. It occurred to her to light the candles, but she changed her mind upon second thought. It was better to leave the table like this. Like an immaculate picture. Untouched. Unmoving.

Then she grabbed the suitcase she had earlier prepared and left her house. As she walked out, she murmured one of Shams's rules. "*It is never too late to ask yourself, 'Am I ready to change the life I am living? Am I ready to change within?'*

"Even if a single day in your life is the same as the day before, it surely is a pity. At every moment and with each new breath, one should be renewed and renewed again. There is only one way to be born into a new life: to die before death."

Aladdin

KONYA, APRIL 1248

Blowing hot and cold, changing my mind every passing minute as to how I should behave toward others, three weeks after Shams's death, I finally mustered the courage to go and talk to my father. I found him in the library, sitting alone by the firelight, as still as an alabaster statue, shadows leaping across his face.

"Father, can I talk to you?" I asked.

Slowly, hazily, as if swimming back to the shore from a sea of reveries, he looked at me and said nothing.

"Father, I know you think I have a role in Shams's death, but let me assure you—"

All of a sudden, my father raised his finger, interrupting my words. "Between you and me, son of mine, words have dried up. I have nothing to hear from you and nothing to tell you in return," he pronounced.

"Please don't say that. Let me explain," I begged, my voice shaking. "I swear to God. It wasn't me. I know the people who did it, but it wasn't me."

"My son," my father interjected again, the sorrow draining out of him, replaced by the chilling calmness of someone who has finally accepted a terrible truth, "you say it wasn't you, but there is blood on your hem."

I flinched and instantly checked the ends of my robe. Could it be true? Was there blood on me from that evening? I inspected my hem, and then my sleeves, hands, and fingernails. It all seemed clean. When I raised my head again, I came eye to eye with my father and only then understood the little trap that he had set for me.

By inadvertently checking my hem for blood, I had given myself away.

It is true. I did join them in the tavern that evening. I am the one who told the killer that Shams had the habit of meditating every night in the courtyard. And later that night, when Shams was talking to his killer under the rain, I was one of the six men eavesdropping by the garden wall. And when we decided that we should attack, because there was no going back and the killer was taking things too slowly, I showed them the way into our courtyard. But that's it. I stopped there. I didn't take part in the fight. It was Baybars who attacked, and Irshad and others helped him. And when they panicked, Jackal Head did the rest.

Later on, I lived that moment over and over in my mind so many times that it is hard to tell what part is real and what part a figment of my imagination. Once or twice I conjured a memory of Shams escaping from our hands into the pitch-black night, and the image was so vivid I almost believed it.

Though he is gone, there are traces of him everywhere. Dance, poetry, music, and all the things that I thought would vanish once he was gone have stayed firmly planted in our lives. My father has become a poet. Shams was right. When one of the jars was broken, so was the other jar.

My father had always been a loving man. He embraced people of all faiths. He was kind toward not only Muslims but also Christians, Jews, and even pagans. After Shams came into his life, his circle of love became so vast it included even the most fallen of society—prostitutes, drunks, and beggars, the scum of the scum.

I believe he could even love Shams's killers.

There was, and still is, only one person he could not manage to love: his son.

Sultan Walad

KONYA, SEPTEMBER 1248

Beggars, drunks, prostitutes, orphans, and thieves . . . He distributes all his gold and silver to criminals. Since that awful night, my father has never been the same. Everyone says he has lost his mind to grief. When asked what he is doing, he tells the story of Imra'ul-Qays, the king of Arabs, who was very well liked, notoriously rich and handsome, but one day, unexpectedly, walked out of his perfect life. Qays put on dervish robes, gave up all his wealth, and from then on wandered from one landscape to another.

"This is what losing your beloved does to you," my father says. "It dissolves your king-self into dust and brings out your dervish-self. Now that Shams is gone forever, I am gone, too. I am not a scholar or a preacher anymore. I am the embodiment of nothingness. Here is my *fana,* herein my *baqa.*"

The other day a ginger-haired merchant who looked like the worst liar on earth knocked on our door. He said he had known Shams of Tabriz way back from his years in Baghdad. Then, dropping his voice to a confidential whisper, he swore that Shams was alive and well, hiding and meditating in an ashram in India, waiting for the appropriate time to emerge.

As he said all this, there wasn't a trace of honesty on his face. But my father got delirious. He asked the man what he wanted in return for this wonderful news. Without the least bit of shame, the merchant said that as a young boy he had always wanted to become a dervish, but since life had taken him in another direction, he would at least love to have the caftan of a scholar as famous as Rumi. Upon hearing this, my father took out his velvet caftan and handed it to him, just like that.

"But, Father, why did you give your precious caftan to that man when you knew so well that he was lying?" I inquired as soon as the man was gone.

And this is what my father said: "You think a caftan is too high a price to pay for his lie? But my dear son, imagine, if he were telling the truth, if Shams were really alive, I would have given my life!"

Rumi

KONYA, OCTOBER 31, 1260

By and large over time, pain turns into grief, grief turns into silence, and silence turns into lonesomeness, as vast and bottomless as the dark oceans. Today is the sixteenth anniversary of the day Shams and I met in front of the Inn of Sugar Vendors. Every year on the last day of October, I retreat into a solitude that grows in weight day by day. I spend forty days in *chilla,* thinking of the forty rules. I remember and review each of them, but there in the far reaches of my mind there is only Shams of Tabriz, glittering.

You think you cannot live anymore. You think that the light of your soul has been put out and that you will stay in the dark forever. But when you are engulfed by such solid darkness, when you have both eyes closed to the world, a third eye opens in your heart. And only then do you come to realize that eyesight conflicts with inner knowledge. No eye sees so clear and sharp as the eye of love. After grief comes another season, another valley, another you. And the lover who is nowhere to be found, you start to see everywhere.

You see him in the drop of water that falls into the ocean, in the high tide that follows the waxing of the moon, or in the morning wind that spreads its fresh smell; you see him in the geomancy symbols in the sand, in the tiny particles of rock glittering under the sun, in the smile of a newborn baby, or in your throbbing vein. How can you say Shams is gone when he is everywhere and in everything?

Deep in the slow whirling of sorrow and longing, I am with Shams every day, every minute. My chest is a cave where Shams is resting. Just as a mountain keeps an echo inside itself, I hold the voice of Shams within. Of the scholar and preacher I once was, not even the smallest speck remains. Love has taken away all of my practices and habits. Instead it has filled me with poetry. And though I know that there are no words that can express this inner journey of mine, I believe in words. I am a believer of words.

Two people have helped me through my hardest days: my elder son and a saint named Saladin, the goldbeater. It was while listening to him work in his small store, beating leaves of gold to perfection, that I had the most wonderful inspiration to put the final touches to the dance of the whirling dervishes. The rhythm emanating from Saladin's store was the same as the pulse of the universe, the divine rhythm Shams had talked and cared so much about.

In time my elder son married Saladin's daughter, Fatima. Bright and inquisitive, she reminded me of Kimya. I taught her the Qur'an. She became so dear to me that I started referring to her as my right eye and her sister Hediyya as my left eye. That is the one thing dear Kimya proved to me long ago: that girls are just as good students as boys, if not even better. I arrange *sema* sessions for women and advise Sufi sisters to continue this tradition.

Four years ago I began to recite *The Mathnawi.* The first line came to me one day at dawn apropos of nothing, while I was watching the sunlight slice the dark. Ever since then the poems spill out of my lips as if by a force of their own. I do not write them down. It was Saladin who painstakingly wrote out those early poems. And my son made copies of each. It is thanks to them that the poems survived, because the truth is, if asked to repeat any one of them today, I don't think I could. Prose or poetry, the words come to me in flocks and then leave just as suddenly, like migrating birds. I am only the bed of water where they stop and rest on their way to warmer lands.

When I start a poem, I never know beforehand what I'm going to say. It could be long or it could be short. I don't plan it. And when the poem is over, I'm quiet again. I live in silence. And "Silence," Khamush, is one of the two signatures I use in my *ghazals*. The other one is Shams of Tabriz.

The world has been moving and changing at a speed we human beings can neither control nor comprehend. In 1258, Baghdad fell to the Mongols. The one city that prided itself on its fortitude and glamour and claimed to be the center of the world suffered defeat. That same year Saladin died. My dervishes and I had a huge celebration, passing through the streets with drums and flutes, dancing and singing in joy, because that is how a saint should be buried.

In 1260 it was the Mongols' turn to lose. The Mamelukes of Egypt defeated them. Yesterday's victors became today's losers. Every winner is inclined to think he will be triumphant forever. Every loser tends to fear that he is going to be beaten forever. But both are wrong for the same reason: Everything changes except the face of God.

After the death of Saladin, Husam the Student, who has matured so fast and so well along the spiritual path that he is now called Husam Chelebi by everyone, helped me to write down the poems. He is the scribe to whom I dictated the entire *Mathnawi*. Modest and generous, if anyone asks Husam who he is or what he does, without missing a beat he says, "I am a humble follower of Shams of Tabriz. That's who I am."

Little by little, one turns forty, fifty, and sixty and, with each major decade, feels more complete. You need to keep walking, though there's no place to arrive at. The universe is turning, constantly and relentlessly, and so are the earth and the moon, but it is nothing other than a secret embedded within us human beings that makes it all move. With that knowledge we dervishes will dance our way through love and heartbreak even if no one understands what we are doing. We will dance in the middle of a brawl or a major war, all the same. We will dance in our hurt and grief, with joy and elation, alone and together, as slow and fast as the flow of water. We will dance in our blood. There is a perfect harmony and subtle balance in all that is and was in the universe. The dots change constantly and replace one another, but the circle remains intact. Rule Number Thirty-nine: *While the parts change, the whole always remains the same. For every thief who departs this world, a new one is born. And every decent person who passes away is replaced by a new one. In this way not only does nothing remain the same but also nothing ever really changes.*

For every Sufi who dies, another is born somewhere.

Our religion is the religion of love. And we are all connected in a chain of hearts. If and when one of the links is broken, another one is added elsewhere. For every Shams of Tabriz who has passed away, there will emerge a new one in a different age, under a different name.

Names change, they come and go, but the essence remains the same.

Ella

KONYA, SEPTEMBER 7, 2009

By his bed she was sleeping on a plastic chair when she suddenly opened her eyes and listened to an unexpected sound. Somebody was saying unknown words in the dark. She realized it was the call to prayer coming from outside. A new day was about to begin. But she had a feeling it would also be the end of something.

Ask anyone who has heard the call to morning prayer for the first time and he will tell you the same thing. That it is beautiful, rich, and mysterious. And yet at the same time there is something uncanny about it, almost eerie. Just like love.

In the stillness of the night, it was to this sound that Ella woke with a start. She blinked repeatedly in the dark until she could make sense of the male voice filling the room from the open windows. It took her a full minute to remember that she was not in Massachusetts anymore. This wasn't the spacious house she had shared with her husband and three children. All that belonged to another time—a time so distant and vague that it felt like a fairy tale, not like her own past.

No, she wasn't in Massachusetts. Instead she was in another part of the world altogether, in a hospital in the town of Konya in Turkey. And the man whose deep, steady breathing she now heard as an undertone to the call for the morning prayer was not her husband of twenty years but the lover for whom she had left him one sunny day last summer.

"Are you going to leave your husband for a man with no future?" her friends and neighbors had asked her again and again. "And how about your kids? Do you think they will ever forgive you?"

And that is how Ella had come to understand that if there was anything worse in the eyes of society than a woman abandoning her husband for another man, it was a woman abandoning her future for the present moment.

She switched on the table lamp and in its soft amber glow inspected the room, as if to make sure nothing had changed since she'd drifted off to sleep only a few hours ago. It was the smallest hospital room she had ever seen, not that she'd seen many hospital rooms in her life. The bed occupied most of the floor space. Everything else was placed in relation to the bed—a wooden closet, a square coffee table, an extra chair, an empty vase, a bed tray with pills of varying colors, and next to it the book Aziz had been reading since the beginning of this trip: *Me & Rumi.*

They had come to Konya four days ago, spending the first days in the city being no different from the average tourists—visiting monuments, museums, and archaeological sites; stuffing themselves with the local dishes; and taking pictures of every new thing, no matter how ordinary or silly. Everything was going well until the day before, when Aziz, while having lunch at a restaurant, collapsed on the floor and had to be rushed to the nearest hospital. Since then she'd been waiting here by his bedside, waiting without knowing what to expect, hoping against hope, and at the same time silently and desperately quarreling with God for taking back so soon the love he had given her so late in life.

"My dear, are you sleeping?" Ella asked. It wasn't her intention to disturb him, but she needed him awake.

There came no answer other than a fleeting lull in the rhythm of his breathing, a missing note in the sequence.

"Are you awake?" she asked, whispering and raising her voice at the same time.

"I am now," Aziz said slowly. "What is it, you couldn't sleep?"

"The morning prayer . . . " Ella said, and paused as if that explained everything: his deteriorating health, her growing fear of losing him, and the absolute folly that love was—everything encapsulated by those three words.

Aziz sat straight up now, his green eyes unblinking. Under the wispy light of the lamp and surrounded by bleached white sheets, his handsome face looked sadly pale, but there was also something powerful about it, even immortal.

"The morning prayer is special," he murmured. "Did you know that of the five prayers a Muslim is supposed to perform every day, the one in the morning is said to be the most sacred but also the most testing?"

"And why is that?"

"I guess it's because it wakes us up from dreams, and we don't like that. We prefer to keep sleeping. That's why there is a line in the morning call that doesn't exist in the others. It says, 'Prayer is better than sleep.' "

But perhaps sleep is better for the two of us, Ella thought. *If only we could fall asleep together.* She longed for an easy, unperturbed slumber no less magical than Sleeping Beauty's, one hundred years of absolute numbness to ease this pain.

In a little while, the call to prayer came to an end, its echoes drifting away on retreating waves. After the last note faded, the world felt strangely safe, but unbearably silent. It had been a year since they'd been together. One year of love and awareness. Most of the time, Aziz had been well enough to keep traveling with Ella, but in the past two weeks his health had deteriorated visibly.

Ella watched him go back to sleep, his face serene and so very dear. Her mind filled with anxieties. She sighed deeply and walked out of the room. She passed through corridors where all the walls had been painted shades of green and entered wards where she saw patients, old and young, men and women, some recovering, others failing. She tried not to mind the inquisitive gaze of the people, but her blond hair and blue eyes made her foreignness incandescent. She had never felt so out of place anywhere before. But then Ella had never been much of a traveler.

A few minutes later, she was sitting by the water fountain in the hospital's small, pleasant garden. In the middle of the fountain, there was a statue of a little angel, and at the bottom of it a few silver coins shone, each bearing somebody's secret wish. She groped in her pockets for a coin but couldn't find anything there other than scribbled notes and half a granola bar. As her gaze fell upon the garden, she saw some pebbles ahead. Smooth, black, and shiny. She picked one of them up, closed her eyes, and tossed it into the fountain, her lips murmuring a wish she already knew would not be realized. The pebble hit the wall of the fountain and bounced aside, falling right into the lap of the stone angel.

If Aziz were here, Ella thought, he would have seen it as a sign.

When she walked back half an hour later, she found a doctor and a young, head-scarved nurse in the room and the bedsheet pulled over Aziz's head.

He had passed away.

Aziz was buried in Konya, following in the footsteps of his beloved Rumi.

Ella took care of all the preparations, trying to plan every little detail but also trusting that God would help her with the ones she couldn't handle. First she arranged the spot where he would be buried—under a huge magnolia tree in an old Muslim cemetery. Then she found Sufi musicians who agreed to play the *ney* and sent an e-mail to Aziz's friends everywhere, inviting them to the funeral. To her delight, quite a number of them were able to come, from as far away as Cape Town, St. Petersburg, Murshidabad, and São Paulo. Among them were photographers like him, as well as scholars, journalists, writers, dancers, sculptors, businessmen, farmers, housewives, and Aziz's adopted children.

It was a warm, joyful ceremony, attended by people of all faiths. They celebrated his death, as they knew he would have wanted. Children played happily and unattended. A Mexican poet distributed *pan de los muertos,* and an old Scottish friend of Aziz's sprinkled rose petals on everyone, raining over them like confetti, each and every one a colorful testimony that death was not something to be afraid of. One of the locals, a hunched old Muslim man who watched the whole scene with a wide grin and gimlet eyes, said this must have been the craziest funeral Konya had ever witnessed, except for the funeral of Mawlana centuries ago.

Two days after the funeral, finally alone, Ella wandered the city, watching the families walk past her, merchants in their shops, and street vendors eager to sell her something, anything. People stared at this American woman walking in their midst with her eyes swollen from crying. She was a complete stranger here, a complete stranger everywhere.

Back in the hotel, before she checked out and headed to the airport, Ella took off her jacket and put on a fluffy, peach-colored angora sweater. *A color too meek and docile for a woman who's trying to be neither,* she thought. Then she called Jeannette, who was the only one of her three children who had supported her in her decision to follow her heart. Orly and Avi were still not speaking to their mother.

"Mom! How are you?" Jeannette asked, her voice full of warmth.

Ella leaned forward into empty space and smiled as if her daughter were standing right across from her. Then she said in an almost inaudible voice, "Aziz is dead."

"Oh, Mom, I'm so sorry."

There was a brief lull as they both contemplated what to say. It was Jeannette who broke the silence. "Mom, will you be coming home now?"

Ella tipped her head in thought. In her daughter's question, she heard another unstated question. Would she be going back to Northampton to her husband and stopping the divorce process, which had already turned into a maze of mutual resentments and accusations? What was she going to do now? She didn't have any money, and she didn't have a job. But she could always give private lessons in English, work for a magazine, or who knows, be a good fiction editor one day.

Closing her eyes for a moment, Ella prophesied to herself with jubilant conviction and confidence what the days ahead would bring her. She had never been on her own like this before, and yet, oddly enough, she didn't feel lonely.

"I've missed you, baby," she said. "And I've missed your brother and sister, too. Will you come to see me?"

"Of course I will, Mama—we will—but what are you going to do now? Are you sure you aren't coming back?"

"I'm going to Amsterdam," Ella said. "They have incredibly cute little flats there, overlooking the canals. I can rent one of those. I'll need to improve my biking. I don't know. . . . I'm not going to make plans, honey. I'm going to try living one day at a time. I'll see what my heart says. It *is* one of the rules, isn't it?"

"What rules, Mom? What are you talking about?"

Ella approached the window and looked at the sky, which was an amazing indigo in all directions. It swirled with an invisible speed of its own, dissolving into nothingness and encountering therein infinite possibilities, like a whirling dervish.

"It's Rule Number Forty," she said slowly. *"A life without love is of no account. Don't ask yourself what kind of love you should seek, spiritual or material, divine or mundane, Eastern or Western. . . . Divisions only lead to more divisions. Love has no labels, no definitions. It is what it is, pure and simple.*

"Love is the water of life. And a lover is a soul of fire!

"The universe turns differently when fire loves water."

Acknowledgments

Dost means "friend" in Turkish. I owe a bigger debt of gratitude than I can ever express to friends everywhere—Istanbul, Amsterdam, Berlin, and London. Many people inspired this novel with their stories and silences. I am deeply grateful to Marly Rusoff, my literary agent, who has believed in me from day one and has always seen through me with that third eye of hers. Thank you to dear Michael Radulescu for his continuing support and faith, and for just being there when I need help. I am indebted to my editor, Paul Slovak, for his many valuable contributions and inner wisdom, as well as for his indispensable suggestions as the manuscript traveled between Istanbul and New York.

I owe a special thanks to Sufis all around the world, those I have met in the past and those I have yet to meet, carrying perhaps different names and passports, but always the same amazing ability to see things from two points of view, their own and that of another. Thank you, dear Zeynep, Emir, Hande, and Beyza, for your time, patience, amity, and precious contributions. My heartfelt thanks to Mercan Dede for his generous heart and unique friendship.

Finally, to Eyup and my children, I thank you for showing me, a nomadic soul, that it was possible to settle down in one place and still be free. This book owes you more than I can tell.

Glossary

baqa: permanency that comes after annihilation, a higher state of life with God

baraqa: blessing

dervish: someone who is on the Sufi path

fana: annihilation of the Self while physically alive

faqih: a scholar of law

faqir: a Sufi practicing spiritual poverty

ghazal: a type of poetry common in Indo-Perso-Arabic civilization

hadith: the words and deeds of the Prophet Muhammad

hafiz: a person who has memorized the Qur'an

hamam: Turkish bath

Insan-i Kâmil: the perfect human being according to Sufism; the stage is genderless and is thus reachable for both men and women

inshallah: "if Allah wills it"

khaneqah: a center for dervishes

kismet: luck, fortune

kudüm and rebab: musical instruments

lokum: Turkish delight

madrassa: college, school where students are educated in a wide range of fields

maktab: elementary school

maqamat: stages of development

nafs: false ego

ney: a reed flute played mostly by Malawi dervishes

qibla: the direction Muslims face for daily prayers

salwar: loose pants

saqui: one who serves wine

sema: the spiritual dance of whirling dervishes

semazenbashi: a dance master

Shafi, Hanefi, Hanbali, and Maliki: the four schools of law of Sunni Islam

sharia: 1. a set of Islamic laws and regulations; 2. the mainstream; main venue

tafsir: interpretation or commentary, usually of the Qur'an

Tahafut al-Tahafut: *The Incoherence of the Incoherence,* by Averroës, in which the author defends Aristotelian philosophy in Islamic thought

tariqa: a Sufi order, or the way, the mystical path

tasbih: a rosary

zikr: remembrance of God

Sources

While writing this novel I benefited greatly from my readings of the Mathnawi by R. A. Nicholson and *The Autobiography of Shams-ı Tabrizi* by William Chittick. I am indebted to the works of William Chittick, Coleman Barks, İdris Shah, Kabir Helminski, Camille Helminski, Refik Algan, Franklin D. Lewis, and Annemarie Schimmel.

The poems by Rumi were from the following sources:

William Chittick, *The Sufi Path of Love*, Albany: State University of New York, 1983
Coleman Barks, *A Year with Rumi*, New York: Harper Collins, 2006, and *The Essential Rumi*, 1995
Kabir Helminski, *The Rumi Collection*, Boston: Shambhala Publications, 2005

Poems by Omar Khayyám from Richard Le Gallienne's translation as found on http://en.wikipedia.org/wiki/Rubaiyat_of_Omar_Khayyam

Of the two translations of the verse Nisa, the first is by M. H. Shakir (*The Qur'an*, translated by M. H. Shakir, 1993), the second is by Ahmed Ali (*Al-Qur'an: A Contemporary Translation*, Princeton, NJ: Princeton University Press, 2001)

Dreaming in English

'Why do you write your novels in English when Turkish is your mother tongue?'

It is a question I hear often. Each time, I need to pause for a split second. How can I explain? I try to offer a compact, rational answer. Yet I also know deep down that my urge to write stories in a language other than my native tongue was an irrational choice, if it was a choice at all. I did not exactly decide to write in English. Rather than a logical resolution, it was an animal instinct that brought me to the shores of the English language. Perhaps I escaped into this new continent. I sent myself into perpetual exile, carving an additional zone of existence, building a new home, brick by brick, in this other land.

Being a foreigner and an outsider in the English language intimidates me sometimes. My children make fun of my accent: they find it fascinating, an odd blend of unlikely ingredients. It is a challenge to write in English, both intellectually and spiritually. Yet the joy and the pleasure I derive from the experience are so much greater than the fear. And whatever pain there is, it is certainly less than the pain of feeling like a stranger in my motherland. Somehow, that is heavier.

I started learning English at the age of ten when I became a student at a British School in Madrid, Spain. It was the flexibility of its anatomy and the versatility and openness of its vocabulary that struck me most. Soon I was scribbling secret poems and stories in English.

When I took the step of writing my novels in English first, about fourteen years ago, I was already an established author in Turkey. Immediately there was a negative reaction in my motherland. They accused me of betraying my nation, an allegation I had heard before. They claimed I was 'forsaking' my inherited language for the language of Western Imperialism. 'How can she be one of us now?' declared a critic. 'If she writes in English she is not a Turkish author any more.'

I have never understood this either/or mentality. All I know is the more they want me to fit in, the more my soul resists. I refuse to make a choice between

English and Turkish: in truth, it is the commute back and forth between the two that fascinates me to this day. As a nomad, I pay extra attention to those words that cannot be ferried from one continent to the other. I am more aware: of idioms, colloquialisms and street slang; meanings and nuances; linguistic cracks, gaps and silences. Languages shape us while we are busy thinking we are in charge of them.

I write my novels in English first. The English is translated into Turkish by professional translators (whose work I admire and respect), and I then take the new Turkish version and rewrite it with my rhythm, my energy, my vocabulary. I love using old Ottoman words, many coming from Arabic and Persian, which have been plucked out of the Turkish language by a modernist nationalist elite in the name of 'purity'. Critical of this linguistic xenophobia, I use both old and new words while writing in Turkish.

Separation can be a form of connection. Writing in English creates a cognitive distance between me and the culture I come from; paradoxically, this enables me to take a closer look at Turkey and Turkishness. *The Bastard of Istanbul* is a novel that concentrates on an Armenian and a Turkish family and the unspoken atrocities of the past. Had I written this in Turkish, it might have been a different book: more cautious, more apprehensive. But writing the story in English first freed me from the cultural and psychological constraints I internalize unconsciously in Turkish. Sometimes, absence is actually a bond and distance can help you to look closer.

I respect novelists and poets who see their mother tongue as their primary source of identity but I sincerely believe my own homeland is none other than Storyland: a vast expanse where static identity is replaced by multiple belongings and the boundary between dream and reality is fluid. This is what keeps me going despite my broken accent and enduring foreignness. I believe that if we can dream in more than one language then, yes, we can also write in more than one language.